THE WAR
IS OVER

THE STONEHOUSE SERIES
Mike & Dianne Heintzeman

THE WAR
IS OVER

TATE PUBLISHING
AND ENTERPRISES, LLC

Published by Tate Publishing & Enterprises, LLC
127 E. Trade Center Terrace | Mustang, Oklahoma 73064 USA
1.888.361.9473 | www.tatepublishing.com

Tate Publishing is committed to excellence in the publishing industry. The company reflects the philosophy established by the founders, based on Psalm 68:11,
"The Lord gave the word and great was the company of those who published it."

Book design copyright © 2013 by Tate Publishing, LLC. All rights reserved.
Cover design by Amber Gulilat
Interior design by Joel Uber
Edited by Katie Heintzeman

Published in the United States of America

ISBN: 978-1-62902-466-0
1. Fiction / Christian / Historical
2. Fiction / Christian / Classic & Allegory

13.07.26

Jonathan
&
Katie,
Thank you

PROLOGUE

Bitterness filled his mouth, alkali dust and chalky white; it had entered with his breath and turned to mud. Specks of sand, driven by the wind, they stung him in the face, collecting in the corners of his eyes. Settling in his hair, smaller grains slid through drops of sweat and down his neck.

There was no growing garden here.

Twenty-seven miles of travel had brought him to this place, only now to wonder what it was that would be found. Soon he would know, soon everyone would know. Had the jaws of death closed down upon his friend and swallowed, or would the man begin to breathe once more and die again another day?

If a seed is pushed beneath the dirt shall it come to life?

Buried in the ground... who can tell?

Summoned by the sisters, he had sent help on ahead, although in this savage place there was no sign his help had made it through.

He pushed on through a windbreak-tree-line. Thick, bushy and short, it was a stand of junipers, their branches jumping in the wind.

Fifty feet in, he felt some relief and pulled a soggy scarf away from his lips. Bits of sand swam between his canines and settled on his molars, grinding between his teeth when he bit slightly down. He raised a leather water skin to his mouth, flushing his teeth with the warm liquid; he swished the tepid stuff around and spat it out.

What is it they have done?

Was there nothing grown from what was given?

He looked back to rehearse the way he came, sand dunes like snow drifts made their way among the trees. He moved further in and found a new and hopeful place. The ground beneath his feet dropped sharply downward, and he followed a donkey trail which led him through a valley.

Who can explain the secrets of a seed... or tell the way it grows.

One can but plant it in the ground... or throw it to the crows.

He continued on, searching.

Tucked into a cove, on the valley's north side were signs of life, a round pointy-top tent home near the hillside cliff, and a fence around a patch of ground, a garden with growing corn inside.

And this one... what else has this one planted?

This is more than an existence... these are signs of life, of hope.

Batting at his hair it felt like old switch grass, stiff and brown with summer's end. Scratching at his scalp, his fingernails filled with sand. He pushed against the unruly stuff, trying to flatten it down.

I should have worn a hat.

CHAPTER 1

Two small but strong hands worked a polished Roman spear-point, *plunge-push, plunge-twist, stab, stab, stab!*

As large as her hand and shining in the morning sun, it found another mark.

Plunge-twist, plunge-push!

Although the tool of war had lost its razor edge, today it fully served the purpose of its new owner, and the war which she now waged.

Lunge-stab, stab-stab-twist, and a right hand darted forward, ripping out both stem and root of her intended target.

Wedged beneath fallen timbers near an ancient battle site, the blade had laid for years before the young woman found it, protected from the ravages of time. The spear's broken hardwood handle she recut and rounded over, just short of its splintered break.

Holding the blade's short shaft tightly in her right hand, her body close to the ground, she pressed both sets of knuckles into broken dirt and with strong arms she pulled her body forward. Drawn to a kneeling position, her legs tucked under and with her bare feet dragging along behind, she set upon her task again.

Twisting slightly right, *stab, stab-twist,* rip it out by the roots, twist to the left, *stab, stab, twist,* and rip it out, stem, roots and all.

Across the way her sister's voice called out while splashing in a water bucket, washing off some dirt, "I'm heading in Mary, it's almost time for lunch."

"Okay Martha, just got a few more weeds to pull in this row, is there any honey butter left from what you made?"

Plunge-twist, plunge-push, rip, plunge-twist, rip, stab, stab, stab.

"No… your brother ate it all."

Lunge-twist, rip, stab-stab-twist.

She looked back over her left shoulder, "Laz, how could you?"

"Really… it was very easy… and I would do it all again… if there were more biscuits and honey butter."

Mary gathered up the pesky weeds and stood to her feet while whacking dirt clumps off their roots. Collecting four more piles she threw them in a compost pit and left them there to rot.

Martha had placed her right foot on the first stone step outside their home's western door before Mary called out to her sister, "Martha, what's for lunch?"

"Hard boiled eggs and cornbread."

Lazarus wondered after her, and although Martha could not hear, Mary heard, "With no honey butter?"

"Yeah Laz, what's she thinking?"

Lazarus was about one third of his way through watering their perennials and had parked his two wheel cart next to the family's stone-lined water well. Suddenly, looking rather flushed, he leaned back against the stonework of their well, and rubbed at his eyes. "Why is the sun so bright today?"

"My brother, it's hi-noon and almost summer! Soon we will be planting seeds in our food garden, what do you expect, some life of softness? Like your fluffy pillow? Maybe you want a cushy job in town, counting someone else's beans?"

Surprised with his lack of response in their usual brother-sister banter, Mary turned to fully look at her best friend.

"Laz, are you okay?"

Both feet of Lazarus had slid forward, and his body slid down, till he was almost sitting on dusty ground.

He rubbed at his forehead with both hands.

"I... I don't know... all of the sudden... my head...it hurts!"

Tipping to one side Lazarus began wrenching; throwing up what little was in his stomach.

"Martha! Martha! Come here now! Martha!" Mary called for help and ran to her brother's side. He was crawling out of the dirt, towards some shade and green grass. "Lazarus, what's wrong? You seemed just fine a minute ago! You eat something weird? Mushrooms? Did you fall and hit your head?"

"I... doon't... kknooow...I," Lazarus answered, slurring his words.

Laz folded to his side and rolled onto his back in the grass, his world was spinning; he was telling his eyes to close... the sun was too bright... but his left eye would not respond.

"Marrry... whaat... is hhaappenning to...mee?"

Martha was beside them now, kneeling, with her left hand on Lazarus' forehead and her right hand clamped around his wrist.

"Lazarus, tell me, what's going on? You're not overly hot, the sun hasn't gotten to you, it's not that warm outside, and your heartbeat is steady and strong. You didn't eat some of those mushrooms that I said to leave alone... did you?"

"Noooo Martthaa... anndd... I wwass oonly teeassing... yyyou aabbout... thheee... musshhrroooms... haa... hhaaa!"

Lazarus laughed with a lop-sided grin, part of his face was not responding, looking like something not connected, sliding downhill.

Martha spoke directly to her sister, "Mary, run to Simon's house. Get Hannah... now!"

Eccentric Simon was four years older than Lazarus and his childhood friend, and Hannah was his black-skinned slave.

With a frozen face of ashen color, Mary questioned, "Martha? Do we need to do this?"

"Mary, look at your brother!"

Moaning, right hand covering his eyes to block out offensive light, saliva escaped through the left corner of his mouth.

Her heart ached for her brother, "Yes Martha, I will get Hannah!"

The House of Simon, the estate of Simon, one mile south, it would take Mary six… maybe five minutes to get herself there.

Simon, a man who had been exiled to die in a leper colony. A man whom Jesus, the wandering prophet, had healed and restored to life.

Simon was the youngest offspring and only son of parents now passed from this earth. He was also owner of the estate his father and grandfather had acquired and built; land, vineyards, horses, oxen, employees, wine, and slaves. Two slaves, Hannah, and her half breed daughter had been purchased ten years ago by Simon, on a business trip to Corinth, a most ungodly city and place.

Even though Mary said, *'I will get her,'* still she had not moved. *Fear, reach down your throat, and grab you by the heart, fear,* was trying to lay its hold on her. Seeds, in the form of pictures, more thoughts and pictures, they flashed through her mind, magnifying the condition of her brother.

"Augh!" Mary screamed, as she kicked against the fear, "No!"

Mary's right hand shot out and clamped onto her brother's beard. There was no response, not a muscle twitch, not a flouncing comment, not a screech of pain; she had clamped her hand onto a dead fish.

"Lazarus! Look at me!"

Both eyes moved, but only one eyelid raised, his left eye rolled up under its lid.

"Lazarus! Listen to me! You will live and not die! You hear me? You will live and not die!"

Mapping out in her mind the things she must do, Mary jumped to her feet. Her eyes shot down the stone cluttered gravel road heading north, and then to her sandals beside their garden gate. She spent the ten seconds it took to put them on, tying them too tight.

Hannah, tall, slender, black and beautiful, she was also a best friend of her sister Martha. Mary wondered how it would have been, to have known Hannah before she was a slave. Taken from her home on the northeast corner of the southern continent when she was just a teen, she was first sold in Egypt. It was there her daughter Esther was born from her first Egyptian master. It was with the daughter Esther, to whom Mary had become a friend.

What a tangled world we humans weave!

Mary's breath was coming harder now, covering the first quarter mile running slightly up hill; soon Stonehouse would be visible through a scattering of trees and on the far side of a valley.

Hannah, where are you?

Esther, are you watching?

You are always up to something!

Be up to something now!

It wasn't Esther who was up to something, it was Hannah, but all it was, was feeding Simon at his veranda table.

Simon was not the average man, nor was he the average slaveholder. True, he was her master, but he had purchased both Hannah and her daughter to rescue them from what he saw their future held for them in Corinth; continually to be sold for money in a brothel. Now she served Simon in his household, but she also shared a room with her husband within the lower level of Simon's home. Esther's room was next to hers.

Esther was also a different type of slave.

At the moment she was singing a song about aardvarks while she worked through her kitchen cleaning chores. And then she looked out her kitchen window.

What?

Mary?

Is that you?

Why are you running like your hair is on fire?

"Mama!"

No answer.

She left her mama's kitchen and found her way to Simon's favorite place to be, his sunlit veranda, back-dropped with mountainous cliffs and a valley floor fifty feet below.

"Master Simon, sir?"

Hannah was standing near his table, silently, observing the fantastic beauty of her Stonehouse home surroundings.

"Esther, will you please call me Sim...," he looked up at her face, "What's wrong?"

"Mas... ah... Simon, it's Mary, from the house of Lazarus, she is on her way here."

"Yes, and? She is often at this house; the same is true of her brother... and her sister."

"She is flat out running up the road! As fast as she can go! Look!"

From his veranda observation post Simon saw this was true. Holding up her robe so as not to interfere with her running legs, she was almost flying, but Simon, having never seen so much leg before, gawked a moment, and then looked away.

"What in the world?"

Dropping out of their line of sight as she approached the house, all three left the veranda and went to meet Mary at the lower level door.

Through the house, down stone steps, around the corner, through an archway and out the door they went.

"Mary! What is wrong?"

Gasp... for breath... "Lazarus!" *Wheeze... inhale,* "Something's wrong!"

She fell against a doorpost, grabbing it with both hands, "Augh!" She screamed while drawing in another breath, "He was fine...," *exhale... inhale,* "We were working in the gardens and in the greenhouse... he was watering nard plants... and then... augh! Then he just collapsed! He threw up on the ground! His face, it is not working right! It looks like half of it is sliding off the wall!"

Overwhelming concern covered Hannah as she wrapped an arm around her friend.

Simon spoke with understanding, "Hannah, you get your kit together, take Esther and go back with Mary now, do what you can. I am going to find Benjamin."

Mary looked up, "Benjamin? Why?"

"He may know where Jesus is... the description of your brother... of Lazarus... his condition... there's only so much Hannah can do."

The finality of Simon's statement slapped Mary in the face, "Oh no! Lazarus! Simon! Lord God help! Help us now!"

Still wrapped with Hannah's arm around her shoulder, Mary hovered at a tipping point.

Hannah, with her left hand, lifted Mary's chin and spoke into her face, "Mary, God is always good, his help is always near, and he will help us now. Come with me, we will see to your brother. Simon will find the runner, your friend Benjamin, he knows things… and he may know where Jesus is!"

With imploring eyes, Mary looked to Simon, observing his perfect skin and hands, remembering what the leprosy had taken from him, before Jesus found him, healed him, and gave to him new fingers and skin. "Simon, when you find Benjamin, send him with this message, 'Lord, the friend whom you love is sick,' that is all."

"Mary, this is very serious, he is not just sick."

"My brother will live and not die!"

"Maybe something of a more… ah… hurry up and come here message?"

"I will not give place to fear! Lazarus will live and not die!"

"Alright then, that is the message then, 'Lord, the friend whom you love is sick,' you go now, I will find Benjamin."

From the center of the soul, at the place where words like seeds are planted in the garden of the heart, a north wind blew. A young woman guarded her black earth ground from every form of corruption. What grew in this place was her sustenance for many tomorrows; she attacked her surroundings with a vengeance. First she eradicated every unwanted plant from her plot, and then she headed north, into the prevailing wind, cutting down or digging out any weed that could send a seed her way. Sow thistle, stinging nettles, purslane and chickweed, they all met the ax.

CHAPTER 2

Benjamin was either going to be home or he wasn't. As a runner, Ben had seen more of Israel than any person Simon knew. Today it appeared he was home, one-half mile away, on a spot of ground just past the Stonehouse's southwestern boundary.

In Ben's yard were two rows of fence posts, five on each side, with a six foot space between them, a fishing net was stretched tightly between the posts. What appeared to be a full bale of freshly laundered wool was spread out on top of the net and drying, it still dripped water into the grass below.

Simon stepped up to the stone-block flat roofed home.

Knock, knock, knock.

"Enter"

Benjamin was seated near an open eastern window; his right foot was pumping a spinning wheel treadle as he fed wool fibers into the contraption, which in turn wound as yarn on a bobbin. Several full bobbins formed a mound by his left side.

"Benjamin, don't you ever stop moving?"

"Ah, Simon!" Ben responded without looking up, "So good to see you! What brings you by today? A new robe? Blanket? Maybe a..."

Ben looked up from his wheel, "Simon... what's wrong?"

"Do you know where Jesus is?"

"Ah… yes… he's out at the spot where the baptizer, John, spent so much time… why?"

A large loom sat beneath a closed, board-covered skylight, Simon moved into the room and placed his left hand on top of the machine. A beautiful, patterned wool blanket appeared to be almost done.

"Lazarus."

"Mary's Lazarus?"

"Yes, I sent both Hannah and Esther to go back with her ten minutes ago… but… Mary… her description… ah Ben… there is only so much Hannah can do."

Ben's mind moved faster than his weaver's shuttle, whatever had happened, Jesus was the only hope Lazarus had.

"I can get there, to where Jesus is out beyond the Jordan, by midafternoon, what's the message?"

"It's well over twenty miles Ben."

"From here it's twenty-seven miles, what's the message?"

Benjamin was already to his feet and tying on his running sandals. He swung a leather water skin over one shoulder and a packed bag over the other.

"Lord, the friend whom you love is sick."

"Tight message."

"It's not like it takes a lot of words."

"Nope."

"I'll let the sisters know you're on your way."

Lazarus was laying in the shade.

Martha was on her knees, only feet from where she was when Mary left. She had taken the blankets from her bed and laid them down next to her brother, and then rolled him onto them. Her pillow was under his head; his only movement was the rise and fall of his chest.

Hannah knelt across from Martha, "He is still breathing… that's good."

She listened for a moment, to the childhood song Martha was quietly singing to her brother, both her hands gently held his right hand.

"Any change?"

"How? What kind?"

Hannah had already checked his temp and breathing, calculating with each symptom, as Mary had presented them.

"Does he come any closer to you, say something... move... open his eyes... or does he just move further away?"

"He said there was two of me... and that his head hurt awful bad... and then he went away."

Hannah watched his breathing for a moment, pulled up one eyelid at a time and looked into his eyes.

"Martha, Mary... I am so sorry... I... Simon, he is... maybe Jesus will get here in time."

Martha questioned, "You sent for him? Where is he?"

Mary answered, "Simon thought Ben might know where Jesus is, and that Ben would bring a message to him."

"Good... he will get here in time."

The breathing pattern of Lazarus changed, becoming erratic, and he moved as if he were fighting something in his sleep. Martha held tightly to his hand, but she spoke to her brother as if he were walking up their steps and through the door, "I made rooster pot pie for lunch... your favorite... early this morning... while you were sleeping...I know I told you lunch was hard boiled eggs and cornbread... I wanted to surprise you... Lazarus! Please don't leave us... don't go! Lazarus, please!"

Martha bit her lip; tears were streaming down her face, dripping off her chin, landing on her brother.

"Augh! Lazarus!"

No response

"Mama!" Esther pleaded, "Do something! You always know what to do!"

"I am sorry Esther, he is not sick, something is broken... I cannot fix the broken part."

Although the body of Lazarus did not move, and no human saw him leave, Lazarus did leave his earth suit, after a moment of silent watching.

To the four crying women huddling around him, what they saw were dead eyes open wide and lock in place, as his heart stopped beating.

Lazarus, at first, once disconnected from the anchor of his body, laid the same way he was, with both eyes wide open, looking up at those around him.

Martha!

What's wrong?

Did someone hurt you?

She was sobbing; massive tears were running down her face.

He glanced to his left.

Hannah?

What are you looking at?

And why are you here, kneeling next to me?

Laz looked at her tanned leather shoulder bag, its top portion clenched tightly by her left hand.

You have brought your bag of stuff?

Why Hannah?

Did someone break a leg?

Someone cut a thumb while butchering chickens?

Lazarus sat up, looking at those around him, trying to get their attention.

No one, not one person, would look back at him.

This is too weird.

Esther, you are here too?

And Mary?

Emotional women!

What is wrong with you?

I am getting up.

As Lazarus stood up, a hand reached out to help him to his feet.

Huh?

Finally, someone here who will pay me some attention!

But, who are you?

"Do I know you? I can't say I've seen you before, but you seem familiar."

"I am an angel, your guardian, you can call me Floyd."

"Hum… alright, Floyd, my… ah… guardian angel, what's the matter with them?" Lazarus asked, motioning back towards the four crying women.

"You have left them, their lives will never be the same, each one will miss you severely, and for them… many things will change. Change is… usually disliked… complicated… and often difficult. They are… sad…and afraid."

"What? I'm not leaving! I'm not going anywhere! I like my life here just fine, thank you!"

"Lazarus, you have already left. Look at what they are crying over."

Laz stepped to the side for a better look, the women were all kneeling, hunched over some clumpy something beneath a canopy of silver birch trees dressed in springtime leaves.

"Ah… that… hum… guy… he sort of looks like me, who is it? Do I have a cousin or something?"

"That's your earth suit."

"My what?"

"Earth suit, you used to live in it, now it's empty."

"Why?"

"It's broken, you cannot live there anymore."

"Broken? How? Can't you fix it?"

"It's called a brain aneurism, and no I can't fix it, that's outside of my ability and jurisdiction."

"Martha!" Lazarus shouted.

No response.

"Mary!"

Nothing there either.

Lazarus gently placed his hand on Mary's back, but it never made contact, just passed right through. "Augh! I don't like this! It's not as if I am very old, I've never even been married… or anything… it's not my time to die!"

"No… it's not, not that you have a *'time to die'*, or a thing remotely close to a… a… specified time to die."

"Then… how did this happen?"

"An attack from the enemy kingdom, mixed with an access door he got from you, not much, but collectively it was enough. I'm sorry; we did our best to keep you in one undamaged piece."

"What happens now?"

"I will escort you to the place of protection, and your sisters will place your earth suit in a cave, or bury it in the ground... where... eventually, it will rot away to dust."

"Ah... no!... I don't want to go!... Not yet...I don't want to leave them here alone!"

Lazarus knelt on the grass, to be close to those he loved and lived with all his life, each one precious to the other.

Esther held the left hand of his empty earth suit; she held his hand in both of hers, while she gently kissed each knuckle, folding his fingers mixed with hers. Tears were streaming from her eyes, falling on their fingers and running down to thirsty ground.

Floyd reached his right hand out to Lazarus as he said, "Come," and although Lazarus did not choose to comply, nor did he move on his own, he moved just the same.

Sliding across the ground beneath a canopy of silver birch trees, Lazarus promptly found himself seated on green grass next to Floyd.

"Time to go," his angel said as he took hold of Lazarus by his right shoulder.

The instant contact was made between the guardian and his charge; both started sinking, down into the earth.

"Whoa back! Just hold on here a bit! Where are we going? You said you were taking me to the place of protection, right? You know... heaven, that's up, isn't it?"

"A little bothered, are we now?" asked his angel, as they slipped beneath the surface of the earth.

———

As we move through our world around us, we travel firstly on roads, rivers and trails; they're our fastest avenue of travel, unencumbered, with nothing in our way. Going directly between two points may be shorter, but such routes are often interlaced with obstacles which impede our travel.

Beneath the earth's surface, things are not that much different for creatures of the spirit arena. There are what could be called, rivers, roads and trails, all of which present easy passage; there are also swamps, mountains and canyons, so to speak, which may slow your travel to a crawl. It is expedient to have a knowledgeable guide, willing and able; to bring you where it is you need to go.

Floyd, as a standard guardian angel, had a *basics-plus* set of programs contained within the hardware of his operating system. Utilizing his subterranean-maps feature, he set both his location and destination, with route planning, on his mind screen and then chose *initiate*.

"I am supposing that you know where we are and where we are going?"

"Not to worry, as long as I don't lose hold of you, you'll be fine."

With both hands, Lazarus took a firm grasp of the canvas jacket his guardian wore.

"Good idea... I wouldn't want you to get lost down here... and be stuck inside some piece of stone."

Lazarus focused on their surroundings; he held the perception of moving in a fog. True, they were walking through a gravel vein, granite encased all around, but he could see some distance, ten and sometimes twenty feet.

"How long will it take for us to get to where we are going?"

"Do you ask, *are we there yet?*"

"I suppose."

"There are faster ways to travel... but I have been told to... ah... kick back... and take my time."

"We could take longer... that would be good... if we are not going to heaven... I'm not in a hurry... not any hurry at all... how about a tour of the earth? I have never been far from Bethany."

"What?"

Lazarus was dutifully following his guardian, but he also had his doubts about where they were going.

22 | Mike & Dianne Heintzeman

"Listen Floyd, if you're not taking me to heaven, I don't want to go! Let's do something else! Aren't there places you would like to go? I have heard of this giant ox called an elephant! Hannah has spoken of them; I would like to see an elephant! Please, let's go see one!"

"Lazarus! What are you thinking? I'm not taking you to hell... I don't do that anyhow; you are being taken to the place of protection! Abraham's bosom is what the place is sometimes called. You have believed Lord God, you watch for the messiah, you trust Jesus to be that messiah, and you go to the place of protection!"

"That's a relief! I thought you had made some sort of mistake!"

"The place of protection... there are many there, gathered from the dawn of time."

"When is heaven?"

"Not until Jesus completes his chores, and makes full payment to his Father."

"Oh."

The two were walking slightly downhill, and Floyd radiated light, not a great deal of light, but enough. He changed his brightness level as they moved through different types of earth, right now they were in some extremely clean sugar sand, easy going.

"How long have you been around? Around me, that is."

"I have watched over you from the time of your conception; however this is the first time you have seen me, although I've been with you all along."

"You could have said something... along the way that is... waved and said hello."

"Not without direct authorization and such a thing may happen only once or twice in a lifetime... and with some humans, never at all."

Eighteen minutes into their journey, and Lazarus was becoming accustomed to their surroundings, and Floyd's twisting, turning choices. Although he could only physically see a short distance, sometimes out to twenty feet, at times he could *feel* or *perceive* out much further.

"Is there a real open tunnel up ahead? Not a gravel vein but a real tunnel?"

"Well done Lazarus! We will enter Abraham Avenue within thirty minutes."

"How did I know that?"

"I occasionally connect to the Spirit Helper data stream for updates in information. It is possible for you to receive information fragments from Spirit Helper through that connection."

"If I let go of your jacket, would I get lost now?"

"Hum… let go and see what happens."

Lazarus let go of Floyd's canvas jacket.

Instantly, for Lazarus, all movement stopped. His body, or his spirit form, felt frozen, not cold, but immovable, encased in earth. Although with his eyes he could see Floyd begin to disappear into the fog-like gravel up ahead, his body would not budge; he could not even move his mouth to scream.

CHAPTER 3

Three miles from Bethany and twenty minutes away, Benjamin needed to make some adjustments; adrenalin could not be pulled upon as the long term energy source for his journey.

Lazarus my friend… what has happened to you?

Their message centers on some sickness;

It also pulls on Jesus' ability to fix you… and burn the sickness out.

Lazarus was not known for being overly adventuresome or exploratory; he expressed a peaceful contentment with his farmer/gardener type of life, which he lived with his two sisters. The only outside interest those around could ascribe to the man, was for one beautiful slave girl named Esther, but she was owned by his friend and her master, Simon.

Benjamin moved over to his next row of thoughts.

Martha…

To me you are as my motherly sister…

A place in which Lazarus truly stands…

Although you need your brother and the work which he does…

You love and serve that man with all your heart.

Your own mother and father have been gone for more than ten years now…

You must not lose another so close to your heart.

Martha had assumed the role of parenting-sister, when both their parents passed. She nurtured and held together what so easily could have been torn apart.

Mary...

Here Benjamin became flustered, conflicting emotions were already present in the garden of his heart. He carried a desire to protect Mary from all pain, and to rescue her from any evil. Through the window of his mind, he saw himself take and hold her hands, gently wipe the tears from her face with his fingers, and then gazing into her eyes, in his imagination, he told her everything was going to work out all right.

Benjamin could notice performance changes come to place in his body, chemical components and systems were shifting; running was becoming easier as his long distance mode was cutting in. He continued on in his practice.

Simon...

My neighbor and my friend...

Although you to me have been somewhat distant...

I have always known I could trust you.

I remember when it showed that leprosy had taken you...

Blotches of your skin turned white and your fingers falling off...

One knuckle at a time.

We all felt the loss...

But Martha wept for you most of all.

As master of his Stonehouse estate, Simon had managed for many years to keep the disease hidden, eventually his practiced diligence came to an end, and he was banished to a colony for the living dead. He was one of a group of ten who were healed, one who came back to worship God at Jesus' feet.

Benjamin slowed to a walk for a moment, took a few swallows of tepid water, replaced the stopper and then continued with his long distance pace and practice.

Jesus, who are you?

Ben Adam?

God in an earth suit?

You fixed Simon's skin and gave him back his fingers...

Rather amazing…
No ordinary man could do that…
Only God could give a man his fingers back.
What is it you will do with Lazarus?
Some fantastic thing?
Shake the earth from Jordan's Valley all the way to Bethany?
With words spoken from your mouth?
Will you shout, 'Stand up Lazarus!
Place both feet upon the ground!
Disease, get off the man and to hell with you!
Life be Lazarus!
Stand up!
Hmm, Jesus,
What is it you will say and do?

For Benjamin, his quest to find Jesus out beyond the Jordan would be much easier than his return trek. His feet were crossing a tipping point, a spot quite the same elevation as the level of the sea; it was all downhill from here. He was moving towards the oxygen rich environment of the lowest point on earth, an oddity, dry earth, twelve hundred feet below the level of the sea.

Lazarus thought about screaming but he felt no fear, only the odd sensation of being weightless and frozen, not cold, but immoveable. He pushed against his gravel encasement with every particle of strength he possessed, all to no avail, couldn't even twitch a finger.

Hum…
I feel like I've been packaged for shipping in some box to be sent to Egypt.
Floyd… my faithful guardian… do you think this is funny?
Come back and get me if you please…
Come and get me even if you don't please!

A minute later Floyd was there, he had circled around behind his charge, to sneak up and touch Lazarus at his elbow. Instantly, at contact, Lazarus could move once more.

Lazarus squawked as he reached around and took a tight hold onto Floyd's coat. "Floyd, you're a guardian… huh?… Do you think that's funny?"

"You asked," Floyd responded as he continued walking towards Abraham Avenue.

"I asked you if I would get lost if I let go of your jacket!" declared Laz as he twisted around for one last look at his gravel cage.

"Did you get lost?"

"Well… no."

"Lazarus, for twenty-eight years I have watched over you, constrained within a requirement of not letting you know I am here."

"Yes… so?"

Floyd lowered his illumination level, their gravel vein encasement had transitioned from black granite to white quartz, and its reflective brightness was intense.

"I thought a small demonstration was in order."

"What? A demonstration of what? Turning me into a statue?"

"A presentation so you might understand how much difference just my being close to you has sometimes made."

"Oh… well… hum…thank you… for all the times you have helped me when I didn't even know it."

"You Lazarus, beloved of Lord God, are welcome. What I do is done in service to my King."

"Maybe… I should thank him instead?"

"You should, Lord God is the one I belong to, and he is the one I serve."

"Hum… what's that?" Lazarus asked, drawn towards an anomaly in the transitioning earth layers surrounding them.

Laz quit moving, but kept a tight hold to his guardian's coat sleeve, Floyd responded to the tug on his sleeve and also stopped, "What's what?"

"Mixed in with the white rock, the yellow layers, the sheets of yellow stuff?"

One entire side of their gravel vein encasement was magnificent, translucent white quartz; it was layered with thick yellow sheets, almost vertical, flat-sheets of a yellow material which Lazarus couldn't see through. Some of the yellow flat-sheets were three to four inches thick, and looking large enough to use building a flat roof on a small home, an entire roof from just one piece.

"It's gold, pretty, isn't it?"

———————————

Simon arrived walking; there was no reason for him to run. All which needed to be done would be accomplished by Hannah and the sisters. Simon held complete trust in their abilities.

"Benjamin is on his way, he said Jesus is out beyond the Jordan, where John the baptizer spent so much time. It's twenty-seven miles; Ben says he can make it there within three hours… that's very good… Jesus could… arrive… here… by… late… tonight."

All four women were on their knees forming a small circle around Lazarus, in the shade of silver birch trees. Simon had begun speaking as he approached, from a hundred feet away, and as the distance between them diminished, so did hope in what he saw.

Martha, unmovable, unshakable Martha, weeping like a little girl, her face pressed down against her brother's chest. Hannah, Esther and Mary, each one crying too.

Circling around silver birch and crying women, Simon knelt beside Martha. Both eyes of her brother were open wide, but there was no life inside, he reached out and silently closed them. "I'm sorry… this is not what I expected… you sent for help… Benjamin is on his way… Jesus will be here soon and Lazarus was not supposed to die."

Martha leaned into Simon's shoulder, asking, "What do we do now Simon? What do we do?"

She took Simon's left hand in both of hers, "These are fingers which once were gone."

Simon finished for her, "And Jesus gave them back to me. Dead is only dead. We will do two things at the same time, we will prepare his body for the grave, and we will watch for Jesus walking up from Jordan's road."

Speaking to all four, Simon said, "If you three hold the blanket from your side, Martha and I will take this side, all together we can bring him into the house."

The War Is Over | 29

From the center of the soul, five people watched the sky, they glare into the wind. Storm clouds, deep purple mixed with green, rolling, tumbling, they were piling up in the sky above them. Raging updrafts with swirling winds, plus the type of heavy green clouds that dump hammering hail, and each one feared what that could mean. All their fences, all their planting, all their weeding, all their hopes and dreams, it all meant nothing if smashing hail descended from the sky.

CHAPTER 4

"You said Abraham Avenue is an open tunnel, is it very big? Very long, I mean?"

They had passed through King Solomon's treasury, (a name ascribed by Floyd to the area where their passageway-vein brought them through translucent white quartz, the spot layered with vertical sheets of gold). After the treasury, Floyd began identifying other interesting rock formations along the way.

"There are thousands of miles of branch tunnels; we will only go through one limb and the primary trunk."

"Once we enter the avenue, will we go back to this type of stuff? Walking through dirt and coal and stone? Maybe another diamond field? I liked that place, especially when you showed me how the stones could look if they were cut."

"No, Abraham Avenue will bring us all the way in."

"Hm... are there many people there?"

"Where?"

"In the place of protection."

"Lazarus, think about it, every human ever conceived is in one of three places. If their body is alive, they reside on the earth's surface, that's one place."

"Okay, the place I just left, what's the other two?"

"If their body has become uninhabitable, they are either in the place of protection, or across the pit in hell."

"So… there are a lot of people there… yes?"

"Yes, on both sides of the pit."

"Oh… ah… how about on the protected side, are there many people there?"

"Millions."

"I don't know that word."

"Let's say if one grain of sand represented one person, there's more sand than you could move in one day."

"Wow!… That's a lot of people!"

"Millions."

"Some have been there for a long time, yes?"

"Yes, for Adam and Eve, it has been four thousand years."

"Oh my word, what do they do all day? They are awake, aren't they? I mean they aren't knocked out or something, are they? I don't know if I will get sleepy, and I don't sense a need to eat… much of my time on earth was spent growing food to eat, cooking, or making clothes to wear! What do they do with all of their time? What will I do with all my time? I'm not very good at doing nothing!"

"Lazarus, that's the one question everyone asks before they arrive… watch your step."

Lazarus hadn't noticed the collective force required to push his soul and spirit self through an environment of dirt, stone or gravel; he had been leaning forward, looking like he was walking through chest deep water.

At Floyd's warning call of 'watch your step', the two were transitioning from walking through solid rock, to a cave filled with only air.

"Wha!" was all the angel heard as Laz pitched forward, passing Floyd on his right hand side. Losing his grip on Floyd's sleeve, Laz landed spread eagle across a gravel floor.

"Hough!… Ouch!… Huh…? That felt… just like it did back at home… interesting… I felt… pain?"

Floyd helped him to his feet.

"What's that noise?"

"Ah yes, the noise, they like to do that for new arrivals."

There was definitely sound coming their way, although it was rather faint.

Laz looked around, they hadn't entered at the end of a tunnel, rather, they had come in through its side; the tunnel went in both directions from where they stood.

"Which way do we go?"

Descending to his right at an angle of approximately three degrees, Floyd headed downhill and towards the noise.

At first it was an even sound, then its pitch rose a bit and fell, followed by a spell of humming, some snapping, a slapping sort of clapping and a hush... followed by a roar!

"Floyd... I think... someone... is singing!"

"Could be, we should check it out."

> *Halleluiah...* (Soft, slow and low, very baritone)
> *Halleluiah...* (Lower still and with a whisper present)
> *Halleluiah...* (A little higher mixed with tenor)
> *Halleluiah...* (All mixed together with a sultry, warbling, woman's voice added, and higher, with maxed out decibels, from what sounded to be about one mile away)
> *All the saints and angels singing...*
> *Ain't my Jesus grand!* (Way loud, but still a mile away)

Prickly sparkles danced up and down Lazarus' spine, they went up to his ears and back to his toes, then Laz dropped to his knees, centered on the cave floor as both hands shot straight up into the air.

"Yes! Yes! Yes! Jesus!"

"Floyd! They are here! Miles underground, how do they know?"

"You were wondering what they do with all their time? Maybe you would like to find out?"

"Yes! Of course! Come on!"

Lazarus started running downhill, calling out, "Come on Floyd! I need your *glow in the dark self* to see with! Come on!"

Floyd caught up, but let Laz run in front, allowing him to be first in line to see all those who welcomed him in.

Laz broke out of Abraham Avenue tunnel, spell-bound. There before him, singers, shouters, and a crowd of people whooping and hollering. Some he recognized, some he thought he knew, but with many, he didn't have a clue who they were; but they all looked to be about his same age, and they were all cheering!

First his mom and dad grabbed him and hugged him, then he was spun around and someone else hugged him. Hands slapped him on the back, voices shouted and people cheered.

"Wha... wha... what? I just died! You all make me feel like I just... won something! Like I'm... the winner!"

"Lazarus! You got it made forever!"

"Yeah Laz! And you get to see what happens next!"

"Uh huh! From right up front, in the center of it all!"

Lazarus seemed confused.

Two people stepped up next to Lazarus, a man and a woman, they appeared to be related, brother and sister maybe, cousins perhaps. The man spoke to all around, "Give the man a little space, we are all excited to see him. Let him acclimate and get adjusted, he has only just arrived!"

"Who are you?" Lazarus asked, somewhat perplexed.

"I am called Mordecai."

"And I am his niece, Queen Esther."

"Queen Esther?"

"Yes," she answered appearing slightly embarrassed, "most people here call me Esther, but on earth I was Queen Esther. They thought it would be a positive, if uncle and I helped..."

Laz cut her off, "You! You even look like her! You are the one my... Esther... my friend... she was named after you... but... she...I."

Mordecai nodded slightly towards Lazarus' parents, and his mom, who looked no older than her son, moved in next to him and put her arm around his waist. "Laz, honey, you're here, this is wonderful, and if you stay here... well..."

"Mom! What do you mean, *'if I stay here?'* I thought everything was settled! Floyd! What's going on?"

Mordecai responded, "Not to worry Lazarus, while you are here, as a new arrival, Queen Esther and I are to assist in your... ah... assimilation, but there are... other things in play."

"What? You're making me more confused, what more things could be going on than what already is! This is all too up and down wild!"

Lazarus was making animated motions, flinging his arms in the air, spinning in a circle. Both hands settled on top of his head.

Queen Esther touched Laz on the shoulder, "Lazarus, your sisters... they... they sent a runner, your friend, Benjamin, they sent a message to Jesus."

"Huh? Fine, but my body died, my angel, Floyd, he said I had a brain... a brain... something or other, and that my sisters will bury my body or put it in the family tomb, probably in the tomb."

Mordecai spoke, "Lazarus, we understand all of what you speak, but you see, Jesus has raised others from the dead, and... you my friend, well... we will wait and see. Until then, like everyone else, we desire to make you welcome."

"Ah, thank you... I guess."

CHAPTER 5

Mordecai was on the right of Lazarus and Queen Esther stepped around to his left, taking his elbow with both hands.

"Come; let's walk a bit, and go for a newbie tour."

They began a slow meandering stroll. The three could have been going somewhere special, or just puttering along, Lazarus didn't care, he felt safe, but in need of adjustment, calibration to his surroundings.

"This morning I was watering plants in our garden… and now… I am here."

Queen Esther spoke softly, "That is the way leaving so often is."

Mordecai spoke up, "You and your sisters have built some fine gardens."

"You talk as if you've seen them."

"We have, they contain a look of… faithful diligence."

Lazarus felt eyes on him, glancing to both sides he saw others walking with; the three were being intently observed as they moved along.

"Why are they studying us so closely? You must get new arrivals on a regular basis… don't you? They are staring, is there something wrong? Are my ears on upside-down… and backwards?"

Queen Esther explained, "You will need to give them time, they have watched you on earth, they know you are a friend of Jesus."

"Oh… okay."

Laz was looking at rock formations as they slowly moved by; he had observed a similar assortment near the Dead Sea and En Gedi. Pillars, small canyons, stone archways and shelf rocks, all laced with nooks and crannies.

"I don't understand… how could they have seen me talk with Jesus?"

Queen Esther started, "Lazarus, what Lord God has done for us here is uniquely special."

Mordecai questioned, "Do you want to tell him, or should we show him?"

"Showing is more fun."

"Alright, I will give a short explanation, and then you show him how it works, something mild to start with."

They were near a rectangular table rock, one of several Laz had seen as they walked along; places for gathering and visiting, with spots for sitting. At these areas fifteen or twenty people were sometimes gathered, often they were laughing.

"Very good, may I show an excerpt of the Haman dinner?"

"If you so desire. Alright, short explanation. We all have recorded memories in our minds, things which we have lived and seen. Lord God filters through those memories and arranges some for us to let others see."

Laz wondered, "To see? How do you see a memory?"

"Like this."

Queen Esther sat down and placed both hands, palms down, on their table. She then focused her eyes on the end of the table, a flat but moving picture appeared at the other end. The moving picture was of Queen Esther at a fancy dinner with the King and one other man. There were several maid servants attending to their food and comfort.

"What! How did you do that? It's like I am watching you through a window! And I can hear you talking! But your voice comes from the moving picture, not from where you're sitting! How are you doing that?"

Mordecai answered, "Lazarus, it is not what we have done, as with all else of any value, it is what Lord God has done."

Queen Esther lifted her hands and the moving picture disappeared.

"What about Mary's garden, how did you see that? My memories are here... with me!"

"Again, the short answer; there are things seen through an angel's eyes Lord God allows us to see. Esther's moving picture had a mixture of her memories, and what was seen by her guardian or another angel."

"My guardian, Floyd, he spoke of a Spirit Helper data stream."

"Uncle! Lazarus may be good with presenting short answers also."

"Can I do this too? Show a moving picture?"

"I would suppose Lord God has yours ready, try."

Queen Esther did not move from her spot, Laz sat down beside her, placing both his hands upon their table, palms down.

Mordecai gave instructions, "Focus on a memory, only the filtered ones will show, and Lazarus, the truth of what was seen is what will be displayed, with this system you cannot present a lie. And you may stop at any time; just lift your hands from the table."

"Alright... thank you."

Lazarus focused on a thought, and at the end of their table was a moving picture. Mary, his younger sister, was digging weeds, using a short Roman spear for a shovel.

Lazarus lifted his hands from their table, "I'm happy and sad at the same time."

Observing shades of loss unfold across his new friend's face, Mordecai attempted to counter the encroaching grief with a value added positive.

"Lazarus, is there some particle of history which you desire to more fully comprehend?"

"What?"

Queen Esther translated her uncle's kindness, "Is there some past event, a happening, which has... bugged you... that you would like to understand?"

Laz considered their offer for a moment before responding. Leaning forward, and cautious to not allow his hands to be placed palm down upon their table, he finally answered. "Yes, there is something that has... *bugged*... me. I dislike snakes, and my Esther hates them. What

I wonder is this, how could Adam and Eve ever allow themselves to be fooled by such an ugly creature as some cursed snake!"

Queen Esther only whispered, "Uh-oh…"

Lazarus heard her *uh-oh* and wondered what she meant.

"A perfectly valid request, let's take it to its source!"

Mordecai stood up… leaving… not waiting for the others to follow.

"Come! I believe they are in the hill country with their rocks, only minutes away, it's the closest thing we have to a real garden; underground as we are there is nothing green which grows here. I do miss the color green, to see green alive and in its fullness!"

The two were walking quickly to catch up, and Laz called out to Mordecai, "Who is they? You know, the ones we are going to see?"

"Who? Well… Adam and Eve, of course!"

"Really? They will answer? They will tell us?"

Laz glanced behind them and saw residents observing their new arrival, walking swiftly with his hosts, deciding it a good idea to tag along.

Knowing what was coming next, Queen Esther only answered, "Your question Lazarus… is on the top ten list of those most often asked and answered."

Their surroundings were transforming as they traveled, the further on they went the more characteristics changed. Where they had been was an abundance of knee high rocks, suitable for sitting, now the rocks were bigger, and varyingly different. Of course there was no grass or greenery ground cover, but there was a consistency of pea sized pebbles placed as ground cover. Set amongst a sea of pebbles were, for lack of a better term, decorator rocks. Tall rocks, skinny and equal to the height of a man, perfectly round rocks and rocks shaped like Juniper trees. They were a beautiful assortment of subterranean rocks.

How uniquely different, an Adam and Eve rock garden!

Through a hollow and a slight distance off was a large, round table rock, again with smaller rocks around for sitting.

Mordecai called out, "Hello Adam! Are you around?"

"We are over here," replied a woman's voice.

"Excellent! We have a new arrival who desires to observe the *tempting cursed snake!*"

Again came a woman's voice, "Is it Lazarus from Bethany? We hoped he would stop by."

Mordecai answered, "Yes, it is, plus about forty others who have followed along."Mordecai led the way and the entire group moved in and stood around Adam's table.

A beautiful woman and a handsome man came into sight. The woman, Eve, spoke directly to Lazarus, "Your friend, Benjamin, the runner, he is more than halfway to where Jesus is, he is making good time."

Lazarus answered, "Ah... thank you... um... Eve."

Adam and Eve sat at the stone table, one across from the other.

Adam identified the obvious, obvious to all but Lazarus, "Of what you are about to see, all is factually and visually correct, except Lord God has added to us clothes, understood? Back then we were the only ones around... and... well...Eve looked absolutely magnificent without them... so I was content with the arrangement."

"Adam! Stop that!"

"Yes dear," Adam replied with a slight smile, "Shall we continue? Palms down."

Simultaneously, both Adam and Eve placed their hands on the table, palms down. Instantly, appearing centered on the round stone table was a miniature, exact to scale moving replica of Adam and Eve in the Garden of Eden, with nice robes on. Many of the watchers were cheering, calling out to the little figures on the table, who of course could not see or hear them.

"Whoa now, how'd you do that? The picture is not flat... it has depth... and presence... aliveness... and it covers the entire center of the table!"

On the table stood a man and woman about six inches tall, and some garden trees, some of which were up to three feet tall.

Laz asked again, "Mordecai, how are they doing that? It's as if I am there! Really there and watching!"

Queen Esther spoke first, "Uncle, just the short answer, please?"

40 | Mike & Dianne Heintzeman

First he took a stick and waved it through the moving figures saying, "They are only a projected image, there is no substance present, understood?"

"Yes sir."

"Now the short answer… memory record through multiple eyes allows full view with depth perception. Minimum requirements are two humans plus two angels. The more eyes present, the more data which may be filled in."

"Well done uncle, thank you!"

Lazarus watched intently, searching the tall grass and trees for one slimly, ugly snake. Caught up in his feelings and his watching, and believing he saw a slithery movement, Laz shouted, "Adam, look out! Grab a stick and whack him in the head!"

Those around him laughed, watching Laz, behaving like a little kid, leaning on the table, his knuckles resting on smooth stone, his face only inches away from trees and a garden that was thousands of years long gone.

Queen Esther teased, "Look out Laz! Don't get too close! The snake might bite you on the nose!"

Laz wondered, but he still moved back a little, pulling in a more encompassing view, when a flock of large birds dropped in from above, all but one landed in the trees.

"Wow! This is amazing, and I smell… oranges! Look! The leaves! They wiggle with the wind!

The one lone bird circled, gliding, floating on bone and leather wings, "That's quite the handsome bird Adam, but kind'a different. It has wings like a bat, with each wing as long as its entire body… sleek… muscly, with a slender tail, and no feathers?"

Laz moved closer in again, reaching with his right hand, as if trying to get the flying thing to land on a finger. "I've seen pictures… drawings of something like your leather-wing bird, but yours is quite stately, and kinder looking, yet powerful, a thing you could trust, like a dog I would let play around my cousin's kids."

Queen Esther asked, "And this creature which you saw, in a drawing, did it have a name?"

"Oh... yes... but there are none around, I don't know if there ever was... it was called a dragon... what... no way! Is this one? What happened? I would love to have one for a pet, to have such a grand animal for a pet! Forget a dog! I want a dragon!"

Mordecia spoke up, "Quite majestic, is it not? The problem is... you just can't trust a dragon... any more than you can trust a snake."

"What? No! Say it isn't so! That's no snake! Look at it... it's beautiful... it's... it... oh... oh no... is it really?"

Mordecai continued, "This is what it was before Lord God cursed it, to eat dust and slide forever on its belly, for allowing our traitor and enemy to move in and speak through its persona. This is what it was."

"Adam... Eve... I am... so sorry... I had no idea."

Adam answered, "It is what it is, and this is no excuse for what we did. We all need Jesus for our savior... true? Just as true for me as you."

Laz, all wrapped up in the fun of having so many new friends around the table, and the joy of visiting with them, asked, "Is there another?"

Queen Esther tipped her head slightly, asking, "Pardon? Another what?"

"Another something... like this... except," Laz said, gesturing towards two small figures with a dragon landing in a fruit tree. "Another memory story picture show, but one with a happy ending? With a victory of some kind? Where an ugly enemy gets whacked in the head?"

Mordecai surveyed those who were watching, standing near Adam's table. In his mind he paged through memories which they carried, stopping at one their guest was sure to think he knew.

"David, I see you are here with Jonathan and one brother. Would you care to satisfy our guest's request?"

David asked, "And that would be how?"

"As a shepherd boy against Goliath."

CHAPTER 6

In order to get himself to where Jesus was out beyond the Jordan River, Benjamin chose the only road there was, which brought him slightly north. It descended on a winding path through rocky ground, mountainous up and down hills that continually rose and fell, with very little flat. In the terrain descending to the Jordan Valley, flat was only a foot or two wide, just a transition space before you went back uphill. His road somehow found a way between those hills creating one steady descending grade.

With his face set towards some of the most desolately beautiful landscape of his nation, Ben caught short glimpses of a spot of green and memories which it held. Jericho, the first city besieged by Abraham's descendants and began the taking of their promised land.

As Ben ran, he thought upon the battle that brought it down.

Jericho had been a primary fortification of invincible walls, eight hundred and fifty feet below sea level, and surrounded by twelve square miles of magnificent, spring fed farmland.

But Jericho was also a place of debauchery, and obedience to its total destruction was Israel's gateway into their Promised Land.

If only I could have stood in this place where I now run...
And watched the walls fall down!
To see with my own eyes...

The stories I've been told...
And the written word that I have read!
Jericho, a one thousand foot diameter circle fortress, with the city's finest homes and shops built into its outer walls. On special occasions, chariot races took place on the flat roof road, built above those massive castle walls.

Joshua, leader of the three million Israelites and groomed by Moses as his successor, had sent two men into Jericho to spy out the city. Found out and running for their lives, they took refuge inside a house of ill repute, a grand house, a house built into the outside wall.

Rehab...
Quite the name for a harlot...
I suppose most watchers considered it only normal when two strange men knocked upon her door.
Unique...
For her help in hiding the spies...
To Rehab and her family was protection promised...
And they unharmed survived.

The green fields of Jericho came into sight once more as Ben rounded a curve. They would be continually visible for the next twenty minutes, until another mountain slid over and obscured his view.

Huh...
After forty years wandering in the wilderness...
And only a few days after Passover...
600,000 warriors marched around those walls in absolute silence...
Once a day for six days!

The feet of marching soldiers, *columns, four-hundred men wide and fifteen-hundred men long,* the feet totally crushed every plant and clod of dirt in a giant circle, one mile in diameter around the city. Priests blowing trumpets in the front line met the soldiers last in line as they completed each day's march.

From the written record in the book of Joshua, Benjamin tried to picture the seven day sequence in his mind. Seven laps around the walls on the seventh day, one massive connected circle of marching men spread around the doomed city with the inhabitance hiding inside. Six laps in silence… and on the seventh… six hundred thousand marching men shouted as priests blew ram's horn trumpets, and the Jericho walls fell down.

Lord God, they believed you!
You washed the promised land of those who loved sin and hated you!
Your people moved forward…
Acquiring their inheritance…
Just the way you told them to!

At the end of the seventh circle of the seventh day, when the ram's horn blew and soldiers shouted, the wall tore loose from the harlot Rehab's home within the wall and began rolling inward, an impossible thing to do. Falling inward, the stone walls, with their foundations, all were vomited up and out of the ground from where they were anchored. Beginning at Rehab's house, and running the wall around, the walls rolled up and out of the ground from where they were set, killing many of Jericho's inhabitants as they fell.

In the end, only those of Rehab's house still stood and lived, and nothing else inside was left alive.

And you let a harlot and her family live…
Why?
Because she helped the spies?
Tied a scarlet cord from her window and let blood-red color flow down the wall? Because she hated sin?
Or because she looked to you and lived?

Jericho, still five miles away, passed out of Benjamin's view as his road shifted slightly south.

Never to be rebuilt as a fortress city.
Lord God…
I'm sure you had good reason…
But why did you have Joshua curse the sons of any man who would rebuild those fortress walls?
It must have been a terribly wicked place…
Or was it just that Jericho was not to be your Jerusalem…
A rebuilt heathen hall?

As a protection to future generations, eventually the men of Israel hauled the Jericho stones away, to be used for other things, anything else, just never a Jericho castle wall.

———————————

On the outskirts of the little town of Bethany, two miles southeast of Jerusalem, five with sad faces carried the dead body of their friend and brother.

Bethany was a small farm town and close-knit, filled with neighbors who were friends as well. It's also a world where the survival of one often depends on the volunteered assistance of another.

Central to smooth flow and function of any place where people dwell is an element which keeps it running smoothly. This is especially true when times are tough, as they were now, and so entered the element called tradition.

Tradition, good hearted, best of intentions, this is what comes next cause that's the way it is… tradition.

Simon spoke decisive words, "Martha, Mary, listen to me, this is not the time to quit. Dead is only dead."

Martha, on Simon's right and holding tightly to the blanket carrying Lazarus' body, asked, "Simon, what?"

"You have sent a runner to find Jesus, he could be here late tonight; it is only the body of your brother which is dead, he is somewhere else."

"Yes… and?"

"And I don't know how to stop what happens next. Even now, watching eyes see us carrying your brother inside. Very soon, help will be knocking at your door."

The five carrying one were maneuvering up stone steps and sidestepping through the open western entry. Once inside, they hovered for a moment as Esther scurried over and cleared dishes off the table where they gently set Lazarus' body down.

"And what comes next?"

"People, neighbors, the Rabbi, those who will press you to prepare his body for the grave. You may be able to hold off his burial until tomorrow, but that is the best you could hope to do."

"And if Jesus doesn't arrive tonight?"

"Save your fight for where it matters most. Plant a picture in your heart of Lazarus alive. The people who will be here soon are not your enemy; don't make them your enemy."

Martha had been holding her brother with her eyes, she lifted them to Simon and placed her left hand on his right, "Will you stay? And help?"

"Yes, yes of course, all three of us, we will stay and help."

Gravel footsteps on the step announced the arrival of a neighbor.

Knock, knock, knock.

From the center of the soul, five people watch the sky, wind, lightning, thunder, torrential rain; all had left their mark and then passed by. From the shelter of a roof they watch the last drops fall. First was eerie, intense quiet, almost a vacuum, then straight-line winds followed by horizontal rain, falling in sheets, buckets of frog-strangling rain, but no hail; finally, stepping into wet grass they go to check their gardens.

Corn?

The stalks were all askew, fallen, twisted laying on each other, roots exposed, each as a hand with many fingers. With washed out roots, what is an anchor to the soul?

The War Is Over | 47

CHAPTER 7

Those seated around Adam and Eve's table gave space to allow Jonathan, David and his eldest brother to settle in.

When all were seated, David spoke to Jonathan and Eliab, "Ready brothers?"

All three placed their hands on the table, palms down.

An entire battlefield appeared before the eyes of Lazarus and the rest.

Philistine warriors were assembled for battle; Goliath and his five brothers walked among them. Rolling hills and green meadows were covered with chanting fighters. On one side was assembled Israel, the armies of King Saul, on the other were Goliath and the Philistines. Between them laid the valley of Elah, arrayed for mortal combat, a place for blood to flow.

Goliath, a massive giant standing almost ten feet tall, strutted his arrogant self, owning the valley. He beat upon his silver-mail armored-chest with shovel-sized hands, shouting profanities into the air. His huge head, equal in size to a five gallon water bucket, was covered with a bronze helmet, gleaming in the sun.

Close within his reach were his tools of war, a massive sword sheathed at his hip and a monstrous shield which was held before him by his armor barer. In his right hand was a tree-size spear, waiting to be thrown through whoever was fool enough to fight against him.

In the prelude to this battle, this scaled down thing which sat on Adam's table equaled in size to a circle three hundred feet in diameter, and the people were about one inch tall. As Laz watched, the moving picture was pulled in closer and Goliath was growing taller, until he stood a foot tall, cursing and swearing, strutting back and forth through the valley of Elah, yet all took place on Adam's table.

"Mordecai... how... where is David?"

Near where Lazarus stood, a scrawny teenage shepherd boy emerged, running forward, shouting as he ran. Hardly half the height of the ugly giant, he carried a shepherd's staff in both hands.

Laz leaned further out and stared at Goliath's pock-marked face, his shoulder-length oily black hair and braided beard dyed the color crimson. The red beard accented his green and yellow teeth. A necklace made of human thumbs hung around his neck.

Laz gasped, "Augh! That's bad... I can smell his breath!"

David ran towards the giant, holding his shepherd's staff in both hands.

Goliath poked at him with his spear, and David deflected the spear with his staff.

Goliath shouted at the shepherd boy, "Am I a dog that you come to me with sticks?" And the Philistine cursed David by his gods.

David shouted back, "Come to me! And I will give your flesh to the birds of the air and beasts of the field! You come to me with a sword and spear, but I come to you in the name of the Lord God of Israel! Today he has given you into my hand! Today I will strike you down and cut your head smooth off!"

Lazarus was watching closely, and he saw David drop his shepherd's staff... then he saw Goliath stagger a bit... and the giant fell forward... with his face to the ground at David's feet.

"What! What happened? Why did he fall down? Is he getting up again, what happened?"

David ran up to the fallen giant pulling Goliath's own sword from his sheath. He held the sword up in the air and jumped up and down on

Goliath's back with both feet! Next, David circled slightly around and lined up at Goliath's neck and chopped his head smooth off!

"David, what happened?"

David was interrupted from his focused chore, but his hands were still palms down on the table. He asked, "Lazarus, is there a problem?"

The entire battle scene was still there, but it was locked down, not moving, Lazarus gawked at it, asking, "What happened? Why did he fall down? I didn't see you do anything!"

David said, "Maybe you should have watched a little closer."

"I always thought you hit him in the head with a stone from your sling?"

"I did."

"How, I didn't see you do it, and I am standing right here, I watched you cut the monster's head off!"

"I had to come in close… close enough to come up almost under his helmet with the stone… I couldn't let Goliath know I had a sling."

"What?"

"Here, we will back it up, you watch, and we will show you once more."

David, Jonathan and David's oldest brother worked together, focused, and ran the scene back about two minutes.

And then they played it forward… very slowly… five seconds equaling one minute.

Queen Esther said, "Lazarus, look at what he has in his hands… hidden behind his shepherd's staff."

Laz looked intently. There was the sling latch and loop in David's right hand, with his left hand pulling tight to the basket and stone. All were hidden in his hands or behind his shepherd's staff.

As Laz watched, David let go of his staff, swung the sling-stone just one quick loop over his head… released the stone… drove the stone up through Goliath's right eye and into his brain… all before David's staff hit the ground.

Laz was amazed, "Wow, that was fast, Goliath never saw it coming! How… who?"

"Lord God told me how and what to do," David answered.

"But… I… how did… uagh!" Laz spoke in frustration, not understanding.

"Goliath was a man of war from his youth. I could not afford to let him see me as a threat… or to see the threat. The target area was small. To kill him, it was needful to have the stone enter deeply… preferably through an eye… I could not give him time to turn his head."

"Oh… okay… and his helmet?"

"Yes, it protected his entire head. The stone trajectory required an upward angle of at least twenty degrees. He needed to see me as a nothing, navel lint, a boy with a stick, letting me get close, only feet away, close enough to strike."

From back the way they came, from where the greeters were when Laz had first entered through Abraham Avenue, there arrived a woman.

"Mordecai, pardon me, David, Est… ah… hum… Queen Esther."

Mordecai asked, "Anna, you have an update? Is there news?"

"The runner, Benjamin, he has visual contact with Jesus, from across the Jordan, he is only minutes from delivering his message."

"Very good, thank you. Were you able to see Simon?"

Lazarus watched a transformation, the woman's face brightened, almost glowed, and her verbal presentation was as of a giddy little girl, with happy tears running from her eyes.

"I saw him! Only for a moment, but it was Simon! With perfect skin! And Mordecai… Jesus delivered new fingers to him also! They are beautiful!"

CHAPTER 8

Miles away a mob has gathered, for some the time has come to face a reckoning with the law. Three guilty persons, one woman and two men, stood huddled with sad faces, each one admitting to their sins. Around them, near a shoreline stood a dozen who were chosen, and collectively they will administer, watch and bear record.

"It is time," declared one of two which will carry out the chore. Each takes firm grip of the woman near her shoulders; they then pull her to walking backwards, further out from shore.

Waiting, silent, they stand in hip-deep water.

On the river's edge are more watchers, witnesses; some shed silent tears for the woman, some wipe around their eyes with empty hands, yet each watcher understands the need of what is being done.

Both men together, with a nod between each other, push the woman backwards and under water. One, born from compassion, looks into her open eyes and speaks words which she cannot hear.

At first there is a struggle, but then all struggle stops. Finally, confident their deed is done; they pull her body up from the water and bring it back to shore.

Next, a man with flowing tears steps to his place, knowing that he was next in line. He goes without a struggle.

With this one their timing was slightly different, and he heard some of their spoken words before they forced him down and into death. "I baptize you…" is all he heard before he was immersed into a relationship picture of death, burial and resurrection.

Raising him up a moment later, Peter and John took his hands and led him back to shore, John informed him as they walked; "Pushed beneath the water portrays your old man dying, guilty under the law, held below the water was that of being buried, and then rising is the life of God coming alive brand new inside of you, a thing that Jesus declares is soon to happen, yes?"

"Yes! Thank you!" the joyful man responded hugging John, causing the mostly dry upper portion of John's half drenched body to become more wet.

"You are welcome… next," John said moving back out to deeper water with one more disciple of Jesus to baptize.

Two miles south, the murky water in which they stood flowed through the River Jordan's mouth, forever to be entombed within the Dead Sea's stone enclosure. Northeast, near Bethabara, a flock of black feathered ravens speckle the horizon. Gazing five miles northwest and slightly uphill, were green fields, the spring fed cropland of Jericho. Closer by, a hundred feet away and on the eastern gravel banks of the Jordan River was Jesus, telling stories, parables, to a captivated crowd of a few hundred people. Most were struggling to understand the mystery of his words. The day was peaceful, an early afternoon, bright blue sky with a slight southern breeze; all this was clothed in a balmy seventy-five degrees.

Jesus continued with another story.

"A farmer went out to plant his fields, casting seed into the ground. And it came to pass as he sowed the seed, some fell by the wayside, where birds came and devoured it up."

Peter and John had the next man ready to baptize. They held their charge by his shoulders and pushed him under water. With both his hands under water, John looked up and over at Jesus, trying to hear his story.

"And some fell on stony ground, where it had not much earth; and immediately sprouted up, because it had no depth of earth: But when the sun came up, it was scorched; and because it had no root, it withered away."

Peter, gazing down into the man's eyes they were holding under water, asked, "What story is he telling now? Can you hear?"

"And some fell among thorns, and the thorns grew up, and choked it, and it yielded no fruit."

John answered as together they pulled the man back up, "The one about a farmer planting wheat seed in a field."

"And other seed fell on good ground, and did yield fruit that sprang up and increased, and some brought forth thirty times what was planted, and some sixty times, and some a hundred times what was planted."

Peter continued in his conversation with John as they brought the man back to shore, "I don't get it. What does he mean? What does planting seed in a field have to do with anything, other than eventually eating a loaf of bread?"

Jesus was silent for a moment, watching a running figure across the river, about a quarter mile away.

Wondering about the meaning of his story, people in the crowd tipped their heads and scratched their chins, some murmured to the person standing next to them.

"You seem to understand his stories… if he tells one about catching fish."

Peter whispered back, "His fishing stories usually make more sense."

In conclusion to his story Jesus shouted, "He that has ears to hear, let him hear!"

Peter and John stood on the shoreline, both dripping water and with no more people to baptize at the moment, John asked, "Why don't you just ask him what he means?"

"John! It will look like I don't know!"

"Huh… isn't that the point?"

Jesus, keeping one eye on the approaching runner who was less than two miles out now, traded another story for a question, asking, "What should we say is like the kingdom of God? Or with what comparison should we compare it? It is like a grain of mustard seed, which, when it is sown in the earth, is the smallest of all seeds that are planted."

The runner's identity could now be told, it was Benjamin, of Bethany, from the house of Heis.

"But when it is planted, it grows up, and becomes greater than all herbs, and sends out large branches; so that the birds of the air may lodge under the shadow of it."

CHAPTER 9

In the place of protection, Mordecai orchestrated the outline of events which followed Anna's arrival and message.

"Lazarus, we must have you and… are your parents here?"

"We are here!" answered a woman's voice.

"Very good… come… come to the table, you too Anna, you should add an amount of adjoining detail. Anyone else?" Mordecai called to those standing around Adam and Eve's rock garden stone table. "Anyone else with close association to Lazarus or those involved, possibly someone from the house of Heis, or a relative of Benjamin?"

"Grandfather," a man called out.

"Good… you could give us access to Benjamin's thoughts… come… sit… very good… yes… alright, everyone ready?"

"Wait!" Lazarus called out, "Mordecai, refresh my memory please… this all works… how? What you do around the table?"

"This is what Lord God lets us see through his Spirit Helper data stream, he makes it very simple for us to use within his rules. This is only what has been seen and recorded by his people or angels, and once in a while Lord God lets us *hear* a person's thoughts, but that is very rare. Alright, ready? Yes? Very good… palms down."

Back on the surface of the earth, Benjamin, with a half mile to go, was reading the scene before him. On Jordan's eastern bank and facing south was a tight-knit crowd, two hundred and fifty, maybe three hundred people. Twenty feet in front of the crowd was a man making animated gestures with his arms as he spoke to the people.

That must be Jesus doing the talking.

Three men were in the water, one was standing backwards.

They must be baptizing people today,
But then they probably do that every day.

The two push the standing-backwards man under water.

Those two look like Peter and John!

Benjamin watched, holding his breath during fifty feet of running.

Come on guys!
Bring him back up!
What are you trying to do, drown the guy?

Peter and John pulled the waterlogged man back up, allowing Benjamin to breathe once more.

Well!
It's about time, don't you think?
Hum… the water looks fairly deep,
What do I do, take my clothes off to keep them dry?
With all these people here?
That doesn't seem right…
A proper runner would never deliver a message almost naked!
Do I swim the river and then run back to Bethany in wet clothes?
I can wring them out once I am out of sight…
They will dry along the way.
What will Jesus do after the message is given?
I wonder…
Jesus can just speak the word!
Yes!
Speak the word, Jesus!
Heal Lazarus from where you stand!

Yes!
You can do that!
Then I will listen for a while,
And I walk back home tomorrow!

Benjamin held his food bag and water-skin over his head as he swam the river, looking like a wet rat emerging on the other side.

Both the crowd and Jesus were watching, waiting as Ben dripped his way up to where Jesus stood.

"Benjamin my friend, so good to see you, do you bring a message? How was your journey? It is a beautiful day for running."

"Yes Lord, an excellent day it is!" Benjamin responded with the expectation of a miracle unfolding while he watched.

"The words you bring, they are for me or for another here?"

"For you Jesus, from Mary and Martha."

Here Benjamin assumed his *message delivering runners stance.*

Standing at attention Benjamin said, "Lord, the friend whom you love is sick."

Benjamin watched, intently looking, searching for an impact in Jesus' eyes, trying to read what he saw, looking forward to what was coming next.

Speak the word!
Shake the whole Jordan River Valley!
Strike the river with a stick and send me back across on dry ground!
Say it Jesus!
Stand up Lazarus!
Set both feet upon the ground!
Look at me Lazarus!
I am talking to you!

"Benjamin, this is my exact message for you to deliver to Mary, Martha and those there with them, *This sickness is not unto death, but for the glory of God, that the son of God might be glorified thereby.* Do you understand? Repeat it for me."

Slightly baffled, Ben responded, "Sir, yes sir, *This sickness is not unto death, but for the glory of God, that the son of God might be glorified thereby.* Is that all?"

That's it?

Aren't you going to part the River Jordan?

Send some thunder and lightning?

Anything else?

Something else?

Are you going to Bethany now?

Later?

Tomorrow?

"That's it."

"Anything else?" Ben questioned, hedging, digging around for another something... more to deliver.

"No, you have my words."

"When do I leave?"

"Now."

Benjamin slogged his way back into the Jordan holding his food bag and water bottle over his head with one hand and swam to the western shore with the other.

In the place of protection Lazarus asked, "That's it? But I'm still here? What happened? How can it be as Jesus said? My body's dead and I'm still here!"

Mordecai spoke, "Slow down Lazarus, it's not over yet," Mordecai said, "apparently, but this isn't going to be an easy fix, I thought it was, and now it's as if your... um... position here... could go either way."

"My position?"

"Yes... whether you are a visitor... or a resident."

"How... I don't understand? I thought Jesus was going to fix my body from there... and that I was going back... to my sisters... now!"

Lazarus was floundering, rising from the table he moved around to stand in front of Mordecai, wanting to look into his face as he talked, trying to understand the thoughts he was expressing.

"Jesus has been shown the conditions he has to work with... by Spirit Helper... and has seen a bigger picture. He can only work within the laws of God his Father, like any other man."

"What? Jesus is not, *just a man! He is God!*"

Now Lazarus was exasperated, and Mordecai evaluated what he could, or should explain to the man. If he went back to his earth suit now, after this much time, he would surely be made a target by the enemy's kingdom. Weighing his next words Queen Esther caught his attention as she whispered, "*Let him know.*"

Exhaling slowly before he started, Mordecai said, "Lazarus... Jesus... his spirit self...Jesus is, he was, and will always be... right now he is God in an earth suit. Soon he will forever be God in a heaven suit. To make this function, to make his mission function... he took on flesh. His mind... his earth suit mind... he needed to learn, with his mind, who he was, and is... through the word of God, even though he is the Word of God made flesh. On earth, he made himself to be subject to the limitations of man, and he must work with the tools at hand."

Lazarus brought his right hand up to his chin and scratched his bearded face, "What tools?"

"The laws of God, and seeds are part of that... the people involved, they have words to plant."

"Huh? Who has what to plant?"

"This all depends on who does what with the word seeds Jesus has given them to sow."

"You mean my sisters?"

"Yes, your sisters are first choice, they are the closest to you, but Benjamin may also have something to do with your future, Simon too. There could be several who become a contributing factor, it all depends on what they grow, weed seed or good seed, and what becomes the dominant over-story in each garden."

"Oh my... how much time is there? To raise me from the dead I mean, time makes a difference, yes?"

"The Jonah factor, he is the record holder. From the time he was swallowed by a whale until he was spit up alive on shore, seventy two hours; three days and three nights."

Benjamin crawled out from the Jordan's west bank in like condition as he had gone in, dripping wet. Not one sound was heard from those behind him; a crowd of hundreds, twelve disciples and Jesus, all were silent.

At least my food bag's dry…
And my water-skin is uncontaminated from that murky Jordan River…
Can't say the same of me.
My clothes are going to stink!
Bad attitude Ben…
Shake it off!
Just as soon as I am out of sight…
I will wring them out…
Carry my robe like a flag on a pole and let the wind dry it!
What am I going to tell Mary?
Here's twenty-one words…
I hope they do the trick?
Quit it Ben!
I wish he would have said he was coming…
Today…
Tomorrow…
Something!
Augh!
I was sent to get Jesus!
I feel like I am returning with a hand full of beans!

Jesus silently watched Benjamin's leaving until he was out of sight, a mile away and around a bend, hidden behind the bottomland scrub-brush of Jordan's valley.

Then he addressed those who had been silently watching with him, "So is the kingdom of God, as if a man should cast seed into the ground."

Ten minutes had been forever to be silent, and with so many people waiting for what would happen next, they listened closely, wondering at his words.

"And he should sleep, and rise night and day, and the seed should spring and grow up, he knows not how. For the earth brings forth fruit of herself; first the blade, then the ear, after that the full corn in the ear. But when the fruit is brought forth, immediately he puts in the sickle, because the harvest is come."

By the river's edge Peter and John were still wearing soggy clothes, and Peter whispered, "Farmer stories."

To which John whispered back, "Will you just ask him what he means? There's no way Jesus is going to leave Lazarus in the grave!"

"Humph… you ask him!"

"I will… later."

CHAPTER 10

Lazarus, his parents, Benjamin's grandfather and Anna were still seated at Adam's table, silence hung in the air.

Mordecai addressed those who were seated, primarily Lazarus, "Sometimes there are more questions than there are answers. I'm sorry Lazarus… what is happening is happening; we have no ability to change a thing from here, we can only watch… and then it's only bits and pieces which we can see."

Lazarus was trying to put a good face on things, and he let his mind and eyes wander, soaking in the sight before him. Seated across the table were his mother and father, both looking no older than himself, although he was sure it was truly them.

Taking thought, Laz spoke, and as he did a grin appeared upon his face, "Not to worry, as my father used to say, it's not over for the rooster till his neck gets stretched… although that was a good thing for papa because a rooster pot pie usually followed."

His dad squirmed a bit but his mom spoke up, "Laz, honey, remember when you were a little boy, and Simon, even though he was four years older than you, was your best friend? Remember? Well, there is someone here I would like you to meet, she arrived here about the same time you were born, her name is Anna."

Jericho came back into sight, but for Benjamin it didn't generate any happy thoughts of victory this time. He was having as much trouble with his feelings as with the constant uphill grade, plus he was running in direct sun with hardly any breeze… and sweating profusely.

Most often when he was hired to deliver a message, it was a written something secured with a wax seal carried in a leather satchel where he would never know what was in it. Simply deliver the letter, wait for a return message, deliver that and get paid, simple.

Mary didn't do the usual and neither did Jesus, they used spoken words, words he had to memorize. Now those words were rattling about in his mind, fussing around like some half-digested something which left the wonder of whether it was going to come back up and out… or go down.

Obviously alone in his surroundings, Ben weighed their words and actions while delivering verdicts on scales of justice in his mind.

Mary sent her message,

'Lord, the friend whom you love is sick.'

Jesus, Lazarus needs your help!

And this is what you give?

'This sickness is not unto death but for the glory of God, that the son of God might be glorified thereby.'

Augh!

Jesus… I will tell you…

Lazarus does not want to be sick!

There is no glory there!

While Benjamin's eyes told him he ran this road alone, his mind fought against opposing thoughts as hard as his feet pounded gravel, sand and stone.

The words you send allude to some unexplainable mystery…

Coupled with a hopeful expectation of glorious victory by Almighty God and the Son of God!

Like gently falling leaves, ideas, pictures, which weren't his own, drifted into Ben's mind. Some, with tentacles reaching, tried to burrow in, tap roots searching for a hold.

How can that be?

And son of God who?

Who is the son of god?

Guardians, demons, God, creatures from two kingdoms which most humans never see, both were using tools as weapons, each were hopeful to move the mind of one man.

You Jesus?

The son of God?

Do you presume?

Hmm?

All were throwing pictures, structured to plant a thought, to grow an emotion, to push or pull Ben towards a chosen action, or the total lack thereof.

You didn't make one motion of coming back with me!

Nor mention going to Bethany on your own tomorrow!

You didn't speak to Lazarus...

Or his body...

You didn't shout...

You didn't holler or nothing!

You didn't do anything I expected you to do!

Benjamin's mind struggled with the choosing of which thoughts to entertain, dark thoughts wrapped in pride, anger and resentment, or thoughts of doing good in the brightest light of day.

Augh!

Surrounded, what Benjamin didn't know, and what he couldn't see, were the places, hidden from human eyes, where those spoken words of Jesus were already busy working. The enemy's kingdom was having a fit; the massive rock they were trying to roll over the tomb of Lazarus had met resistance. The demons behind this murderous scheme had come face to face with twenty-one force-filled words spoken by Jesus.

Something somewhere was going to give. The bones of demons were snapping... cracking... joints were popping and their blood was running, all from the applied pressure of Jesus' words. The rock they were rolling was beginning to roll back on them.

Another place those words were working was in the garden of Ben's own heart. Jesus had given him words to remember, they had entered his mind, he was forced, in a manner, through the obligation of his chores, to think them, repeat them, remember them. Eventually, somewhere along the road between Jericho and Jerusalem, Benjamin allowed those words to be planted, planted in the garden of his heart.

Back at Stonehouse, Joseph, Hannah's husband and overseer of Simon's slaves and workforce had become watchful, something was not right.

This is more than the setting of a broken bone...

Pulling through some stitches or the applying of a poultice and administration of a tincture...

Something else is wrong.

Hannah, my doctoring wife, what are you up to?

Joseph opened a locked doorway in the back corner of Simon's crushing and processing building. Through practiced ease with flint and stone he lit a candle, and descended a circle stairway into the cave below. For a moment he was lost in thought while surrounded with flickering shadows and hanging skins.

Determinedly he pulled himself back and began his weekly inspection, the examination of each wineskin; none could be allowed to leak.

We live in a world of interacting relationships functioning within laws; and the laws are always constant, even among variables.

Example: Satan's kingdom is always a parasite to a complaisant human, drawing life out of the human. On the other hand, to the human desiring a positive relationship with God, the Holy Spirit is always Paraclete, the one who adds life to the human, often with synergism, unity working together.

Around us, plants and animals often interact in symbiotic associations, like the crocodile which opens its mouth for the bird that picks trapped food fibers from around the crocodile's teeth. Another example is between creatures which require oxygen and that of plant life; one breathes in oxygen and exhales carbon dioxide, the other breathes in carbon dioxide and exhales oxygen.

The perennial gardens of Lazarus and his sisters functioned in a symbiotic relationship which their father had uncovered. A primary plant which they raised was called spikenard, it craves growing ground laced with silver birch tree roots and biodegrading silver birch leaves, and spikenard also likes casual shade from the trees.

It was late winter before Lazarus had finished processing last season's harvest of spikenard roots, rendering its fragrant oil from the plant. Today his sisters used one pint of the heavy perfume, worth about a year's wages for the average worker. After washing the body of their brother, they, with the help of their Rabbi, neighbors and those from Stonehouse, collectively prepared the body of Lazarus for the grave. First coating his body with spikenard oil and other spices, and then wrapping it from head to foot with grave cloth.

It was into this arena that Benjamin was about to enter.

Martha glanced up through their open eastern window, staring out into the encroaching darkness as if her constant looking would cause someone to appear, but once again, there was no one there.

A few hours before, a fireball setting sun was sending horizontal sunshine towards the Jordan, where with her eyes and her memory she could see all the way to the river bottoms, out to the spot where John the baptizer so often preached.

Their chores almost complete, she picked up a candle and went to stand at the opening, just to be a little closer to her hope.

All direct sunlight had long since gone away, and any shadow seen was cast from either star or moonlight. She set her candle on the windowsill and left it burning there, calling for Jesus to come.

Movement by her side pulled her face towards Simon; she gazed up into his kind eyes saying, "Save my fight for what counts, yes?"

Simon slowly nodded as he spoke, "I went to hear John once, out where we sent Benjamin this morning. John had a voice that could break rock, and as he taught he pointed to Jesus, off in the distance, and he shouted it out, *'Behold! The Lamb of God! He takes away the sin of the world!'* He is the one we have watched for."

"And he is the one I watch for now."

"It's black dark outside Martha, a person would need excellent night eyes, just to move around."

There were seventeen friends and neighbors about the home of Lazarus, most had red and puffy faces from crying, all were there to show support, to help in any way they could.

Taking Martha's hand, Simon said, "Come, the people will be leaving soon. You must thank them for their kindness, most will return in the morning, when we take his body to your family tomb."

"Simon… will you speak for me… I… I…"

Martha was interrupted by a knock upon their western door, and Mary went to open it.

It was Benjamin, sweaty, wet and smelling like the muddy Jordan River.

Mary, her mind numb with pain and loss, simply held the door open until Ben stepped inside.

For Benjamin, even the dimly lit room seemed bright after running in such darkness, and for a moment he took note of his surroundings.

The heavy plank entry door was hinged open to his left, a leather work apron which Lazarus often wore hung by a forked branch hook on his right; his sandals were neatly arranged below the apron.

A small stone cooking and heating place which vented through the ceiling was in the kitchen area, further in and on his right. A crowd of people were scattered throughout the room, with Simon and Martha directly across from him and in front of Martha's eastern window. A lighted candle, which he had focused on for the last mile or more sat on the windowsill. Several oil lamps, set on shelves gave flickering light and dim shadows throughout the room.

Bedroom doors were to his far left, but in front of Ben was their dining table, and Lazarus, his body prepared for burial, lay upon it.

Sadness as a shroud was worn in varying degrees by every face in the room; this was not a happy place.

Standing at attention while dripping sweat, and speaking with the same voice inflection and determination as what he heard, Benjamin presented the packaged message. "These words are from Jesus of Nazareth, he said they are to be delivered to Mary, Martha and those here with them. *'This sickness is not unto death, but for the glory of God, that the son of God might be glorified thereby.'*"

There, it was given, and Ben studied what followed next.

Years later he would describe what transpired as something which he saw, although he always identified that it wasn't seen with eyes, but just a way to explain what resulted in the days which followed.

This is how Ben eventually described what took place, *'As Jesus' words left my mouth they came out as many shooting streams of water, one stream directed towards each person in the room, and I watched the affect those words had on every person there. Some closed their eyes and ears to what they heard, some covering their faces with their hands, although no one actually moved. Others were unflinching, but the stream of words bounced off them and landed on the ground. The words struck Mary in the chest, just below her neckline, penetrating, they disappeared inside. With Martha and Simon, those words hit them right between the eyes and sunk into their foreheads. Martha shook her head slightly and repeated the words, and as she did so, those words came out of her mouth as a mist, circled around and entered into her right ear.'*

Once Ben delivered the return message from Jesus he was silent.

Martha was patient, waiting for something more, but when Ben only stood there she went to asking, "Well?"

"Well what?" Ben answered.

"When will he be here?"

Ben slightly grimaced, "He didn't say."

Martha's right foot started tapping, loud enough for Ben to hear, "He is leaving tomorrow, in the morning, yes? And coming here?"

"I don't know... he didn't say."

Martha began a slow pacing back and forth, only two or three short steps in one direction and then turning back the other way. "Benjamin, he must have given you some idea of his arrival time, something!"

Ben was starting to squirm, "Ah... no."

"Is he coming at all?"

"Oh... ah... he... um..."

"Benjamin, what did he say?"

Perplexed, Ben would rather have faced an upset Army General than this one scrappy woman. Still standing at attention, he began again, "This is what Jesus said, 'Benjamin, this is my exact message for you to deliver to Mary, Martha and those there with them, '*This sickness is not unto death, but for the glory of God, that the son of God might be glorified thereby.*' And then he said, 'Do you understand? Repeat it for me.' So I repeated it for him, and then I left... to return here."

Martha looked to Simon, who stood his ground but only shrugged his shoulders with one raised eyebrow.

Turning towards her eastern window, the Jordan River, and Jesus out there somewhere, she continued in a solemn voice, "Very well then, come by in the morning and I will pay you, for now, you may go."

With that, Ben quietly left, closing the door behind him.

The sound of the gently closing door matched the sensation which Martha had, it was as if a feather floated from her head and landed in the pit of her stomach. Things of the day did not add up.

70	|	Mike & Dianne Heintzeman

CHAPTER 11

Benjamin was awake but he had no interest in trading his warm bed for frigid morning air. He rolled over, pulling one of his beautiful wool blankets up and over his head.

After a minute of rebreathing his own exhaled air, the temperature did increase, as did the humidity, but within his tiny tent the oxygen level was falling. Finally he stuck his nose out into early morning coldness, exhibiting at least some sort of courage to face the day.

Looking about he pulled up first one knee and then the other, rubbing out what sore spots he could reach. Squirrelling around in his bed he slowly stretched out sets of muscles, warming up his body to movement once again.

Martha…

You want me to stop by in the morning to get paid?

That's not something I want to do.

I don't want to deal with any mourners…

They could already be at your house!

I don't want to see Mary crying for her brother.

I don't want to bury Lazarus.

And today…

I don't even want to get out of bed!

He began to adjust his agenda to fit what he would rather do.

I want to know what's going on from the message Jesus sent!

Having been fed a crucial piece of information, Benjamin now possessed a deep desire to observe how Jesus' words would play out, assuming what Jesus said was true.

He went to find some breakfast.

This sickness is not unto death?

Two completely alternate realities could not both exist at the same time… Something's got to give!

And…

I'll watch what happens from a distance.

The house of Lazarus was built on some sort of a divide, rain which fell by their chicken coop eventually made its way to the Dead Sea, rain which fell at their front step ended up in the Mediterranean Sea. A similar thing was true at Stonehouse, and halfway between those houses. Below some cliffs on the Dead Sea side of the divide were the caves of the dead; their family tomb for many generations was at that place. Benjamin decided to go to a watching spot, about a quarter mile south of the tomb.

Within an hour Ben was there, just in time to watch Mary and Martha step out of the tomb. The bones of their parents were there, and now so was the body of their brother.

Simon and two others leaned into the cave's cut-stone disk and rolled it back into its place covering the entrance. Once the stone was set, Simon spoke with Martha and she shook her head as if saying *'no'*. A moment later, Simon, Hannah and Esther all left for home.

Mary was weeping with the mourners but Martha appeared rather detached, unwilling to cry, and unable to leave, but looking for a way out. Caught between two places, Martha looked up and locked her eyes on Ben's hillside vantage point as an old woman approached and put a hand on her shoulder.

The old woman spoke and Martha found her way of escape.

Martha looked back at the old woman, broke free of her hand, looked over at the mourners, and ran for home. Benjamin watched her run until she passed Emil the goat herder's empty sheep pens and was out of sight.

Hmm...

Martha responded positively to the words I brought from Jesus...

And she behaves differently from all others now.

I wonder...

Is she thinking what I am thinking?

Wanting to talk, Ben followed after her; it would be some time before Mary and the mourners left the tomb.

Martha was standing inside the open door holding her brother's coat as Ben came up the steps. She turned at the sound of his feet, her knuckles white from clenching Lazarus' coat; lines of tears ran down her face.

"Don't let go, Martha."

"Benjamin, tell me again what Jesus said," Martha softly asked.

Answering gently he complied, *"This sickness is not unto death, but for the glory of God, that the son of God might be glorified thereby."*

From the center of the soul another friend has joined together in pursuit of their cause. Clear a space, pull all weeds, till the ground, plant good seed, mend each fence, keep the rabbits out, water the ground and watch to see what grows from the seed which was planted.

Benjamin had been standing in the doorway, with the brightness of early afternoon sunshine behind him. Leaving the entry and walking down three steps, he left his silhouette burned into Martha's vision.

She closed the door and walked to the other side of the room, where she sat by her window looking eastward towards Jordan's valley.

Martha sat there thinking, holding her brother's coat and rolling words around in the garden of her heart.

Who are you Jesus?

Your words…

'that the son of God might be glorified?'

Who are you talking about?

Your mother's name is Mary…

Wasn't Joseph your father?

Martha had listened to the prophecies about the messiah, from the time that she was a little girl, everyone had. The messiah would come.

Mary's Joseph died years ago.

John the baptizer taught about one who would come.

The Lamb of God!

Could our Jesus be that one?

Sixty miles north of Bethany and a little west was the city of Nain. The city was surrounded by a protective stone wall with a primary gate and was only a two hour southwest walk from Nazareth. A year earlier Benjamin returned from a message delivery with an eye witness account from that town. This is the recounting of that story which he told to Lazarus and his sisters.

"*I had finished my delivery, collected my pay and was nearing the city gates to leave town when a funeral procession blocked my way. Being in no hurry I climbed up a flight of steps and sat upon the wall above the gate to watch and wait.*"

"*Turns up that seated next to me, a man as old as I, was the young man's cousin who had found him dead the day before, fallen from a cliff. The cause of death being blunt force trauma from multiple head wounds, plus broken bones, loss of blood and being very dead.*"

"*The man was exhibiting symptoms peculiar to one losing his cousin and best friend, bouts of weeping between him telling me of his sad tale.*"

"*In the midst of it all, a commotion ensued as a large group of men began to push their way in through the city gates which the funeral procession was attempting to leave town through. It appeared as if the altercation might come to blows when the apparent leader of the mob presented himself to speak before the dead man's widowed mother."*

Mary asked, "What sort of man disrupts a funeral? Did they run him out of town? Did the widow woman scratch his eyes out?"

"This is where the story gets interesting, you see, I recognized the leader of the mob to be one we all four know, the man was Jesus!"

Martha was incredulous, "What? No way, why would he do such a thing? That was so disrespectful!"

"Some would say it was but let me finish! Jesus told the widow woman, 'Do not weep!' (The cousin said he knew of Jesus and Jesus knew the family having grown up in Nazareth only a few miles away.) Anyhow the woman quit crying and the funeral procession quit walking."

"Ben, get to the point, what did *our* Jesus do next?" Lazarus asked.

"He spoke to the dead man saying only, 'Young man, I say to you get up!' And the dead man sat up! The people carrying the stretcher he had been laying on set the thing down on the ground and the dead man who was now alive got up from the dirt and went to stand with his mother who was now beside herself gone wild, shouting, hollering, 'Thank you Jesus! Praise you God! Thank you Jesus!"

"And that is what I saw," said Ben, finishing his story.

Martha asked, "What about the broken bones?"

"From what Aaron, for that is what the dead man's name was... from what Aaron displayed and said there was nothing broken any more, not even a limp and no scars."

Shadows were getting long before the door opened and Mary walked in, her face caked with dust and streaked with tears. Looking to her older sister she cried out, "What are we going to do Martha, he has left us, and we are alone!"

Hanging her cloak on its hook by the door, Mary's gaze fell to her brother's empty sandals in their place below his leather work apron.

"We could never do our chores and his too! I miss his face, his laughing eyes, I even miss the way he would tease me about the chickens!"

Tears were once more sliding down Mary's face.

Martha went to her sister, placing an arm around her shoulder while still holding her brother's coat. "Mary, we are not without hope, Jesus will be here soon, I am sure of it!"

"And what good would that do now?"

Drawing from a memory Martha answered, "Do you remember Aaron from the town of Nain?"

Mary's face was all puffy red from crying and she rolled out of Martha's embrace before she answered, "Yes, I heard the stories, and some said he wasn't really dead! Some said that Jesus splashed cold water in his face and he woke up!"

Her crusty voice matched her face and eyes.

Mary threw her shawl on a table and marched on, "And if Jesus had come when we sent Benjamin it might have made some difference! But he didn't come, and Lazarus is still dead!"

Mary's brow was furrowed and she leaned forward as she spoke, both arms were muscled down by her side with her fists clenched.

Sternly but gently Martha continued, "Mary, do you remember when Jesus was here, and this house was packed with people; do you remember what I told him?"

Mary remembered the pleasure from Jesus' praise, "Yes, you told him to tell me to get up and get to work!"

"Yes, I did… but he said that you had chosen to do the better thing, you were listening to him… you were sitting there on the floor, soaking up every word he said!"

Mary looked down at her brother's coat held tightly in her sister's hands. "Yeah, so?"

"Jesus was right; I was scurrying around like a squirrel! Doing things that really didn't make any difference… but you absorbed his every word! His words were alive to you!"

"Mary, Jesus said that this sickness is not unto death! Jesus said the son of God would be glorified by it!"

Mary silently sat down in her sister's eastern window chair as Martha forcefully continued.

"Mary, that man in Nain was dead! But dead is only dead! All Jesus did was say something to his mother, and then he told him to sit up! Jesus didn't splash water in his face to wake him up... the man was dead!"

Mary looked to her sister with hope-filled eyes. "Martha... I want to believe our brother will walk in through the kitchen door and ask us what's for dinner! But I helped wrap his body... I touched his cold dead skin! Martha, his body was there... but he was gone! Can Jesus bring him back through that door?"

"Mary, Jesus has never lied to us, and he said this sickness is not unto death! Now, I don't know exactly what that means, but I do know it's something different than what is! Please! Just believe him with me! Don't let go of what he said! Believe with me, please!"

"Martha, I know that if Jesus had been here, our brother would not have died! I do not understand what Jesus said... but yes! I will believe him!"

From the center of the soul young life has arrived! Bursting, exploding through black moist earth, young buds, tiny leaves, one sporting an earthy crown, a case fragment portion as a hat, wearing part of the seed hull it was birthed from. Gentle stems, tasty morsels, succulent leaves; guard them from the bunnies, those adorable, furry, cute little garden eating bunnies.

The War Is Over | 77

CHAPTER 12

In the place of protection, only a handful was come together, and as in all of the area that Lazarus had so far seen, the place was illuminated by an irradiant ceiling. Some areas offered mellow light and others were quite bright, some even changed in lighting depending on the number of people present and the activity going on. In some sections the radiant ceiling was almost reachable by your hand, and at other times it could be one hundred feet above, but at many places it was supported by natural stone pillars, honeycombed hollow mountains and caves.

Lazarus was reminiscing, "Soon it will be morning, Martha is almost always the first from her bed, forever on a mission, and she must accomplish something. Start a cooking fire, fetch some water, pick the eggs, but only if all eggs in the house are gone for she usually leaves the egg picking chore for Mary."

David's articulate voice responded, "Faithful family is a precious thing, and they both stand strong with you."

Queen Esther wondered, "Will Jesus arrive at the house of Lazarus today? I thought he might be there by now... but...Uncle... his plan... do you know?"

The five, for Jonathan was there also, had retreated to a favorite place of David's, one of cliffs and caves and magnificent rock formations.

"If you pick a melon before its time it will just be hard and white inside." His niece questioned, "What?"

David continued with Mordecai's thought, "Jesus has but one opportunity, he must not release the string until the arrow is at full draw, consistency is expedient to accuracy."

She asked another way, "Will someone answer who won't speak in warrior jargon... or of one who hobbies as the gardener?"

Again Mordecai only responded with his practiced *short answer...* which she so often called for. "Once you pick and cut the melon all growing time is gone, he must wait till it's ripe."

"Jonathan, can you give a proper answer? These two are talking riddles!"

"I will try... there is a thought which Jesus has often presented... and it is this, *'So is the kingdom of God, as if a man should cast seed into the ground. And he should sleep, and rise night and day, and the seed should spring and grow up, he knows not how. For the earth brings forth fruit of herself; first the blade, then the ear, after that the full corn in the ear. But when the fruit is brought forth, immediately he puts in the sickle, because the harvest is come.'*"

"Oh! I get it! He waits for Mary and Martha! For his words which they planted in the garden of the heart... to grow and ripen! Yes?"

"Yes, for those two first, but others such as Benjamin could also help. Jesus' great love for Lazarus and his sisters... his love compels him to wait until it is time to go."

Now Lazarus was curious, "And... what if nothing ripens?"

"Then what's the point of going?"

"Oh... hm...I see...ah... I guess being a resident here... wouldn't be so bad."

David offered, "Much better than the alternative... the other place to go I mean."

Lazarus sat with his back to a tapering cave, a tunnel entrance appearing much like a giant mouth. Near the onset, at twice the height of a tall man... the mouth was open wide, displaying rows of teeth. Long, shiny white and slightly pink with warbled smoothness, they hung down from the cave roof while matching teeth protruded up from the jaw. Drops of milk slowly fell from canine uppers to matching lowers, often minutes between each drop.

"The… other place… where is it? Can you see it from here?"

Queen Esther answered, "Oh Laz! It's a very ugly place," Queen Esther answered, "you don't want to go there!" She hovered between desire and necessity for a heartbeat and then continued, "But you probably should."

"Then it's possible? To see it… ah… from a distance… without actually going there?"

Behind Lazarus, past irregular rows of pearly white teeth, at the point where the cave's roof came closer to its jaw were other pillar teeth, which over time had come close and grown together. Some stood guard on either side of the tightening cave to form a throat of sorts. In the center of the throat was another hanging thing which someone had rearranged, carved, to be as the little waddle doodad in the back of a person's throat.

David answered, "We can show you the place as you were shown Goliath, or we can walk down to the canyon's edge. From the iron fence you can look across the pit and into hell. The best observation point is at the narrows."

Hope.

Godly imagination towards a desired end began to take on substance, and Mary let the horse run wild.

Early morning and snuggled beneath her warm fluffy covers, long, thick, wavy black hair all a mess, she opened the window of her mind and pictured only what she wanted to see.

Jesus walking up the Jordan valley road, and as always, he was surrounded by an ever present crowd.

She could see Jesus, knocking on the door, taking the girls, one by each hand to the family tomb.

Jesus, magnificent in power, shouting at the storm clouds, rebuking the wind, and sending the darkness straight to hell!

Jesus, giant angels at his beckoned call, 'Uriah' he says to one, 'take the stone away!'

The mighty angel picks up the tomb cover stone and throws it to the side, it smashes to broken pieces.

Jesus, shouting, his flaming voice scorching darkness, shattering boulders, declaring, 'Lazarus! Life be! Stand up! Place both your feet on solid ground! Come out here! Now!'

Her brother rising up, fully alive, running out of the tomb!

And then minutes later, Lazarus, clomping through their western door, fussing about her chickens, wanting something to eat while carrying Matilda, her favorite laying hen, tucked under his arm!

Lazarus! You put Matilda back! I will find you something to eat, but it's not going to be my favorite chicken!

Mary saw it, she could see it all. In absolute victory she threw back her covers and went to brew some tea.

In the place of protection, Lazarus asked, "Will you take me to the narrows?"

Mordecai responded, "Lazarus, if we go there… well… it will be a picture burned forever in your memory."

"I understand… but I believe it's something I must see."

"Very well then… who goes with, anyone?" David asked.

Queen Esther glanced at Jonathan and her uncle, they both nodded, "We all will."

"Not that it makes any difference, but how far away is it?"

"Couple miles."

Below Martha's window, two empty teacups rested on a small table set between three chairs. Two chairs were empty, one for Martha who was up fixing breakfast and the other was kept in place for their brother. Mary continued to watch the Jordan road.

The War Is Over | 81

Martha spoke as she broke eggs in a pan, "It's an eight hour walk Mary, if they leave after breakfast they won't be here until mid-afternoon."

"Will Jesus come today?"

"I don't know… but friends… mourners; they will be showing up here soon."

"I don't want them here!"

"They are not our enemy," said Martha as she brought their breakfast and sat down.

"Will they come tomorrow also?"

"Tradition will push them to mourn for Lazarus at least a week."

"Then Jesus needs to show up here today!"

Acrid smoke from burning coal laced with sulfur caused their nose hairs to twitch, nostrils close, and made their eyes water.

For the last half mile of their journey they observed only a few sporadic groups of other agonizing watchers.

They moved cautiously, and even though they were on God's side of the pit, the five traveled in a small tight cluster.

Across the divide, hell was not illuminated by an irradiant ceiling above, far from it. Red light rose from burning coal and lava, flowing in a multitude of tiny streams. The intertwining molten rivulets created thousands of small, black, pointy-end islands.

David had delivered Lazarus to the narrows, a skinny spot between their protected place and hell.

Blocking their way from falling into a long narrow gorge was a massive iron fence.

David broke the silence, "This fence you can touch, not so on the other side, it barks sparkling blue fire if any fool should lay his hand upon it."

Lazarus took hold of two vertical bars and peered down into the abyss below them; with his forehead pressed against rusty iron he could not begin to see the bottom.

By his left side, David picked up a rock the size of a chicken and tossed it over the fence and into the pit below. It bounced and clunked distinctly for fifteen seconds or more, dragging other dislodged rocks and boulders with it on its journey. It was a full minute before all crashing rock reverberations ended and the pit was once more silent.

But there were other sounds.

Deep, guttural, heinous snarls floated towards them on acrid air.

Queen Esther covered her ears with both hands.

Chains, countless sliding, clanking chains, held captive creatures of malicious evil.

Studying hades, Laz saw that almost every lava island imprisoned a condemned demon on it.

Stakeout spikes anchored one end of each chain with the other welded to a collar clamped around some demon's neck.

Cursing, swearing, vial outbursts were mingled with anguished human cries.

Demons struck without abandon while the chains imposed limits to their pleasure. Quite often they caught a human victim and burst forth with the horrific roaring of an attacking lion, wolf or bear.

The imagination of Lazarus could not have prepared him for what he saw.

David explained, "Sometimes in their movement to escape the lava's heat, humans get too close to a chained and waiting demon. Lazarus, what you hear are demons, chained and fallen angels, each lashing out at some incarcerated human. This is where they exist for now, and neither one will ever die."

Moments later a shredded human form was thrown some distance by a screeching demon, landing in a lava stream. It sizzled, popped and snapped, presently, as the lava vein slightly shifted, the blackened carcass laid smoldering on stark black rock.

"Is he dead?" Lazarus wondered.

Mordecai answered, "They never truly die, he will rejuvenate to movement once again, in about an hour or so."

Nearer, the closest person across the pit was about a hundred feet away.

Watching the carnage around the man, Lazarus whispered, "I don't want anyone to go to hell."

On hell's side of the pit, this *closest man,* was sliding his body over cooling lava rock and spending great effort with each movement. He set his face towards Laz, staring.

Laz was looking back.

The man changed his course of travel and began to drag himself towards Laz and the other four.

From hell, he cried out in a rasping hissing voice.

"Water!"

"Water, please!"

No one moved.

"Lazarus! Just one drop to cool my tongue!"

"Lazarus, please! I beg of you! Help me!"

Prickly sparkles laced with shivers danced down the spine of Lazarus.

"Who are you? How do you know my name?"

"Lazarus! Help me... please!"

"Who are you?"

Another voice answered from fifteen feet behind and slightly higher, for he was standing on the hillside. "It's not you he calls for... it's me. My name is also Lazarus, and in Jerusalem that man was a wealthy man."

"And he knows you?"

"I was often laid at his gate to beg for food, or a bit of coin, until my body died. And now he is here... but over there."

The onetime beggar called across the pit, "I'm sorry friend, but I cannot get to you! There's no way across the pit!"

"Then go back and tell my brothers, please! They are just like me! Unless they turn their face towards God they will join me in this place!"

David answered to the man, "They have Moses and the Prophets, they must listen to them!"

"No! They are too much like me! I didn't listen to the word of God, but if one was raised from the dead, then they will listen! Lazarus! Will you do this... please?"

Mordecai responded this time, "The word of God is stronger than a man raised from the dead. If they don't hear the voice of Jesus, they won't hear a man raised from the dead!"

"Augh! They must not die as dead men and join me in this place!"

The other Lazarus answered, "I'm sorry rich man… there is nothing to be done for you."

"Augh!"

"Augh!!"

"Augh!!!"

Both the Lazarus' felt the agony of the rich man's future.

Queen Esther sought to cut this pointless sorrow off, "Come… we need to go… we don't need to be here anymore."

CHAPTER 13

Time crawled along and minutes moved like hours, Martha saw every mourner just the same as every hour of the day. She was grateful when each had come and gone.

Mary, emotionally exhausted, was already sleeping in her bed.

Martha, refusing to surrender, needed to be in motion with a common chore, a simple something to keep her body busy so she might more clearly think.

Lighting oil lamps, she set to straighten up around the house.

Methodically, as Martha went through the motions of picking up and putting away, in her mind, she picked up the words of Jesus. She held his words in her hands, turned each over, looking at them backwards, and then forwards, struggling to comprehend.

Jesus…

What is the meaning of your words?

What am I to do with what you say?

She allowed the ideas those words presented roll around on the table of her mind. They were marbles to play with and she was entertaining guests, welcome friends, they were pictures, talking in whispers, strolling back and forth, and she watched where they would walk.

As they traveled she followed close behind, curious of their journey.

They led her into places she had never before gone. *'That the son of God,'* was a blood-red marble that sent shivers through her body. *'This sickness is not unto death,'* was a silver marble which moved about but only delivered one destination; it always brought Lazarus back through their front door. *'But for the glory of God,'* was translucent-gold... it seemed to follow her as she followed Jesus.

The morning of the third day arrived, and after breakfast Mary returned to their eastern window. She settled into her chair with a wool blanket and a cup of hot herb tea which she wrapped her hands around, warming her fingers.

She pulled up memories from years ago, of going to hear the baptizer where Benjamin had found Jesus.

Benjamin made it to the Jordan and back in one day, almost sixty miles, but he is a runner, fast and lean.

Steam rose from her earthen cup and she caressed its warmth while gazing east, her eyes methodically searching the miles of roadway she could see.

I can understand Jesus not leaving the first day when Ben delivered my message; he needed to finish what he was doing. There could have been hundreds of people listening to his stories; he is doing what is right.

She blew gently across her cup of tea and took a sip, then, exhaling, steam exited her mouth; the morning was fairly cool and Mary had pushed Martha's shuttered window open wide.

When we went to hear John the baptizer, we got there in one day, stayed there two days and returned in one, four days total. The trip was fairly easy, but we walked both ways, and Jesus only has to travel one. What's taking him so long?

From the corner of her eye, on Mary's right-hand side she saw some movement; it was Martha exiting the henhouse with an apron full of eggs.

When Jesus taught from our house, we fed him and all of his disciples. We treated each one like a proper guest, but where is he when we need him? It took a full day to clean up after all of those people left!

Mary's cup had grown cold and she took the last swallow of tepid liquid as she put her cup away and went to greet the mourners at their door.

From the center of the soul things are changing. One garden is presenting head height corn with ears growing and a little corn silk showing. Another garden has beautiful pea and bean plants climbing, reaching for the sky, with a hopping furry bunny come close to see, sniff, and then to eat. Oh how did that cuddly bunny find a way inside the garden fence?

It is the fourth day, and very early in the morning.

Pressure ripples appeared on the otherwise smooth surface of the Jordan River before the breeze blew smoke across Peter's sleeping face. He rubbed his nose and rolled over.

Water began to boil in a pot as Jesus poked at his cooking fire with a stick; streamers of sparks chased each other up through the smoke. Their breakfast was almost ready and soon it would be time to leave.

Jesus walked over to John's snoring form and nudged the bare foot which was sticking out from beneath his blankets. His bleary eyes looked up at Jesus and then at the star-sprinkled sky behind him.

"Good morning John, time for breakfast, get the others moving, we are going to pack it up."

They traveled light, they always did, but there were a few things which were consistently needed, such as a change of clothes, a coat, bedroll, and drinking water. There were also times, like now, when life was a continual camping trip and they took turns being the cook and carrying the food packs. As it was, by the time the sun was up breakfast was finished, their camp was packed and they were ready to go, somewhere.

Jesus left, so they followed.

Heading north, he went upstream to a place where they crossed the Jordan in knee-deep water. As they came up from the river, Jesus headed southwest instead of north towards Galilee, where the disciples thought they were going.

"Uh… Jesus… where are we going?" John asked.

"Judea… we are going to Judea,"

They wanted to stop moving, but Peter cleared his throat as they trudged along and said, "Teacher, they just tried to kill you a couple of weeks ago in Judea. In fact, there are a lot of people in those towns who want us dead… and I think that being stoned to death would be a very uncomfortable way to die."

Jesus spoke loud enough for them all to hear, "If you walk in the day you will have plenty of light to see and you won't fall, but if you walk in the night you will fall, because there is no light in you."

Those words brought his twelve disciples back to an angry mob incident in Judea, at Jerusalem-an angry mob with lots of stones. Jesus never had to say much to that type of person in their self-righteous robes to have a whole flood of ugly come pouring out of them, and that's what happened a few weeks ago in Solomon's porch at Jerusalem.

They tried to stone him, again.

It all started so simple, Jesus only said, "Follow the evidence of miracles and see where they lead."

They didn't like that.

Then Jesus said, "I and my Father are one," and that popped the cork out of the bottle and all of their ugly gushed out.

There were about two dozen people out of the crowd of hundreds who grabbed up rocks preparing to throw them at Jesus when he said, "Look and see with your eyes with the same volume of light as you have in your heart."

For all of those holding stones, their eyes went blank.

Everyone holding stones looked just the same, blank-faced. As if they had just stepped from bright sunlight into a very dark room, and their eyes could not focus on anything.

One by one, they dropped their stones and started waving their arms around out in front of themselves searching for something to hold onto. If they took a step, it was as if they were trying to avoid some unseen obstacle.

Some just fell to the ground.

It only affected those who had been holding stones, and the rest of the people started to laugh.

The laughter only made those with blind eyes madder still, which only made them funnier to look at.

Emil, the goat herder, reached out and grabbed one by the beard with a sharp jerk. "What! Who did that?" the bearded man hollered, as Emil pulled roughly on another beard and jumped out of the way of his flapping arms.

Jesus then walked through the middle of them all and left. His disciples followed, but for a long ways they could hear the laughter of the crowd, mixed with the angry voices of those with temporarily blinded eyes.

Judea would be an interesting place to return to.

From the center of the soul grows the garden of the heart. Garden dirt has no knowledge of what is planted; dirt's determined purpose is to cause a sown seed to grow. Thistle or corn, green beans or thorns, each are only seeds to dirt.

Still dripping Jordan River water with wet sand clinging to his sandaled feet, and with Spirit Helper's help, Jesus looked into the gardens of his twelve disciples.

You have some good things growing… but nothing from the twenty-one words I gave you to plant for my friend Lazarus… humph.

I will let you consider for a while, where we are going, and what we are going to do there.

Later, I'll try planting in you a super-grow something, and hope to get a crop.

Five miles before a fork in the road, the green fields of Jericho came into sight.

Jesus spoke distinctly to his twelve, "Lazarus is sleeping, but I go to wake him up."

Peter perked up, "Jesus, this is good news! If he's sleeping that means he's getting better! His fever must have broken... yes?"

The others all agreed...

Humph... they don't get it... and they don't know... he's been dead four days.

I will try again.

"Lazarus is dead, and I am glad I wasn't there!" Jesus said, "Now you can see something happen that no man has ever seen before! This will be better for you! Let's all go to Lazarus right now!"

At first no one said a word, no one even moved.

Some looked at their teacher through puzzled eyes, blinking, and thinking.

Hugh?

What?

Has he gone crackers?

Finally, John stepped out from the cluster of men. He took three steps forward and turned so he was standing at Jesus' side. He didn't say anything; it was just in his own mind he had made a choice.

Glaring at John, and without moving his feet, Thomas folded his arms and spoke for the rest, "Yes, let's all go to him, then we can all die together! I am sure they have stones enough for us all!"

The others mumbled some incoherent words among themselves, but really, they had nothing else to add.

Humph... then I don't want you with... and we will go alone.

Five miles came and went and the fork in the road arrived.

The road led to Ephraim eleven miles north. It was where they were going in two days; Jesus was sending the eleven there now.

"Peter... John and I are going to wake Lazarus up, you take the rest to Ephraim, and we will meet you there in three days."

CHAPTER 14

With one on each side, Queen Esther and her uncle led Lazarus from the narrows, David and Jonathan followed close behind.

Laz whispered, "What a horrible place!"

From two steps behind, Jonathan commented, "Each one is there by choice… or by the lack thereof. The price will be paid for each of them; just the same as us, only they will never taste of God's goodness, they didn't have to go there."

"How can that be? And who could pay a ransom for so many?"

"The debt is owed to God Almighty; Jesus will make it paid in full to him."

The sound of rapid footfalls broke through to their hearing; someone was running full speed towards them.

A woman's voice, shouting between gasping breaths made herself known, it was Anna.

"Thank God!" *breathe… gasp,* "I found you!" *gasp… breathe,* "Jesus!" breathe… breathe, "He is more than," *gasp… gasp… exhale… inhale,* "halfway there!"

"Halfway to my sisters? From the Jordan? Then he's still hours away?"

"We have been," *inhale… a bit less struggle… catching her breath… exhale… inhale,* "looking for you… since he left… this morning… five hours ago!"

Mordecai responded, "Our apologies to you and the others Anna, we were walking and at the narrows… it seems time has gotten away from us."

"It's all still good… there is enough time to walk back to Adam's table… they are gathering at the gardens… now!"

Laz wondered, "Gathering? Who? How many and what for?"

"There were hundreds, then thousands, probably millions now!"

"Millions?… I've heard that word before… uncountable… like sand!"

"They are at the table… we get to watch what Jesus is going to do!"

From a rocky outcropping high above the Jordan road Benjamin sat unseen.

Cold remnants of a morning campfire were behind him, an open sided canvas shelter was positioned so he could see the Jordan road from his bed, other food stuffs and gear were scattered about his camp.

To the south was the tomb, west was the house of Lazarus, and further on is Jerusalem, but his focus was northeast towards Jordan's valley.

The stones of this spot were worn smooth by those who used this vantage point to watch who was coming and who was going. The tomb was only a half-mile to the south, but Benjamin could see several miles along the Jordan road.

Jesus would be easy to spot- there was always a crowd of followers around him.

Afternoon traveler traffic was sporadic.

There was a man and boy leading donkeys with saddle-packs, an hour later he saw what appeared to be a family with five children approaching from the east. The family disappeared from view for the last hundred yards or so, down below the cliff he was watching from. Two minutes later, the sound of their voices reached his ears as they passed below him, with excited chatter about seeing their grandma.

About a mile out were two men traveling alone. Ben got up to stretch a bit, as he was getting stiff from sitting. He gathered a few sticks for a fire and went to watch for Jesus and the twelve again.

John's stomach growled. He rummaged through the clothes and personal gear in his shoulder bag for a bite to eat, searching for even a dried up chunk of tasteless milk cheese.

Nothing.

What does Jesus have?

John looked but already knew the answer. Two shoulder straps, one fastened to a goatskin water bottle made by Emil, the other connected to a canvas shoulder bag made by Benjamin, but no food pack.

I wonder if he's ready to talk yet.

Walking single file since Jesus sent the others north to Ephraim, John had decided to give his teacher a little space.

"Say… um… Jesus, do you have any food in your bag? An old biscuit or a lump of goat cheese maybe?"

"Five minutes John; you can have a snack in five minutes."

How? From where?

John looked around, they were nowhere. Blocking his view to the left were vertical cliffs, on his right were some sheep, or maybe they were rocks, it was hard to tell that far away. Ahead was more dirt road.

"Good… good… glad to hear it, 'cause my stomach's getting kind of noisy."

The two were walking a fairly steep uphill grade at the moment, and as their road transitioned with the embankment on their left, Jesus doubled back, tracking a goat path up the back side of the cliff they had been walking next to.

Is this where food is?

John followed, winding between brush and boulders for a few hundred feet. Near the plateau top a patch of canvas was serving as a tent… and a man was kneeling in the dirt, blowing on a bunch of sticks. A curl of wood smoke rose up above his head.

"Hello Benjamin."

The man jumped and spun around on one knee.

"Who!… Wha?… Jesus!… How did you? I've been watching! Where did you come from?"

"I saw you up here all alone, thought you could use a little company."

"Where are the others? Isn't there more than just you and John?"

The slightest smile showed through on Jesus' face, little wrinkles at the corners of his eyes, "We will have to be enough, where's Lazarus?"

"In their family tomb... his body...they put his body there... three days ago."

"And the message I sent back with you?"

"Delivered it the same night you sent me back."

"Very good... and?"

"Ah... most... um."

"Benjamin... continue."

"There were twenty people at the house, Mary, Martha, Simon... and seventeen others, most... ah... only a few... what I saw... it was odd... I think... I... *saw*... some believe you."

"Martha?"

"Yes sir, rock solid she is Jesus!"

"Mary?"

"She... ah... at first she did... believe you... that is... it's been hard... a bunch came from Jerusalem, mourners... but Martha won't have nothing to do with them... Mary did good... for a while."

"Would you find Martha, and bring her back... you will find us here."

"Sir, yes sir, right away!" Ben looked down, his smoky sticks had popped to flame and the fire was burning bright. "My food pack's over there, help yourself if you're hungry... I'll get Martha!"

John moved towards the food cash as Ben headed downhill.

Ben ran a parallel track to the house of Lazarus and stopped running a quarter-mile north of the house. There were always people watching and he wanted to get to Martha without attracting attention. He approached the house from behind the chicken coop on its eastern side.

Martha was straightening up after lunch, gathering up the table scraps.

"Mary, I am just going out to feed the chickens, I will be back in a few minutes," and Martha walked out the western door.

Circling around the house and carrying a bowl of leftovers brought running hens from every corner with their flapping wings and squawking. Martha threw the scraps in several directions to keep them from fighting over their food.

Watching the hens peck and cluck brought some sense of normality to her mind.

Hearing the crunching sound of dry brush she looked up to see Benjamin peeking at her from around the corner of her chicken coop.

What in the world?

"Psssss! Martha!" Ben whispered, "Jesus is here... and he's calling for you!"

Martha looked back at the house, and then she stepped towards Ben. She set her bowl down on the chopping block to the side of chicken coop and walked behind the building and out of sight of those in the house.

"Benjamin, what are you doing?" Martha demanded, and then asked, "Where is he?"

"I'm sorry, Martha, but it was just you he called for," said Ben.

Martha looked back at the house. She could still hear their blubbering noise from behind the coop, "Good idea."

"Jesus is at my cliff spot, just above the Jordan road. He is waiting for you there, Martha... it's just Jesus and John."

Jesus... who are you?

A man?

The son of God?

God in an earth suit?

Whoever you are, I trust you with my life...

And John is one of his best students...

And a friend.

Martha was silent for a moment, studying Ben's eyes... and thinking.

Benjamin...

It looks like we do this together.

Then Martha bolted, running... flat out... calling over shoulder, "This is it! This is what I have been waiting for!"

Caught off-guard, Ben stood there for half a heartbeat with his mouth hanging open... before his mind caught up with his spirit self and Martha's running feet... and then his body started moving.

She's fast! Wow! Martha... I hope you know where your goi... humph... oh yah... I told you... he's at my cliff spot!

Ben pushed it but he didn't catch up with Martha until she reached the transition point with the road and his lookout cliff.

Jesus stood there waiting.

John was there also, nibbling on the last date-nut cookie he had found in Ben's pack.

Motivated by her expectation for what she saw was coming next, Martha wasted not one word. "Lord," she said, "if you had been here, my brother would not have died. But I know, that even now, whatever you ask of God... God will give it to you."

"Your brother will rise again."

Jesus?

What?

Your eyes Jesus, they twinkle!

You toy with me!

And you are not afraid!

I can do this too!

"Yes, my Lord, I know that he will rise again, in the resurrection at the last day."

Well said Martha...

Try this on...

And I will see what else is growing in your garden.

"Martha, I Am the resurrection, and the life: he that believeth in me, though he were dead, yet shall he live: And whosoever liveth and believeth in me shall never die. Do you believe this?"

You Jesus!

You are the one the prophets have foretold!

The one we have waited forever for!

Yes!

Martha's knees turned to chicken gravy, her stomach floated upside-down; she desperately tried to maintain some control of her body, to remain standing in one place instead of floating away. She bit her lip and then continued.

"Yes Lord," she managed to say. "I believe you are the Christ! The son of God! The promised one come into the world!"

Hum… for now this is enough.

"Martha, will you bring Mary here to me?"

His question brought her back to the moment and the present condition of her brother. "Yes Lord, I will go and get her."

CHAPTER 15

In the place of protection, Laz covered his ears with both hands as he yelled loudly, "Mordecai! How can they hear what's going on? They're all cheering for Jesus! How can they tell what he's saying?"

Mordecai shouted back, "How do you hear him?"

"With my ears of course!"

Mordecai shook his head hollering back, "Listen closer!"

Only feet in front of Lazarus was the 'Jesus, Ben and Martha' scene perfectly presented, as if he were watching *top-side* from a hundred feet away. Jesus was speaking, *'Martha, will you bring Mary here to me?'*

"What? How cool is that! Mordecai! I hear him talking from the inside out! I don't need my outside ears to hear Jesus!"

Seeing how things were shaking down, and how his leaving could be coming at any moment, Lazarus was getting curious… and maybe a little nervous.

"So… what happens? … When someone leaves this place… and goes back topside I mean."

"Both Queen Esther and I were in attendance, when the young man from Nain left this place… and was reinstalled into his renovated earth suit."

Laz still had to shout, "And? What happened? What was it like?"

"When he left? At first he glowed a little, and then sparkled from the inside out, like a hundred candles burning. A moment later was a big burst of light, with a wind, as if a great deal of air left with him. All in all, it only took four, or maybe five seconds."

"Will I know beforehand?"

Mordecai shrugged his shoulders saying, "Most are here watching because they have never seen anyone leave, it usually happens fast, you will be given very little notice; but you will have the opportunity to choose, of whether to stay here… or to go. Oh, my! Lazarus, look! Ben and Martha have returned, they are back… at your sister's chicken coop!"

Martha and Benjamin retraced their steps to the chicken coop, and Benjamin waited for her there. Picking up her dish from the chopping block she glanced towards the home's eastern window.

Mary was seated at there, her eyes locked on the Jordan road.

Martha snuck up to the northeast corner of the house and slid along the wall.

"Mary," whispered Martha through the open window.

"Martha, what are you doing? And why are you whispering?"

"Ssshhh, Mary! Be quiet!"

"Why? What's going on?"

"Oh, Mary!" Martha wanted to shout instead of whisper, "I have seen Jesus! He's at Benjamin's cliff, he called for you, and he's waiting for you there!"

"Oh, Martha!" Mary started to cry again. "If he had only come sooner… it might have made a difference… but Lazarus has been dead four days!"

"Mary! What are you saying?" but Martha couldn't finish. Mary was getting up and making noise, "Mary… no wait!" but Mary was already heading across the room, making more of a fuss.

Making a show of grabbing her shawl with exaggerated tears, Mary headed for the door.

There were twenty-seven other people in the house, half had been present when Ben arrived with Jesus' message that first night, the others had come from Jerusalem to take part in mourning the death of Lazarus.

Each one took their traditions and positions seriously, and each responded immediately to Mary's cue. She was going to the tomb to weep there, and they were going with.

Mary knew where she was going, and headed for the roadside cliff. Twenty-seven people didn't know where they were going... but followed Mary.

It was only minutes and she was running up to Jesus, kneeling at his feet.

The mourners were close behind, but instead of arriving at the family tomb, they found themselves facing off with Jesus. Some had unpleasantly encountered him before.

Mary was weeping loudly, tears dripping on Jesus's sandals.

Some of the twenty-seven had their hackles up, and were scowling, roughly repeating among themselves their displeasure of Jesus' tardy presence.

Benjamin and Martha were about fifty feet behind the mourners, wondering how everything had gone so suddenly wrong.

Mary said, "Lord, if you had only been here, my brother would not have died!"

Where were you!

Why didn't you come when we called for you?

It's your fault my brother is in the grave!

If you cared at all you would have come here right away!

Jesus appraised the mess before him, twenty-seven wailing or belligerent mourners and a weeping Mary.

He looked out past the crowd of people, to a host of demons, beings who press to beg, borrow or steal a living human body to work their *magic* through. Creatures, mixing up their concoction in a blackened caldron, and cooking up the mash.

Don't let the enemy's use of these people push this sideways!

They're only confused people...

Providing fallen angels a human voice!

Pull in the harvest…
Bring Laz back…
And turn this all around!

Jesus heard the demons laughing in the distance.

Calling to the watching people, he asked, "Where have you placed his body?"

Determined voices answered, "This way Lord, come and see!"

Lord God my Father…
Of all these precious people…
Only two stand here with me!

Twenty feet ahead walked Ben and Martha, leading the way to her brother's tomb.

I will not leave my friend Lazarus in the grave!
He is coming back!

Hot tears rolled down the face of Jesus, he caged the anger held towards the worthless religious practice of so many.

Why do you choose to disbelieve my Father's goodness…
And resist the knowledge that he and I are one?

Whispered voices rose from those who walked beside and behind him.

Humph…
The laughing demons have moved a little closer.

Thinking they were safe, demons mocked Jesus through the willing voices.

"Look how he loved Lazarus, see, he is crying!"

They are vultures sitting on the shoulders of the willing.

"Oh really? Then where was he when Laz lay dying?"

They are crows feasting on the good seed that I sent and planted.

"Yeah, he healed others, why didn't he heal his friend?"

They are demons passing pictures to human minds…
Whispering words…
Using their lips.

"Jesus had Mary believing he would raise her brother from the dead!"

They are rabbits allowed to eat at the gardens of my friends!

The tomb was a cave, covered with a large stone, which was cut to the shape of a disk.

Together, waiting for instructions, both Ben and Martha stood beside the grave of her brother.

Thirty feet away, and five feet higher in elevation stood Jesus and John.

Father...

You have more people to be in place here...

Where are they?

Emil, the goat herder, arrived from somewhere unannounced, and stood close to Ben and Martha.

Well now!

How grand is that?

Thank you!

John moved down to stand by Ben and Emil, Martha moved up and stood by Jesus.

Now Mary, where are you?

In the hollow space, halfway between where he stood and the tomb, Jesus saw Martha's sister, sobbing and centered among weeping, wailing mourners; Mary, with empty hands, and an empty heart.

Humph...

Well then...

This will have to do.

"Take away the stone!"

Slapped in her face with a wet rag, Martha responded with her first thought, "Lord! By this time his body stinks! He's been dead four days!"

Oh my!

Did I really say that?

"Martha, do you remember the words I told you, that if you would believe, you would see the glory of God?"

Lord God...

Jesus...

Your eyes...

They are twinkling again!

From the center of the soul, Martha saw the garden of her heart. The words of Jesus planted, they'd been guarded, protected, and now were bursting forth with life! She scooped up giant armfuls and piled them up around her brother! She yelled it, she screamed it, and she triumphantly hollered it out, "Benjamin! Emil! John! Get your backs into it! Roll that stone away!"

The three men didn't hesitate a heartbeat, they threw themselves into the cover stone and rolled it back, and the stink did come floating out the cave.

Jesus observed each one's reactions, as a southeast breeze carried the dead man's odor past the party of twenty-seven.

Some turned to escape the stench; some held their breath, waiting for the wind to change.

Martha swallowed hard without breathing, her eyes started to water.

The fragrant smell of their spikenard perfume wrapping had been overwhelmingly overpowered by the decomposing of his body.

On the winds of time, memories are often carried by things that are not consciously considered. "We win," Jesus told Martha. "And this is a moment in forever which will always be remembered. I want all people to know how… and why… we win. I want them to see, to hear… and even to smell… and remember."

Looking to heaven, Jesus said, "Father."

Everyone heard, but some, a minority, didn't like his words.

What!

He did it again!

He called God his father!

How dare he call Almighty God his Father!

But they did what any coward does, when they were small in strength and number, they clenched their fists and whined to one another.

Jesus continued on by saying, "I thank you that you have heard me."

Verb confusion slid down past the eyes of the twenty-seven.

Hugh?

What?

Did we miss something?

I thought your first words were, 'Father'.

Now you talk as if you said something more?
You are just too weird.
"And I know you always hear me."
Will you not understand?
Four days ago I sent my words ahead!
For you to plant and guard to grow!
"But because of the people that stand by I said it, that they may believe you sent me."

Martha had her eyes glued on the door of the tomb, and she was ready to run to her brother when he walked out.

In the spirit arena, Benjamin, John, and Emil were all pulling life out of Jesus and throwing it right in the cave mouth to Lazarus. They were still running hard and doing their part. In this race to rescue Lazarus, the five of them were getting to the finish line at the same time.

And then there was Mary.

Her heart ached as if her garden had been rooted up by a pack of feral hogs.

I am a hollow empty vessel!
Both my hands are empty!
I have brought forth nothing grown in my garden from your words!
Oh God help me!
I am so alone!

With a loud voice Jesus said, *"Lazarus, come forth!"*

In the silence which followed his commanding words, a gentle breath enveloped them all.

Mary dropped to her knees, sobbing; she put her face in the dirt.

Through the tears and grime, that fresh breeze brought a distant memory past her nose. She was twelve years old, and her father was standing in her doorway with a gift. It was a small plant with bell-shaped lavender flowers on it. The flower had arrived with a caravan which had come from the mountains of a northern country. Her father had only said, *'Many people associate sadness with this plant, but the pretty purple flowers reminded me of you. Keep this for me.'*

The plant was Spikenard, and Mary smelled the sweet oil aroma from its purple flowers. She stopped crying and looked up to see where the smell was coming from.

In the distance she could hear the shuffling sound of tiny steps as Lazarus inched his way out the door, wrapped from head to foot with grave cloth.

Watching him try to walk, Jesus said, "Loose him, and let him go."

CHAPTER 16

In the place of protection, Lazarus, watching closely knew this was it. Having only seconds, he, for only a fraction of that time, reflected on his newfound friends seated with him around Adam's table.

Queen Esther, although you could be my own Esther's twin, your personality's quite different, very nice you are, only uniquely different from my Esther.

Mordecai, you have become my articulate and educated friend.

David, on earth you were King, but you speak to me as equal.

Jonathan, you are a most insightful and honorable man, I would like to know you better, but that will have to wait.

Mom and dad, your daughters are going to hear of you, and the adventures you have today!

And you Anna, how do you fit in?

You stand at a distance, bubbling over with excitement!

What secrets do you know?

'Lazarus! Come forth!'

Jesus' words came through loud and clear to every person present, and Laz simply *thought* his answer.

Yes!

Millions of watchers went absolutely wild! They were shouting, screaming, causing the cavernous expanse of the protected place to shake and quiver!

Lazarus' guardian angel, Floyd, with his running shoes on, switched off *standby mode* and went to *active.*

Laz began at first to glow, then came the hundred candle sparkle, a brilliant flash of light, followed by his place at Adam's table, empty, and instantly, Laz was somewhere else.

The revitalization of Lazarus' body was instantaneous, and although Emil wondered where the maggots went, what mattered most, is that they were no longer there.

Ben jumped down into the cave entrance, shouting, "Laz! You are back! Here, let me help you!"

Ben jerked the head-cover off his friend and then grabbed for his elbow, still held captive below the grave-cloth wrapping. Emil took hold of his other elbow and together they brought him up from the cave.

And then Martha was there, with her arms wrapped around her brother.

"Lazarus! Thank God! You are back!"

Laz was still a little groggy after the reentry into his earth suit.

"Martha?"

Lazarus buried his face into his sister's wavy black hair and drew in a deep breath of air through her curls. Opening his eyes he saw Jesus watching, smiling from ear to ear.

Emil had a knife out, and was cutting off the grave-cloth; Benjamin took his outer robe and placed it over the shoulders of his friend, tying it around his waist.

"Martha, where is my little sister?"

"She is here... give her a moment... this... your... ah... it's been rather hard on her."

And then there was Mary, somewhat shaky, standing in front of him.

She reached out and took his hand… it was warm and strong and calloused.

Mary looked up into his eyes and said, "Lazarus… I was so afraid! I thought you were gone forever! I didn't think I was ever going to see you again!"

Tears were pouring from her eyes and dripping off her face.

"Well… I am not gone… I am standing here looking right at you, and I will be here with you, for a long, long, time." He reached out and pulled her close, and felt her salty tears on his chest.

Hearing the sound of crushing gravel, Lazarus turned just in time to see the stone drop back into place with a thump, sealing off the tomb. Emil, Ben and John had returned it to its resting place and then stood as guardians around Lazarus and his sisters.

And then Jesus was there, "My friend, so good to have you back again!"

"Jesus! We watched you call my name! From Adam's table! Lord God you are amazing!"

Martha wondered, "Lazarus, what?"

The mourners, who were no longer mourning began to gather round.

Jesus stopped him, "Lazarus, you must keep what you now know in a very small circle, understand?"

"Yes sir, we will talk later?"

"Later… yes."

The demons, they're not laughing now!

Sulking, red faced, and separating themselves from the other mourners, two men peeled off, quietly moved out of sight, and went to find their superiors in Jerusalem.

The transition time was easy for Martha.

She had expected to see the glory of God, and see it she did.

Mary, on the other hand, was still somewhat bewildered, riding on waves of emotion. She took hold of her brother's left arm as they walked back to their house. Every few steps along the way, she would pull his arm up to her nose and sniff it, as if recording a smell to remember.

News was spreading fast, the eye-witnesses were charged with the reality of what had transpired, the stinky dead Lazarus raised from the dead.

They were following Jesus, Laz, and his sisters back to their house.

As each one saw someone they knew, he, or she, would run out and say, "He was dead! His body stunk! And Jesus said, *'Lazarus, come forth'* and Lazarus walked out of the tomb... alive!"

Once more, and with her eyes closed, Mary lifted the left arm of her brother up to her nose and smelled it, drawing in a deep breath through her nostrils.

As her eyes opened, her brother asked, "Mary, what are you doing?"

"It's the smell Lazarus! You were dead and now you're alive! It's the aroma of life! Not death!"

"I am sorry Mary, but I don't know what you are talking about. It was my body that died; I was alive, just someplace else. I suppose my body did start to smell bad after being four days dead, but that doesn't explain why you keep smelling my arm?"

"After your body died and we prepared it for the grave... we smeared it with spikenard oil. Then after Jesus said, *'Lazarus come forth,'* there was a breath of air that came with those words, and it carried this smell! I took a deep breath of an *alive spikenard fragrance*, and when I looked up, and you were standing there! You were all wrapped up, but even after they unwrapped you, you were still covered with the smell of this perfume! It's such a beautiful scent! It's a smell of life and hope! I'm so glad that you're back here with us! I love you so much, Lazarus!"

Lazarus wrapped his arms around his little sister and spun her in a circle, her feet lifting from the ground, "Here we are Mary! Martha! God is always good, and we have it made forever!"

Mary squealed like a little girl, "Lazarus...!" and then she started laughing, spinning in his arms, "You... are... going... to... make... me... dizzy! My... brother! Aaaahhhh!"

Slowing... spinning slower, gently, Laz set her down, but not letting go, only to keep her from falling, she was kind of wobbly.

Her world still revolving... moving in and out, Mary asked, "My brother... what would you like? Now that you are home... is there something I can get you, anything at all?"

"I'm kind of hungry... it feels like I haven't eaten in forever!"

"Oh Lazarus! We've got tons of food! People kept bringing things! Piles of stuff! We could never eat it all! What would you like? Lamb chops? Biscuits and gravy? Simon even sent a wagon down this morning! Hannah and Esther fixed it up... he sent a message with... said it was all your favorites... said you would love it!"

Here Mary burst into tears once more, happy and sad, joy to be alive, emotional-overload-happiness-tears. "Lazarus! Simon... he expected you to be alive!"

Laz glanced around, looking at the crowd... when he exited the tomb there was maybe thirty people there; walking from the tomb to the house they had gathered at least another thirty more.

Laz jumped up to the house steps, "Welcome! Welcome to you all! You came to help... to show support to my sisters... to mourn... a body which had died... but... as you can see... I'm no longer dead at all... but very much alive! The funeral food which you have brought... I believe it would be better served... as a feast! A celebration! Martha will direct you, you who came to help, let's move it all outside, where we may all celebrate together!"

Within only moments a caravan of food flowed out the door, with Martha directing, Mary running back and forth. She created a special plate for her brother, and brought it straight to him.

Together, they ate, and talked, most got a turn to gawk... staring at the man who once was four days dead... but now totally alive. Some reached out to touch a hand... or some to touch his face... but all were in awe of the one who gave him life.

Behind the scene, those who came to help, kept things running smoothly, cleaned up the mess, and as darkness came, they gently helped maneuver the guests on to moving home.

Finally, Lazarus, his sisters, Jesus and John, moved inside and were standing there alone.

From just one step inside the door, Lazarus surveyed their home. With his right hand, he reached over and felt the oiled leather of his work apron, below the apron were his sandals, sitting in their place. To his far left, both doors to the bedrooms were closed, and in front of him sat two empty tea cups on the table at Martha's window, his coat was draped over an arm of Martha's chair. He looked up at Jesus who had been watching him, and whispered the words, *"thank you."*

Mary wondered, "Hum?"

Something seems a little strange, who is it that isn't here?

"Martha, where's Benjamin? I haven't seen him for hours."

"I don't know Mary, Emil's gone missing too."

In the place of protection, those who had been around Adam's stone table with Lazarus and watching Jesus at the tomb, (up until the point where Lazarus began to shine brightly and then disappeared), simply shifted to watching Jesus with Lazarus in his earth suit, and shuffling his way out of the tomb, (in full three-D of course).

From that point in time, *(of Lazarus leaving Sheol and moving forward in his earth suit)*, the watchers were of course still watching, but they spread out once more, utilizing every stone table in the place of protection.

Each table went to watching in real time, live feed mode, tracking different players on the earth. One could always tell which watchers were watching the same scene and people, for at key moments a matched cheering response could be heard throughout Sheol's caverns.

There was left about a dozen, seated around Adam's table.

"Uncle Mordecai this is so wonderful! Lazarus, he made it back to his earth suit! His sisters, they got their brother back!"

"Absolutely grand, is it not? And, in the process he set a new record, four full days and nights before his body was... um... raised up... fixed... and refurbished, with no maggots!"

David spoke up, "Grand it is Mordecai, and Jesus, even restricted to an earth suit is nonetheless quite amazing. Limited to the laws he built for man, and still he got it done!"

"Uncle, do they know who Emil is yet?"

"Emil, the goat herder?" David wondered.

"Yes... you know... where he was... who and what he's seen... do any of them know?"

"No, I'm quite sure they don't, except Simon may know a little. Those who are close to him, they weren't even born when it happened, and he never talks about it, not ever."

"What about Anna? And Stonehouse? Or Stonehouse and Simon? Who knows?"

Here Anna answered, "Simon's parents never spoke to anyone but Simon about my life at Stonehouse, and as far as I know, Simon has never spoken to anyone, except his parents about me."

CHAPTER 17

Where are those two going?

Lazarus hasn't been out of the tomb five minutes and they leave?

What for?

I don't get it.

"Emil, those two, they're leaving? Who are they? And why go now, I don't get it?"

Turning towards Jerusalem to answer Ben's question, Emil grunted his reply, "Humph... those two? Jannes and Jambres, pitiful examples of humanity, they are probably going back to report in."

"What?"

"They're spies."

"Spies? Oh, come on now... spies? Emil... really? At a funeral?... What for? Who would do that?"

"This ain't no funeral anymore."

Mary got herself up out of the dirt, wiping some grime off her face with her robe sleeve. Cautiously, slowly, she moved towards her brother as Ben put his outer robe over Lazarus' shoulders.

"I'm going to follow them."

"I can do you better than that, I can tell you where they're going. You get in front of them, run and arrive there first; hide, then you can hear what they have to say."

"No way!"

"Yes way. King Solomon's stables, under Solomon's porch, across from the Temple. Seen 'em go in there before, with three in particular, Korah, Dathan and Abiram… Chief Priests… from Jerusalem… expounders of the law… lawyers… disgusting lot."

"What if they go somewhere else? We'll miss them."

"I'll track 'em from this side, that way one of us is bound to hear them."

"Okay… let's go!"

Twenty minutes later and Ben was making his way, torch in hand, through a labyrinth of stone archways under Solomon's porch, hallways and small rooms, each being maybe twenty feet square.

I hope you're right Emil,
There's only one active traffic path through this place,
Everything else is covered with cobwebs…
And fat spiders!

Ben was in his hiding place with the torch doused only minutes before he heard the first swishy sound of sandal leather on cobblestones strewn with gravel.

Three new torches were set in iron sockets anchored to the stone wall, by three Chief Priests-Jerusalem lawyers. Korah, Dathan, and Abiram, had arrived.

The two funeral spies, Jannes and Jambres, appeared from the opposite direction and set one more torch in a wall socket.

"We went there just as you told us to," Jannes said glancing around the apparently empty room. "We told everyone what a counterfeit that Jesus really is!"

Priest Korah agreed, "He's just a traveling trouble maker!"

"Just a trouble maker!" dittoed Priest Dathan, listening as more footsteps approached on stone cobbles. "He abandoned Lazarus there to die. I mean, if Jesus actually healed a man born blind, then surely he could have kept Lazarus from dying!"

"Well... of course, that's true," agreed Priest Abiram. "But he let Lazarus die... too bad. So, is there a problem?"

"Well... we stayed there four days before Jesus ever showed up."

"Four days, that's plenty of time for someone to get someplace," Priest Dathan pointed out. "And besides, after that long, the body of Lazarus would have been infested with maggots, and it would stink something awful!"

"It did stink something terrible," recounted Jambres. "When they rolled the stone away... oh... the smell that oozed out... made my eyes water. Oh, he stank!"

From Jerusalem's Temple, the High Priest Caiaphas, entered through the room's single archway entrance.

"What?" demanded Priest Abiram. "What do you mean, they rolled the stone away? On who's authority? Does that man have no respect at all for the dead? We could charge him for any number of laws which he has broken!"

"W... w... well," stammered Jannes, "actually Martha, Lazarus' sister, she gave the order... to move the stone."

"They had better have put it back!" declared Priest Korah.

"Well... eh, yes...um... they did put it back," sputtered Jannes, "but Lazarus came out first."

This got the attention of the High Priest Caiaphas, who never took part in trivial conversations, "What do you mean *but Lazarus came out first*?"

Jannes explained, "Well... eh... they rolled the stone away and then Jesus told Lazarus to come out. He just sort of shuffled his way out of the cave, still wrapped in all of that stuff, but he didn't stink no more! It was that Jesus who did it, it's his fault!"

It looked like High Priest Caiaphas was going to have a fit, "No! No! No! We can't have this happen! Do you have any idea the consequences... if people find out about this? Do you have any idea at all? The Romans, that's what will happen! The people will follow after Jesus! We will lose our control over the people! They will start to think for themselves! And the Romans will blame us!"

Priest Abiram added, "If he had only done this once, it wouldn't be so bad, but he persists in doing things like this over and over again!"

"We must put a stop to this," High Priest Caiaphas shouted, "and we must put a stop to it now!"

Priest Dathan agreed, "Yes, we must! For the good of the people, we must stop this!"

"If we don't do something, then the Romans will come and take our place and our nation!"

Flickering torch-light bounced from face to face as the six men continued in their heated conversation.

Ben listened closely, horrified.

Augh!

How wicked can they be?

We always and forever have watched for the Messiah!

And now he is here!

This is a good thing!

Not bad!

Priest Abiram identified, "For the good of the people, they need us to lead them. That fly-by-night Jesus just wanders around all over. If people follow him, the people will wander all over."

Priest Korah wondered, "If the people follow him, they might give Jesus our money. We can't have them give their money to him, he would just waste it, this is where the Temple is, we know what to do with our money!"

Ben's mind reeled.

You would trade in our Messiah?

For money?

For power?

Have you gone mad?

"You people know nothing at all!" declared High Priest Caiaphas. "Don't you know that it's more needful for one man to die than for an entire nation to perish? We will kill him… to save the nation!"

"And what about Lazarus?" asked Jambres… perplexed, "Should we kill him too?"

The War Is Over | 117

High Priest Caiaphas said, "That's an excellent idea, kill Lazarus too!"

"Both of them?" asked Jannes... somewhat stunned.

Ben thought of jumping out, and cutting them to pieces with a sword, but he didn't have one.

Caiaphas, you are God's High Priest!

Your office...

People trust you...

Because of where you stand!

But you!

You are gone mad!

Priest Dathan said, "What's the matter with you? You little whiner, do you have no stomach at all?"

"Gentlemen," said High Priest Caiaphas, "I have seen this kind of thing before, someone dies, gets raised from the dead, and people start asking them questions. Questions like, *'Where were you? What did you see? What did you learn?'* He will confuse the people, so for their sake, we must also kill Lazarus."

"Kill them both?" questioned Jannes. "The people would quit following you if they thought you had something to do with killing Jesus... and Lazarus."

"We won't be the ones who kill him," mused the High Priest.

"What? Then who will kill them?"

High Priest Caiaphas said, "We will get the fanatical people that follow him to kill them."

"And how will we do that?"

"With words," said High Priest Caiaphas. "With Jesus' own words, how did he say it? *'You steer a big boat with words,'* or something like that, but we will take some of his own words and steer the people against him. They will kill him... we will just help them do what **they** want."

And then they were gone.

Ben sat in total darkness.

No light, no torch.

No flint to kindle flame.

Slumped in his hiding covey, Ben's head pounded.

118 | Mike & Dianne Heintzeman

His mind… it blurred with anguish.
How could they be so wickedly corrupt?
Lord God, my God!
Help me… how?
How can we stop their putrid plan?

From the center of the soul, six spirits war with weapons grown in rose, grape and plum tree plots. Savor the crowned achievement of their lives.

A collectively developed creation enhanced through malicious guidance of plant characteristics and grafting technology. A cut and slice here, a grafted thorn there, twist a truth, plant a lie, add some fear, mix in a dash of greed, and what do we have? A magnificent grapevine with leaves as big as two hands placed together, fruit protected by guardian thorns so long and strong, one could enter through your palm and exit out the other side.

For our king, we will weave some for a crown.

CHAPTER 18

"Jesus!"

"I saw them!"

"So many I couldn't count them all!"

"My guardian angel, he's called... Floyd, he said... there are... millions!"

"King David! I saw King David! Walked with him, talked with him... and his best friend Jonathan, I saw him too!"

Lazarus turned around, opened the door, quickly looked around outside, came back in, slammed the door and locked it with a crossbar.

"We are here alone! I can tell you! Everyone was so amazing! They're cheering you on Jesus! They're cheering all of us on! And... watching us... when they can."

His older sister was concerned, "Lazarus... slow down... and take a breath!"

"Martha! You would love the people there, I visited with Adam and Eve, she kind 'a looks like you, a little around the eyes. They assigned transition helpers to me, a niece, and her uncle, who both appeared the same age as I, but then... they all look equal in age...they showed me around the place, we went for walks. And Martha! They were from my Esther's favorite story in the scrolls, the one she calls her own, the book called Esther! And Mary, get this, my Esther could be Queen Esther's twin!"

Laz went to sit on his chair at their table but closed the shutters first. As he set its locking crossbar he found himself eye to eye with a tiny hole drilled through the upper middle of the central shutter board.

Twenty years ago my father drilled that hole in my mother's new shutter boards; Hum...

How unique...

I remember it like yesterday.

"Samson, ask me something about Samson... go ahead... you would never guess, a full head of long hair... and... this is it... he's just a normal size guy, no bigger than me! I thought he would be a giant!"

Laz slowed down a bit, and he took on a solemn face. "Jesus, they are waiting for you, all the people there, they are waiting for you to come and get them."

Pushing the subject back to lighter thoughts, Jesus made a statement, which he accented with a grin. "You set the record Lazarus! The longest time with your body dead, and then returning to enter back into it once again."

"They thought I might... do I get some sort of award? A prize?"

"Sorry Laz... no prize... no award."

"How fun is that?"

"What I want to know is this... the people in the place of protection, what do they know of me coming to get them?"

"How is it you ask me, Jesus? You have the power to raise me from the dead, and heal my body, but you ask me what they know? I would think you know everything, I don't understand?"

"He is the Christ!" Martha declared, looking at Lazarus and watching his eyes. "The Son of God!" Then turning to Jesus, she said, "Jesus, you must know everything."

"I was, I am, and I ever will be. I am the word become flesh, but I had to empty myself to enter this body of flesh. From before we formed Adam from the clay of this earth, this plan of redemption has been in motion, to get the ones who are waiting for me is a page of that plan."

Mary timidly entered into the conversation, needing her questions answered. She looked down, brushed at some wrinkles in her robe, looked back up and asked, "Who was Joseph? Your mother Mary's husband, wasn't he your father?"

Standing up, Jesus walked to the stone fireplace near the spot where the cook usually stands, at his side were wooden spoons worn smooth through use.

"Joseph was more than a good man. He was my dad, but not my Father. Mary agreed to allow my body to be formed in her womb, but she never had physical relations with Joseph before my birth. The word of God is the seed which grew in her womb."

Jesus reached up with his left hand he removed Martha's burning oil lamp from its perch on the wall and set it on the worktable in front of him. "We cut a blood covenant with Abraham, and we had it recorded, *And it came to pass, that, when the sun went down, and it was dark, behold a smoking furnace, and a burning lamp that passed between those pieces.'* It was my Father and I that walked with Abraham through the blood, Abraham saw our footprints through the way of blood. My Father is that smoking furnace, I am that burning lamp."

"Eventually, down the river of time, the day came when Abraham placed his son Isaac on the altar as a willing sacrifice. Abraham's faithful actions played a major part of arranging my arrival here."

Martha said, "We have heard and read of those words forever, I see you in the written word Jesus!"

Jesus continued, "The book of covenants contains my path to follow, we put hundreds upon hundreds of prophesies in that book for me, that word has been my food."

"Remember what Moses recorded of the leading of God, with the children of Israel, when they ate manna in the wilderness? *And the Lord went before them by day in a pillar of a cloud, to lead them by day; and by night in a pillar of fire, to give them light; to go by day and night.'* The book of covenants is full of pictures of my Father and I, the pictures were put there so that you would identify me."

John was befuddled, "Jesus, you keep saying we, and us, but the Lord our God, he is one God!"

"Yes, you are right John, my Father and I are one," Jesus said. "I am the word of God made flesh. Remember how it is written, 'And God said, Let us make man in our image, after our likeness.' We made man in our image so my body could be made in Mary's womb and so you could be born of God!"

"I know what my Father tells me, I do what I see my Father do, and I know what we put in that Book for me. The Spirit is my blood, the word is my flesh, I and my Father are one. I know who I am because I eat that word and I drink in that Spirit."

Lazarus lifted the lamp from the table and stared into its flame, "And you ask me what they know, in that place where I was!"

"Because I emptied myself, and allowed myself to be placed in this earth suit. While I am here, I am restricted to function within the limitations of this body, like you, under this covenant, that is the only way we could buy you back. In the same way that Adam failed, I must succeed!"

Lazarus was becoming exasperated, "Jesus, you talk as if this isn't all done! Like it isn't finished! They said that you are the Lamb slain from before the foundation of the earth! Sounds very finished to me."

Finishing his walk around the stone fireplace, Jesus settled onto a box bench with a cushion and leaned against the western wall, it still gave off heat from the evening sun. "Failure is not an option, but failure has always been a possibility. That is why this is real, that is why it counts."

"And what if you failed?" asked Lazarus, as he returned Martha's oil lamp to its place on the wall.

"Then everything would cease to exist," Jesus declared.

"Oh... hum... okay... I wouldn't like that at all... but I think I understand."

Then answering Jesus' original question, Lazarus said, "They remember all that happened on this earth. And collectively, they know everything that is written in the book of covenants. They understand where we are on the timeline, and they understand the price that you will have to pay."

Laz sat on his chair by the table, and turned it so he was eye to eye with Jesus on the cushioned bench, four or five feet away, "It was David who talked the most about this. King David, son of Jesse, but it's a bit different there, more of a circle than a string with two ends, but it was still King David."

"Mordecai and Queen Esther led us to the narrows; David and Jonathan were also there. At the divide you can see across the pit, right into Sheol, hell. The pit is very deep with iron fences on either side, no one can get across, you can see into hell if you want to look, but it's a very ugly place."

Lazarus retold parts of their conversation, "David said, Jesus is the one that I was talking about, when the Holy Spirit inspired me to write, *'Thou hast ascended on high, thou hast led captivity captive: thou hast received gifts in the man; yea, the rebellious also, that the Lord God might dwell.'* Jesus is coming to get us."

Lazarus continued, "And then David said, 'Lazarus, we are the *'captivity'*, all of us being held on this side of the divide. This is a place of protection, and Jesus is coming here to take us *'captive,'* and bring us home!"

The eyes of Lazarus picked up the vacant look of a *twenty mile stare*, as if he had gone back to Sheol, and was standing next to King David. From that place, Laz said, "We looked with David across the divide, listening to the gut-wrenching cries coming from the other side, watching the torment of their affliction. And David said, 'but before Jesus can come and get us, he will be thrown into hell, to pay the price for us. Once the final price to his Father is paid, in front of all of us, and them, Jesus will totally defeat that fallen angel, the devil, and seal his fate forever. Then he will take us with him, and present his blood of the New Covenant to his Father.'"

CHAPTER 19

Sunshine's early morning sneaky kiss to Martha was accompanied by a full chorus of clucking chickens scratching out their favorite rendition of 'Oh please release me and then feed me!'

Tripping a wooden flip-flap latch, Martha first tugged their cage door slightly open and then she wiggled her hand around inside to push the hen house door open wide. A half dozen floor birds bolted first, flapping their way to a bug and clover breakfast.

Squawking chickens spread across the yard, but Martha delayed her advancement towards picking eggs, as one by one, roosting pole fliers flew past her head at nose height. She felt poofs of wind and bits of debris strike her face, elements released from flapping feathers and beating wings.

Ugh!

No wonder I usually let Mary fetch the eggs!

And she thinks chickens are fun!

Go figure.

I'm going to give the fliers more time to clear out first.

Reaching into the feed box, she brought out a full scoop which she dumped in little piles near the coop.

Twenty-six.

Twenty-seven.

Twenty-eight?

That's not right, where are they?

Cautiously Martha stepped inside.

Five chickens were *hiding out* in henhouse nesting boxes.

Making a basket from her apron, Martha shooed the *wanna-be-sitting* hens off their nests and gathered eleven eggs.

"Soon enough, girls," Martha pledged to her protesting hens. "By Passover you will each be sitting on a nest full of eggs."

Stepping back into the house, Martha detected a slight tinge of wood smoke in the air. John and Jesus had a fire going, and Lazarus set a kettle of water on to boil.

Gazing across the room, Martha gathered up the sight before her and gently slid it into her memory box.

Mary slipped out, wrapped in a blanket with her hair all messed up. She managed to wrap one arm around her brother before Martha threw her a *go-get-dressed* glance. As Mary scampered back to her room, Martha found herself focusing on dust stuck to the bottoms of Mary's feet.

Martha,

It is a happy day…

Enjoy the journey!

"I believe that we all need an extra day of no work, what do you think John?"

"Well now, Martha, what an excellent idea! What do you say Jesus?"

"We must meet up with Peter and the rest in Ephraim, and that's a fifteen mile walk," he answered while observing the hopeful faces of his friends. "But we don't really need to leave until tomorrow."

"Yes!" John said, with a little bit too much enthusiasm.

Lazarus patted his stomach, "So… who's fixing breakfast this morning?"

His older sister answered, "I will, if you all stay close enough for me to hear the conversation."

"Deal, it looks a bit chilly outside anyhow."

Against the home's western wall was a long built-in storage box. It had several separate lids and was long enough to serve as two beds, but was mostly used as a bench, cushions and pillows were scattered along its length. Furthest from the door, and with a couple of cushions between himself and the bedroom wall was Jesus, listening to happy conversation with his feet up.

Lazarus landed on a cushion near Jesus and asked, "Why?"

"Why what, Laz?"

"Why are we made like we are?"

"These bodies are so fragile, and most people only live seventy or eighty years. I talked with Noah's Grandfather, and he lived to be nine hundred and… whatever-it-was."

"Nine hundred and sixty-nine."

"Okay… nine hundred and sixty-nine years, but these bodies are so limited… we could have been made unbreakable… forever! Jesus… you know exactly what I am talking about!"

"Hum… I do, you've seen a lot of things that are now stuck in your mind forever. What did Adam tell you about that? You did ask him, didn't you?"

"Well, yes… but they still only know what's written… and what is prophesied… and what has happened up to now. That's the end of what they know… I think you know a lot more."

Martha could see from her window that some chicken had uncovered an entire covey of tasty grubs; it gobbled what it could until another hen spied its frantic feeding which triggered several more chickens to descend on the first hen's private stash. In a flurry of rust-colored feathers, yellow beaks, and rake scratching scaly red feet, the big white worms were soon gone.

"Good answer, although there are limitations on me because of this flesh and blood body… plus there are some things I won't tell you."

"Okay… that's fine… I understand."

John and Mary were all ears… and Martha was cooking without making any noise.

"Martha… you watched those two the Chief Priests sent over… there were five to start with. What do you know of the two who ran back to Jerusalem?"

"How do you mean… what do I know of them?"

"You kept an eye on them… what's their heart condition?"

"They came here with the intention of undermining you; they were intent on keeping Lazarus in the grave by casting doubt and unbelief on the words you sent to us."

Mary pushed her bench pillows around trying to get comfortable and added, "They took turns talking to me…it seemed like they kept stirring up the same feelings with different words around them, but they all wanted me to be mad at you, like it was somehow your fault Lazarus was in that hole in the ground."

"John… you saw them, how old do you think they were?"

"Thirty-five, maybe forty… why?"

"All five were confronted with the truth, and three turned towards God."

Mary finished her answer, "And the other two headed straight to their handlers back at Jerusalem."

Jesus continued, "You understand what they have seen, if they had another four hundred years to choose, would they choose to repent towards God, or stay in rebellion?"

Looking back over her shoulder at Jesus, Mary concluded, "they made up their minds almost immediately… so I would say more time would not make any difference."

"Very good, Mary… each individual person will have their opportunity to hear the good news, everyone will have the chance to choose life or death, blessing or cursing, but choosing life is much better."

Lazarus wondered, "So can I say it like this… we were placed in these flesh and blood bodies, where we can only do so much good, or so much bad. In this limited condition, we have to make one primary choice that lasts forever, and that choice is which one of the two kingdoms we will belong to forever. Whatever kingdom we belong to when our body dies, that is the kingdom we belong to forever. From what I have come to understand, there is not a way into it yet, only a protected spot waiting for it, but something that you, Jesus, are going to do, in the near future, will allow you to be the door into that kingdom, the only door."

"An acceptable answer… is it yours or Adam's?"

"Well… it's a little bit of both."

"My Father will never allow rebellion into his house... not ever again."

John's ears perked up, "Jesus, how did rebellion get into heaven?"

"I'm hungry," Jesus said, "it smells like breakfast is ready, what do you say Martha, eggs up?"

"Wash, bless, and eat... in that order," said Martha. "No rebellion in my house either!"

CHAPTER 20

Lazarus was poking at the cooking fire with a stick, Martha was watching, thinking.

What is it with boys and fire?

Sparks were popping around and some wisps of smoke were entering the room instead of going up the chimney.

She went to the east window and opened the shutter a bit to look out. The clear morning sky had given way to clouds and a misty rain was falling. After closing the shutters she turned back to observe her brother.

He was still poking around the fire, but now he was adding more sticks. It was a good day to be inside and looking out. Picking up the kettle, Lazarus added more water to it and set it back to heat.

It was mid-afternoon and Jesus was beginning to stir, he had taken a nap amongst a pile of cushions on the western wall bench.

After preparing two cups of tea, Lazarus went and sat next to his friend and handed one steaming cup to him.

"When my body was in the tomb, and I was with David and the others, David kept talking about what's coming, all stirred up about how it is going to be so different for the people on earth, how different can it be?"

A slight smile appeared on Jesus' face... and he began to answer, "The words David wrote *'You have ascended on high, you have led captivity captive,'* they are only a portion of what Spirit Helper inspired him to write. He went on to say, *'You have received gifts in the man'.* David was writing about what I will do."

"I know that with you, Jesus... words are an extremely precise thing. I believe what David wrote... is about you receiving something specific from your Father, and placing that part of Himself into an individual person. That's what I want to understand, that's my question."

"Lazarus... this is something which has to be comprehended from the inside-out, with the help of Spirit Helper. And... His day is not here yet, but I can tell you what to look for, and where to dig."

"That's good enough... I know how to dig."

"John, I want you to come over here and sit on this bench next to me... and Lazarus, I want you to sit over there... with one sister on each side of you."

Each one took their place and sat down.

"Okay... John... tell me what you see."

"What do I see?"

John was flustered. "I see a man with his two sisters sitting next to him. What do you mean, *'what do I see'?*"

"John, come on now... look at them... they are brother and sisters... can you tell that by looking at them? Tell me about them."

"Oh! Alright, I understand! Now you gave me something to work with. All three have thick black hair, but Martha's hair has large loopy curls, and comes to the middle of her back. Both Lazarus and Mary have the same wavy hair, but Mary's hair is very long, but it's the same kind of hair as Lazarus. Mary and Martha both have a nice, slim, straight nose, but Lazarus' nose... it's a little bigger."

"Hey, John, don't you go picking on my nose, I got it from my father... and he has a very fine nose."

"So sorry," John mocked. "I never saw your dad".

"That's okay, John, I saw him three days ago."

"You saw Papa?" both girls asked at the same time. "Lazarus! Why didn't you say something?"

"Sorry… I forgot… in all that was going on… but I did tell him all about the two of you."

"Okay," John said. "Let's get back to the faces. I'm looking at eyebrows, on the sisters, the same and quite attractive… feminine. Laz, you must have gotten those bushes from your father, also. But now the ears, very nice and all the same."

"They are from our mother," Martha said. "I always thought that she had such beautiful ears."

"She still does, Martha."

"Oh, Lazarus, you saw her too!" Tears just burst out and ran down Martha's face.

John pretended to complain, "Hey… come on now you guys… you are going to get me sidetracked here!"

Mary concluded, "Okay, Jesus, you made your point, it's very obvious… we have the same mother and father, and you can tell that just by looking at us, but everyone else can see that too. Tell us something we don't know."

"When you are my sister… spirit you… the real you… you will look like me."

Jesus continued, "As each one of you choose to accept the Covenant that I will cut for you, each one of you will be born of above, born again, not of something corruptible, but of what is incorruptible, by the word of God that lives and abides forever. You have heard me use this term… *born again*… many times before, you need to understand… this is not starting over… this is becoming a new creature. This is not only being washed and forgiven; this is the seed of the word of God taking root in *spirit you,* and you being recreated, instantaneously from the inside out."

The four sat in stunned silence… as if Jesus had told them that they had been anointed to be Kings and Priests.

"By birth, you will be sons and daughters of the Most High God. As you receive what I am going to do for you, you will become, by birth, Kings and Priests unto our God and Father. As a seed falls into the ground and dies, your old self will die, and you will be raised to newness of life."

Jesus paused for a moment… but no one said anything… so he kept going… "Because it is by the seed of the word of God that you will be born again, there will be a lot of stuff which everyone who is born of my Father will receive, similar to the reality that in your flesh and blood bodies everybody has the same elements, even though you all look different… ten toes… ten fingers and so on. Equipping abilities of the nature and character of God my Father will also be implanted in you. This will be part of your inheritance from him. Faithfully following and making use of your inheritance will direct the course of your life. Because this is you being born of my Father with his nature and character and empowering ability implanted into you, you will look like me. In the reality of the truth, you, and I, will both look at Almighty God, and say '*Abba, Father.*'"

"Now, Lazarus… does that answer your question?"

Mary looked at Jesus… then she looked at John. She leaned out and looked over so she could see her sister, and then she focused in on her brother's nose. Finally, Mary asked, "Jesus, when this happens, will I be able to recognize John and my brother and sister?"

With John there were more than smile wrinkles around his eyes. Lazarus sucked in a breath, Martha let out a gasp, and Jesus gave a hoot and stifled a laugh. He tried not to laugh, he put a hand to his eyes, but it slid down his face to cover his mouth. Mary was serious.

Mary stiffened. "You said! You said we will… we will… look like you!"

Looking through happy tears, Jesus replied, "Mary, you are a sweetheart, and you are absolutely right."

Mary gave her sister an *I-told-you-so* look.

Lazarus' mouth just sort of dropped open.

"Mary," Jesus said regaining his composure, "never, not ever, has anyone… and this is a tremendous credit to you… so totally received this truth. This is a moment I will remember."

Mary beamed, but the rest didn't know what to think. Martha tipped her head to the right, raised an eyebrow, and looked at Jesus.

"I think… I will need to explain this a little bit further."

"Mary, you are a spirit, you have a soul, and you live in that body of yours," Jesus recounted. "When you are born of above, your body will not change. Your soul will not change, but you are a spirit and you, your *spirit self,* will be born of God, that is where the new birth and implantation of the nature and character of my Father will be, that is where you will look like me."

Jesus was watching Mary's reaction.

He took a breath and continued.

"You have physical characteristics from your parents and grandparents, your soul or heart is made up of your mind, your will, and your emotions, and they are also inherited elements from your parents and grandparents, but when you were conceived... that is when *spirit you* came into existence. You have natural ability which you have had from the moment of conception within body, your mind and *spirit you.* From *spirit you* is where the words *I will,* or *I will not,* come from. It is *spirit you* that will be born of God, and *spirit you* that is born of God will be perfect and complete, and that is where the implantation of his nature, character, and ability will reside. From there, that new birth nature works back through your soul, and eventually has an effect on your body. His inheritance in you is at the central core of your being, **spirit you.**"

CHAPTER 21

Martha entered a place of contemplation in her mind, and from there she turned her imagination free.

Although she was sitting at her eastern window with the shutters closed, in her mind she was standing near the Jordan River's shoreline, waiting her turn to be baptized by John the baptizer.

You said you were not the Christ…

But that I would see him soon.

How right you were…

John the baptizer.

Rising from her chair Martha went and stood before the closed western door of her home. This time, in her mind, while gazing towards Jerusalem, she watched herself walk up a long flight of steps leading to Solomon's Porch, where from that place she could see the Holy Temple.

Jesus…

You say things are going to change…

And that change will be cut in you.

You will be the door and doorway to God my Father?

What is it you will do?

In her imagination, standing with her back to Solomon's Porch, solemnly, silently, at the top step of that long and open stairway, Martha took her memory box and set it unprotected at her feet. In her memory box were the contents of her soul… every tradition, hope, dream and knowledge of her heart.

Jesus…

Am I willing to walk into tomorrow with and through you?

With the toe of her right foot, Martha nudged her memory box until it teetered precariously on the top-step edge.

I will!

I do!

In the imagination of her mind, and with one final motion of her toe, Martha watched the contents of her soul tumble down, bouncing, spinning, tumbling on a wild ride into her tomorrow.

Martha's shoulders shuddered as if she had a shiver, then she walked over to a tall open water jar where she washed her hands up to her elbows. After thoroughly scrubbing her hands she dried them on a clean towel which she left hanging on its hook.

John, dealing with his own thoughts had been watching Martha's practiced washing, and he said, "Jesus, when we were at the wedding… where you performed your first miracle… will you tell that story… and your explanation?"

Mary perked up, "A wedding? Where was it? Who got married? Who was there? What happened?" She also needed to move around a little, standing up, she stretched a bit and went over by the cook-stove where it was a little warmer.

Lazarus went to the cupboard and pulled out a bowl of dates, took a few for himself, and set the bowl on the table as he took a bite of one, avoiding the pit.

"Well?" Mary called across the room, "What about the wedding?"

Going to the same cupboard, Martha retrieved a jar of honey and a plate with five small loaves of bread. Setting the plate on the table she picked up two cushions for herself and threw one to her sister.

John reached out his hand and brought it back with one of the five loaves. He broke the loaf in half and drizzled honey generously across the bread, letting it soak in to the bowl-like shape of delicious goodness.

Four more dates left the little pile and as Jesus bit into the first one he said, "John, why don't you tell them the details of the wedding while I eat that piece of bread for you, and I will trade with you later?"

John took one bite of the bread and handed the rest to Jesus. He then scratched his back against the fireplace stones that he was leaning against and began reciting the particulars of the event.

"It really started three days before the wedding, at the place where John the baptizer was teaching."

Mary began checking details, "The same place we sent Benjamin to, yes?"

"That's right, at Bethabara, out beyond the Jordan, a bunch of Pharisees had showed up asking John the baptizer under what authority he was baptizing people. In their puffed up voices they asked John, *'Who are you, are you the Christ?'* and John said, *'No, I'm not even worthy to untie his shoelace... but what's odd is this, you walk right by him! He walks among you! And yet you don't recognize him for who he is!'"*

"So... the next day, day one... here comes Jesus, and John sees him from some distance off... now this is with Pharisees and Priests, Chief Priests and people all around... hundreds of them... and John the baptizer shouts it out... he just hollers in his rain barrel voice, *'Behold! The Lamb of God! The one who takes away the sin of the world!'"*

Mary spouted a comment, "I wish we had been there that day!"

John continued, "Simon Peter's brother, Andrew, he was there on day one, he had been a disciple of the baptizer, but he left John to follow Jesus. Anyhow, the next morning we left for Cana of Galilee, and Cana was about sixty miles away, it was nonstop walking for almost two days. We made it to the wedding three days after the fuss with the Pharisees."

"Cana is just three or four miles north of where Jesus grew up near Nazareth, and his mother was helping with the wedding. Both the bride's family and the grooms were good friends with Mary, so they invited Jesus and all of us to the wedding party. I think that was a total of nine or ten of us at the time."

"So, who got married John?" Mary asked.

The War Is Over | 137

"Sorry, Mary, I had never met them before, but they both work with her Dad's farm at the same place… but that isn't the main point of the wedding, anyhow."

"John?" Mary quizzed, "How can the bride and groom not be the main point of the wedding?"

"It's just not the main point of the story… Mary… quit sidetracking me! We were just enjoying the food and the fun like everyone else when Jesus's mom comes up to him, and she's all upset. I don't know how, someone must have goofed or something, but they were out of wine."

Martha was surprised, "That would have been bad etiquette, and it would have cast a dark shadow on the family to run out of wine at a wedding."

"Yeah, so she looks up at Jesus and says, *Jesus, they don't have any wine.*"

Lazarus wondered, "What did she think Jesus was going to do? You did say this was the first miracle Jesus performed… so he must have done something about the wine shortage eventually."

"I'm getting there, Jesus looked back at his mom and says, '*Woman, what have I to do with you, my hour is not yet come.*'"

"What!" exclaimed Martha giving Jesus a look, "You called your mother '*woman*'?"

Jesus only grinned… very slightly.

John continued, "Well, she drug four of the house servants over to Jesus and told them, and I mean that she just drilled it into them, she said, '*You just do whatever it is that he tells you to do! Got it?*' and she left to do something else, but she was gone."

"This ought to be good," Lazarus said. "What did he do next?"

"Yeah, well… this is where it's gets interesting! Hum… ah, you know the big jar of wash water that you keep near the door? They had six of those all in a row, for all of the guests, but instead of always dipping a little water out all of the time, they set it up really nice for everyone. With all the jars in a row, you would just walk up to the first jar, rinse up to the elbow, go to the next jar, rinse up to the elbow, and so on. It worked really well, those jars were over three-feet tall and they held from twenty to thirty gallons of water each. The first jar, of course, had the dirtiest water in it because they washed in that one first, but the stuff would just settle to the bottom. The last jar in line held the cleanest water, but the thing is… it was a very practical… and nice way for everyone to get their hands clean."

Martha remembered, "I have seen that before, it works very smoothly, and I would call it elegant, but what does that have to do with wine?"

"Jesus told the servants to top off the water jars. The servants figured Jesus was just giving them busy work… while he was figuring out what to do… but they filled them to the top, anyway."

"Wouldn't the water spill out?" Martha wondered, "You know… when someone put their hands in there? It would just run all over."

"That isn't what happened next."

Martha whimpered, "Oh no… John… please! He wouldn't do that! My thoughts will not let me go there! Tell me that he didn't have them dip out *dirty wash water!*"

"Yes, he did, Martha. Jesus looked at those servants and said, *'Each one of you… take a wine glass… and each one draw out of a different jar… and take that full cup to the Ruler of the Wedding Feast.'*"

"No one died?" asked Lazarus, "Something must have happened, because the Ruler of the feast could have lifted their heads for that! I mean… that water had *donkey dung and camel slobber in it!*"

John worked at containing his excitement, but he kept going, "It was a good thing that Jesus's mom was somewhere else… she would have had a fit!"

Mary was still after the details, "So, did the guy get sick or what?"

"No… I have to give those servants credit, they put a good face on it, and brought the wine glasses to the Ruler, full of what was in those jars… and he drank it."

"No way!" Mary exclaimed, "Is he still a friend of the family?"

"He drank from each cup," explained John. "The Ruler of the wedding tasted from each wine glass… then he called the bridegroom over."

Martha put one hand to each cheek… exclaiming, "Oh, no! Not in front of everyone!"

"Oh, yes! In front of them all he said, '*Everyone sets out the best wine first, but this man is an amazing man! He has saved the best wine for last!*'"

"No way!" Mary exclaimed. "It turned to wine?"

"Not just wine, but the best wine, *and all that was in those jars turned to wine.*"

Lazarus added it up, "John… that's more than one hundred and forty gallons of wine! That's a lot of wine!"

"Well, they didn't run out after that."

"Hmm…"

CHAPTER 22

The story tellers traded places but Jesus dealt with another item before he explained the story.

Looking at Lazarus, he rehearsed a memory, "Martha, Mary, the morning you sent Benjamin to find me… you were looking for my help. Before I tell you about the wine, I would like to explain to you how I am looking for your help."

Lazarus, taking note of the serious expression on his friend's face, announced, "Jesus, it is a great honor to be your friend, and I know on this we three totally agree, if there is anything that we can do for you… ever… forever… just speak the word, and we will do it!"

Jesus explained, "There are things coming, responsibilities I must fulfill. What I am asking of the three of you, and you too, John, is for you to add your faith to mine, to help me complete this, knowing these are things which must be accomplished and fulfilled."

Lazarus spoke for them all, saying, "We will stand with you Jesus, however you need, wherever, forever!"

"Very good… thank you," and then Jesus began his explanation, "The turning of dirty water into wine is a picture painted by Spirit Helper of what is coming. But first I will be identified by a friend who betrays me to those who will kill me. In Jerusalem, I will be beaten, whipped, and hung on a cross and there I will die, spirit, soul, and body.

I will take upon myself the sin of all people, past, present, and future. I will go into hell and suffer there. On the third day, I will overcome death, hell, and the grave. I will make a show of them openly and be raised into newness of life, alive forevermore. I will be the one payment for sin, for all of time."

Lazarus had been standing with a sister on each side as Jesus started to speak. He reached his right arm around Martha's shoulder and pulled her close to him on one side; and he reached out his left arm and pulled Mary close to him on his other side. And then he said, "It is as David and the others prophesied, it is as it is written, so shall it be. We will add our strength and faith to yours my friend, my Lord, and brother."

Mary spoke up, "This time I will be a help to you, Jesus!"

"For all of time, we have watched and waited for you… and now we see you… our Messiah. Even though I do not understand what it is you must do, I believe you, and will honor your request, whatever you want us to be Jesus… we will be," said Martha.

John added, "Even though these are things which you must do Jesus, it is hard to hear you talk of them. If there is any way for me to serve you, or to keep covenant for you, just speak the word and it is done, all that I am, all that I have, it is yours."

"Thank you, each one of you. It is because of you, and those like you, because of the joy of bringing you life, I will get through this to the other side. All right, enough of words like that for now, this should be a good time to tell you about the wedding wine!"

"I like the sound of that," Martha announced through her tears. "We could all use some happy thoughts."

"Okay… find a comfy spot!"

Each one shuffled around, grabbed a cushion and a blanket, moved a lamp, lit a candle… in a moment or two all were settled in, a private audience with Jesus as their friend, teacher and story teller.

"Ready?"

"Alright, here we go, I will start with a couple of details first… a parameter."

"This of course happened on the third day, and it is on the third day that I will be raised up. They wanted wine, but they didn't have any wine. You want life, not just to have your sins covered for another year. Lazarus, when your body quit working, you went to that place of protection called Abraham's Bosom, instead of hell, because you were looking for me. There was no way for you, or for the others already there to be with my Father yet. But the next time your body quits, you will go directly to be with my Father… and I will be there also."

"But Jesus!" Mary interrupted, "That won't be for a long time, will it?"

"Not to worry, Mary, Laz will be here, with you, for a long time."

"Yes… here we go…we formed the body of Adam from the clay of this earth. Those jars were formed from clay. The jars were filled with water as a representation of natural birth. They, like you, were different size vessels, and when they were filled with water, they were similar in size and weight to a man. There were six jars, and the number which is attributed to man is six. The water became contaminated with the dirt of this world, some a little dirty, some a lot dirty, the same way a person is corrupted with the sin and the sludge of this world. The one word from my mother was that she told the servants to do what I say. The servants brought dirty water to the governor of the feast, calling it wine, but remembered where it came from. Each one of you will present the New Covenant to many, bringing them to my Father, and you will have to deal with the memory of where they came from. The ruler of the feast tasted the dirty water which was transformed completely into the best wine. No one was looking for clean water, or filtered water, or boiled pure water, we were expecting total complete change. As you turn towards my Father and have faith in me, and faith in what I will accomplish for you, you too will be transformed completely into a new creature that never existed before! This is not just having your sins forgiven; this is being born of my Father! Sons and daughters! I will be the first begotten from the dead! You will be seven, eight, nine, and ten begotten from the dead!"

"Wow!"

"Yes!"

Martha bubbled, "Jesus! What a beautiful picture you paint for us!"

"Jesus, you are cutting a new covenant, is that correct?" Lazarus asked.

"Yes, that is correct, because what is taking place is the fulfillment of the existing covenant."

"And you, you are going to be the door into that new covenant, is that also right?"

"Yes, correct again my friend."

"And the promises of the covenant, will they be new also?"

"Absolutely, a new covenant, based upon new and better promises!"

Martha wondered, "Jesus, what was it about the first day? Why was that day a marked day?"

"John the Baptizer was in the line of the priesthood, and he is the primary one who cut a path in front of me. John was the son of Zacharias and Elisabeth, both righteous before God. Zacharias was a blameless priest and his wife was of the daughters of Aaron. It was John... standing in his place on day one... before all people... he identified me as the Lamb of God that takes away the sin of the world."

CHAPTER 23

Raindrops were landing in puddles around the house of Lazarus and Mary's chickens had retreated to the protection of their coop. The chill of late winter weather was kept at bay by Martha placing a few more sticks on the fire. This cold snap was a feeble attempt to hold back the approach of summer. Warm weather was coming, and just as light drives back darkness, the warmth of summer would soon be here to stay.

Lazarus had his feet up on a pillow and was reclining on three more; his face was pointed towards light coming from an oil lamp set high on a shelf. Lost in thought, his eyes were focused on nothing; he was drifting along in the midst of a seven mile stare.

Mary had been watching him. He still smelled of spikenard, as he would for several more days. After a few minutes she picked up a pillow and threw it at him, as the soft fluff bounced off the side of his face, Mary asked, "My brother, where are you?"

"I was wondering."

"Wondering what, my brother?" She playfully asked… listening… wanting to hear him talk, she didn't care if he was contemplating the smell of garden dirt, she just wanted to hear his voice.

"I am still hovering around the *why* question."

"Why? Why what?"

"I can see how being born of God benefits us, but I don't understand, what's in it for him?"

From where he stood, leaning against warm fireplace rocks, Jesus responded. "Real companionship, but to obtain father /son, father/ daughter camaraderie, he is faced with two opposite things. On the one side, he is looking for a family, people that he can have fellowship with and be good to forever. On the other side, even though it is his will that all be saved and to come unto the knowledge of the truth, he is not willing to let rebellion into his house ever again. Both of those things must be worked out at the same time. It's his desire tempered with reality."

Laz continued with his question, "Okay... so... how is this new covenant that is coming, different for your Father than what has been?"

"The primary modification is you will be spiritually alive instead of dead. If he touched you in your present condition, his touch would kill you. Just the brightness of his presence would burn you to a cinder."

Martha wondered, "Is it something like when a man touched the Arc of the Covenant and died? Back when David was King... here on earth... alive... his body alive... I mean... um."

Oh bother!

Stumbling around with my words!

How do you talk about a man whose body has been dead for hundreds of years... But Laz walked and talked with only two days ago?

Ugh!

Jesus, smiling at Martha with an understanding of her challenge answered, "Yes, similar."

Laz continued to pull for more, "What else?"

"Do you know how long of a time it was from when Adam and Eve broke covenant with my Father, until the time when Abraham came along?"

"Well, no, I have heard, but I don't remember... I do know that it was a long time."

"Long time it was, especially since we were looking for Abraham from the moment Adam sinned."

"Why couldn't you find Abraham? How could you lose him?" Mary wondered.

Jesus chuckled, "It wasn't that we were looking for a man called Abraham... we were looking for a person who was willing and able to do what we needed him to do. It wasn't an easy chore we needed him to accomplish."

"Every person was examined," Jesus continued, "we approached Adam and Eve to see if they could walk out the steps which were needed. The person we were looking for would have to believe the word of my Father above and beyond what they could see and feel. In reality, Martha and Mary, what we were looking for was similar to what was needed in you to get Lazarus out of the tomb. But with Lazarus, the stand in faith, believing my word and growing something from it was only four days. The person we were hunting would have to stand in that faith place for twenty-five to forty years, depending on how you count it."

Martha was not used to having so much time without work to do, she was methodically moving through the home's central room in a *straighten up and put away mode*. With an armful of pillows she responded to Jesus' statement saying, "The more that I chose to believe you, and what you said, the easier it was to believe your word and your promise to me. To myself, I said, *'I choose to believe you, Jesus. I bend my will to match yours.'* After choosing, I was just playing a part, and waiting to see how what you said was going to be carried out, was going to happen."

Everything in front of Martha was destined to be *put away*; Lazarus chose to get out of the way first. He gathered up his assortment of cushions from the floor and went to the west wall to sit next to Mary on the long bench.

Mary added, "For me, I let my emotions and the words of those around turn me away from your words to me. I will not let that happen again."

Still leaning against warm fireplace stones Jesus continued, "Job, was the first person who got close to what we needed to work with, but not close enough. Even so, we believed it would be profitable for you to add the record of our interaction with him into the book of covenants. Job is a covenant man and tremendous things were accomplished through him, especially if you consider the fact he had no written word to stand on. Also, Job did not know there was an enemy out there; he did not know the kingdom of Satan existed. Job thought everything that happened was God's will, everything that happened was God's fault. Job believed God was a twisted sort of sovereign King where everything that took place was God's will and design."

Jesus continued, "This earth was made and given to mankind to be a *man-planet*, where man is the authority. When Adam broke covenant with my Father, Satan acquired a big piece of that authority. Soon, as a man, I will get the authority back, plus much more."

"Soon, nothing will happen here, from either kingdom, without having a human as an authorizing agent in-between. Of course, Job was functioning under an incorrect assumption, believing Satan did not exist, and it cost him dearly, but he still chose to serve God, and that is commendable."

Without hardly allowing Jesus to take a breath, Lazarus continued, "Another *why* Jesus. Isaiah and Ezekiel both talked about things they had written about Satan and his kingdom. They told me they could not step out and expose much of Satan's kingdom; each said they were kept to writing things in a covered or hidden manner, why?"

"Well… finally… an easy question to answer. Satan is a *dead-spirit*, until I finish my work here; I am the only *alive-spirit* on earth. If we exposed too much of that *dead Satan spirit*, way too many people would have followed him, because of *like-association*. Chickens gather together with other chickens because they are *like-creatures*. After Adam sinned, man's *dead-spirit* was too much like Satan's *dead-spirit*. Exposing Satan would have put you, and people like you, at too much risk, a thing we were not willing to do. It was better to just get blamed for what Satan did, to protect you from following him."

"Okay, let's go back to my original question. How is this new covenant that is coming, different for your Father than what has been?"

"After we cut covenant with Abraham we had an inroad to this earth, we had a voice here. There are characteristics in Abraham that are conducive to a good working relationship with my Father. This question of yours, Lazarus, the answer to it is right in the middle of the biggest byproduct of the new birth."

"So… I ask a pretty good question… hmm?"

Mary moved over a little closer and gave her brother a pat on the back, "Way to go, my brother!"

Martha wrinkled her nose at both of them and asked, "So, what's the byproduct?"

"Well… I told you how we searched for a long time to find Abraham, and through him we had an inroad into this earth. We cut covenant with him and had ongoing communication with him. He also talked to others about my Father, and as a result, others entered into that covenant with my Father. By the time Abraham's descendants left Egypt, my Father had formed them into a great nation of millions of people."

Martha questioned, "I don't see how that is a byproduct."

"I'm not there yet, it's a big question. This fact of having millions of people to choose from did make things much easier, but often the people with certain desired characteristics could not be found, even among so many people."

"What did you do when you couldn't find the right person for the job?" Mary wondered.

"What we could not do was what we did with Adam and Eve in the beginning. We made Adam and Eve from the ground up… so to speak."

"Yes… I suppose you did," said Martha, laughing.

Jesus had moved over from the cook stove and all five friends were now reclining on cushions, on or near the long bench seat in the home's big room as he continued. "We could not do that again, because Adam's sin was so far-reaching, technically, the earth did not belong to us. So, because we could not just make the person that we needed, we designed one instead."

Lazarus was scratching his chin in a contemplative manner as he commented, "I see the difference between making something and just designing something. But if you couldn't just make the person you needed, wouldn't you still need a man and a woman to have a baby? And if they were to have a baby, how does designing one make any difference? Wouldn't you still need someone, somehow to implement the design? I don't understand how you could do it."

"Okay… we are going to have a moment of creation education. The woman carries the egg; the man carries the seed, thousands upon thousands of seeds. Each one carries one-half of the ingredients for one unique person, only one of the many thousands of seeds will join with the egg. When the two come together, there are millions of variables branded. Just for the physical body alone there are thirty thousand lines of information that are identified and mapped in an instant. At that same moment in time, the soul is printed and the spirit comes into existence. A complete human now exists who only needs time to grow and come forth."

John, who had been rather quiet until now, said, "Awesome, design Jesus, but how do you get the design you want?"

"By the request of the parents, Isaac was the first. Abraham and Sarah wanted a son; we wanted a specifically designed person. With their covenant request, over the course of time, we were able to bring one specific egg and seed together that would match the design we needed. Rather than go to the beach to find one precise grain of sand on the seashore, we designed and aligned, but Abraham and Sarah built that one grain of sand and called him Isaac."

"Amazing! Did you ever do it again?" John asked.

"Many times… some are recorded in the book of covenants, some aren't. John the baptizer was the last of his kind."

Lazarus wondered, "If he is the last, what will you do now?"

"This is where the benefit to my Father really shows up. Although we can start with the parents, we no longer have to begin at your conception. We can implement my Father's design at the new birth."

"Oh my Lord Jesus! It's the water to wine!" Martha exclaimed.

Mary looked at her sister with scrunched up eyebrows. "What?"

Lazarus saw it, "Born of God! Dirty water turned into wine!"

Mary's eyes lit up. "Yes! Jesus, my brother, I will look like you!"

"At the time when you are born of my Father, He will add to you that part of Himself to match the design we need you to be. You will be brand new from the inside out… and you will be alive… and you will look like me."

Mary pondered, "I will look the same on the outside, but *spirit me* will look like you… because I will have nature, character, and ability of our Father in me. Hum… *spirit me* will be perfect… complete… and equipped."

Back on her feet again, and this time it appeared the fireplace was going to get some of Martha's attention. She pushed the coals around a bit, added some small sticks which almost instantly popped into flame, next a few larger sticks were added. She surveyed her work, and confident something had been accomplished, she returned to her place to listen to Jesus again.

"Once you are born of my Father, beware; don't let the words of others rob you of the inheritance you have received from him. Instead, open the gate in spirit you and let his nature, character, and ability flow from spirit you to affect your mind, your will, your emotions, your body, and everything around you."

Martha wondered, "Jesus… you have been talking about this new birth from the direction of how we will receive things from our *soon-to-be-Father* that are like you, but may be different from each other. Are there things that all of us will receive… that will be the same in all of us?"

"Sure… take a lesson from your dad. You have the same number of bones as he has. Also, except for the male-female elements, all of your blood vessels are in the same place. You have two ears and one nose as your dad has two ears and one nose, but the design of them is from your mom and not your dad."

Martha exclaimed, "Thank you, mama!" as she entertained an image in her mind, it was a picture of Lazarus talking with her mama, but she was young again and her body wasn't broken, and Laz was telling her how good her girls were doing, and how much they missed her. Martha wiped tears from her eyes and said, "Sorry Laz, you do look good with your ruggedly handsome nose… but I prefer mama's nose on me!"

Jesus was grinning as he continued, "There are characteristics of my Father which everyone will receive, fruit if you will. For example, He is covenant love, everyone receives the fullness of love. The same is true about joy or life and shalom, so to answer your question, yes, there are many elements of my Father that everyone who is born of him will receive. On the other side of that thought, we do not want… or need…

everyone to have the ability to be the governor of a city. Neither would we want to give carpenter ability to everyone, the same is true for a cook or blacksmith or teacher. Quite often, it is the blending of abilities of my Father, and the subsequent training, which finds the same ability of my Father in a blacksmith, a stonemason or a seamstress, but different abilities in the farmer, gardener, or shepherd."

Martha asked, "How do you mean, *everybody?* There are a lot of people who don't like you, Jesus… not even a little bit."

John also wondered, "How are you going to keep the rebellion out if this is for everyone?"

"It's true I am paying for everyone… past, present, and future, but my Father will not force anyone to be part of his family if they do not want to be part of it."

John observed, "I think the heart of rebellion wants what you have… but wants nothing to do with you, Jesus."

"That was the fall of Lucifer, and his followers end up looking like him."

Lazarus identified, "But now Jesus, I am slightly confused. David wrote of you, and it was recorded, *'He who took captivity captive and gave gifts unto man, yes unto the rebellious also that the Lord might dwell.'* That says to me there are rebellious people involved."

"Lazarus, the characteristics you received from your father of your flesh… like your ruggedly handsome nose… you will have, regardless, if you are a good son, or a bad son. You are his son because you carry his characteristics, he cannot take them back. Good son or bad son, you received them from him."

"No person will be able to be in rebellion with my Father and me, and enter into my Father's kingdom at the same time, but it is possible for them to have rebellious moments as a son or daughter, but we will not cut them off, or kick them out. We will teach them and train them and try to lead them through Spirit Helper. When I leave, I will send Holy Spirit to teach you and train you… to be helper to you… he will work with you from the inside out."

John wondered, "What if they want out of your family, can they get out?"

"It is possible, but it doesn't happen in a day, or a week, or a month. Even if one of Peter's young sons ran away and cursed his father, Peter would receive him back again because the young man was only flopping around in the ignorance of youth. But a mature son or daughter who had eaten fully of the goodness of being a son or daughter, that one could eventually reject my Father and me, but if they did, there would be no way back in for them."

Mary wondered, "Why would anyone want out?"

"Throughout all of time, there will be people who live in and face exactly the same circumstances. One will turn towards my Father and receive life; the other will stay in Satan's kingdom. There is pleasure in sin, but only for a little while."

Mary asked, "When my time comes, what of my Father will I receive? Will I receive and know it all at once, or will it just settle on me like dust?"

"In the space of a heartbeat Mary, spirit you will be transformed, perfect and complete."

Beneath the surface of warm moist soil, at a place where no man sees, tiny seeds were breaking open, releasing the life they contained.

CHAPTER 24

With her left hand resting on her kitchen windowsill, and her right hand holding tightly to a leather pull cord, Martha held the single window shutter slightly open, peaking out at a cold drizzling rain.

It would have been a horrible day for travel!

Satisfied she had no reason to be outside or working, Martha pulled and tied the window closed against early nighttime coldness.

I would feel sorry for even a goat to be out in such miserable, drippy, weather.

Her ears registered a sound before her mind could identify its source.

What's that?

Wet sandal leather pressing down and turning slightly on wet stone covered with a thin sand and gravel topcoat?

Some person's walking up our steps in this weather?

She started moving towards their western door only slightly before a feeble knock sounded on its vertical boards.

Who would be out in this ugly stuff?

She pulled the latch and peered outside.

"Benjamin!" Martha exclaimed, gawking at Ben's icy looking, raw red face and hands. Cold water was dripping off his chin and running down his neck.

"What are you doing! Come inside, before you are frozen stiff like winter laundry! You are soaked to the bone!"

"Lazarus! Take him to your room and get him into some dry clothes, I'll build up the fire!"

Her brother was already tugging Ben's wet clothes off, and pulling him towards his bedroom door. Jesus caught hold of Ben's other arm, keeping him from falling.

"Then get him right back out here! He can stand on the warm rocks by the fireplace, and we'll cook the ice out of his bones!"

Martha grabbed small kindling sticks that would burn both fast and hot, and threw them on the bed of coals where they quickly burst into flame. She added some bigger blocks of wood and backed away from the heat.

One, maybe two minutes passed before they emerged with Ben in a dry cotton robe with Laz half carrying him to the fireplace. His teeth had started to chatter.

Spasms of shivering convulsed the runner's body; both Jesus and Lazarus held their friend near the fire's heat.

Mary ran to her room and returned with her best woolen blanket, one she had received as a gift from Ben the year before. She draped it over his shoulders and pulled a chair to the front of the fireplace.

A minute later Ben melted into it, and the shivering had stopped.

With a ladle, Martha dipped hot chicken broth from a kettle hung above the fire, it contained their evening meal. When the heat penetrated out through the mug, she placed it in Ben's hands.

"Ben!" Mary questioned, "What were you doing out in this weather? You're not wet from walking here from your home across town? You must have been out there for hours... what were you thinking? Are you trying to freeze to death?"

"Yesterday... after Lazarus came out of that tomb... Jannes and Jambres... they're not good men... they left for Jerusalem right after we unwrapped your brother."

Lazarus was remembering, "Your face... it was the first I saw... you lifted the cover off my head. The first few moments... after I got back... they're a little fuzzy... but I remember seeing your face... but... I don't remember seeing you after... not till now."

Mary thought out loud, "I looked for you later... I wanted to thank you Ben, but I couldn't find you. Why did you leave so soon?"

The skin of Benjamin's face had transitioned from cold-red to hot-red. Soon, he would have to back up his chair a bit, when the fire's warmth penetrated a little deeper.

His muscles were starting to relax.

"I managed to... ah... overhear those two... with their handlers... Chief Priests... in Jerusalem; it's not good Jesus."

Ben paused... his face pointed at the floor.

Martha questioned, "What's not good? Out with it Benjamin! What are those people up to?"

For some time, Martha had refused to call *those people*, by their highly-prized titles, because their reputations walked before them.

Looking up into Jesus' eyes, Ben continued, "They put the word out this afternoon... they marked you... Jesus... their plan is to kill you!"

Martha exclaimed, "What! Have they gone mad? They have done some bad stuff before, but this is insane! They could never get away with this! We must stop them!"

Jesus spoke gently, "Martha, they cannot take me before my time... and... have you forgotten your promise to me?"

Martha stopped and bit her bottom lip as tears formed and threatened to spill from her eyes... she shook her head, "No... I haven't forgotten."

"It will happen, but by my Father's timetable and plan... not theirs."

Ben looked back and forth between the only family he knew, "What are you saying, Jesus? You're not serious... are you?"

Mary reached out and put her hand on Ben's arm, "It's okay, Ben. There are things coming that will hurt a lot, but only for a little while. It will be like Lazarus coming out of the grave, but someday Lazarus will die again. When Jesus comes out of the grave, he will be alive forevermore... and when he finishes what he's going to do... he will be my brother!"

Ben looked like a chicken staring at a new coop, he didn't know if he wanted to go in there or not.

"Mary… what are you talking about? The Chief Priests have marked Jesus for death… but you think it's okay… because he's going to be your brother? Are you all there or what?"

Martha answered, "Benjamin, Jesus is indeed the Messiah… like we talked about, but the plan is bigger than we ever imagined… much bigger!"

Martha brought another chair over and set it next to Benjamin's.

"Mary, why don't you sit down… take your time… explain some of this to Ben while we get supper on the table? Okay?"

Mary settled into her chair and started recounting from the time Ben left to follow Jannes and Jambres.

Jesus set bowls on a small table in front of Ben and Mary, and others on the big table for the rest of them. Lazarus snatched up the soup kettle, Martha brought out more small loaves of bread and honey.

CHAPTER 25

Above all else, Benjamin was a seeker of truth, it was what he lived for, and this passion carried him from person to person. People had tried to hire him to carry a known lie to another, but even at ten times the normal rate, his answer was always, No. He knew lies are often told to cause the innocent to receive the punishment of the guilty, or to prop up what should be torn down.

Knowing the truth and yet having to watch the presentation of a lie purchase for a corrupt person a senate seat, or governorship, was what Benjamin often had to live with. The twisted plans of High Priest Caiaphas, who led the plot to kill Jesus, were an abomination to the obligations and responsibilities of the office which he occupied, but this time, Ben was going to see truth prevail. The ultimate liar, that fallen angel called Satan, was going to get caught in his own trap and hung with his own rope.

Jesus…

What you are doing…

This is so much more amazing than anything I ever imagined!

And as I live and breathe…

I get to watch you place it into motion!

The warmth of heated stones from the fireplace was a great comfort to Ben's feet, but he needed to move around, to loosen up the muscles that had gotten so cold in the penetrating rain. He stood up slowly, but kept the woolen blanket around his shoulders, gratefully allowing Mary to refill the mug in his hand with more hot chicken broth.

From the center of the soul stormy winds focused their intensity on one small garden at the edge of town. Isolated hail threatened to destroy it, but the storm had been driven back by the constructive actions of friends. Now, through their assistance, even the marks of the storm were being removed.

Night sounds began to enter the room as daylight was fading, Martha was moving about the home lighting more lamps when the yip of a distant coyote pulled Lazarus to his feet. Putting on his chore coat on his way out the door he called to no one in particular, "Just taking care of the chickens, back in a minute," John followed him outside.

Moving silently through evening shadows around the house towards the chicken coop, theirs was only movement in the yard, a misty rain was still falling; crickets and tree frogs were making their presence known.

They're all here...

All her sleeping chickens lined up on roosting poles...

All is well!

Laz closed the henhouse door.

"I missed the sounds of home" Lazarus thought out loud. "There were countless numbers of waiting people where I was, but after four days, I have to admit, I missed the life and sounds of home."

Walking back to the house John placed a hand on his friend's shoulder, "I'm glad you're back, especially for your sisters, they count on you, not only as their brother, but also for what you do. Their life would have been a tremendous struggle without you."

"Yes... I know... and it was for them I returned... when Jesus called my name, I knew I had a choice, I only thought the answer yes, and the next thing I remember is trying to walk all wrapped up like I was. What

I wonder now… is what will we do… when Jesus is gone… how will we get along?"

Sand and gravel footsteps on wet stone announced their return before Laz opened the door and they removed their wet coats. John stood warming by the fire, looking into its glowing embers and asked of Jesus.

"When we were at Jerusalem, the Pharisees wanted to stone you for calling God your Father. You said to them, *'Look and see with your eyes with the same volume of light as you have in your heart.'* For over an hour they walked around like blind men, but they weren't able to stone you, because they couldn't see anything. Is that something we could do?"

"If you follow in my footsteps… the things I have done, you will be able to also do. My Father and I give to you the authority, and through Spirit Helper, the power will be resident in your spirit self."

Benjamin's mind was dealing with a flood of information, since he found himself in this place where he was privy to the plans and words of Jesus, and now he had a wonder. "Emil has two locks of hair, tied to a pole in his house. He said they came from the beards of the blind. Am I to understand that they were acquired that day, in Jerusalem?"

Jesus chuckled, almost laughing, looking slightly down; he slowly shook his head from side to side, "Oh yes… Emil… my favorite goat herder… he also has a lot of sheep and he has had many temple contracts to supply lambs for Passover."

"Three years ago he contracted to deliver twenty-four spring lambs for Passover sacrifice, but he marked them in a way that he could only see."

Mary asked, "What? Why would he do that? The lambs are watched and checked very carefully… to make sure that they don't have any spot or blemish."

"He was curious to know the answer to what he thought was going on… and then he watched and counted. Those twenty-four lambs were sold fifty-seven times by his count."

"That doesn't surprise me one bit!" Martha squawked, "They're supposed to take the lamb someone brings or buys and offer it up as a sacrifice for the one who brought it! It's terribly wrong to take a lamb out and sell it again, but those people would do it!"

Mary, responding to her sister's break from her usually controlled demeanor, shook her open right hand up and down, as if it were hot, "Yes mam Martha! So... ah... Jesus, what happened next?"

"He confronted the Chief Priests about his count, the two who were primarily responsible for the wrong."

Mary clapped her hands together, "Yes! He caught them in the act of all sorts of nasty things! They stole sacrifice lambs and sold them again! That's very bad!"

Jesus was grinning again, "Those Chief Priests are the two who have a piece of their beards hanging from a pole in Emil's house."

"What!" Mary exclaimed. "That is just too weird! Why would he do that?"

Jesus explained, "Those two told Emil... they said, *'Because the lambs have been marked, they are no longer lambs without spot or blemish, they are not worthy to be sacrifice lambs, we will not pay for them.'* What those two have planted in the garden of their heart has changed the course of their life."

Benjamin's mind was running in exploration mode, "Jesus, this... ah... *Spirit Helper*... you speak about... who is he... and what does he do?"

"He is the strength of my Father... he speaks to your spirit self... he's the one who told me Lazarus had already died before you arrived with Mary's message. I heard him speak the words which I sent back with you, and when his words were planted in a human heart, the harvest of them pulled Lazarus from the grave."

Martha wondered, "Can anyone change the course of their life with the words they speak, and plant, in the garden of their heart?"

"Life and death are in the power of the tongue. When you speak what you believe, you are planting in your garden, when you speak what you feel... you are also planting in your garden. When you believe and speak my words from Spirit Helper, your harvest will be very good. The course of your life will follow what you grow."

"I have been listening to your words Jesus," said Lazarus, "and it's obvious you are heading in a chosen direction on a mission for your

Father. What can we do to help you? It sounds like you are going to Jerusalem soon; do you want us to go there with you? Would we be a help to you there?"

"Lazarus, because of where you have been and who you have talked with over the last few days, you have more understanding than any other person as to what I am going to do. John will be there, Peter also, and some of the others. It would be of little value for you to also see what you know will happen. The same goes for you Martha and you to Mary, but there is something that I would like you to do for me."

Lazarus said, "Just name it, Jesus, and we will get it done!"

"Yes!" Martha added, "It would be our pleasure to... ah... what is it you would like us to do?"

"Tomorrow, John and I are leaving for Ephraim to meet up with Peter and the rest. We will be back here in Bethany six days before the Passover. I would like you to prepare a meal for us when we are here. There would be about two-dozen people to feed."

Martha answered quickly, "A dinner party? Yes of course, we would be pleased to prepare that for you... and whomever you invite, but... twenty-four people... they would never fit in this little house."

John agreed, "This house is a very comfy home, but you are right, with twenty-four people in the big room, it would be quite tight."

Benjamin perked up, "Jesus, what about my neighbor... Simon, the one you healed of leprosy. His home, Stonehouse... you could fit three dozen people just in the big room... I believe he would be pleased to do this... for you... besides... he's kind 'a sweet on Martha."

A little color rose in Martha's cheeks, but she answered in a smooth voice, "Benjamin presents a functional idea, and both Mary and I work well with Hannah and Esther... as long as Lazarus doesn't become a distraction," Martha added, shifting the attention onto her brother and Esther.

"My dear sister, they are both good cooks, as are you Martha, and mama taught us, to always treat the cook with kindness, it's the correct thing to do."

"Yeah," agreed Mary, rescuing her brother, "And if you didn't treat mama well you went hungry! She knew what got your attention… and obedience!"

Lazarus made his choice, "Jesus, leave this to us, we will take care of the dinner… and I will make the arrangements with Simon."

"Sounds grand Lazarus, I will consider it done, and leave the details in the hands of you and your sisters… thank you."

It was getting late, and Benjamin started making his goodbye's when Mary gently elbowed her brother in the ribs.

"Say, Ben, there is no need for you to go out there in the rain again, and having one more guest for the night is no problem."

"If you are sure that it's okay, it would nice to stay warm and dry."

"No problem Ben, besides, you're still wearing my robe, and I wouldn't want that to get all wet." he added with a grin.

"Oops, I guess I got carried away with the conversation," said Ben as he stood there, with Mary's winter blanket hanging from his shoulders.

Martha went and stirred up what was left of the fire and added more sticks to it. In a few moments, a flame popped up and she added some bigger blocks of wood.

Lazarus brought the wash-water kettle and hung it on its hook above the fire. After ten minutes in the flames, Lazarus brought the kettle to the girl's room and poured about a gallon of hot water into their wash-basin and left them in the privacy of their room. Back in the big room, he hung the kettle on its hook and added more water.

CHAPTER 26

Early morning sunshine cast a beam of light through a small hole drilled in Martha's shuttered window which looked out to the east. The beam of light made a dot the size of your thumb on the western wall inside of the home. The western wall was their calendar wall, the dot of sunlight marked twenty-seven days to Passover.

Clean clothes hung from hooks around the fireplace, they also covered most of the chairs. John and Jesus had washed out their change of clothes plus their everyday robes before each found a place to sleep. Jesus had patiently responded to questions from the mind of Benjamin until the man finally drifted off to dream up more things to wonder about. He was like a giant sponge in search of truth.

Martha's feet made a slight swish-pha swish-pha sounds as she moved towards her domain, from there she searched for live coals among the ash.

Here's one, not very big, hum… ah… two, three, yes! I can make this work.

From her kindle box Martha drew a small handful of slivered wood fragments which she strategically placed and then gently blew into them. A small cloud of smoke raised up and next a poof of yellow flame.

Yes!

Well done Martha!

In a crisscross fashion she placed some thumb sized sticks and then glanced at her wall calendar.

Three and a half weeks till Passover...

Hum...

One more week of gathering eggs...

And then the hens can nest...

Fifty or sixty new chickens...

They'll give Mary something to fuss about.

Draped over almost every chair, bench and table were drying clothes.

Hmm...

They were busy last night.

I wonder if they're dry.

Martha checked folded places and hems.

No moisture... dry as a bone.

She gathered up an armful and moved them to a side bench; sleeping bodies covered every other flat surface in the room.

Mary silently entered the big room from her bedroom door, fully dressed and with her hair in one long braid.

Really?

You're up and dressed?

Already?

Interesting... what are you up to?

Mary snatched up the egg basket and went to visit Martha's chickens.

Little sister silently picked her way through a chicken yard obstacle course and snuck up on the coop.

All her sneaking was in vain, the floor birds were piled up against the door.

Flipping her braid around front she pressed her back against the coop wall, and with her right hand tripped the flip-flap latch and flung the door wide open. Rushing wind bounced off her face, flung there by furiously flapping red fathered wings.

Martha watched her sister from the window.

Twenty-plus years old,

And there's still wild eyed wonder from fat flying chickens...

Go figure.

When Mary was just a little girl, Papa added the boardwalk inside the coop. It was a plank at shoulder height connecting the upper roosting pole to the edge of the door, giving the hens a place to fly from. Mary thought papa had some practical reason for coaxing her chickens to fly, like causing them to lay seven percent more eggs or something. Martha knew that the only reason that he added the takeoff runway was to put a smile on Mary's face and hear her laugh.

Mary patiently kept her place and waited for her favorite chicken.

Every second or two, another set of wings blasted through the doorway, but Matilda was still inside.

Cautiously, Mary peeked around the corner.

The room was empty.

Mary stepped up into the coop and began looking into nesting boxes gathering eggs as she went, looking for the old chicken. Farthest from the door was the hen, in her nest, with her face towards the opening, flattened out to cover as many eggs as possible. Mary reached into the box to shoo Matilda out, but got a double peck for her effort.

Pursuing her first reaction, Mary pulled her sleeve up over her hand and was ready to force Matilda from her nest, when instead she stooped over and looked in through the small opening at Matilda's face. A low growl, as much as a chicken can growl, reverberated from within all of those feathers.

"Matilda… you are sitting on our breakfast!"

In steadfast determination, Matilda hunkered lower down, becoming a red-fluff egg guardian.

She looked into her basket and began counting eggs; one, two… thirteen, fourteen, fifteen. *That should be enough*, she thought. "Okay, Matilda, I will plead your case before my sister, but no guarantees, got it?"

Sensing victory Matilda's growl changed to a humming coo as Mary left the henhouse.

Wood smoke with some hotness warble things floating through the air…

Almost ready for cooking!

I wonder if the others are up.

And she hurried for the house.

Low tones of morning voices could be heard through the wooden door as Mary scurried up three steps and entered.

"I have fifteen eggs, Martha, but Matilda is determined to stay on her nest. I know it's a bit early, but she really wants a brood of chicks following her around. Do you think it would be okay if we just let her set? Babies would make her sooo happy! I told her I would ask you... and tell her side of the story."

Martha glanced back at her calendar. The sunshine dot was moving down the wall and was more than halfway to the floor. "Mary, you know she could only be sitting on one or two right now. Yesterday morning I gathered every egg in the henhouse."

"Well... yes... you are right... she would add to her clutch for about a week before she would really stay on the nest, but you know how she likes to be out in the yard with her brood while the rest are still sitting on their nests, waiting for their chicks to hatch. She is lonely to be a mama-hen!"

Squeaking hinges broadcast the arrival of Lazarus into the room. "Letting her set now would mean we could have rooster pot-pie one week earlier. My vote is for Matilda."

"Lazarus!" Mary pouted, "At least let them hatch and eat some bugs in the yard before you cook them in a pot!"

Jesus was watching his three friends with his blanket pulled up to his chin. Across from him the sunshine dot made a direct hit on John's right eye. The brightness caused him to squirm in his disorientation. He raised his hand to block out the light.

Lazarus poked at Mary with his words, "Now sister, you know every puppy turns into a dog, it's only a matter of time, but I would rather eat a chicken tomorrow than to have one extra egg for breakfast today."

Mary saw sparkles in the eyes of her brother, and refusing to get caught in his teasing, she simply said, "So good to have you back my brother!" and threw a pillow at him.

Jesus was sitting up and leaning against the wall now, still wrapped in his blanket, surrounded by the sweet taste of victory.

John propped himself up on his left elbow and rubbed his eyes with his right hand.

Benjamin was still staring at the ceiling, drifting between thoughts and his earlier conversation with Martha.

"Mary," said her sister, "let's go see how Matilda's doing and give the boys time to get up and dressed."

The two sisters left the house.

In all of his lifetime, Benjamin had seldom dared to dream of having such firsthand access to truth. Over the past twelve hours, Jesus had fed him answers to questions he had considered for as long as he could remember. His thoughts were being placed in proper value sequence order; some were thrown into the trash where they belonged.

There is freedom unlocked through truth!

This is so much more than just information!

Truth is the only absolute…

Unbending,

Unchanging,

Forever the same,

Absolute truth!

As the three houseguests dressed and straightened up their room, Ben formulated his next question which stretched beyond the borders of his country and his lifetime.

The sisters peered in at their feathered friend.

She was again making that, *'I'm not moving,'* sound.

Mary explained, "I told her I was going to talk to you… she's still waiting to hear your answer."

"She seems kind of set in her ways."

"Reminds me of someone else I know."

"I have had to make adjustments."

"The proof of the correction you made is sitting in the house instead of lying in the grave… thank you, Martha."

Martha turned to face her younger sister, there was five years between them, almost the same amount of time their parents had been gone. And now, Martha was amazed how just a few words from her sister could pull them so close, for too long she had behaved more like a mom than a sister.

"Let's just let her be," agreed Martha.

"Yippee! You hear that Matilda? You get to fill up the nest and hatch a whole batch!"

Watching joy expressed over so small a something reminded Martha of her need to store strength by the moment as part of preparing for tomorrow.

From the center of the soul, in a place where flowers grow, buds were forming, growing into flowers which would brighten their homes only days from now.

CHAPTER 27

Martha took a full scoop of feed and spread it around for her birds.

"Eat up girls," she said. "Setting time's soon coming."

Then she and Mary walked back to the house.

Upon entering, they found Jesus fixing breakfast; Martha was slightly flustered and shot a glance at her brother.

"Don't look at me;" said Lazarus with his mouth half full, "He started it."

"Martha, I hope you don't mind," said Jesus, "I'm a pretty good cook… and I won't burn your biscuits. Besides, we have eaten here so often I know where everything is. How about an egg in a hole?"

Now both girls looked bewildered.

Without waiting for an answer, he poured some biscuit batter into the shape of a circle in the already hot pan. Next, he broke an egg into the center hole, waited just long enough for it to firm up, and flipped the entire cake and egg over and let it cook the other side to a beautiful golden brown.

"Try one, Martha," said Lazarus, with bit of honey dripping off his bearded chin. "They are very good."

Martha was still standing.

"Martha," Jesus said, "I know this is hard for you, but this is something that you, and every person like you needs to understand. I didn't come to be served, I came to serve. You cannot just give all of the time. You also need to be able to receive, and to receive without earning. What I have to give cannot be bought and paid for, neither can it be earned, it can only be received."

Struggling with being a guest in her own house and served by her Master, Martha looked to her sister for something, but what was it?

Having just come in from seeing Matilda in the chicken coop, Mary did the first thing that came to her mind. She clucked like a chicken and said, "What's one more adjustment?"

Lazarus was caught between thoughts, so was part of his breakfast. It had stopped moving halfway to his mouth and honey was running down his hand.

Martha found a place to sit and said, "I would like to try the house special. I think it's called, *'Egg in a Hole,'* with a little honey, please."

"Excellent choice madam, one house special, coming right up."

Jesus slid the over-easy golden brown goodness onto her plate.

"And for the sister?"

"You know this is easy for me," responded Mary. "I'll have the same, with a spot of butter."

Turning to Benjamin, he added, "And you sir, what will you be having today?"

"Ah, yes... I will have the same as Mary, with a side-order of one question."

"I wondered," said Jesus as he poured more batter on the skillet, "How you were going to fit that in. This is the same theory you were discussing with Martha earlier, isn't it?"

"Yes, it is... but I thought that everyone else was asleep."

"I was sleeping just fine," John said, "until that blast of sunlight hit me in the face. What were you talking to Martha about?"

"People who have never heard, this earth is a big place and we live on one small speck of it."

"Heard about what?" John asked.

"What is common knowledge to us, we have knowledge of God going all the way back to the creation of mankind, and even going back to before the fall of Lucifer."

John answered, "Well, of course, we are God's chosen people, we should know all about him."

Ben asked, "Would God love someone less and send them to hell, just because they never heard of him? Would not the Judge of all the earth do what is right?"

"And what is right, Ben?" Jesus asked, "My Father has placed the knowledge of his existence into the heart of every person ever conceived on this planet. Everyone has the opportunity to choose life."

"How, I have heard about God all of my life, what have they heard?"

"Maybe it's time you see him."

"Huh? How can I see God and live?"

Jesus spoke to them all but addressed his question to John, "That dot of sunlight which woke you up John, did you know what it was?"

"Well... no... not at first... but after a moment I got my bearings and remembered the wall calendar."

"And what about the wall calendar?"

"Every year, at the same time, at the same place, the sun and earth will be in exactly the same position. Therefore, sunlight shining through the hole drilled in the shutter marks a specific spot on the wall. On this day of the year, every year, for as long as this house has been here, or will be here, the sun will mark exactly the same spot at the same time, forever, but everyone knows that, that's why you can have a wall calendar."

Jesus explained, "It is the word of God that holds the planets in place. The accuracy with which the planets are held in place is a characteristic of my Father. That is the way he is, perfect in every way. You can see him in what we have made. In all of creation you see my Father, and everyone will have the opportunity to choose, but if you see the truth, and reject the truth, a choice has been made. The problem comes when people do not want to hold the knowledge of God in their heart, and instead create another god of their design to match their personal motive or rebellion. Often people create their own god for the purpose of exerting control over the people around them, or they create, or find, a god that fits the lust of their flesh and mind."

"So... what's the difference between what some of the Chief Priests do," John asked, "when they use your Father God and his word to us...

attempting to manipulate and control us, or those who create another god out of wood or stone or animals or of the earth? Each one is doing so for the purpose of manipulating and controlling the people around them! The Chief Priests and Pharisees have taken the Ten Commandments and turned them into over six-hundred commandments! And that's only the nice side of what some of them do!"

Jesus poured some more batter into the pan and cracked an egg in the center before he answered. "For some there is very little if any difference, for others, they think they can keep the law, and try to force others to do the same. The primary purpose of the law is to show you that you can't keep it! It's impossible... you need a Savior! ... You need to be born of God, and you can't do it on your own! You need the life of God in you to be able to walk in the love of God! All of the righteousness of man is like used grave-cloth... it stinks!"

Mary leaned back slightly at the forcefulness of Jesus words...

Wow...

Hmm,

Yes,

I agree!

Ben set his plate on the cook's table and looked at his sizzling breakfast in the pan, he sniffed the air.

Yummy, that does smell good!

"But... how does that answer my question about the God of Abraham, Isaac and Jacob? What about those who haven't heard of him? What about those who haven't heard of you, Jesus? There will be people who will die two months after you complete what it is you need to do, and if those people die without knowing about you, what happens to them?"

"My Father has placed the knowledge of his existence in the heart of every person. The person who says in his heart that there is no god... he is a fool, because he has deceived himself and denied the truth."

"Jesus, my question is still unanswered! What about the *Lazarus* who lives on some island in the sea, and has never seen your face or heard your name? The person who doesn't even know this chosen nation of Israel exists? The person who has chosen to love the one who created this earth and all that is in it because he has seen the face of God in the work of his hands? The person who knows you exist because of the acknowledged knowledge of God which has been placed in his heart... but has never heard of Abraham, Isaac, or Jacob! What happens to that person?"

Removing the skillet from the flame Jesus slid Ben's breakfast onto his plate and handed it to him. Turning back to the fire he poured more batter and cracked another egg.

"That person will walk with me in Glory... but it's his friends and family which are much harder to reach. Most will die separate because they have not heard from someone who will carry the truth to them. I know this is a difficult thought... because I... like my Father... I am not willing that any should die separate, but they do."

Benjamin said, "Thank you... that helps me to understand. Are you going to send someone to the island... to bring them the truth?"

"Once I finish my chores, things will be in position where I can call everyone, and I will send some. As an act of their will they can reject my call or answer my call, for those that answer my call, my Father equips them through the new birth. Born of God they will be able to receive the teaching, training, and covering of Spirit Helper. And just as the Father has sent me, I send you, as sons and daughters of my Father, called, equipped, empowered, and anointed... *take You the gospel into all your world.*"

"Jesus, may I have another... ah... *House Special?*" Mary asked.

"One more, coming up."

"You are right, Jesus," said Martha, as she looked at her empty plate.

"Is that just a general statement?" Jesus asked with a smile, "Or are you referring to something in particular?"

"You are a good cook," continued Martha. "May I have another also? This time I am going to watch close so that I can copy you later."

"Very good Martha... oh... and by the way... I have been meaning to ask you about your gardens and greenhouse, how are they coming along?"

Lazarus answered, "Surprisingly well, considering they used up a year's wages worth of spikenard oil on me, I will smell like that purple flower for another week or more."

Jesus joked, "Look at it this way Laz, it wouldn't have been wasted if your body had stayed in the grave."

"Humph… when you put it that way… I don't mind smelling like the girls' flowers."

"Come and see the gardens," Lazarus said, "we are close enough to summer now; things are starting to green up and look good. We are producing enough mature nard plants to only harvest those which are three to four years old. The older ones yield a much higher percentage of oil, but we don't even have sawdust left when we are done, every part of the plant is used. We did lose one group of our customers, though, and I am very glad that we did."

John asked, "How is that? And why would you be glad to lose an entire customer group?"

"Yes! And it was your fault, Jesus." Mary added with a sneaky smile.

"Now Mary! You stop that." Demanded Martha, then to Jesus she added, "It was the leper colony you healed, they used the nard oil mixed with sesame oil and rubbed it into the skin at the back of their neck as a sedative."

Mary explained, "Jesus, you know I'm very grateful you gave those people their lives back. And unless their families were well able, I never even charged them for the oil. The mixture seemed to ease their pain."

"Yes, I know what you three did… Spirit Helper told me."

Lazarus and Mary were leading the way out to the gardens.

Finishing the last bite of her breakfast, Martha began gathering up the plates and utensils.

Humph… this can wait!

Martha left everything sitting where it was and followed Jesus out the door.

Walking along the first garden fence just south of the house, Jesus was looking across rows of sprouting plants, three to four inches tall. In the places where flatland broke away to hillside were Silver Birch trees.

Turning his gaze towards the nard plants Lazarus asked, "There are some things I would like to ask you about concerning other plants we raise. Also, there has got to be an easier way to get the spikenard oil out of the roots… now… considering the fact that you made the plants, maybe you could help us out?"

Looking into the eyes of Lazarus Jesus said, "Lazarus, you were there with Abraham, David, and the rest, you saw many, many, people… a lot of different colors of people… people like you have never seen before in your life!"

"Yes I did, there were some as black as a moonless cloudy night and others as white as chalk… with red hair… it was amazing… why?"

"When Ben had his question earlier, you knew the answer, but you were quiet. Why?"

Unlatching the first garden gate, Mary pulled it open and led the way along its path between the rows of sprouting plants.

"I saw things from one side but wanted a bigger picture… and you gave it to me."

"Now you have questions about plants… and you want answers… like a hungry man waiting in line to be given a fish to eat. If I just give you a fish, you will get back in line tomorrow, but if I teach you how to catch a fish you won't be hungry anymore."

"I'm not hungry," Mary said, "you can tell me about the plants."

"Young lady, it's time for you to learn about fishing poles and hooks and worms and where the fish are!"

"So… where are the fish?" Mary asked.

"The fish are where you find them," said Laz, "I know that much."

"My Father's Kingdom contains all of life and godliness, therefore, any knowledge which has anything to do with life or godliness can be obtained through my Father and me… anything."

CHAPTER 28

Opening the garden's southern gate, Mary turned left and led the way to the family's most treasured possession, a stone-lined well. Beneath the rocky Judean hillside was a labyrinth of tunnels, more often than not they were rivers, veins of rock and gravel encased in hard packed earth and stone. Within miles of Bethany there were only three places where people had been able tap into gravel veins and draw out the life-giving water which they contained. One was here at the house of Lazarus, one was in the town center of Bethany that the town was built around, and the third was on the estate of Simon, at Stonehouse.

In the spirit arena a freelance warrior angel named Malbec had just arrived, Floyd didn't want to look, he didn't want to talk.

"Floyd, Uriah, are you tracking time?"

The guardians of both Jesus and Lazarus did not respond.

"Comrades, we must get them moving!"

Uriah glanced his way but did not speak.

"We have advance teams prepping at Stonehouse."

"Time is not a factor there," Uriah clarified.

"It is in Jerusalem, we must place all three in a protected place... soon... and... sir... Scarface is back in town."

"Jasper knows?" questioned Uriah.

"Of course."

"With what's coming... I don't want to rush my charge... these people are his friends."

"Then let Spirit Helper give to him a bump, but Commander, we must cut Ben out, and get him moving, soon!"

"We still give you minutes Malbec... sometimes you give us only seconds... and occasionally, half a second."

Perplexed, Malbec understood his commander's dual accented meaning; he just did not care to be on this side of the waiting game. "We must lead both Benjamin and Emil to Jerusalem... together... for their, ah... chores, Ben will not come with me as long as Jesus remains here...at the home of Lazarus... I think it's very simple."

"Understood... Malbec... that is all for now."

"Sir, yes sir... Godspeed Commander."

Lazarus, his sisters, plus Benjamin and John, were all totally absorbed in a conversation with Jesus about acquiring knowledge from God about the world around them, and how to use that knowledge for their benefit.

"The knowledge of life and godliness includes what we grow... in our greenhouse and gardens?" Lazarus asked.

"Does what you are growing bring life and the quality of it to you and people around you? If so, then yes, ask away."

"I did, and you said that you are going to teach me how to fish. And I am not hungry, I just had breakfast."

"*Humph*, then I will teach Mary," responded Jesus with a grin.

Lazarus said, "Slow down! I was only kidding! I have got my fishing pole right here ready to go, lead on Jesus!"

"I am, I was, I always will be, we talked about that. Except for the fact that my flesh and blood, blood line comes from my Father and not my dad, I am as limited on this earth as you are. Even though my Father and I made the plants, in order to get information about the plants, I have to get the information the same way you will have to. Once you are born of my Father, you can function as I am now, and you can get help and information through Spirit Helper, just as I do now."

"We believe you," said Martha. "So how can we make it work?"

They were all standing around the well now, trying to see light's reflection and water at the bottom. John talked into it and was listening to the echo of his voice.

"My words are spirit and they are life, the seeds which you plant in your garden are like the words that I speak, full of potential and life. Anything that I have, or anything that I have said to you or will say to you, any promise that I have given or will give to you, is fully yours. The same is true of my Father. All that the Father has is mine. I will take of mine and give it to you. If you pay close attention to what I give to you, and say to you, and you follow it *home*, just as you would focus on a candle's light shining from Martha's window on a cloudy, moonless night, walking home from Jordan's valley. Just as you would follow that light, focus in on, and follow my word and eventually Spirit Helper will be able to show you, and give you the full truth of what you are looking for. Eventually, you will come to that light. In that, you will see and know as I see and know, what I have done, you will do."

Jesus continued, "Benjamin, when you came to find me at the Jordan River, you filled your water flask at Jason's spring, twice. That's an artesian well of pure water bubbling up and overflowing. That is like the life which will be in you, and in all who are born of my Father. The life bubbling up from the inside of you will be the life of God in you. Don't let things from your mind or body or the world around you get thrown into the gateway of that spring of life, and plug up the flow of life and godliness. Make good use of what you are given, by doing so you will bear good fruit. My Father is glorified when you bear good fruit."

"Even for our garden and greenhouse we can do this?" asked Lazarus.

"For anything, that has to do with life and godliness. For the food you eat, for the clothes you wear, for the health of your body, for the renewing of your mind, for the word of God coming alive in you, for the house you live in, for the way you travel from place to place, for the workers in your fields, for the governing of your cities and nations, for the things you build, for the way you communicate with those around you, and for all of life and godliness. For the length, width, and height of my Father's Kingdom. As you live this, you bring glory to my Father… and it is my Father that swore an oath saying *'As surely as I live the whole earth shall be filled with my glory.'* The life of my Father flowing out of you is the fulfilling of that oath; as his sons and daughters walk in the fullness of life and godliness, that is the fulfillment of his oath. These are some of the things we are giving to you, it is treasure hidden for you."

Above the well was a simple bucket winch, two vertical poles with a crosspiece, crank and handle. Benjamin had lowered its bucket into the water and was turning the crank to bring it back up.

"Spirit Helper, he will show us all of this?" Lazarus questioned, "But you are basically describing everything that we say and do!"

"Yes… I am… and if you get yourself into agreement with my word, my word will work for you."

The sisters, Benjamin, and John looked at Lazarus, and Martha said, "While you were away, we got a crash course on learning this. The evidence of this truth is you standing here in your flesh-and-blood body… looking at us with your mouth wide open."

"If you agree with the word of God, even before you understand, by speaking and acting accordingly, the understanding will come, the light will come. Spirit Helper will see to it."

Laz asked, "When Benjamin found you, you knew my body had died… Spirit Helper told you… didn't he? How do you do it so fast?"

Ben set the full water bucket on the stone wall, and with a ladle he began to drink water from it, when he was through he handed the ladle to the next person. Eventually each one had a drink of water from the well.

"I continually tune in to his voice, the voice of Spirit Helper. With practice, as a born of God person, you can learn to listen *fast* also."

"With garden stuff?" Clarified Lazarus, "And finding an easier way to render the nard oil out of the spikenard roots? Spirit Helper will show me, and tell me how? I think I am going to like this!"

"Lazarus, for many years I worked with my dad doing the work of a carpenter, with instruction in that life arena from Spirit Helper. I often went to him for assistance to do what we needed to do, and he helped me. Spirit Helper and I are here with you now, but it is going to be even better for you when I go away."

Martha wondered, "Now, that thought is still fuzzy to me, how can it be better when you go away?"

"Look at it this way, when you sent Benjamin to get me, you were sending to get the help that we, Spirit Helper and I, the anointed one and his anointing, bring, and there was time and distance to deal with. Once I go, you can have the anointed one and his anointing in you, with no time or distance to deal with."

"And we can talk to your Father like you do?" Martha asked.

Jesus clearly answered, "As a born of God person, he will be your Father also, and with the anointed one and his anointing dwelling in you, yes, you can."

"What if two people are talking to him at the same time?"

"Even if every person on this earth was one of his kids, and each one was talking to him at the same time, he could still respond instantly, personally, with each person, no problem."

"Wow, he is very big!"

"Heaven is his throne, the earth is his footstool, but it is his sons and daughters that are most important to him."

Mary was beside herself, "And he, Almighty God, wants to help me with my greenhouse and gardens? This is just so wonderful!"

"When you look at a good father here on this earth, and say, *'Wow, he is just such a good father to those kids,'* and if he really is, even in his limited human condition, he got that from my Father."

Benjamin asked, "And the power, where does the power come from? When you said *'Lazarus come forth'* it took some sort of power! Something to heal and restore his body… and then pull him back into his earth suit! And you are telling us… that you are limited… in that flesh-and-blood body… like we are limited, but we will be able to do what you do? And even greater things than what you have done… because you are going to your Father! When you do what you do, where does the power come from? Is it the same place that we will get the power from?"

"The power comes from the same one, from Spirit Helper."

"Does this, ever get easy to do?"

"As you renew your mind with the word of God, and train your body, walking in the Spirit will become a natural thing... but there will also be times when it will be as if you are walking up from the Jordan Valley Road in the absolute black of night. All around you will be darkness... and it will seem like the only thing to guide you will be a candle light in the window and Spirit Helper in you. You will slide your feet along the path, not even daring to lift them off of the ground for the blackness around... but you will focus in on the light, you will keep moving, and you will arrive safely home, because Spirit Helper will not leave you, not ever, he will always be with you."

Glancing at the position of the sun and considering the time, Jesus said, "Martha, will you pack us a lunch to go? John and I need to head north soon, in order to meet up with the others tomorrow."

Martha apologized, "Oh... yes... I am sorry Jesus; we have gone and done the twenty questions thing to you again."

"Not to worry Martha, I started it when I asked about the garden. Besides, I like being here... and by asking about your plants... I was also stalling our departure. It has been so good to be here... with all of you."

"You have excellent travel weather today," Lazarus stated, "and we will see you again soon, for the dinner!"

"And you will be there also? Without the grand entrance?"

Mary grabbed her brother's hand, "He will be there also, with no grand entrance, just a constant peaceful presence... thank you very much, Jesus."

As they left the gardens Mary closed the gates and then caught up to the others as they entered the house.

John and Jesus loaded their backpacks as Martha gathered travel food. The morning had become a sparkling clear sixty-five degree day... and they had reached the time when no one wants to say goodbye.

Martha handed the food pack to Jesus with tears threatening to spill from her eyes. *Thank you Jesus,* was the only words she could get out before her voice choked.

"I know… I'm glad to have him back here too." He tried to wrap his arms around all three siblings at the same time. "We will see you again soon."

He grabbed Ben with both hands, by the shoulders, and looking straight into his eyes he said, "It will be good to have you as my brother, this worked because you did your part. Thank you… and I also have a request for you."

"What is it Jesus?"

"Talk to Emil, I want the two of you to keep an eye on Lazarus and the girls, and keep them safe. Will you do that for me?"

"Yes… of course… we will do that, sir."

Glancing at Mary, he added, "I know that you, as your sister has, you have made adjustments in your heart."

And to Martha he said, "You have brought my Father Glory, and he is grateful. Thank you, Martha."

To Lazarus it was a bear hug and, "I will see you on another day my friend."

Then Jesus walked down the steps with John, and took a turn towards Ben's lookout spot and the road north to Ephraim.

As Spirit Helper someday would, Jesus walked through the individual gardens of his friends, working with, and helping them deal with what was growing there. Weeds, and their destructive effects were removed, as understanding of planting and protecting good seed was given… all for the purpose of bringing in a full harvest of life and godliness.

CHAPTER 29

His attention was focused on the individual strands of curly hair; they glistened with scented oil in flickering candlelight. Careful attention had obviously been given to their proper brushing and arrangement. Each of the two collections appeared to be a small handful, as if cut off near the base of a braid. The foundation-ends had been doubled back to form a loop, and then tightly wound with heavy thread as you would to the strands of a bowstring, leaving a handbreadth of flowing hair. The two graceful bundles were caught in a leather thong hanging from a rafter pole in the home of Emil the goat herder.

"I would rather have been paid in cash for the twenty-four lambs," Emil said to Benjamin's unasked question, "But payment by a piece of their beards will have to do."

"I saw them both at their secret meeting with Jannes and Jambres, in the tunnels beneath Solomon's porch; their beards have never grown back in those places. They have to comb other hair over from the side to cover the bald spots. Did they ever find out who has a piece of them hanging from a pole?"

"No one has bothered to tell them… I am only one of many who hold reason to have extracted payment by force. Some have offered to buy my two trophy beards, but I have grown fond of seeing practical justice."

"We should be back in two or three days, what do you have worked out for your sheep and goats?"

Emil was moving around the room placing items in his shepherd's bag, a canvas cloth bag with a flap lid; it had a long strap that went over his left shoulder as the bag rested on his right hip. It was large enough to hold a young lamb... or two if they were newborn.

"My youngest sister's oldest son, Moshav, he will watch the flocks while I am gone. He is a good boy; my sheep will hear his voice."

"Wasn't it three years ago, when you marked the twenty-four Passover lambs delivered to the Temple?"

Looking around as he was talking, Ben was impressed with how neatly organized the one room home was. The collected *stuff* of one man's life was in here, but everything was in order, and if something was not in use, it was put away.

"It's not like I didn't know what they were doing. They just needed to know their wickedness wasn't really hidden, not that they care. God knows the condition of their heart, there is nothing hidden from him."

"There is nothing concealed when light shines on it, let's get going, we can talk on the way. I would just as soon travel light and not too fast, we'll get there soon enough."

"Sure, I have flatbread, dates, milk-cheese, goat-cheese, a water flask, bedroll, and a wet weather tunic. What is it you hope to find in Jerusalem anyhow?" Emil asked, closing the door behind them.

The faces of a hundred sheep turned to look as Emil stepped outside, some moved expectantly towards the gate, Emil scratched around the ears of one as he walked by.

"I'm not quite sure; I told you what was said, at their secret meeting under Solomon's porch. I suppose I'm wondering what they are up to, if they still plan to kill Jesus and Lazarus."

A dozen sheep were standing at the gate now, making their baaa, baaaa call as their shepherd walked away... down the road... leaving them alone.

"Those people will do whatever they consider necessary to stay in power, whatever it takes. There is no goodness in them, their lust for power, money and control has sucked all of the goodness out of them."

Rounding a curve and cresting a small knoll, Bethany was left behind and Jerusalem came into view.

"There must be someone who can talk some sense into their heads... isn't there?"

"Benjamin, you know this as well as I do, the religious leaders in Jerusalem have become a privileged club. Anyone with a true heart towards God is sent out to some little town... or big town for that matter, but they are sent away. They do what they do trying to cover their own black hearts. The local people around the country have a representative of God who is true and kind... and a servant of the Most High God. All the while the real money-hungry power brokers have turned the Jerusalem Temple into a den of thieves."

"You sound like you have come to know them rather well."

"Two months after Passover, I will be fifty years old. All of my life I have delivered lambs to the Temple, as my father did before me, and his father before him."

Emil...

You talk of family and tradition.

Why didn't you ever marry?

How come you have no sons to carry on after you?

"Yes... I suppose... you see the heart of a man when he takes his coin purse out."

"After delivering the... ah... *twenty-four sheep,* I went back to collect, happened to be the same day Jesus showed up at the Temple... with a whip. He really tore the place apart, Jannes has scars from that day, and Jambres got bloodied up too. Jesus can handle himself quite well... and I got to see him do it!"

Three years ago...

And I can see it like yesterday!

His whip snapping and cracking...

Blood running and people diving after money!

Temple guards backed up against the walls...

Too scared to move!

But Lord God...

I think you need to clean your house again.

Ben asked, "Have you known Jesus very long?"

Emil kept his eyes forward facing.

Should I tell you?

The first day I saw him?

A world away?

A lifetime ago?

"Very long? It was thirty-three years ago in Bethlehem when I first met him. I was there, seventeen years old, guarding sheep for my father's brother who had broken his leg. We were on the edge of town when the angels came, mighty giants of the Most High God; the sky was full of them, announcing his birth. We went to see the newborn King in a cave stable."

What!

Emil…

You never told me!

You are like a father to me…

My best friend forever,

Why did you never tell?

"Emil! What? You've never said a word! Angels told you? Why didn't you say something? This is a really big deal! It's a shout it from the roof top kind of thing! How come I never knew? Does anyone know? You must have told someone!"

"You know, for a snoop, you sure don't know much!"

Hey…

Don't be so hard on him!

He's clueless…

It all happened years before he was even born!

The walls of Jerusalem were just up ahead, and from where they stood they could see a small piece of Herod's palace built into the upper western wall.

"Oh bother… I shouldn't be so hard on you… none of us talked about it after Herod killed all of the baby boys. I knew forty-two of the children who were slaughtered by that madman. One was my own son…my wife… she was never the same after that, she withered away and died before the next lambing season came around."

All movement stopped, but Emil kept walking, and Ben stood still staring at the back of a man he thought he knew.

Emil?

Your son?

Your wife?

I never knew!

Dear God in heaven...

I'm so sorry!

You don't live alone in a one room home out by the graveyard!

You live near the tomb of your wife and son!

Emil...

All your silent memories!

What a thing to mark the arrival of Messiah!

Emil stopped and turned around... there was no anger... no vengeance... towards evil yes but not towards men.

Now is when you wonder Ben...

With your eyebrows raised...

How often is the will of man in conflict with the will of God?

"Ben, God is good, he's good all of the time. It's the goodness of God which leads a man to repentance. The goodness of God sent his own son, Jesus, to this earth to pay for Herod's sin of murdering my son. Forgiveness was available for Herod if he would have bowed before God to receive it. When the Israelites wandered in the wilderness and were bitten by serpents, they died by the hundreds, but when they looked to the serpent fastened to a pole, they were healed. Even Herod could have received forgiveness had he looked forward to Messiah, fastened like the serpent to a pole."

"You don't blame God for what happened?" asked Benjamin.

As much as he had tried to remove them, the pictures were still there, so were the sounds.

Six men that held me down,

Filthy creatures who taunted my wife before they murdered my son.

In the middle of the mess my Rachel broke loose,

Attacked the men and tore a chunk out of the face of one.

Well done my love.

"How can I blame God? He didn't do it... and he did not authorize it! You must examine to see where an action originates from! Don't be deceived into blaming the God of Abraham, Isaac, and Jacob for something that should be laid on the neck of a fallen angel! It's true, some people allow themselves to be puppets in the hands of the pervert, but I know upon whose neck hangs the murder of my only son! He, with his followers, will spend forever in the fires of hell!"

"Emil, how can you look at Herod and what he did, and come to the conclusion he could be forgiven?"

"There is no evidence he stepped forward to receive the forgiveness which was available to him. Even so, the depth of Herod's badness doesn't come close to the height of God's goodness! It took thousands of years of faithful diligence on the part of God to bring his son here, to buy our forgiveness, and get us back! Jesus has not come for one... he has come for a multitude... but Herod was among those that he came for... even though Herod's now in hell."

The two started walking again, entering Jerusalem through its southeastern gate, people were everywhere. Eventually Benjamin stated, "You talk about this as if it's already has happened."

"For thirty years I have studied the words of Jeremiah, David, Moses, and others, I've observed unchangeable things in God's plan... what he has said will happen. We can dig around here in Jerusalem... poke around and listen... but what Lord God has cut as a plan will happen, only the peripheral details can be changed. I believe Lazarus must be kept safe from the wickedness of those at the Temple... but Jesus as a serpent will be nailed to a pole!"

"Your wife and son, was that changeable?"

"Looking back, I can say yes. It was inevitable Herod would kill some, but Mary and Joseph escaped with Jesus, so did others. Just look around at the men who are thirty-two or thirty-three years old, Satan tried to kill them all just to get the one he missed!"

"So, what are we supposed to do, just sit back and watch as wicked people do whatever they want?"

"No! First we are to be students of the word! We work with Almighty God and the plan he has put forth. Second, within our sphere of influence, spirit, mind, and body, we resist every twisted plan and action from that fallen angel and his puppets!"

"And how do we do that?" questioned Ben.

"Go back to what we do first, be a student of the word of God. If we don't, we might find ourselves supporting the enemy's plan by resisting God's plan! We must acquire enough understanding to know the difference."

Ben said, "Jesus has spoken of many difficult things he will have to face."

"I understand Lazarus talked to David, I have studied what God said through him. What God said is what will be and is not changed by my opinion. Jeremiah wrote of Herod's slaughter of the innocent. Some were students of the word and escaped; I was not and did not. I will not again do what an ignorant person does… and I will not fight against the plans and purposes of Almighty God."

"Then we will continue, learn what we can, weigh what we find with the written word of God… and do what is necessary to keep Lazarus and the girls safe."

"Well said, and it is very easy for me to work in agreement with you in that direction."

"Good… now… will you tell me more about that night in Bethlehem, when the angels showed up?"

"Ben… behind you, no… don't move… don't turn around."

From the center of the soul, high above a quiet valley two silent eagles flew. Circling, watching, for the twitch of a gray ear, or maybe a hop or two out into an open place. They would kill and eat the rabbits, before rabbits do what rabbits do.

CHAPTER 30

From the far side of a valley which she had been in before, Martha looked to the southeast. On the distant hillside sat a large stone house, and behind the house, sharp cliffs dropped off more than a man could climb without gear.

Originating from somewhere below her, a flashing movement captured her attention. She continued moving forward, but focused her eyes towards the questioned spot, on the east side of the valley floor.

Movement again burst forth, escaping from behind a treetop which had blocked her view… a dark shape, a horse, struggling. Sunbeams burned through from behind a cloudy sky and struck the horse, reflective light bouncing from the animal's sweat-drenched sides.

The black creature reared up on its hind feet, fighting against ropes which anchored it to its unfolding horror. One rope was hanging loosely and tied off to a heavy timber post, a second rope was held tightly by the left hand of a man near the post. He was clothed in a tunic; it was tied at the waste and left his arms and legs half naked.

Glaring down at his tormenter, with his ears laid back and nostrils flared, the black horse pawed the air above the man. Majestic though the black horse was, he fully fought his fear of entering the controlled dominion of a sweaty human.

Throwing his head from side to side while searching out his target, his black hoofs raked the air above tunic-man's hairy head, coming down upon him.

Martha screamed, "Augh! It kicked him! The horse kicked him in the head! Oh God help him now!"

Is he dead?

Kicked in the head and killed?

His head bashed in by some wicked horse?

But no... the man spun around... rolled down beneath the rope and came up on the other side with a heavy leather whip.

Captivated by the sight before her, Martha shouted out instructions, "Beat the rebellion out of him! Hit him harder! Teach him not to use his feet like that again!"

Drawing back with his heavily muscled right arm, tunic-man hammered the black horse. He hadn't struck the animal before its violently attacking action, and Martha doubted if he would have to hit the horse again.

The big black stallion was being driven through an invisible fence, kicking and screaming he went, being encased within the command of a man.

With a solid grip, he approached the dripping beast, its sides heaving with air surging through its lungs. The man slowly reached up with his right hand and took hold of its flowing mane while staring into its left eye, and with his left hand he moved a bridle up while guiding a bit into its mouth. Then sliding his hand up over the horse's sweaty face, he exchanged handholds on the mane, and with one fluid movement, he threw himself onto its back, and the two as one were off, pounding around the ring.

Minutes went by and his frantic fight became empty, his days of living for himself were gone. The horse was now in service to his master.

They were close to the man now... close enough for Martha to see lines made by dripping sweat, through the dust, leaving tracks on the man's bare arms and legs, she looked away, embarrassed for her looking.

Lazarus saw the flush of her face and said, "Martha, what? You were gawking at the man? It's only Simon! You have seen him... and talked with him... many times before!"

Mary observed with a smirk, "Yes, but never while he's out here breaking horses... covered only with that windblown tunic of his."

"Enough," stated Martha. "We are here on business... maybe we should come back another time."

"No," Laz said, "this is the appointed time... just look at your feet for a while... you'll be fine," he added with a quizzical sound to his voice.

Martha was studying her toes... and stones... on the ground... around her sandals... as Simon approached all three.

"My friends, it is so good to see you. I would greet you properly, but then you too would look like a dusty Bethany road."

"And greetings to you Simon," answered Lazarus. "It's good to know... you really do have arms and legs... and with healthy skin, I might add," stated Lazarus, throwing his sister a glance.

She was pushing a stone around with her toe.

Simon responded, "Jesus has a way of fixing things completely, if he's given the space to do so. I see the mole which was at your hairline... the one that used to be above your right ear... is also gone."

Martha spun around to look at her brother, she hadn't noticed, but yes, the mole was gone!

Lazarus pulled up his sleeve and checked to see... the other one, just above his left elbow, it was also gone!

Simon addressed his guests, "We will have dinner on the veranda. Mary, I believe Esther has returned to her room, could you find her?"

Then turning to Lazarus and Martha, Simon continued, "Hannah has things ready for us. Why don't the two of you go on up, and I will join you in a few moments?"

"Yes, Simon, very good," answered Lazarus, "we will see you there."

Without looking back, Simon turned and walked towards the stables.

Lazarus was studying his sister. Her face was pointed towards stone steps leading to the house, but her eyes followed Simon... entering the stable.

My sister... she is... twitter pated?

Humph!

Gawking after Simon?
Humph…
I should have known, I suppose I really did…
They have both hinted it enough…
Augh!
Simon and my sister?
What am I to do, what will Mary say?
True…
He is a Godly man, but… he owns like half the town!
With servants!
Humph!
They call him lord and master, owner!

Esther turned at the sound… Mary knocking at her door… within the servant's quarters of the house.

"Is that you mama?" she called out.

The room of her mother and stepfather was just next door.

"Esther… it's me… Mary."

"Oh, Mary! Come on in, I've been waiting for you!"

Mary stepped into the room. Esther was off to the side pulling on a clean robe.

Esther tied a colored sash around her slender waist.

"Come… I must keep moving… I have vegetables prepared… outside, on the step… I need to grab them first, and bring them up… to the kitchen; I must finish building the salad… and serve the meal."

Around Simon's veranda table three friends sat.

Undisclosed history held them together as well as their love for each other. Each one lived in the same house where they were born, and in that thought were hidden mysteries.

In the silence which surrounded them, Lazarus looked towards his childhood friend.

"Simon… when I was born… you were four years older than me… and yet by the time that I was five, you were my best friend. You know… I have always wondered… but have never asked… how is it you survived? You grew up in this house, here in this town. There are no other men alive… from Bethany to Bethlehem… who are within sixteen months of your age. How is this possible? You survived when others died."

Simon sat with his back to the cliffs behind him. In front of him, beyond his friends, doors, windows and archways were positioned in a manner where he could see and monitor the functioning of his estate.

At his feet was a hemp floor mat.

Beneath the floor mat were three small drains, to pipe away water, to keep the stone floor of his veranda dry.

With his right foot he slid the mat to his left and sounds from a conversation taking place between Mary and Esther, just outside the lower entry of the house, could be heard through the pipe at his feet. He slid the floor mat back.

"My great grandfather built this house; he had a sister by the name of Anna… and… my friend… if I answer your question… I not only trust the two of you with my past, but I also trust you with my future."

"It is my expectation that days are coming when the secrets of this house… this home… should not be hidden to you."

Turning his gaze to Martha, he added, "All of my life… I have been fond of you, Martha, but the first sign of leprosy showed up before my father died. As the youngest of my family and the only son, I was afraid and hid the symptoms. By the time Jesus healed me, twenty-five percent of my skin was affected. Because of the leprosy, certain relationships could not be established… but that was then and this is now. I know these are precarious times, but there is much strength in unity… and since your father is not here to ask… I will ask your brother."

Lazarus felt the blood drain from his face and his mouth went dry. He looked at his sister. She was biting her lower lip to keep from giggling like a little girl.

"Lazarus, I am asking you… for your sister's hand in marriage… on the condition… of course… for this to be agreeable with your sister."

"How....when...uh...Martha?" Lazarus stammered, looking at his sister, who simply nodded to her brother. Looking back at Simon with wide eyes, Lazarus swallowed hard and said, "Yes?"

The chatter of Mary and Esther came around the corner from Hannah's kitchen, but they stopped... and sort of stood there.... watching... as Simon... kneeling by the side of Martha's chair... very delicately... placed a kiss upon her lips.

"We must have missed something," stated Mary with both her hands bolted to her hips. "What is going on here?"

"It's, ah...okay... Mary," answered a flustered Lazarus, "He asked me first."

"What?" Mary demanded, "He said, *'It's nice that you brought your sister over here, oh, by the way, can I kiss her?'*"

"No," replied Lazarus. "He asked me... if he could marry her."

"Yes! Way to go, Master!" yipped Esther. "Kiss her again!"

196 | Mike & Dianne Heintzeman

CHAPTER 31

"Wow, Martha," Mary exclaimed, "when you make adjustments, you make adjustments, nothing stays the same. Hmm… ah… I guess that you don't have to just look at your feet anymore."

A pinkish shade of red rose up in Martha's cheeks.

Esther spouted, "Mama will be so happy, she has always loved you, Martha!"

Lazarus was squirming and changed the subject back to the mystery woman, "Simon… your great grandfather's sister… Anna?"

"Oh… yes… now that my question has been answered, I am willing to answer yours… understanding… what is said here, among family… stays here. There's much about this place and its history… which even Esther and her mama do not know."

Esther's ears perked up. She brought the back of her right wrist up to her forehead and went into some melodramatic spiel about her adopted daddy keeping secrets from her. When she slowed down enough to actually look at Simon… with one eye open and one eye closed… she stopped her performance mid-sentence and said, "You all must be hungry, I will bring dinner to the table," and waltzed off to the kitchen.

Watching her leave, Simon said, "Her antics kept me going when I felt like just giving up and dying. There is a treasure in that girl that I hope is forever polished."

Martha spoke up, "You have given her a life when most slave owners would have taken it away. Joseph and her mama know it for sure, and it speaks volumes of the goodness of your heart."

"Simon," Lazarus voiced again, "who is Anna?"

"My great, great grandfather's name was Phaneul, Anna was one of his daughters, she warned her brother, my great grandfather, of things which were coming... before he ever started building this house."

Martha asked, "Simon, isn't this house one hundred years old this year?"

"Parts of it are, it took them a few years to build it, and to keep the secrets of it hidden. It's built on three chimneys, vertical shafts that lead to a matrix of underground tunnels."

Preparing the table for dinner, Esther did not walk into the room, she floated. First she twirled at the door, glided across the floor and placed fresh flowers at each end of the table. All the while as she moved through the room, she kept her head turned, and her eyes looking, so they could not make contact with Simon's eyes.

"Did the tunnels have something to do with you living when other babies were murdered?" Lazarus asked.

"When Jesus was born in Bethlehem thirty-three years ago, his birth was announced to a group of shepherds by angels, a great big bunch of angels. Emil was among the shepherds who first went and saw our Messiah, Jesus, within hours of his birth."

"Emil?" questioned Mary. "The same Emil I know? What happened to him?"

"I will get there in a moment, Anna had been married at the age of fourteen, and lived with her husband for seven years before he died. Then, for the rest of her life, she was either here at Stonehouse, or at the Temple in Jerusalem, watching for the arrival of our Messiah. She was at the Temple watching... waiting... on the day Mary and Joseph brought Jesus to the Temple to be dedicated to the Lord, forty days after his birth. She was one hundred and five years old at that time."

The next items to arrive were dinner plates, held in the crook of Esther's left arm. As she moved around the table, she did not turn, she spun, again somehow managing to give no chance of receiving a visual command from her master.

Martha asked, "How did she know to be there? Did Emil tell her?"

"No, I don't think so. There was a lot of time and distance between them. My father and mother were convinced Anna was a prophetess, and so was her brother, my great grandfather. Out of all the babies she saw brought to the Temple for years and years, when she saw Jesus, she knew he was the one she had been watching and waiting for."

Martha identified, "Spirit Helper told her."

"Yes he did," responded Simon, looking into Martha's eyes. "I'm so glad you understand that, Martha, you are a treasure."

"Well, thank you, my husband-to-be," Martha chirped.

Laz interrupted, "Martha, will you keep him on track! I still don't know how Anna rescued Simon!"

Then came chilled water glasses, somehow being fastened to a silver serving tray through centrifugal force, one set before each guest, but as she swirled past Simon, his slightly moving foot caught her toe. Set off balance, a flying silver tray with one last water glass separated above Simon's head. With what looked like a graceful bow, the tray was caught by Esther's hand as Simon, his left hand just above the floor, rescued the water glass and placed his still full glass upon the table.

Without even one ruffled feather, Simon continued, "She warned them, my parents, before I was born, of what was written by the prophet Jeremiah. She told them, *'I don't know how, when the wickedness of Satan's kingdom will spew forth and the blood of babies will cover this land like a blanket, but you will know when it will be safe for your only son to see the light of day.'* So my parents hid me, I lived in the caves under this house until I was four years old."

Mary asked, "And what of Emil?"

"His son and I were born the same year."

"His son?" asked Mary. "I didn't think he had ever married... let alone had a son!"

Martha looked up with saddened eyes. "Then Emil's son was one of the babies murdered by Herod the Butcher! That's a wound that only the goodness of God can heal."

"What about his wife? I have never heard a word about her," Mary wondered.

"They are buried in the same tomb. She died somehow, within a year of the boy, and he was almost two at the time."

Martha thought out loud, "He would have been old enough to have toddled around after newborn lambs. It must have cut the heart out of his mama to have her baby taken like that."

Simon continued, "Yes, but Emil chose to live on. I have often seen a tremendous depth of kindness in the man, but at the same time, he has the strength and action of a broadsword. He is a man you want at your side."

Returning with one last item, and walking into the room, was Esther, with beautifully folded cloth napkins which she set before Simon and his guests.

"And Anna, what did she do after she saw Jesus," Lazarus asked, "did she stay at the Temple?"

"No, she had finished her mission; she moved into the caves below this house and had a primary part in raising me. Anna was my constant companion… she was with me until the day her body died, the same day my parents brought me out of the caves. The change was terribly intense… to go from the darkness of the caves I had always lived in… to the sunshine brightness. As a protection for my eyes, for many days, they wrapped strips of cheesecloth around my head to keep the brightness of the sun from damaging my eyes."

Both Hannah and Esther served the meal, and Esther was, only when her mama couldn't see, presenting short pantomimes, all depicting segments of a Jewish wedding. Martha was having a hard time keeping a straight face and swallowing her food. At one segment, Mary almost broadcast her green beans across the table. Hannah knew her daughter was up to something, but was trying to ignore her.

"Hannah," Simon finally said, "I have an announcement to make that will affect this entire household."

Hannah drew in a deep breath, looked down, and responded by saying, "Master, please forgive my daughter. The exuberance of youth and her creative nature sometimes carries her away. I will see to it she is under control. Please don't deal harshly with her."

"Oh no, it's nothing like that, Hannah, what I have to tell you is good news! News Esther has just heard. I have asked, and Martha has said yes... to be my wife!"

"Oh, Master! I am so glad! She will be an excellent wife to you... and give you many children!"

Martha blushed and looked at her feet, changed her mind, and looked at Simon with no words, only mischievous eyes.

"All in time, Hannah," Simon said as Hannah joyfully went back to her chores.

"We will set a day, not too far away I hope. There will be many things to accomplish before that time, but there must also be another reason for this gathering you arranged, Lazarus."

Simon continued, "I had my purpose for assembling with you, and it has been accomplished. But Lazarus, I still don't know why you wanted to talk to me. You only sent word we needed to meet around a meal. I had Esther and Hannah prepare one for us to celebrate what I hoped would be good news. Was there something else? The message the runner brought was very vague."

"What did the runner tell you?"

"He said, *'A message for Simon at Stonehouse from Lazarus... Simon, we need to meet around a meal.'* That was it, word for word."

"Lazarus, are those the words you sent?" Martha asked.

"Ah... no... they aren't," answered Lazarus scratching his head. "Benjamin was out of town... so I sent Thomas. The message was *'Simon, we need to meet about a meal.'* That's an entirely different message... although I do have to say... this was an excellent dinner, best that I have had in a long time. Thank you, Simon, and I send my complements to the cooks. As a side note, Esther's dinner theater idea could catch on, I greatly enjoyed the performance."

At those words, Esther gave an exaggerated bow. "You may send flowers to this address!"

"I didn't question it," Simon said, "it looked like the perfect setting for what I wanted to ask, so I just started planning."

Martha's face went slightly white, "You planned the horse bit for me? Why?"

"My life seldom has clean clothes of white robes, I needed to know if I was still appealing to you covered with dirt and dripping with sweat."

Martha's face went whiter still, but Mary answered, "You knocked her right out of the saddle Simon. Your real life will be very interesting."

Martha bristled, "And if I hadn't been attracted to you, all dusty and dripping, what then?"

"That, my beautiful bride to be, is a question I thankfully was never presented with."

Laz interrupted again, "Can we get back to the message and the meeting, please?""Do we have to?" questioned Esther. "I'm writing this down in my diary as the most fun day ever!"

"Yes, of course, something about a meal?" Simon answered.

Lazarus stated, "Six days before Passover, Jesus will be in town, and he asked if we will prepare a meal for him… and two or three dozen guests. We volunteered your house as the place… our house is too small, but we of course would help with the meal… and preparation. We were hoping you would say yes."

"Lazarus, Jesus has given me life… I would give him my house if he asked me for it. Of course, yes."

A movement in his peripheral vision caught Simon's attention, and he jumped from his chair in time to catch Hannah as she slumped to the floor.

"Mama!" called Esther, as she landed on the stone floor by her mother's crumpled form. "Mama! What's the matter? Are you hurt?"

Martha was there and checked her heartbeat and breathing, "I think that she just fainted. The things that this woman has been through and the thought of Jesus coming to this house cause her to faint, go figure."

After a moment or two, Hannah's eyes fluttered and opened. "Did I?" Hannah wondered. "The room just sort of drifted away."

"Are you okay, Hannah?" questioned Martha.

"Yes, I believe so. This hasn't happened for a long time… please forgive me."

"Let us help you to the cushioned chair in the shade."

Lazarus and Simon gently brought her to the comfy chair to rest.

In the quiet of the shaded corner Martha asked, "This happened before? When Hannah?"

"Almost twenty years ago, not to worry, I will be fine in a moment or two."

Esther was wide-eyed, looking at her mother. "You take the evening off Hannah," Simon said, "Esther will gladly finish your responsibilities of the day, isn't that right, Esther?"

The daughter was nodding her head up and down, but her mouth was not moving, a noticeably uncommon moment.

Martha said, "Simon, it might be good for Hannah to sit in on the discussion about the dinner. We will be working together on its preparation and serving."

"Do you think she is all right?" questioned Simon, as he turned to look at Hannah.

"Oh… I think that she is more than all right, Simon."

"Then yes, of course."

"Very good," said Lazarus. "Now we can come up with the dinner choices."

"My brother, how can you think of food after all of the goodness we just ate?" Mary asked.

"Someone has got to keep us on track here or we won't get anything done. The dinner is only five days away."

Choices were made and Martha took notes on a parchment. A chore list was written out for each person. Simon said he would discuss with Joseph what slaves could be spared from work on the grape vines to help in the dinner preparation.

As things were winding down, Martha walked with Hannah to the kitchens for a look. When they were alone, Martha said, "Hannah."

"Yes, Mistress Martha."

"First, I always have, and always will, value your friendship, and unless proper etiquette around company demands it, I want you to call me Martha and be the same friend to me you have always been. Okay?"

"Yes, Martha." And she gave Martha a big hug. "I am so happy for you. Simon is a good man who has always loved you. For many years

I wondered why he never told you, and now here you are. God is so good."

"What seemed so far away is now as close as the air we are breathing. This truly is a beautiful day. It appears you too, will also make an announcement soon. Have you told Joseph yet?"

Hannah was caught slightly off guard. "I haven't told anyone yet. I am a little afraid. I was only fifteen when Esther was born. Do you think that Simon will be upset?"

"Hannah, Joseph oversees all of Simon's grapevines and wine. He is Simon's most faithful servant. It was years ago when he saw your love for Joseph, and he gladly gave you to him. I am sure he expected babies would come."

CHAPTER 32

The rhythmic pattern of the sound was methodical in nature. It had started in the morning hours and continued throughout the day. Matched with the sound, little puffs of powder escaped from beneath thick pads of leather as they impacted dry, dusty earth. A precise rocking motion at each blow forced small swirls of dust to exit the forward end as each leather pad made contact with the ground. Both of the leather cushions were fastened in place with a series of laces cut from a finer material and tied just above his ankles. The person wearing the sandals had pulled his robe up, and tied it with his belt so the loose cloth would not interfere with the motion of his hairy legs; legs which he now stared down at, as they continued forward in their march towards Ephraim. He looked over at John and then fastened his eyes on the northern horizon.

John was looking at his own hairy legs and dirty feet, "Jesus," he asked, "why did the prophet Isaiah say *'how beautiful upon the mountains are the feet of him who brings good news?'* Right now they just look like dusty dirtballs. I can't even see my toenails under all that caked on dirt!"

"John, look at the words around what he said, he wasn't talking about those things at the end of your chicken legs."

"Hey, don't you go making fun of my legs, Jesus!" John said, as he stopped walking to twist around sideways and look back and down at his hairy legs with dirty feet. "They are a fine set of transportation utensils."

"Okay, John… how about strong and sturdy, but bony legs?"

"Better, but not much… so… if he wasn't talking about my feet, what was he talking about?"

"It's a picture of those who support you, and the vision of your mission. It's your supporters… it's what they do, and the mountain of challenges they face and bills they pay. Your *'beautiful feet'* are the people who take you where you need to go… to fulfill the vision planted in your heart by me. The more time marches on, the more it will cost to go and do what you have been called to do. You must guard and protect those people… and instill in them an attitude of your gratitude. They are the ones that cover the cost and go the distance with you. Those people who support the vision and the mission are the beautiful feet."

Jesus was talking to John, but he was thinking of two families who had consistently supported him on his mission. More specifically, he was remembering his first encounter with two members of those households, Joanna, from the house of Chuza, and Mary from the town of Magdala.

Mary arrived with the entourage she never left home without, with only one addition, she was holding tightly to the hand of Joanna who was leading the way. Three personal servants surrounded the two women, and four bodyguards positioned themselves strategically near their primary charge, Mary, the Magdalene.

To the casual observer, Mary Magdalene was a woman of great authority, treasured wife of Keynes, a powerful member of the Roman senate. Viewed in the spirit arena, the woman was held captive by the demons which possessed her. Seven fallen spirits which continually slid through her body, as other entities charged her mind with pictures of eminent disaster.

Jesus continued, "I will finish the answer to your question, not according to what is, but according to the new covenant that is coming."

"Okay, I will remember."

"In my Father's Kingdom, much of what each one of his kids are called and equipped to complete, are just the chores of life and the raising up of Godly children. Many callings are monitored through market forces placed upon the finished product, plus supply and demand. If there were only one shoemaker and you were not allowed to make your own sandals, he could demand almost any price for the sandals he sells, but there are many sandal makers and only the best get my business because we do a lot of walking and I want the best shoes for my feet, winter and summer. Income to the sandal man comes through the sale of the finished product. The preaching of the gospel has a finished product, but its cost is often covered by those who see the value of the vision, they are the beautiful feet. It's my Father's method of quality control. It works well if each person does his part. Only an idiot would take shoes from one sandal maker and then pay another sandal maker for the shoes. Also, you should not give support to someone who is presenting the gospel poorly, just the same as I would not buy crummy sandals and pay good money for junk. It takes trained effort to make a quality shoe, and for that, I am willing to pay the price."

"That makes sense, but I would like it written out a little clearer if you would please."

"When I finish my chores here, I will find someone who will clarify those words for you, and write it down in the new covenant like this, *'How then shall they call on him in whom they have not believed? And how shall they believe in him of whom they have not heard? And how shall they hear without a preacher? And how shall they preach, except they be sent? As it is written: How beautiful are the feet of those who preach the gospel of peace, who bring glad tidings of good things!'* Is that easier to understand?"

"Yes, much better, you clearly identified the understood subject, the sender, as the feet, thank you."

"Good, when you read that in the new covenant later, know that I did that just for you, okay?"

"Yes, that's good, and I will say this now before it happens, thank you Jesus, and thank you feet!"

Although Jesus and John kept walking forward, Jesus' mind went back to the fate of seven evicted demons.

Approaching Jesus, Joanna found herself pulling hard on Mary Magdalene's arm, turning around to look into Mary's face, she saw wide-eyed terror. The seven demon spirits resident in Mary, each were being scalded by the brightness of Jesus' presence, they were flooding her mind with fears of a shameful death.

Refusing to give up on her friend, Joanna kicked out her own doubts, and looked only at the freedom she knew Jesus could deliver.

They were close enough to touch him now, and the demons were in total panic, flailing around in a pointless effort to stay within their tormented trophy woman, and to escape the dominion of Jesus.

Three hours of nonstop walking was beginning to take a toll on John, he started counting sheep on a nearby hillside to pass the time. Eventually he recorded all the sheep he could see, and he started counting trees, there was not as many.

After a few minutes of silence, John spoke up. "I do have one more question, if you don't mind."

"Hmm, what's that, John?"

"Are we there, yet? My feet need some rest."

"Tell your feet, *Just five more miles, my faithful friends, just five more miles.*"

With desperate eyes, Joanna searched the face of Jesus, as a trembling Mary fell before his feet, pleading with her words, "Help me... please!"

Placing his right hand to where it covered her left ear, Jesus spoke words into her mind and body, "Leave her! Now and forever!"

Seven demon spirits were blasted out of the woman's body; they slammed into the stone wall of a distant building, and then limped off to find a place to hide.

208 | Mike & Dianne Heintzeman

Like a puppet with its strings cut, Mary flopped straight to gravel ground and sloughed off to his right side, her limp hand still held tightly by Joanna. Three personal attendants and four bodyguards were clueless as to what to do.

Mary, slowly, as if waking from a dream, in time became aware of her surroundings, opening her eyes; Joanna helped her to her feet.

———————

"I'm sorry to bug you, Jesus, but I need to ask you something else."

"John, there's nothing I enjoy more than peacefully talking to one of my friends. I don't have much time left here and I would just as soon spend it with you, so ask away."

"I have been thinking about how much you know, and I can understand how you described you are limited because you are in an earth suit like mine, but what about when you go back to where you were, what will you know then? And what does your Father know? Does he know who will get, what you call, *'born again'*? Does he know the nature and character of a baby who will be conceived next month? What about the son or daughter of that son or daughter, does your Father know what she will have for lunch on her fourth birthday?"

"We only have a mile to go, John; you could have asked the question this morning."

"I was thinking about it this morning, does that count?"

"I will start at the beginning of your five or six questions. Because I came here and moved into an earth suit, there are things which have changed forever. Soon, I will be in a heaven suit, as you will someday have, and I will be functioning at one hundred percent, spirit, soul, and body. On this earth, as I am, I can't even walk on water, walk through walls, or fly, except with Spirit Helper assistance. The same is true for you. And as far as your questions are concerned, they have been answered hundreds of times in the written word of God, which you already have."

"Hum… most of my question has to do with what hasn't happened yet. I would expect Almighty God would know everything about everything as it is right now. What about a week from now, or a year from now?"

"John, do you understand how many variables there are at any given moment? Just the number of variables surrounding the conception and birth of one child is in the billions, and if you are talking about two people, then you are looking at billions times billions of variables."

"Well, can't you just look into tomorrow? I mean, can't your Father just sort of turn the pages of a book and look and see what is happening a year from now, or ten years from now? Isn't he all-knowing?"

"John, there are over three-hundred and fifty prophesies written in the Covenant record just about me walking on this earth. Some identify items of supply or covenant action from my Father's side, and some predict wicked actions instituted from the enemy's camp. If my Father could, or would, do what you are describing, then not one of those prophesies would be worth anything. According to his word, he is restricted to working hand-in-hand with a willing human. This is done by first declaring a thing prophetically, and then he watches over his word to perform it."

From within the heart and mind of Jesus a picture was lifted up, one the written word had painted, of a wrinkled up old woman and an even older man who never had any children.

And the Lord God said to the man, Look now toward heaven, and tell me the stars, if thou be able to number them; and he said unto him, So shall thy seed be. And the old man looked into the nighttime sky, overwhelmed with its vast expanse and innumerable amount of stars, but he believed God, and he began to see each star as a child with a face and name.

"That takes faith," said Jesus, "We have to work through people because we gave this planet to man, this is a man-planet. Anytime we work with a man or woman, there must be a live and active faith exchange taking place. We created man as a freewill agent, we will not override the will of a person just because we want or need him to do something."

As the dusty road continued on before them, even so did the pictures in Jesus' memory.

When the old man, Abram, and his wife had not produced a son as fast as they thought they should, they reasoned in their own minds... and Sarai told her husband, you think you can have a son? Then have one by my servant girl, Hagar. So Abram took Hagar and they produced Ishmael.

Jesus finished by saying, "The only things which are a non-item are the things we have full control over, like the planets, the stars, the galaxies, all of the solar systems and all of space, that's easy."

"What happens when people don't believe you, and instead go their own way? If you won't force them, what do you do?"

"Deal with it, or find someone else. Just check out the lives of Moses, or Abraham, or David. Each one of them messed up a bunch of stuff."

"How much of what happens here on this earth is the will of God? Half?"

"Not even close John, anytime someone is not living and moving in the love of God, they have violated the will of my Father, even if they don't break the covenant."

It was fourteen years later, when my Father changed Abram's name from father of a multitude, to Abraham, father of nations. That's when Abraham and Sarah conceived, and bore the son named Isaac, when Abraham was one hundred years old and Sarah was ninety.

From the center of the soul and moving north was a garden, but no ordinary garden, it was the garden of God. Many of the seeds growing there had been maturing for hundreds, and even thousands of years. Each one would come to harvest; it was only a matter of time.

"Here is a thought for you John; the thief comes only to steal, murder, and destroy, but I have come so that you would have life like I have it. You can weigh everything you face with that one truth. If you encounter something that brings you life and the fullness of it, then somehow I am behind the goodness. If you encounter something that has to do with stealing, murdering, or destroying, then somehow Satan's kingdom is behind the ugliness. Of all the things you will face on this earth, my Father's 'Will' is the author of only a very few of those things. In what passes before you, moment by moment, it is very needful for you to comprehend what things to accept, and what things to forcibly resist. Resist everything which has to do with stealing, murdering, and destroying. If you submit your will to my Father, and receive the leadership of Spirit Helper in you, you can successfully resist Satan's attacks and he will run away from you in terror."

In the spirit arena, Emil's guardian, the angel named Jasper, was up in arms.

"Malbec! They've been found out! I'm sorry… I didn't see the rat sneaking over! He was hidden in the shadows!"

Initially Malbec made no comment; instead he wiped blotchy splots of demon blood from his sword. At his feet, a pair of dismembered hands sizzled up some smoke and disappeared. "They can't be more than ten seconds in front of us, we'll find them."

CHAPTER 33

In the darkness, he pressed his back against cold, hammered steel straps.

Just below his shoulder blades, he could feel blunt square nail-heads, fasteners driven through the iron bands and into rough-hewn wooden door planks.

Another drop of sweat wound its way down his neck and he forced himself tighter to the timbers, trying to become one with its shadows. The drop of sweat was sucked into the damp cotton cloth of his robe.

Light from their pursuer's torch flickered on mud-smeared cobblestones at his feet. He pulled his left toe back from the flame's illumination. His lungs screamed out for more air while he forced himself to maintain slow, silent breathing.

Emil!

Where are you!

Across the narrow ally, and maybe five feet to Ben's right was another building entrance, its recessed door tucked back a foot or more behind a mortar-stone jamb. Another shadowy form hiding there tried to hide his labored breathing.

Emil!

Is that you?

Augh!

The old man had sprung like a cat, running through the back alleyways just inside Jerusalem's outer city walls. Escaping their initial confrontation with only surface bruises from two guards, they were able to keep their faces, and identity, hidden. After several minutes, they lost most of those who chased them, only the original guards continued in pursuit.

Bethany's runner and their resident goat herder had spent three days picking through the sludge of those who sell their souls for money. Finally, their search brought them to the ones they now tried to leave behind. Scarface and Tracker had been posted sentries, while religious leaders discussed plans to permanently silence Lazarus and his sisters.

Ben and Emil had slid into eavesdrop range across a string of rooftops, and listened to their planning through an open skylight window. All went smoothly, and they would have laid hidden on the rooftop until pre-dawn silence, but a big brown corn-rat stuck its wet nose into Emil's left ear.

Bickering voices from their pursuers now mixed with profanity, magnifying their frustration. "I don't give a rat's ass how you do it, find them!"

Ben remembered the ugly face which went with the voice, a heavyset man about Emil's age, with a long scar that ripped a path from his left eye and disappeared into his beard.

Scarface declared, "I saw the bastards run in here!" Scarface declared, "This is Yehuda Street! It's a dead-end alley!"

Tracker responded, "And what the hell do we do with them when we find them?"

"They heard too damn much! We make sure that they can't repeat what they know!"

Wet hair on Ben's neck bristled with goose bumps, and chased a shiver down his spine, the slithery sound of tool-steel sliding against sheath leather reached his ears.

They have drawn their swords!

Emil?

Help!

One set of cautious footsteps moved slowly towards his ears, and yet his eyes detected no movement of the torchlight. Ben forced himself further into the inside corner of his hiding place, jagged edges of cold stone bit into his left shoulder. He reached back with his right hand, working the door latch, a silent effort to find escape. The latch softly clicked and Ben pushed against the heavy timber door only to feel the restrictive thud of a locking crossbar.

Tracker's shadowy form was passing his doorway hiding place, but the light behind him had not moved.

Tracker snarled out hate-filled orders, "Move it old man! Get your fat ass down here! I can't see a bloody thing in this blackness!"

Tracker's insolent voice was now directly in front of Ben. He could smell the unwashed stink of stagnant sweat and wine, but all became silent as the man peered into surrounding blackness. Slowly, sliding gravel sounds rose from the man's feet, and directly in front of Ben appeared the left side of tracker's face. Highlighted by the flickering torch, yellow light bounced off of the man's pockmarked oily skin. He had twisted himself around to bark demands at his scar faced accomplice.

Blood pounded in Ben's temples, he was trapped with no place to run.

Looking down and to his right, Ben watched with horror as the shadow line of light moved closer towards his hidden form.

Too late, Tracker was turning to his left as the torchlight exposed Ben hiding in the doorway.

The voice spat out, "Ha! There you are my running rabbit!" and then he yelled, "I have found the hiding hole of our running rabbit! What should I do with him now?"

"Kill him! And then cut off those big ears of his! We will hang them on a string and sell them to Caiaphas for a piece of silver!"

Tracker's eyes focused on his target as he brought his right arm across and down, the tip of his broadsword ticking stone at his left foot. He hesitated starting the backhand blow for one second, pulling out more perverted pleasure from the white-faced panic in Ben's eyes.

But Tracker's twisting movement exposed his open neckline, Ben observed as muscled cords flexed tight and hovered, heart's pulsing bulge rose and fell beneath the man's greasy, yellow-brown skin.

Wha... ah!

Augh… augh… augh!

Tracker misread the sudden added whiteness of Ben's eyes, his cowering against the timber door, and horror in his eyes.

Ben's silent added horror was of Emil's knife, reaching around, digging in.

The old goat herder had struck and withdrawn before the understanding of his action could reach Tracker's clouded mind.

Tracker's blood spurted, pulsed and squirted, spraying Ben's robe and splattered on the ground.

The man's half-severed head tipped forward, falling into the massive gushing wound, his eyes went to hollow gray.

Ben watched gurgling bubbles popping for one moment, and then the lifeless form of his attacker crumpled down into the muddy cobbled alley.

The man with the torch never flinched, he didn't speed up, he didn't slow down, he just closed in on the bloody puddles of the blind alley.

Emil turned to face their last attacker.

This is the same man…

He moves the same…

He has the same sadistic eyes…

The same face…

Except for where my wife tore it up…

With the broken handle of an empty cup!

By their feet lay Tracker's body, twitching slightly, its quivering face made ripples in a pool of blood, its feet pawed the ground in a walking motion.

Scarface said, "I didn't want to split the bounty with him anyhow, he's always been too dumb to breathe. But now me, boys, I'm a killing machine!"

His words flowed out in a cloud of filthy breath.

Emil declared, "Your days of murdering the innocent are over, Haman! Before your torch goes out, you will be burning in the flames of hell! Begging for mercy at the feet of some chained and laughing demon!"

Scarface sneered, "Now who is going to do that, little man? And how do you know my name?"

"It's what they used to call you, before you became one of Herod's baby killers! You sold your soul to Satan! And you will get his reward, you piece of human trash!"

"That is so harsh," mocked Haman, as he turned slightly to slide his torch into a bracket on a doorpost. He pulled a second short sword from his belt and gave Ben space to grab the torch.

"Leave it be, Ben!" shouted Emil. "He will cut you down before you're halfway there! Get behind me... and up against the middle of the wall!"

Ben moved around and backed up against the wall.

"Just giving the boy some space, little man," jeered Haman blocking their exit. "He needs to think he's doing well."

"Your blood ran red the night your face was torn, Haman!" Emil remembered, pulling a second knife from his right-hand sleeve. "But before the new sun rises, the dogs of this city will drink their fill of you, and puke your black blood out into the street!"

Circling in on Emil, Haman said, "I remember you now. You had a little boy, too bad, he died. Serves you right, it was your wife that jumped on my back and ripped my face with a broken cup handle. She did your fighting for you, little man."

"Six men to hold me down! You coward, of a coward king! You never did know who to fight for."

Haman lunged with his broadsword, but as Emil sidestepped the blade, he sliced the big man's wrist.

Emil's razor-sharp blade raked Haman's wrist, severing tendons and arteries. The sword fell useless to the ground, from fingers which would no longer close.

"You have gotten slow Haman, or maybe you have never fought anything but little girls and babies."

Ben stared at Emil's hands, a six-inch double-edged blade protruded from each fist, each finger had a big brass ring around it, and what looked like brass hammerheads protruded out from the heels of his hands.

"You little lizard!" barked Haman as he swung a backhand blade at Emil, with his still-working left hand.

Emil sliced that forearm with his left blade, spun to his right, and drove his right-hand fist up and into Haman's chin, driving Haman's head cracking backwards. His left-hand blade split Haman's bulging belly and his right-hand blade came back across Haman's exposed neckline, swung back up, and made full-pressure contact from Haman's neck to his navel.

Haman's knees buckled and he hit the ground, hovering, kneeling in front of Emil, his body oozing parts and pieces. With his left-hand blade, Emil brought a final slice of the knife across, and just below, the big man's chin.

Haman's body fell forward, into the alley, landing face down next to Tracker.

Ben was stuck to the wall. He couldn't move, everything happened too fast, in the space of one breath the man was cut to pieces.

Responding to Ben's shocked face, Emil said, "Never give the enemy room to move. He will turn around and stab you in the back if you give him space. Haman's end was inevitable, it was just a matter of who and when."

Emil wiped the blood from his blades on Haman's shoulder and said, "Come on Ben, we've got to get out of here, it's almost dawn."

A speechless white-faced shivering Benjamin turned to leave.

As both together, they left the alley, two mangy dogs trotted by.

Ben turned around and blankly watched... gawked... as sniffing dogs licked at bloody bodies lying beneath a flickering torch.

The flame was almost out.

Ben stammered, turning towards home, "We... we need... we need to get Lazarus... and his sisters... all three of them... to a safer place, somewhere... somewhere Caiaphas and his plans can't reach them... at least for a couple of weeks."

"I believe your neighbor Simon can help us there. He has resources that go beyond what you can see."

"He has a lot of stuff I can see, between Stonehouse, the winery, vineyards, horses, and all of that land. What does he have beyond that?"

218   Mike & Dianne Heintzeman

"I am not quite sure, he just has a way of making things happen."

They were at the edge of Jerusalem now, heading southeast and traveling downhill, Emil looked across the Cedron Valley and to the horizon; dawn was half an hour away.

The valley was thick with early morning fog; it deadened the sounds of a city beginning to stir.

"Emil?"

"Hum…"

"Where should we go first, the house of Lazarus, home or Stonehouse? An hour won't make any difference, and I'm a smelly mess. You need to get cleaned up too, and you should switch robes before someone sees you, you're all splattered with blood."

"Hum… you're right," Emil answered, looking at his robe, "I'll burn this, wash up, and meet you at Stonehouse. With the dinner in two days, they're probably all at the House of Simon."

"Sounds good, I will meet you there."

From the center of the soul, and with absolute precession the watching eagle struck, dropping from the empty sky and crashing through its silence. Two rabbits hopping, side by side had broken through the family garden fence, now cut down with deadly force, plunging talons ripped through the cords around their heart. They had been sitting, side by side eyeing up rows of young peas and beans, now they were leaving, hanging silently from the claws of one giant bird.

CHAPTER 34

In Benjamin's mind, each piece of information was systematically being sorted, labeled, and categorically placed in correct arrangement for rapid retrieval and maximum safeguard value. He considered who would be allowed to receive each piece of information and if some things should be presented at all. Little did he know he would be the one sitting down and listening.

"She's what?" questioned Ben, looking at Simon and listening to Mary. "To you, Simon? You're what? When did this happen? What sweaty black horse? She thought what? Oh my…! About Simon? Augh! Cover my ears!"

Emil was sitting in the comfy chair on Simon's veranda, peacefully listening to the excitement of life, and the joy surrounding his friends.

Ben pleaded, "Please, Mary, please! Start at the beginning, slow down, and… tell your story… in some sort of order… and I will try… not to interrupt you."

After forty-five minutes of information from six different voices, Ben and Emil learned Simon and Martha were to be married, Simon had lived in the caves under Stonehouse until he was four with his great great aunt Anna, Anna had been watching for the Messiah and spoke words over Jesus when he was brought to the Temple as an infant, Esther could do an excellent pantomime of both a Jewish wedding and a pregnant woman, the dinner would be the following evening, Simon and Martha were hoping Emil would agree to prepare roast lamb, Simon had hidden the leprosy for over fifteen years, Esther's Ethiopian mama, Hannah, was expecting a baby with her husband Joseph, Simon was very good at breaking horses and Martha considered Simon to be *hot*.

After a brief intermission to let the information settle, Emil and Benjamin explained the danger presented by the plans of Caiaphas. It was concluded that Lazarus, Martha, and Mary would live in the caves beneath Stonehouse, starting immediately after the dinner and stay there until the threat of death had passed.

The primary details which needed to be overcome were the gardens and greenhouse at the House of Lazarus, plus Martha's chickens. Benjamin offered his services as gardener and chicken-tender, and Mary found the solution acceptable. Final arrangements were to be concluded by Mary instructing Ben as to the proper care and feeding of each and every type of plant in the gardens.

From the veranda all eight made their way down layered stone steps set on top of the immovable foundation of Stonehouse. Simon led the way, explaining the structure of the house and characteristics of the rock which it was built on.

"The entire house sits on stone. When great, great grandfather found this spot on his father's land, what caught his attention was the '*whoosh*' sound of air flowing up through a small hole. It was night and he had pitched his tent on top of this flat-top stone cliff. The cliff was then as it is now, it drops off fifty feet straight down and he was camped about one hundred feet from the edge. In the cold silence of night, he heard that whoosh sound of moving air and went to find its source. He found warm air escaping through a small hole at the edge of a large flat stone. In the morning he dug around the stone and pried it to the side, sliding it off the top of a vertical hole. He took a burning stick from his morning campfire and dropped it down the hole. It fell thirty feet and lay on the floor of a cavernous room. There was about fifteen feet of a sort of chimney hole before you got to the cavern. He worked the day to make a rope, and by evening he lowered himself down the hole after throwing a bunch of supplies in first."

Martha asked, "How old was he when he found this place?"

"Fourteen or fifteen… he was just a kid. I think Anna was a year or two younger. He was right here, where we are standing, with the sheep he watched over with his dog."

Opening the door to his wine cellar, they noticed a fresh air smell.

"This room sits below the kitchens. There is also a dumbwaiter which drops down to the caves from the kitchen through a chute near the fireplace. Another vertical shaft sits alongside of the fireplace chimney and the airflow coming up from the cavern leaves the house through a second chimney. They are side by side. The constant air-wash keeps the caves full of clean air."

Lazarus was impressed, "There must be other ways into the cave… for there to be moving air. This room is fresh and fairly dry, not musty at all, I am surprised. Caves are usually stale, damp and musty, not a place you would want to live."

"There are several ways in and out; there are three points of access from the house. How many of those do you know Hannah?"

"Only this one Simon, I did not know there were others. I have never been down there in the dark. It has always reminded me too much of the belly of the ship they took me away in."

"Not to fear, Hannah," comforted Simon. "This is an entire world away from what you encountered on that ship."

Simon made his way to a closet at the back of his wine cellar and opened the door. There were brooms and tools hanging on the back wall of the closet. He reached in, released a latch, and pulled a hook on the far right side next to the back wall which was really a second door. It swung forward and to the left. At his feet was a black hole, and straight in front of him was a large rope that was hooked over to the side. Beyond the rope was an iron ladder, and the top of the rope wrapped around what looked like a bucket winch you would find at a deep water well.

"This is the primary entrance; it's just big enough for a pregnant woman to get up and down. There are two exits which are fairly accessible near the base of the cliff, but they are very well hidden from the outside world and each has a locked gate. This entrance can be quickly locked from the inside with crossbars. There are also three small exits that I could get through when I was a little boy, but I never actually went outside through those holes before I was permitted to leave when I was four. I just peered through, looking at what was out there."

Martha took Simon's hand, "It must have been hard, as a small boy, peeking out at a world that wanted to hurt you."

"Anna was my constant companion," replied Simon. "With her, what I had was a life far richer than a prince in a palace. Wait until you see, it's as if the joy she brought to the cave is still there!"

Esther excitedly expounded, "Yeah Martha, just wait and see, it's awesome!"

"And you, Esther? What do you know of this place? The three entrances, the cavern… caves… and… ah… stuff?"

She began by hedging, "Master Simon, sir…"

But Simon cut her off. "Don't you start with me… I only want to know what you know of this place."

"Yes, Simon… sir… hum… I know of this door and the other two, the upper room, the big room, the bedrooms, the caves, and all of the lower exits."

"You went through thirty-nine candles that I know of. It's a good thing you did your chores so well… and that your mama is such a good cook. Fortunate for you, that is."

"Yes, sir," replied Esther. "Fifty-three candles… that's what I took… before I started making candles myself… I will find a way to pay you back for what I took."

"Did I ever tell you… that you were not allowed down there?"

"Hmm…" Esther perked up, "No sir."

Simon declared her sentence, "You will repay the cost of my candles… by being of service to Martha, Lazarus, and Mary, as they are to be my guests… in my home away from home."

"Really? That's like you paying me to take the candles!"

Simon continued on, "Do you still have a candle stash and tinderbox in the first room below?"

"Yes Mas…ah… yes, Simon."

"Then you go first, and get some light on down there, the rest of us will follow."

"Me too, sir?" questioned Hannah.

"Yes, I think it would be good for you… and I need to know I can send you down on your own… if you are needed there."

Esther grabbed hold of the forged metal ladder rungs on the far side of the hole. She stepped over the blackness and onto the rungs. In a moment, she was down the hole and out of sight.

Seconds went by and shuffling noises, mixed with the clicking sound of a flint floated up to their ears. Off to one side of the black hole were flickers of light and then a steady stream of yellow light. Another moment passed and more lights birthed from the first flame.

Simon asked, "Who's next?"

"I'm game," said Mary, as she walked into the closet and cautiously stepped across the hole and climbed down the ladder. As her feet hit the floor, she let out a, "Wow, this is so cool! Martha, you've got to see this!"

"Home, sweet home," said Martha, as she took her turn, with Hannah following close behind.

"Esther?" called Simon down to the women. "Do you know how to lock the door?"

"No sir, I've never done that."

"Pull the red chain and then loop it through the ladder… hook the chain hook on a ladder rung."

There was a metal-on-metal clanking, sliding sound, followed by a thunk. Three steel bars slid across the hole and into receiver sockets on the other side of the hole. Not even a chicken could get through there now.

"That's very interesting, Simon," came Martha's voice up from her cage. "So how do we get out now?"

"Martha… it's not you who is locked in! It's everyone else who is locked out! You have the controls there with you. You are supposed to… feel safe now."

"I would feel safer…if you were down here with me… showing me how this works!"

"Okay, Martha, unhook the red chain and pull the green chain."

Again there was the metal clanking, sliding sound with the following thunk… and the hole was open again. All four men went down, with Simon last in line, pulling the closet door and the false door closed behind him.

Light was being broadcast from several sconces around the room, and Esther was passing out more candleholders, each with a burning light. The room was full of brightness, the walls and ceiling contained a substance like mica, or else it was mica, a reflective metamorphic rock of a golden color.

Hannah was awestruck, "This is beyond what I ever could have dreamed! To think something might exist is one thing, but to stand in its presence… Simon, this is beautiful!"

They were standing in a small cavern, about twenty feet wide by forty feet long with a rounded ceiling which was maybe fifteen feet high, at its highest. The floor was fairly flat, but they were in a dish-shaped hollow, directly below the ladder entrance. To their side was a low wall about hip-high and on the other side of the wall was a large hole that they could not see the bottom of, from where they were standing. At the far end of the cavern was a circular stairway… made of timbers… that went somewhere… down. Around the room were a couple of sitting chairs, a tall cupboard, a daybed plus a branch tunnel displaying a desk and many pigeon-hole type, deep storage cabinets.

"This is my idea of a get-away place," said Mary listening to her own voice. "I thought there would be more of an echo."

Laz was also gawking, and thinking.

Two weeks down here…

Ben doing my chores…

Not bad,

Not bad at all!

Benjamin noticed the contented happy look in the eyes of Laz, "Just don't get too comfortable... or I might get hungry for some of your chickens."

Martha informed him, "Benjamin... those are my chickens... there's plenty of other food to fix... in the house."

Simon asked, "Ready to see the lower level, where the bedrooms are?"

"Bedrooms? Like more than one? Are you kidding?"

"Three," answered Esther. "They are caves with beds and doors and even an inside ..."

"Esther!" Simon stopped her again. "Let them wonder for a moment."

"Yeah," questioned Lazarus, "what do you do for... you know, when you have to...ah... it's an, ah... an easier question when there is not a room-full of women."

Simon nodded to Esther, "Lead the way Esther."

Martha and Simon let the rest go first while they tagged along behind. "How did this all come to be?"

"My father had his most faithful men work on this while my mother carried me. It was at Anna's insistence. There was quite a bit which had been done to the caves over the years, but the *'Home Touch'* was added in the months just before I arrived. Father knew mom would want to spend several hours a day down here. He did it for her as much as for Anna and me."

As they walked down the spiral stairs, they could hear Lazarus sputtering and Esther laughing, Simon said, "They have found the inside outhouse."

From the center of the soul flowed a joyfully peaceful day, of looking at flowers, checking out how the broccoli is growing, and even in the midst of an approaching storm, to look around and say, all is well.

CHAPTER 35

Morning brightness sparkled in through Mary's interim bedroom window, releasing warmth across her bed and through her covers.

This could be the last bit of sunshine I encounter for some time.

I should stay here for a while...

And store some sunbeams up!

For Lazarus and his sisters, this would be a day unlike any other. Jesus, his twelve, and other followers were arriving in the evening. Emil had chosen two yearling rams for roasting over an outside fire pit. Some of Simon's field workers had been assigned to assist Emil with the rams, and also to helping Hannah in her kitchens. Yesterday, Esther's energetic self was wound a bit too tight, and she found ways to express herself through her clear resonant voice, singing songs about history, working, and milking goats. Through it all she remained a treasured stress reliever, and the household entertainment.

Excitement was pulling Mary from her warm and comfy covers, but valiantly, she successfully resisted.

Even though her daily diligence usually didn't arrive until two hours or more past sunrise, she was often a working machine long after others were done. Morning was her think-time, a time of *'design-before-doing'*.

Why rush off to be busy?

Why make a mistake because I didn't think it through?

Why put myself in the place where I must redo what I have done?
Or do a thing which never should be done?

Soon after Lazarus shuffled out of the tomb, after the fragrant smell of spikenard floated past her nose, past the time she lifted up her face from the dirt, Jesus took the time to teach, and she with those around her took the time to hear, learn, and make adjustments. Together, they examined what he had done, which brought her brother back to life.

Now basking in this sunlit morning she was searching out a plan.

Focus in and find a course of action!
Mary...!
Find a way to be of some valuable assistance!
In a place where before you were none!
Select something you desire to supply.
Find the thought from which your hope will grow.
Plant a seed...
Paint a picture of a...
My Lord Jesus...
Godly imagination!

Without crawling from her bed, or throwing off her covers, Mary spoke out loud and said, "Jesus, I agree with you! I bend my will to match yours! Even though they destroy your body with their whips or on the cross and cast it in the grave, after three days your Father will surely raise it up!"

———

Mary worked the day with Esther, setting up lighting for the evening. Rows of candles were placed in every window, fully ready to be lit, plus every oil-lamp was filled and trimmed. Then, after a few hours of cleaning, they assisted Hannah in the kitchen, with delicious fixings set on a before-dinner table. Finally, they mixed up a concoction Emil requested to brush on the roasting lambs.

"You are so quiet today," stated Esther. "Where are you, Mary?"

"Sorry Esther, I've been trying to find something to be a helpful friend to Jesus... with what he has to do."

"That's very vague, Mary," observed Esther, who proceeded to present a pantomime of a person who was first locked in a jail cell, then escaped through the bars, climbed out of a window and up a rope, ran across a roof, jumped off of that roof and onto a horse and rode away.

Esther explained, "Just paint him a picture which is clearly understood by both of you... what others think is not important."

Mary walked over and scooped up the pile Esther's imaginary horse left behind and dumped it into a bucket which wasn't there.

Mary said, "I like how you think; now I only need to know what the clearly understood picture is."

"You told me about how we will soon be able to be *born of God*, and how Spirit Helper is coming to help. Just ask him for help now. I think he would want to assist you with this."

Mary stood up straight, looked to the sky, waved both her arms back and forth to get his attention and shouted, "*Spirit Helper*... ! Help, help, help! I need to know what to do! What will be a help to Jesus! With what he is going to have to face and do! And thank you... very much... in advance... for your help!"

"Esther... do you think he heard me? Did I say it loud enough? Do you think it worked?"

"I would expect so, but it looked more like something Jesus would have done... when he was four or five years old."

CHAPTER 36

From the cavernous expanse echoed a reverberating rumble which caused his entire body to tremble. It sounded like rolling rocks bouncing off each other as they fell through shifting space. Another sharp, grating sound lifted up with pronounced resonance which prolonged the agony. It was inevitable this would happen… a probability when he chose this course of action… or more accurately, his chosen lack of action. There was an immediate solution to the dilemma he now faced, but unwilling he was to take it.

Rrr…ooo..aaa..rr..oo..aaa..rr!

There it was again.

He glanced at the faces closest to him.

Hum…

They heard it too…

It will pay out…

This was my choice…

And I would do the same again!

Rrr…oart… oooaaa…tarsp!

Think about something else!

Change the thought-line of your mind and then the noise will stop!

John looked over at him and asked, "Getting a little hungry… are we now, Jesus?"

"Yes, a bit, but there are only a couple of miles to go… I can almost smell it now."

"Maybe you should have had some breakfast, or at least a little lunch?"

Jesus answered, "Let's see, Matthew's biscuits or Martha's cooking? I will wait. Maybe they got Emil to fix a roast lamb."

"I can hear you think about it," John replied, referring to the rumbling coming from Jesus' stomach.

Benjamin appeared, running towards them from over a small hill, within a minute, he was standing before the crowd of men.

"A message?"

"Two words only, *'Roast lamb'* and I am to get a head count."

"Twenty-four," answered Jesus.

"By the time I get back, you should be thirty minutes away."

"Thanks Ben, tell Simon, *'we're hungry, and see you soon.'*"

The view of Stonehouse from across the valley was an impressive sight, an elegant stone castle on a hill. Behind them and to their right were fading remnants of a celebrated sunset, in front of them, flickering light was being broadcast from every window in the house. There was a row of candles burning brightly on each windowsill, twin rows of torches up stone steps.

Six stone jars filled with water were lined up near the entry, a refreshing washing place for those arriving at the feast.

Simon and Martha were together… standing just inside the entry to greet their guests.

"Jesus, my friend, it is so good to see you! You and yours are welcome in our home."

"Thank you Simon… Martha... this is so grand… and I am grateful… also… considering your preparations… I would like to ask you, is it possible the two of you have news? It's been some time since I've seen a dinner set like this… about three years now… six stone washing jars for guests, lined up in a row. Sometimes three jars, sometimes four, but it was six jars at the wedding… although they did run out of wine."

Simon clarified, "Until you turned the dirty water into wine. We won't run out of wine here, but the six clay jars were set up at Martha's request. And to answer your question… yes… I have asked for her hand in marriage… and she answered yes!"

"Yes! This is such wonderful news!" answered Jesus as he reached out his hands to his friends.

As they placed their hands in his, he said, "This is an excellent union I forever bless, and always empower to prosper!"

"Thank you my Lord," responded Martha, with little tears of joy escaping the corners of her eyes. "Your words are priceless to me!"

Gazing into the background, Martha watched for a moment as the line of guests moved along the water jars, each washing up to the elbow. Servants were also present to wash the feet of those who so desired.

"There has been a connection between the two of you for as far back as I can remember."

Martha wondered, "And how far is that?"

"You were just learning to walk when I first met you. You were here with your father. I was about five at the time. Simon… I'm sure you remember this."

"How could I forget it? I had never seen any other children before that day, ever. And you came into my home, my cave."

"What?" Martha gasped, "I was down there before? When? Why?"

The entryway was quieter now, most of the guests had gone to find Lazarus and hear more of the story John had been telling them about. Lazarus had become famous, one man… who had first-hand conversations with Adam and Eve, Moses, David and many more. They all planned ways of getting him to talk… and then to sit and listen.

Jesus began his answer, "Joseph and my mother had taken me to Egypt, my dad had been instructed in a dream… by my personal angel… to escape to Egypt and stay there. Years later, my dad had a dream and received instructions from my same angel to bring us back to Israel. As soon as we got back to this area, he went to find the friends he trusted. That was Simon's father, Anna, and your father, Martha. They had become good friends during the year and a half we lived nearby. We came to Stonehouse first, and I think we met in the caves because it was getting hard for Anna to get up and down the ladder."

Then, looking at Simon, Jesus asked, "I'm not telling Martha something about Stonehouse I shouldn't say... am I?"

"No... not at all, I told her, and a select few, but I did wait to hear her say yes before I showed them more of Stonehouse."

"Simon and I walked you around the caves," continued Jesus, "one of us on each side, with you holding onto our fingers to keep from falling. They must have talked for a few hours... and we just kept watch over you and explored the caves. As I remember, it is a beautiful place."

"The caves are beautiful!" responded Martha, a bit bewildered. "I wondered why it looked so pleasantly familiar... Simon, you never told me. Why?"

"I did say... I've always been fond of you... and who you are to me."

Simon led the way to the veranda and comfortable chairs, the temperature was perfect, it was going to be a beautiful night. Jesus let a sigh of relief escape his lips as he relaxed into his favorite comfy chair.

Martha was beaming with brightness, but also wanted to know what came next, and asked, "So then what happened?"

"My mom liked being close to Anna, so rather than stay in the upstairs house, we stayed in the caves that night. Joseph received another dream with instructions, again from my angel, and we left that next day for Nazareth... and lived there."

Lazarus had escaped the disciple's questions for a moment to say hello to Jesus, he walked up and interrupted, "Just as I promised... no grand entrance for me this time... just my own unique happy peaceful presence." He was munching on something.

Jesus smelled what Lazarus was eating and asked, "Is Ben or Emil around?"

"I think they are both out working on the roast lamb," answered Martha. "Maybe Lazarus could take you by the before-dinner snack-table and then to where they are working?"

"That will be good Martha, thank you; we will talk later, Simon."

Two of the field-workers-turned-kitchen-helpers were just leaving with the first roast lamb as Lazarus brought Jesus to Ben and Emil. Jesus was eating fresh fruit from the table but he smelled the second roast lamb slowly turning above the coals, and his stomach rumbled again.

"The three have been kept safe," stated Jesus, referring to Lazarus and his sisters as he greeted Ben and Emil. "This is a good thing… how was your trip to town?"

"One of the Temple guards was going to split me with his sword, but Emil rescued me!"

"They left me no choice Jesus; they were intent on killing us both."

"It was only seconds… and both men were dead! Emil cut them to pieces."

Emil added, "It was Scarface with the guard."

"You have looked to my Father and me for protection," stated Jesus. "It would be wisdom for them to leave you alone."

"Their strength was gone from them… I know I wasn't there alone. Thank you, Jesus."

"It is part of what the Spirit Helper will do when you let him, David's mighty men didn't do what they did on their own, and neither did Samson. Do you have plans in place to keep all three in one undamaged piece?"

Ben was remembering words they had heard, "The Chief Priests are bent on murdering Lazarus… *and his sisters!*"

"My sisters and I will live in the caves for a couple of weeks… and Ben will stay at our place and take care of the gardens."

"That will be enough," said Jesus, and then to Ben, he added, "Don't sleep in the house, have your bedroll in the greenhouse or sleep at your house."

"Yes, sir… I will do that."

Back at the main entry, Esther approached Martha. "Pardon me, Mistress Martha, I've been trying to find Mary. I haven't seen her for hours and hours. She was going to help me with some stuff... not that I need the help... but I'm concerned about her."

"I haven't seen her for quite a while; ask your mom, she seems to be able to track everything and everyone around her kitchens."

Esther left and was back in less than a minute. "Mistress Martha, Hannah said she saw Mary walking down the road, away from the house hours ago."

"What! Find Ben and Emil! Bring them up to speed! Tell them Martha said, *'Please find that girl!'* She shouldn't be out there at all, but now it's black dark outside!"

Within five minutes Ben, Emil, and two of Simon's trained servants were moving north, tracking Mary's trail.

Ben said, "The only thing that makes sense... is that she went home for something!"

"Even so... she should have taken a bodyguard with her. After our trip to town, I don't trust anyone from the Temple. There were voices in that room I have known all my life!"

Their trip to town sat on the doorstep of Ben's thoughts, "Emil, Jesus is going to face a terrible death! Just reading some of what David wrote is more than I can imagine!"

"Every prophesy will be fulfilled... down to the most minute detail... but I have found nothing in the written word about Lazarus and the sisters being damaged. That would be just the fallen angel doing wicked things, and we can stop that, we have the right and power!"

Cresting a small hill, Emil strained his eyes, looking through the darkness.

Torches...

Maybe I should have brought torches!

No...

That would just make us easy to see...

Bad idea if we were ambushed.

Ben was anxious, edgy, and it made him think out loud, "In one place it's written, *'I will smite the shepherd and the sheep will scatter'*, but that's in sequential order, the shepherd gets struck first."

Emil remembered, "David wrote a Psalm… it goes into graphic detail… the beating… Jesus… augh!"

Emil shook his head and tightly gripped the long blade's handle he had strapped on his hip; they were more than halfway to the house of Lazarus.

"Lazarus refuses to talk about it, but I saw him once, he was curled up in a ball, just weeping in agony. I thought that he had gotten hurt or was terribly sick, but when he calmed down where he could talk, he just mumbled something about what he saw… when his body was in the grave… something about Jonah… thrashing in the stomach acid of a whale for three days… and Jesus in hell for three days."

Eight eyes scanned the darkness and they walked in silence for a ways, their ears straining to pick up some distant sound. The moon was just breaking through clouds in the night sky… bringing its reflective light with it.

About one quarter-mile in front of them… a lone figure emerged from dark shadows… cautiously moving towards them.

CHAPTER 37

It was late afternoon when Mary turned to go up fifteen beige stone steps with a cruse of lamp oil to put it away. She stopped mid-stride at the first step and gazed into her jar of oil.

"Yes! That's it!"

She snapped around, looking out the window, to search the position of the sun. Determining she had just enough time, she ran upstairs, put the jar away, and ran back downstairs and out the door.

Mary made a beeline for home… or more precisely, the greenhouse and her hidden stash of processed spikenard oil. Cruising right along, she made it there in less than twenty minutes.

From the greenhouse door, she saw Emil's sheep and goats in a nearby field. To one side was Emil's nephew, Moshav, watching Emil's flock from a small knoll.

Mary waved at the young man as she entered through the door.

Quickly, she walked into the storage room in the northeast corner and closed the door behind her. Next, she got down on her knees, brushed some dirt away, and lifted a cover board from a box buried beneath the counter. From there, she removed a full bottle of spikenard oil. Its value was more than a year's wages for the average worker.

Scrutinizing the bottle for a moment, she blew away the dust and polished it with her sleeve.

She started to replace the cover board when she felt a presence surround her. Prickly hairs stood up on the back of her neck. There was no fear, but there seemed to be a voice... or a thought.

She listened closely.

Is someone talking to me?

"Hello... is someone there?"

Nothing... no response... not heard with her ears.

Who are you? Where are you?

She glanced around, twisting back, looking over her shoulders.

I don't hear him with my ears...

But I do hear him...

I think...

Somehow...

A voice was there... maybe... someone speaking, or passing off a thought, from another room, as through a closed bedroom door.

What?

Again Mary swiveled to her right, and to her left, searching all around... no one else was there.

How are you doing that?

She hesitated, and drew the cover board back. A moment passed, and she moved to return the cover board into its correct place, but there was that presence once more, trying to get her attention. Caught in a current, Mary floated back and forth, stuck in the middle of an *Esther* pantomime.

Augh...!

Really...?

Still on her knees at her hidden stash box under the counter... she leaned forward and looked into the compartment. There were other bottles there, but her attention was drawn to her money bag, a long sleeve-like leather bag with gold and silver coins at the bottom. She reached down and picked it up. It weighed as much as a mug of tea.

The skinny leather bag was as long as her forearm and tied with a heavy leather cord with a loop, just large enough to get her hand through. She slipped her right hand through the loop and closed it around the top of the bag, letting the contents swing back and forth.

This is kind of heavy.
Why carry it back to Stonehouse?
Do I need money there?
At Simon's?

She again went to replace the cover board. This time there was no presence to stop her. She finished by brushing dirt back over her stash beneath the counter, so it looked the same as the rest of the floor.

In a hurry to return, Mary left the building, but noticed cool evening air was settling in. She set the Spikenard bottle down on a work table and went to her house to grab a coat.

From the top step at the house, she reached with her left hand to open the door. From that spot, Mary noticed the same presence she sensed in the storage room of her greenhouse.

She clicked the door latch with her thumb and the door opened, swinging to her left, her left hand still on the latch.

Evening light flowed into the room, and the setting sun was shining on her back.

Pushing the door open, Mary felt a calloused hand grab her left wrist at the same moment that she saw it emerge from the shadows. Turning her head as she screamed, Mary glared down at the hairy hand holding onto her arm!

"No! You... don't! Augh!"

A gruff laughing voice came from behind her on her other side. Looking back over her right shoulder, she saw a man peeling himself off of the wall.

"Ha... ha... ha...! Got ya!"

The two men had been hiding, in ambush, one on each side of the door.

"Not... like... this... you don't!"

Struggling against a tightening grip around her wrist, she used that restriction to push against... as she swung her right hand back... with the heavy leather pouch... at the right temple of her approaching second attacker.

"Augh... hugh... yag!"

The leather bag met the man's head with a high-speed, direct blow impact, and his eyes went blank as he totally stopped moving, hovered for a second... then crashed face first to the floor.

Thunk... donk... paugh!

The first man was pulling hard on Mary's left arm, but also realized there was resistance. He grabbed onto the arm with both hands.

"You... wiry...little... runt!"

Years of digging in the dirt and working in the greenhouse had built a bit of strength into the woman's arms.

"Hairy... ape! Augh... eat... dirt!"

Seeing the victorious results which the leather bag had on the first man, Mary swung with all her might at the left temple of the man who's hairy hands were locked around her arm. With a sickening thud, a pound of gold and silver coins struck the side of the doomed man's head. From there, his forehead bounced against the wooden door, and his hulking frame slid to the floor.

Wosh... wam! Bamm! Caugh... aassssh!

There was silence for the space of one breath and then came the sound of running footsteps on the outside path leading to the steps. Mary turned and began another backhand blow for the incoming intruder, but as the sandaled feet stepped over the door's threshold, and half an instant before the man's brain would be turned to pudding, Mary's eyes met her assailant's eyes.

"Moshav!"

Mary did her best to redirect the swinging club.

As Moshav ducked and dodged, it slammed into the open timber door.

Kasmoosh!

"Wha....!"

"Ah!"

"Wow, Mary, that was close!" exclaimed Moshav, as he began to take in the carnage in the room. "I heard you scream, are you okay?"

"Yes, I think so," she responded, feeling at the red marks on her arm, where the hairy man had grabbed her.

Moshav was scrutinizing the motionless men on the floor. "They don't look too good... who are they?"

Blood was oozing from head wounds on both men.

"It's a long story... but I really don't know who they are."

"They're both out cold," said Moshav. "My uncle Emil will be proud of you, how did you do it?"

"I don't know," said Mary, looking for a chair to sit down in, and adding, "I feel a little queasy."

Moshav was looking closer at the two men. It was getting harder to see, the sun was down, and it was almost dark.

"They are both bleeding; their hearts must still be beating."

Mary stood up, got a lamp and lit it, asking, "What are we going to do with them?"

"We'll tie their hands and feet, and I will wait right here, while you go get my Uncle Emil."

Mary handed Moshav some leather laces and they tied both men's hands and feet.

Moshav found an ironwood pickax handle and said, "If they move, I will hit them, hard in the head... with this! You get Uncle Emil back here as fast as you can!"

Mary held her hand up and looked at it in the lamplight, it was white and shaking. She jumped up, ran out the door and down the steps. She fell to her knees by the side of the house and threw up what little she had in her stomach.

Moshav heard her and grimaced... gave her a moment, and said, "I will watch them. You go find my uncle; I don't think they'll move for quite a while."

"Thank you, Moshav," replied Mary, as she retrieved her bottle of Spikenard.

She went back up the steps, retrieved her desired coat and then said to Moshav, "Be safe my friend... Emil will be here soon."

Mary had only walked a short distance, just a quarter-mile, when she heard the blade of a sword slide against the metal cap of its sheath.

"Who's there?" she shouted, preparing to run.

"Mary!" Ben answered. "Is that you?" He broke from the other three and ran to her.

She met Ben running halfway and threw her arms around him, sobbing into his shoulder.

"You're shaking! Are you okay? What happened? We went looking for you! Where have you been?"

"I...I went to get something... from the greenhouse, but then...," Mary paused.

They were all standing in a cluster around Mary now. She seemed to be lost in thought, or traumatized from her ordeal.

"He did more than warn me!" said Mary with understanding. "He prepared me, and helped me!"

"Who warned you?" asked Ben. "Who was there and helped you? I thought you were alone?"

"I went there alone, but I wasn't alone!"

"Mary," demanded Ben, "Who was there? And what did he do to help?"

"It was Spirit Helper! The one Jesus told us about! There were two men waiting, just inside the door... in the house... waiting for me there!"

"Two men?" questioned Emil. "How did you escape? Did they hurt you?"

"I hit them in the head... with this!" said the adrenalin-stoked Mary as she held up her right arm with her money bag still hanging from her wrist.

"Yes, you hit them with that bag," coaxed Emil, "And then what?"

"They... they are both unconscious... knocked out... lying on the floor. Moshav helped me tie them up."

"So... Moshav was there to help you... to take the two men down! Good! I have worked with him! I spent some time training him!" corrected Emil.

"No... Moshav heard me scream. He got there after the two men were already knocked out... and lying on the floor. He helped me tie them up... and he is waiting for you now. We didn't know what to do with them! They're bleeding all over Martha's floor!"

Emil considered Mary's words... as he stood there looking at this little girl. She was twenty-four years old, probably five foot four and a hundred and thirty pounds with winter clothes on.

This is something new, like a girl-Samson!

"Ben, you take one servant with you and get Mary back to Stonehouse. I will take the other servant with me and deal with the two men Mary sent to *nana-land*. Go figure. You did good Mary! I'm impressed!"

Emil left quickly, interested to see what he could read of what took place from the scene itself, and also from Moshav's input.

The others moved a little slower, one on each side of Mary.

As they walked, Mary leaned into Ben's shoulder, and kept a tight hold on his hand.

From the center of the soul were growing live and active gardens, before the harvest was actually needed, it was already fully grown.

CHAPTER 38

Emil and the servants assisting him had taken them both and tied their legs securely, in a spread-eagle manner with four cross poles. They would not be allowed to move or flop around.

A much larger, long wooden pole *(almost four arm-lengths long)* was then threaded between the cross poles and their bodies. Both sets were then securely fastened to that bigger pole.

Two holes were dug about hip deep; one about two feet in from each end of the big pole.

A large forked branch was solidly set in each hole with dirt packed in around its base.

Next, the large pole with both creatures fastened to it was hoisted up, and set on top of the forked branches.

Emil had taken part in, or had overseen every aspect of the preparation. They had one chance to get this right.

This should ought to work.

Mary's gonna love this... Martha too!

I hope Jesus approves...

And think that it's okay...

I hope...

Hum...

Finally, both of them were slowly turned, by servants, for a few hours... over a large bed of coals... as another servant brushed them with a rich mixture of herbs and spices. When they were both barbequed to perfection, the rams were brought into the feast.

Mary, Ben, and Simon's servant arrived back at Stonehouse shortly after the first ram had been carved up and served.

Although the house was full of people, Mary knew she would not escape Martha's *'what do think you're doing?'* look and questions.

Mary went to find her sister first; she was with Hannah in the kitchen.

Martha called out to her the instant she came round the corner, "Mary! What were you thinking? Did anything happen? It's not safe to be out there! You heard what Ben and Emil said, the things they heard... it's just not safe, Mary!"

"You're right Martha... but I am okay... I will tell you all about it later. It was something I needed to do."

Mary hesitated... evaluating... considering what she desired to tell her sister, "He was there Martha, the one Jesus talked about!"

"Tell me straight, Mary! Who was there?"

"Spirit Helper... he was there!"

Martha was measuring her sister... overwhelming contented joy was oozing from her, and she pushed to see if it was real.

"And you know this? How do you know this?"

"Peace in the middle of a storm! I was in a *'Glory Bubble'* when he was there... and I could do whatever it was I needed to do! And he got me ready... ahead of time!"

"And you're sure it was him... no doubt?"

Although both were close as equals, Martha pressed herself to appear intimidating towards her younger sibling. Elbows pointing out, both hands anchored to her hips, somehow almost towering over Mary.

"Yes, Martha, and I believe that he led me there in the first place... although... I'm not quite sure I did that part completely right."

"And the *'there'* he led you… where was that?"

"To get a bottle of spikenard oil… from our stash… at the greenhouse."

"That oil is your brother's also."

Gazing up into her sister's eyes, Mary saw concern for her, not the price of spikenard oil, "Yes, I understand. Could you find him… and Simon too? What I believe I am to do… it will involve him also."

"Now?"

Martha tried to read her sister, to get inside her head, but she couldn't tell where she was going.

I trust you Mary…

I hope to say the same an hour from now.

"Yes… right now."

"Okay Mary… I will get them… and be right back."

There were conversations interrupted, but Martha returned shortly with Simon and Lazarus. Ben saw them leave, circled around, and met them in the kitchen.

Mary looked into the face of her brother and expounded, "Lazarus, when your body died… it seemed all hope was gone… but Jesus sent us something. With his words he built for us a place to stand… he planted life-seeds in our hearts. Martha guarded and allowed those seeds to grow, so did Ben… Emil, John and Simon too."

Mary spoke directly to her sister… but to the others also, "Jesus was able to reach in through you… and pull Lazarus back to us! I could have stood there with you… but I did not."

Mary spoke matter-of-factly, face to face, there were no shifting eyes, shuffling feet, or staring at the ground.

Simon asked, "Mary… what is Spirit Helper leading you to do? Whatever it is… we will stand with you."

"Jesus has spoken of his death… and his resurrection. You Lazarus, you have told us some of what he will have to face… during his dying time, things David and others wrote about! What I am to do… is to present a picture… against death and for life! What I am to do… is to anoint his head with this oil… and then his feet, and to wipe his feet with my hair. Now, knowing what I am to do… can you still stand with me?"

"That paints a very potent picture… of death, burial and resurrection, and I'm sure Jesus will see it clearly. But Mary, when Spirit Helper leads you somewhere… go there… even if you go alone."

Simon and Lazarus went back to their guests and Ben joined them. Martha brought another food platter out from the kitchen.

Watching silently for a few moments… peeking out around the corner at the crowd of people, Mary quietly asked, "Spirit Helper… when am I to do this?"

At that moment, Esther came and stood beside her, and placing her right hand on Mary's right shoulder, she whispered in her ear. "Just paint for him a picture… which is intensely understood by both of you… what others think is not important."

Mary whispered, "But… there are so many people!"

"Don't let your emotions run away with you, you steer them with your spoken thoughts, and use your emotions for what they are for. You are only the *delivery girl*, delivering a message to one man. Jesus is the only one in the room. It is just like what Benjamin did at the Jordan. You have authority because you are under authority. Follow the lead of Spirit Helper, open your mouth and he will fill it."

Once again, she slipped inside a *Glory Bubble*, and thoughts entered *Spirit Mary* which she then sent to her mind. She first heard, *'Remember the words King David wrote.'* Next, words she had studied, and the understanding of them flowed into her mind, and with the knowing surfaced emotions which accompanied the understanding, tears were sliding down her face.

Turning to her friend, Mary said, "Thank you," and stepped out through the crowd, walking directly up to Jesus.

Breaking the bottle's seal, Mary opened it, and its fragrance escaped into the room.

Tentatively at first, she poured some of the Spikenard oil over the head of her Lord. As she did so, words rose from her heart which left her mouth as a whisper, but they were words Jesus clearly heard. *"Who hath believed our report, and to whom is the arm of the Lord revealed."*

As Mary's fingers worked the oil through Jesus's head of hair, she continually spoke in clear and level tones, whispering words emanating from her spirit self, words Spirit Helper brought to her remembrance. *"Surely he hath born our grief and carried our sorrows…"*

And on she went; somewhat surprised the words of Isaiah flowed from her mouth as smooth as the oil on her fingers. *"For the transgression of my people was he stricken…They parted my garments among them and cast lots upon my vesture."*

As more oil was added, so were segments of the Psalms of David, *"For thou will not leave my soul in hell; neither will thou allow thy Holy One to see corruption…in the midst of the great congregation I will praise thee."*

As Martha watched her sister, the odor from the oil brought before her eyes a memory of her brother, shuffling his way out of the tomb. When they were at the grave of Lazarus… she stood there… with and next to Jesus. She had filled her lungs and heart with that beautiful aroma of life. Tears of joy were streaming down her face. She knew that her Lord would rise again, defeating death, hell, and the grave, alive forever more, purchasing salvation from his Father… for whosoever will receive… just as he said he would.

Mary continued, *"In thy presence is fullness of joy…"* Except for the sound of Mary's voice to the ears of Jesus, the room… to her Lord… was absolutely silent.

"Thou art my Son; this day have I begotten thee. Ask of me and I will give thee the heathen for thine inheritance, and the uttermost parts of the earth for thy possession…"

From his head, she went to his feet and poured the remainder of the flask upon them saying, *"Thou hast ascended on high, thou hast led captivity captive: thou hast received gifts in the man…"* Then Mary began to wipe the feet of Jesus with her own hair, giving voice to the words. *"How beautiful upon the mountains are the feet of him…all the ends of the earth shall see the salvation of our God."* Then, finally, Mary rose up, and gazing into the eyes of Jesus she added, *"I will uphold those who uphold you and favor those who favor your righteous cause."*

Searching her heart, Mary concluded she had completed what was requested of her... and she left the room.

Esther followed her around the corner, down the steps, and into the wine cellar, watching her walk into the closet at the end of the room. Esther waited to close the back door of the closet until she could see light coming up from the caves below.

Mary took the candle and holder in her hand and found Anna's old room. She set the candle on Anna's nightstand and laid upon the bed, pulled up a blanket, curled up into a ball, and fell asleep.

Esther returned to the big room as Jesus was giving one of his disciples a royal dressing-down. It was directed at the one she never cared for... Judas.

"Poverty will always be with you... but you will not always be with me!"

Now is when silence settled on the room, and the house, the only sound in play was Jesus' voice, "What she has done, she has done against the day of my death! But wherever the good news is preached, this will also be spoken of as a memorial to her!"

At that moment, Judas stood to his feet and left the dinner. Some watched him from the windows... walking down a wide path... departing to his future.

CHAPTER 39

In the spirit arena, Emil's guardian angel Jasper, and the guardian of Simon's servant were enjoying a peaceful moonlit walk to the house of Lazarus. Each angel seeing to the assistance of their charge... until Malbec arrived.

Jasper questioned the reason of his presence, "Malbec...? What...? We are on schedule... what has changed?"

The other guardian glanced at the newcomer with shielded trepidation.

"My arrival? You are bothered by my arrival? Seeing my handsome face... how could my magnanimous presence cause to you concern?"

Ahead and on their right Emil's sheep looked like so many moonlit rocks on the hillside. His dog Clipper slept with one eye open among the goats, but Moshav was nowhere to be seen.

The other angel answered, "A whirlwind Malbec...! Your arrival is often from the center of a whirlwind!"

"Comrades... the very center of a whirlwind... it is a magnificently peaceful place to be!"

Jasper wondered, "Oh... I see what you're up to... you were there, weren't you! Mary... her coin purse... the 'girl Samson'? Hmm? That was you?"

"No... it was Spirit Helper's doing... working through the girl... but I was sent as a precautionary measure... and to take notes. Ah... there he *is... see him? Sitting in the shadows, peeking through their open doorway... see... it's Emil's nephew!"*

The two guardians focused on Malbec's index finger, pointing towards the house of Lazarus, and the slightest speck of moonlight reflecting from Moshav's left eye.

───────────────

"Hello, uncle, you never said anything about babysitting, what do we do with them now?"

"Have they woken up yet?"

"No, I did clean their wounds and stop the bleeding... but I couldn't find any vinegar to clean them with, so I just used soap and water."

"Humph... a job hazard of their occupation."

"They are border-line of needing stitches... Mary really smacked them good!"

"And she did this all by herself? Took out two grown men with a purse?"

"It wasn't three breaths from the time that she screamed until I was at the door... if I hadn't ducked... she would have put me in that pile too! What do we do with them now?"

Emil lit a lamp and began poking at them... checking heart rate, breathing, the cords around their hands and feet, staring at both their faces.

Do I know you?

Have I seen you before?

You look to be about thirty or thirty-five years old...

Old enough to know better!

"They probably would have killed her if they had a chance... but I think it would be wrong to cut the throats of two unconscious men."

A damp area on the floor marked the place where they had been bleeding, and where Moshav washed it up.

Next, Emil found Martha's ink and quill, and wrote a note on the front and back of both their robes.

"Moshav."

"Yes, sir."

"Fetch Lazarus' donkey cart and back it up to the steps."

Moshav returned in a minute and held the cart in place while Emil and Simon's servant drug the two men into it.

"What now, uncle?"

"We take 'em to the town square and dump them! Someone will figure out what to do with the reprobates in the morning."

Ten minutes later, they slid both men out in the center of Bethany's town square, tied them back-to-back, gave them each a block of wood for a pillow, and covered them with a horse blanket.

As they put the donkey cart away, Moshav asked, "The words you wrote on them, what did they say?"

"Something they can try to explain in the morning, '*Help Me! I was hit with a purse!*'"

"Funny uncle... do you want me to stay with the sheep again tonight? They're all bedded down... and it's a nice night."

"Yes... no reason to move them to their pens... thank you, I will be back for them by noon... and you can spend the night in the greenhouse... it's warm and dry in there!"

"That will work."

"Good night Moshav, you did good! Be safe."

It was well after midnight when Emil returned to Stonehouse.

The place was mostly quiet, for Simon's dinner guests had retired to the guest house and cozy beds prepared for them.

Candles cast their light from Hannah's kitchen, so Emil went that way, while lingering aromas from a magnificent dinner produced a rumble in his empty stomach.

Hannah and Esther were there working, in a mechanical, *pick it up and put it away* mode, and Jesus was speaking with Simon.

"It will work with you then, to use Stonehouse as our base for the next few days?"

"Yes... yes, we have plenty of room here, and I will let Hannah choose from the field servants, for the extra help she will require. Come and go as you need, there will be food and beds for you and yours, whenever you are here."

"Thank you, Simon, a home base here will help things function smoothly."

Emil began to nibble on some leftovers, but Hannah brought a plate which she had set aside for him. Choice slices of roast lamb, some figs and olives, a thick slice of bread covered with honey butter and a small block of cheese.

Delicious smells from throughout the room again triggered a rolling rumble in Emil's stomach.

"Thank you, Hannah."

Simon brought over a full wine goblet... followed by a question, "This is my favorite, I think you'll like it... you took care of the two?"

"Moshav bandaged their head wounds, although they really needed stitches, I left them tied up in the city square, and someone will find them in the morning. We even gave blocks of wood for pillows, and a horse blanket... not quite what they deserve."

Jesus looked into the face of the weathered sheep herder and said, "You have covered quite the distance Emil, thirty-three years since you saw me first... sleeping in a manger... I'm glad you didn't let your heart grow hard."

"I didn't think you could remember... although... I know you've been around... forever... not quite sure... how all this works."

Jesus smiled slightly, "My mind does not remember the moment... my mother told me of it later... and about your wife and son."

Tears slid down Emil's leathery skin as he replied, "I will see them again... someday."

"I can tell you this, my friend... your wife and son... they are among those I will bring to my Father... very soon."

There was a slight tremor in Emil's shoulders and he bit his lip before he could respond, "Thank you."

"It is to you, Emil, who I am grateful... and those like you... for you have welcomed me, and he who sent me... even in the face of the most difficult things on earth."

Emil fidgeted and changed the subject slightly, "So, what happens next?"

"Tomorrow I ride into Jerusalem on a donkey's colt."

"Hum... a declaration that you are King... and the war is over."

"The war between God and man is over... with my final payment made."

Esther had been listening closely while doing her kitchen chores, "We... all of us here at Stonehouse... we are cheering you on Jesus!"

"Thank you, Esther... Lazarus and his sisters, they have moved into the caves beneath the house?"

"Yes sir, and I will watch over them... just like Simon ordered... no one will know of them, or where they are... ever!"

———————————

From the center of the soul and moving north there is a bridge, not a door which enters in, but instead a path to land, an avenue of growing ground for to replicate, to transmit through seed or spore, chosen elements from within the spirit core... through a wall, across a cavern, through the waters, there is a way.

CHAPTER 40

Tobias sat on his knees at the edge of town.

The little boy had a stick in his hands and was watching ants go in and out of an anthill on a path to a doomed caterpillar. He pressed the point of his stick into the dusty ground and dragged it across their path, creating a cavern about two inches deep.

The ants had surrounded a caterpillar and were lowering the entire bug into the ground, by digging around and under it. The caterpillar was sinking.

Where's my mom?

The little boy's mother held Tobias within her left peripheral vision, about ten feet away.

Humph…

She's still talking at the baker's wife…

They could yack all day!

When they started talking…

Way back when this morning…

My caterpillar was minding his own business…

Crawling across the ground…

Looking for a bush to climb and leaves to eat…

Now…

Augh!

He's going to be a bug lunch!

Tobias gazed down into the ravine he created, halfway between the anthill and his caterpillar.

The ants were forced to march one by one up a ridge, down into a deep valley, climbing out of that valley and up and over another ridge to get to their caterpillar.

I suppose…

They are hungry too…

Tobias took a twig as big as his little finger and put it in place as a roadway over his boy-made obstacle. The ants started crossing the valley on his finger-sized bridge.

From the east and further out of town, a misplaced noise reached his little boy ears.

Hugh?

What's going on?

What are people cheering for?

Did we win something?

Tobias looked up to see what was going on.

Centered in the roadway, the head of a man appeared from over a crest in the hill. Tobias stood up to get a better look.

From his three-foot four-inch tall stature, he could sort of see… through a growing crowd… a man riding on a donkey.

I've seen his face before…

I think.

He squinted his eyes against reflective morning sunlight bouncing off the dusty road. He put a chubby little hand up to his red hair to block out the direct sunlight, and climbed up on a rock to get a better view.

I have seen that man before!

And I remember where!

His eyebrows went straight up, and his eyes popped wide open!

He jumped up and down and fell off his rock!

He got up, ran around, and grabbed onto his mom's robe and started jerking on it.

"Mama! Mama!" squealed the excited boy. "It's him, it's him, it's him! He's the one! I remember him, he's the one!"

His mama wasn't listening. She was too deep in conversation about what Rabbi Gershwin's oldest daughter had done.

Tobias darted out and ran for the man, his chubby little legs just pounding the ground.

The man was surrounded with children. Other people where there also, but children were running back and forth and jumping up and down.

The little red-head hid behind a fat woman's robe and was holding tight to some extra cloth by her hip with his chubby fingers.

He peaked out from around the robe.

A little girl appeared right behind him… she looked over his shoulder and exclaimed, "That man glued my daddy's leg back on! A giant rock smashed it off… but that man glued it back on!"

"My Uncle Aaron was dead!" said little red-headed Tobias to the girl, "And they were going to put him in a hole in the ground… but that man sent words to him! And made him be alive again!"

They both looked at each other… clapped their little hands together… jumped up and down… and ran out with the others.

There was another man holding onto a halter rope, leading the donkey the man was riding on, and a bunch of big people were following along behind.

Tobias stopped a moment to watch some big kids… climbing trees and cutting the big green branch leaves off… and throwing them down.

What in the world?

Other people picked the branch leaves up… and laid them down in front of the donkey.

Why?

They must think he's special too!

Some people took off their coat-robes… and laid them down on the road… right in the way of the donkey! The donkey had to step right on them!

Hum…

Maybe I should?

Hmm…

I think I would get in trouble if I did that!

He ran up next to the man on the donkey.

"I know you! You are the man who made my uncle alive again! He was dead! They were going to put him in a hole in the ground! But you made him alive again! Thank you, Mister!"

Tobias bumped into another little boy and they both fell down.

As they were getting up, Tobias said, "That man made my uncle alive again!"

"Well," said the other boy, "He fixed my nana! She was broken... so she couldn't come and visit us... but he fixed her! And she ain't broken no more! My nana loves me! She made me this robe, see!" he declared, holding his arms out, and showing off his robe.

They were skipping along next to the man on the donkey now.

"My daddy says that man's the King!" shouted another boy.

"Well... my daddy says he's the forever-King!" declared another.

"He fixed my big brother!" announced a boy with a green robe. "He was nutty in the head... and my mom said I couldn't play with him... but he ain't nutty no more! He plays with me now... and he even cleans his room!

Further into the city they went.

A girl with long braids told the boys, "Bad men made my daddy move away... to an icky place... because his skin was falling off! But that man put my daddy's skin back on! And he told my daddy to go home! Now mommy doesn't cry anymore! Cause daddy came home!"

The girl in braids ran up to the man on the donkey and said, "Thank you, Mister! For putting my daddy's skin back on! Mommy's happy now... and she makes pancakes!"

They were at the big stone gate now.

The man got up off the donkey... but he didn't stand up.

The man got down on his knees... in the dirt.

Tobias ran around some legs and got to the man... and gave him a big hug... and he said, "Thank you, Mister!"

The girl with braids was there too... she grabbed his face with both hands and kissed him on the cheek, "That's from my mom!" She kissed his other cheek. "That one is from me!"

More children ran to him for hugs.

After a time the man got up… and went inside the big stone gate.

In the garden of God, hundreds of seeds planted over thousands of years were producing fruit which was all reaching maturity at the same time; soon it would be time for harvest.

CHAPTER 41

This is the final chapter of my journey…

Jesus gazed in through the city gates and towards the Temple walls beyond.

Three years ago I entered Jerusalem through this gate…

Once I painted for them a picture of my mission…

When I transformed six jars of dirty water into wine…

Then washed my Father's Temple with a whip…

Must I clean it now again?

Father…

The shepherds of your people have not received me…

But I will follow where you lead…

And fulfill my chores along the way.

The son of God, with his twelve, entered the arena of his final destination.

From where Jesus and his twelve now stood, everything before them expressed the most magnificent of architectural craftsmanship seen in any century. At each side were massive walls constructed of bordered stone, each block often weighing in excess of forty-tons, all presenting perfect joinery of master craftsmen, the accumulative lifetime accomplishment of countless artisans, master stonemasons.

On display and one hundred yards ahead, was presented the treasure which these massive walls silently guarded, Israel's Jerusalem Temple; a masterpiece of engineering and wealth exhibited genius.

To the naked eye... everything seen presented life and present tense perfection... but this was not the Temple built by Solomon at the direction of Jesus' Father, nor was this the rebuilt Temple raised up after Solomon's Temple was destroyed.

This was the replacement of the rebuilt Temple, authored by the same Herod whom Emil had encountered... the man responsible for the murder of his son.

Herod... a descendant of Jacob's twin brother Esau...

Herod was husband to ten assorted wives, and father to more than a dozen children... of whom he murdered several of both; Herod's kingship was forced upon the nation of Israel... by the power of Rome. The consequences inflicted by his leadership, while it influenced the building of magnificent structures and impenetrable walls, it carried with it a tremendous cost in decadence.

The depravity of Herod, and his sons who now ruled after him, overflowed on those they placed... or allowed... to be in positions of authority and power.

Emil's episode with the twenty-four spring lambs was only a minor infraction when piled next to the mountain of wickedness perpetrated upon the very people the priests of God's Temple were appointed to be shepherd to.

Through extensive posturing of their outward exposure, they presented a picture of high and lofty holiness... while their spirits were dead... and their hearts corrupt beyond measure.

This was the opulent... although decadent atmosphere... Jesus and his twelve now entered into.

His twelve walked along, goggling, gawking... each step through the expansive thirty-seven acres of splendor brought more jaw dropping amazement. The complex they were scrutinizing had been under construction for forty-nine years at this point, and it would take another thirty-one years to finish it completely. Work progressed with a crew of up to 10,000 slaves, plus conscripted and paid workers, all spread across the many preparation, fabrication and construction zones.

On this day, a huge block of bordered stone was being maneuvered into place on a segment of the one-mile-wall which surrounded the entire compound. Peter and several of the others stopped to watch, as 200 men, plus animals, strained to gently slide the forty-ton stone into its resting place. It was only one of thousands cut from Mount Moriah, the giant rock which had been above and behind the Temple Mount.

Moriah was slowly being cut away, and shaped into the massive stone blocks which the walls were constructed of.

The re-manufacture of Jerusalem's Temple had been the first phase of construction. From a remote quarry, each white block of stone for the entire temple was cut, shaped, numbered, and stored, ready for assembly. This was done before the second Temple *(built following the time of the Prophet Ezekiel and after the Jew's release from Babylon)* was dismantled and replaced with the new temple. That construction phase was complete before Jesus was seen by the Prophetess called Anna.

Eventually the group came to the expansive stairway leading up to Solomon's Porch. The twelve lined up across the first step, all twelve on one step.

They spread out a bit to fill the entire space.

From there, they began in unison... to walk up the stairway... and eventually over the road below.

In some sort of a procession, they took a breath, stepped up to the next step, paused, took a breath, and stepped up to the next step... eventually reaching the top. Solomon's porch stretched out before them.

Hundreds of giant columns in four rows supported a massive timbered roof.

Peter and Andrew ran up to the first column, together, they tried to reach around it... but they couldn't quite touch each other's fingertips.

John was overwhelmed; he walked in circles as they progressed across the elevated second floor. Sauntering up to Jesus, he wrapped an arm around his shoulder and said, "Jesus, this place is huge! There has to be two or three thousand people here! Just on Solomon's Porch! And it's not even close to being crowded!"

The other eleven disciples gathered 'round, wanting to hear what their Master would say about the fantastic buildings.

Jesus was seeing things from a slightly different perspective, through the revealing eyes of Spirit Helper.

"Tell me John… why didn't King David build for my Father the first Temple?"

"Because he had blood on his hands… that's what's written… David was a man of war."

"Was he a faithful man?"

"Ah… hm… he is called a man after God's own heart?"

Can you see him John?

As a barefoot shepherd boy…

He learned to lead while guarding sheep.

Anointed to be king…

He killed giants…

He inspired the people of my Father…

To live…

To win…

And to do the thing that was right!

"John… even though it was his heart's desire, my Father told David he could not build for him a Temple; he said it would be Solomon… David's son, who built for him a Temple."

"Yes, that's true," answered John… wondering where Jesus was going.

"What about the second Temple? Was that built according to my Father's instructions?"

"The people… after they were released from being slaves in Babylon… at first they neglected rebuilding the Temple. They did their own stuff first, and it cost them. Then God, through a Prophet, told them to build the Temple first, and then the other stuff would fall in line."

They were standing in the center of Solomon's porch now; Peter studied the massive cedar logs within the roof structure. Those cedar log rafters were supported by the log columns which he and Andrew had tried to reach around. With his head tipped back, Peter slowly turned in a circle while gawking up into the roof structure.

How in the world did they put those giant logs up there?

They are huggahumga big!

And absolutely beautiful!

Jesus pulled John to the center of his question, "Close enough... so tell me, from where did this nation receive the instructions to tear down that Temple... and to build this one?"

John with trepidation answered, "The first Herod offered to do it... I guess it was... ah... his idea?"

"Tell me of your father's brother."

Curious of Jesus' questioning, and John's obvious apprehension, the eleven pulled in close to hear what was coming next.

Not wanting to meet Jesus' penetrating gaze, and shifting to his right, John answered, "I never met him... but he didn't like the eagle!... I know that much..."

Jesus pressed, "And... what eagle was that?"

This was a memory John didn't want to remember... it revealed the internal condition of many powerful people. Powerful people who said things... things which listeners wanted to believe were true, but within their heart... they knew those words were only spiced devil lies. The actions of those leaders eventually proved the corruption of the heart.

"The one that used to be over the entry... into the Temple...nobody liked it! Herod shouldn't have put it there!"

John went silent for a moment, scanning his surroundings, calculating, taking note of who was listening, concerned he would be hauled away... for speaking so... forcefully... about what the previous Herod had truly done.

"It was a giant Roman imperial seal emblem; he should have never put... that thing... over the doorway into God's Temple!"

"And what did your uncle do about it?"

"Twenty eight years ago... when Herod was dying... my uncle... along with about forty others, they went to tear the eagle down."

"And the man who offered to build this temple, how did he respond?"

It was... a thing never talked about... not out in the open... not if you wanted to live... but this... reality... was never far from John's thinking.

John answered while staring at the ground, "The Roman soldiers arrested all of them... all the men... Herod ordered they be tied to poles... in front of his palace. He had wood piled up around them... ordered the soldiers to light them up. Herod burned them all... all of them... he burned them all! All burned alive!"

"Now tell me, John... do you believe my Father would have chosen Herod... over David... or Solomon, to build for him a Temple?"

"No sir... that would be terribly out of character for him," answered John rather timidly.

Jesus started walking again, moving towards the northeast corner of Solomon's porch. He maneuvered the group so they could look over the wall and down into the Cedron Valley, parts of the wall were over thirty feet thick and one hundred feet tall. Directly across the valley they could see the Mount of Olives.

Jesus explained, "There have been more people than you can count... many of them good people... my Father's people... pouring their blood, sweat, and tears into building this place. They will not be forgotten... nor lose their reward, but the primary motivation behind the building of it... was a corrupt man building a monument to himself."

"Yes sir," answered John, considering the thousands of people who died... working with these massive stones. "I hear you."

Peter asked, "Wasn't it the third Herod who had John the baptizer arrested... and murdered, for declaring it was wrong for Herod to marry his brother's wife?"

John considered, "Yes, I think so... although it could have been the second... it gets a little confusing as to which Herod is which, when they keep naming themselves *'hero, the offspring of a hero,'* and then they make everyone around them call them a *'hero, the son of a hero.'* When I look at that man, and consider what he is like… and the things he has done, I know this, he's not my hero."

Jesus addressed his twelve, "Look around you, and watch men gather together to do the will of man! Now consider this, as soon as they finish piling these stones up, they will all be torn down, with not one stone left on top of another! And why? Because they have not known the day of their visitation, when God walked this earth as a man! Neither have they sought the will of my Father! If they looked for him, even now, they would see me, and they would see my Father!"

Peter questioned, "And what of the people this morning? They cut branches from the trees! Laid them on the ground in front of you! The children were dancing circles around you on that donkey; their parents spread their coats on the ground in your path. They were shouting, hollering… and praising you as Messiah! The Christ! They were so loud… the Pharisees got all bent out of shape! Tried to shut them up… and be quiet! Have they seen you?"

Jesus answered Peter, "What the children presented was real… for it came from the simplicity of their understanding. Most of their parents are looking, and hoping, for someone to be a King! Like David! To send Rome home… like a whipped dog… with its tail between its legs! But they don't understand the scope… or placement of my Father's Kingdom!"

"And what did you tell those Pharisees this morning?"

Jesus was looking at the massive stones cut from Mount Moriah, from behind the Temple… the mountain where Abraham set Isaac on the altar, a willing sacrifice. Mount Moriah was being broken up for the building of a wall. "I told them… if the people stopped from praising me… then these stones would immediately cry out in praise to me instead!"

From Solomon's Porch, Jesus was pulled by Spirit Helper to walk throughout the Temple complex, seeing all things through his Father's eyes. The thoughts, the intents of each heart were all laid bare. Pharisees and Sadducees, money changers and vendors, people selling doves for sacrifice, sometimes selling the same dove twenty or thirty times, some vendors were selling doves only once. Others were selling lambs, or selling the services of a lamb inspector, for those who brought their own sacrificial lambs.

They were surrounded with the sale of all things that could be sold for a price, or the sale of what could be done for a price. In all of this, everything and everyone was uncovered before the eyes of Jesus. After several hours of observation, he went back to Bethany, and Stonehouse, with the twelve.

From the center of the soul were observed countless gardens, many filled with thistles and thorns of every shape and type, but very few gardeners willing to go to God and receive from him a crop failure... and new seed to sow... why?

CHAPTER 42

Matilda was in a fowl mood and wouldn't budge, and none of those young chickens with their dainty little combs were going to get her to move either. When at last they were all out of her henhouse, she got up, drank her fill of water, and then went right back to her clutch of eggs.

She watched the last four roosters strut and scratch outside the door.

Do little...

And do nothings...

That's what you boys are.

Two of the four had outlived their usefulness.

Lazarus is gonna catch you by your feet!

You're gonna squawk your last squawk...

Rooster pot pie!

That's what I'm thinking!

Benjamin opened the feed box and removed a small scoop of food... he spread it way inside the henhouse door.

This new guy's kind of impatient...

Wasting feed like that!

Birds came running from every direction... when they were all inside, Ben closed and latched the door.

Henhouse door latched,

House door,

Green house and garden gates...
Check,
Check and check...
And now,
What time is it?
He glanced to the setting sun.
Time to go!
That's what time it is,
Simon was a bit insistant with his instructions,
'After a day in Jerusalem... I want them to feel invited... here! They need
a welcome invitation... and a friendly face!'
He said they would have it ready...
Ben hustled on to his predetermined spot and lit one candle.
Okay Ben...
Slow down...
Take a breath...
You've got your candle burning inside its protective case...
All is well...
Sit patiently...
And wait.

Sunset in the Bethany hills is always a beautiful sight, and this evening was no exception, crisp reds and prancing yellows, with fluttering waves of pink; but the ground beneath his feet began to give up its daytime gathered warmth before Jesus and the twelve reached the eighty yard marker Ben had flagged.

Benjamin took the cover off his candle and lit the first torch. Then covering his flame, he ran to the following torch and lit that one, covered his candle and ran to the next.

Three roadside torches were burning brightly by the time Jesus reached the first, where he stopped, watching as a warm and welcome hope passed over the last half mile to Stonehouse. Running through the blackness, Ben lit another torch every stone-toss of the way. The winding path to Stonehouse was now a tunnel of brightness through the dusk of night.

Simon,

Benjamin...
This is kindness...
Hannah,
Esther,
Joseph,
You are in this somewhere too...
This is beautiful...
Thank you.

Jesus shook off the turbulence which had settled on his shoulders throughout the day; shook it off and left it lying in the dirt.

From the steps of Stonehouse, Esther watched for her signal, much was ready; more would be set in motion soon.

It's black as the inside of a cow...
With his mouth a little bit open...
But that don't mean I look so well...
Benjamin,
Are you somewhere there?

A flickering spot, the reflection in a cat's eye, grew into a flickering flame on the far side of the valley floor.

"Mama! Joseph!"

Feet were washed by servants in heated water, caked-on dirt and troubled thoughts were gently massaged away. Each arriving traveler made use of their own private basin of warmed water for hands and face before they moved on to a well-stocked grazing table prepared by Hannah and her crew.

An hour later, time found Jesus and Simon seated at his veranda table.

"I looked for what should have been there Simon. Every outward sign of that place, from the splendor of the buildings, the number of priests and servants in and around the Temple, to the outward adherence of the law, all outward signs declaring there is Life and Godliness at the Temple to be picked and eaten, but there was none. We both knew what I would find, but I hoped to find at least a fig growing on some remote tree somewhere."

"He takes away the first covenant that he may establish the second. I would not expect the cupboard to be full when it is to be removed and put away."

"Your knowledge of what is written has influenced your ability to see what is to come. Are you still copying the scriptures and storing them in clay jars in caves?"

———

Simon's memory floated back to his first trip to the Dead Sea caves, accompanying his father when he was thirteen, to hide sealed scrolls in dry caves among the cliffs.

'Why father? You and the others, you have worked so hard on this! Now you put them in a place where no one will ever find them! It's such a waste of your time!'

'Simon… you are alive because we believed what was written, and hid you in a cave. Now we who are alive and living in the fulfillment of what is written, we take that same truth and hide it in a cave for those who will someday find it. Hidden for those who will receive the word of God, and our witness of his word… we give it to them… hundreds of years… possibly thousands of years from now.'

———

Simon answered, "Yes, as my fathers before me did. It's an excellent way to study, to copy the written word, word by word, getting every stroke of the pen exactly correct. There is always someone here, almost every day, copying the written word. Some of the copies sealed in jars are stored here. Others are in caves near the Dead Sea. We do sell some copies, of course, but great-grandfather was intent on hiding the written word in a way and place for it to be found many generations later. What else did you find at the Temple?"

The War Is Over | 271

"The same demons that harassed and clung to the Herod who died almost thirty years ago are hanging onto and slithering through this Herod. It's sad how ignorantly deceived people can be, they think they have some generational, or reincarnated leader; in reality, it's just that the same demons have sat on each man's shoulder, and whispered in their ears."

"Humph... no one gets a second walk around the world... I am looking forward to when you can put your laws into the minds of your people, and write them into their spirits. They will be more resistant to the deceptions from Satan's kingdom packaged in the words of men."

"Hmm... yes... and know this Simon, the assortment of laws which will be deposited into them, or have access to through Spirit Helper, those laws cover the distance of my Father's kingdom, much more than 'thou shalt' or 'thou shalt not.' If you look close, you would find some laws cause wheels to turn, others allow birds to fly, or by working a mixture of laws you could pull lightning from the sky and put it in a bottle."

Lightning in a bottle?

Then who would want a candle?

But I would like to fly!

"Laws that allow birds to fly? I want to fly! I have always wanted to fly! If I could understand the laws that cause a bird to fly... then maybe I could build a set of wings... and sail off the cliff behind the house! That would be my idea of fun, way beyond riding a fast horse! To fly like a bird, this is something I want to do!"

"Maybe you should have Martha save you all of her chicken feathers... and you could glue them into that set of wings."

"No thank you! I'm going to get feathers from something that flies a whole lot better than one of Martha's chickens! Besides, flying has to be something more than just the feathers! It has to have something to do with the shape of the wing and the ratio between the size of the wing to the weight of the body. Just look at an eagle wing and body compared to a chicken wing and body! You wouldn't even want to eat an eagle, they're tough and stringy, and there's more meat on one of Martha's chickens then on an entire adult eagle!"

Jesus lamented, "Not a chicken suit? Hannah and Esther could stitch you up an eagle suit, how about that?"

"You think I'm kidding? You brought this up you know! And now you want to smooth it over just because I would like to fly like a bird, by using one law to overcome another law."

"Hold on now Simon, what do you mean to use one law of my Father against another of his laws?"

"But that's what you are doing here," rebutted Simon. "The Law of the Spirit of Life you bring, it overcomes the Law of Sin and Death! That's how you got Lazarus out of the grave!"

Jesus chuckled, "Good, Simon, very good, to see you get your feathers ruffled over the word of my Father, very good."

"You toy with me! Martha said you did the same to her... just before you called Lazarus out of the grave! Now you give me a peek at a treasure and then you pull it away... that's not nice!"

"I know you Simon, I pull it back only for you to want to take a closer look, and what do you see? The Law of the Spirit of Life I bring will make you free from the Law of Sin and Death! Faith growing in the hearts of his people, that is the most beautiful thing my Father sees!"

"So, someday, maybe I will fly like a bird?"

"Here or there," answered Jesus picking up his last piece of honey bread, "I am sure that someday we will fly side by side. More than that, I will spend forever showing you treasures in my Father's Kingdom, and the treasures are far beyond what you can think or imagine."

The two men talked on until their table candles were only little stubs. Laughing, telling stories, dreaming about doing stuff together, building flying wings made with colored feathers.

Eventually, they both sat quietly for a bit, stalling for time, all too aware of what the immediate future held.

"Simon..."

"Hum..."

"The whip I made, is it still hanging in your tack room?"

"Yes... no one has touched it... not since I put it there three years ago."

"Good... I will take it with me in the morning."

From the center of the soul a plague of horrors threatened to spill outside its borders, chickweed, thistle, and thorn seeds from unkempt plots threatened to spread contamination throughout good ground of many hearts. Light the torch, take it to the thorns and thistles and burn them to the ground.

CHAPTER 43

In the spirit arena, Jesus' personal guardian, Uriah, was dealing with Malbec's preparations as the troop approached Jerusalem.

"Malbec."

"Sir?"

"Rehearse for me, stipulations required to be met prior to an angel's... ah, interference with a human action."

"Do you mean the duly granted authorization permitting me to cut a human in half, from the top of his head to his... his miscellaneous parts?"

"If you are referring to the same request and granting sequence for stepping through the waters and cutting off a finger... then, yes."

"Sir, no authorization is ever required to reduce any demon into a discomfited pile of sizzling entrails in the dirt. Dispatching demons from planet earth is part of any angel's standing orders."

Malbec, you are avoiding the question...

"Malbec... you just can't directly damage a human in the process, the demon must be pushed away from, or released by their human host... first!"

"Humph... at least a little bit away, yes, of course... authorized deliverance through the host's inferred request. Three years ago Jesus maneuvered me space to... um, do my chores, in this place where we are going... the Jerusalem Temple, I expect him to do the same... today... soon."

Early morning dew kept the dust down on their walk to town, and Jesus was hungry, he had skipped breakfast, again.

Together, thirteen men approached the city's massive outer walls, while in the distance Jerusalem's Temple came into view through the open gates.

Close to where they were walking, Jesus observed an item slightly out of place, pre-season leaves on a lone fig tree. Although they were past the time of any freezing weather, winter was not quite gone and summer had not yet arrived.

Fig tree, why do you have leaves?
What are you telling me?
That you have fruit?
Huh...?
Fig tree...?
You never have leaves until your first fruits are ripe...
And I am rather hungry...
What do you have for me?

Veering right, he dropped slightly down, leaving the gravel road and then up an embankment, his mouth salivating by the time he reached the tree.

John called out from the others waiting at the road, "Hannah's breakfast was better than anything you'll find on that tree!"

Reaching the fig tree with his back towards the twelve, he gave John no answer, but rather began looking for his breakfast, hiding behind the leaves.

Where are you?

John continued on, "Biscuits and chicken gravy, toasted bread with honey butter, or just toast with butter and a little jam!"

Jesus' stomach rumbled his response while he worked his way around the empty tree.

This is so wrong...
Telling people you have figs...
When in fact you have none!

"Hot herb tea, and some of those *'egg in a hole'* things you like to make, Martha must have taught her how to do it, they were almost as good as yours!"

The eyes of all twelve were focused on their teacher now, searching out an empty tree. He was on the far side and facing them, moving back and looking up higher in the tree.

Anything?

Not one fig?

Somewhat dejected, Jesus let his gaze slowly fall, scanning through the leaves and branches one last time.

Nothing!

Augh!

Standing twenty feet before him was the barren tree; his twelve were slightly lower to his left. Directly in line with the tree trunk and through the city gates was the Temple, majestically displayed in the distance.

There's no food in you either!

Not anymore.

Jesus raised his right hand and pointed at the tree, and the Temple, "No man eat fruit from you, from hereafter and forever!"

The twelve fell back several steps, stumbling, almost to the ground.

Struggling, and first to recover, John caught his balance. Firmly planting both his feet he vigorously shook his right hand up and down, laughing, with animated surprise displayed on his face, "Wow! Kind of close there Jesus, watch where you point that thing! I'm glad you didn't burn a hole through me with your eyes! I thought you might have smoked me for a minute there, but I do pity that poor fig tree!"

You're not the problem John...

It's the perverted philosophies of men.

No one standing there saw a thing, they were just looking at a tree, but Jesus watched as the presence of his Father prepared to leave that Temple made of stone.

The old Temple order was now in flux, the transition was in motion. The old covenant had brought him to this place, but the new covenant would be cut in him.

Continuing their walk to the Temple with the steady stream of people arriving for the coming seven days of Passover, John moved over to walk next to Jesus.

"I have the food bag today," John said, lifting the cover off his shoulder bag, "Hannah and Esther packed it for us last night."

Jesus looked inside; there were small cloth-wrapped bundles, red ones and tan.

"The tan-colored ones are bread and goat cheese, the small red ones are dried fruit, dates with raisins, apple chips, and roasted nuts; a very tasty mixture."

Jesus' right hand reached into the bag and took out a folded red bundle, "Thank you."

"Esther asked that we would return the cloth napkins if we could."

"Yes, of course," said Jesus as he removed the tie-string around it and unfolded the bundle, holding it in his left hand. He tried a dried apple chip, it was creamy white with no peal and as light as goose down, it snapped when he bit it.

"Umm… that's good, who makes them?"

"Esther said Hannah does the dried fruit, the apples and pears are her specialty. I understand she uses several different kinds of apples, some with the skin on and some peeled. I like the chewy ones with the bright green peel; they have a bit of a twang to them."

The raisins had a dusting of saltiness added to them; Jesus picked out several of those and ate them, licking his fingers. Next he chose an apple chip with a bright green peel, placed it on the center of his tongue, and closed his mouth. Slowly, his cheeks sort of sucked in and he closed his eyes. He shifted the apple bite around in his mouth and chomped down on it. He shook his head like a wet dog, but continued chewing the chip until he swallowed and opened his eyes.

"Good, huh? That will wake your mouth up!"

Jesus reached into the food pack and pulled out two more of the red wrapped bundles. "Wow… they do have a bit of zip in them, don't they," he stated as he deposited one in each of his two outer robe pockets.

John watched the trail-mix bundles disappear into Jesus' pockets and noticed the odd braided leather belt double-wrapped around his inner robe. He had seen that braided leather before.

Today they entered the court of the gentiles through a ground-level gate and emerged into a throng of people.

"Master," said John, "there must be twenty-five or thirty thousand people here today, and it's still early in the morning!"

They made their way through the sea of people moving towards the Temple gate. Looking up above the massive doorway, John could make out the broken anchor holes where Herod's Roman eagle had been mounted. The eagle was gone, but the scars remained.

Off to the right side of the stone entry was Emil. There were two men near him with bandages around their heads. One bandage covered a left ear and eye; the other covered a right ear and eye. The bandages were days old and dirty. The men were listening as Emil spoke to them.

Following Jesus, John and the others moved towards Emil.

John noticed red puffiness protruding from under the bandages, and there was a green tint soaking through each bottom edge of the dirty cloth. In an involuntary motion, John covered his nose with his sleeve, protecting himself from the eye watering stench emanating from the men.

As Jesus drew close, both would-be assassins painfully lowered themselves to their knees before him.

They spoke together, "Master, please forgive us for the wickedness that we meant to do to Mary, Martha, and Lazarus, we were so very wrong."

Placing a hand on each head and reading fevers of well over 100 degrees, Jesus answered, saying, "Yes, I forgive you, sin no more."

"When you see that little scrapper of a girl, please tell her… them… that we will do what we can to protect them."

The other added hesitantly, "Not that they need any help… she did just fine on her own."

Jesus was grinning with one eyebrow raised as he answered, "She wasn't alone… but you will look at them with your own eyes… and hear with your own ears... their forgiveness to you, as you tell them of your faithfulness which is now set towards them."

Both men were still on their knees, Jesus' hands on their heads, each looking up through one good eye, green puss oozing out of swollen, infected wounds, both covered with the stink of certain death, flies buzzed around their heads.

"Yes sir," they answered.

In that instant of forgiveness and repentance, both men pulled on the life resident in Jesus to flow into them.

His goodness came like cool honey on their heads, not just covering, but flowing in, as if each man were a giant sponge and the life of God saturated each cell of their bodies.

With a visible line starting at the top of each head and flowing down, each body hair stood straight out, hovered, and then lay flat as the power of God flowed through them, purifying every particle of their physical selves.

As that line of his purifying presence passed down from their ankles to the bottoms of their feet, both men shivered violently, for a fraction of a second, as if an icy backdraft wind burst across sweaty damp skin.

Jesus peeled the crusty green bandages off of their heads, and even though the stink of infection stayed with the bandages in his hands, the skin beneath was totally mended, only gentle scars remained as a memory of their encounter with a woman's purse.

In the spirit arena, Malbec was cleaning his sword to a background sound akin to bacon sizzling in a pan.

"Get ready Uriah, he's about to kick in the door."

CHAPTER 44

Baa...

Baa... baa... baa...

Baa...

Emil turned at the bleating sound of sheep.

Jannes...

Jambres...

Not again!

Jesus' eyes followed Emil's gaze, six men were attempting to herd a few dozen sacrifice lambs through the crowd to their holding pens in the court of the gentiles.

Those boys didn't learn a thing!

Jesus' hand went to the whip handle tied around his waist.

Father...

How do you want me to start this...

The washing of your Temple?

In the spirit arena, Uriah shouted to Malbec, "Take point! I've got right flank! Jasper! Left flank, Phalanx! Rear guard!"

Jasper asked, "Captain, what about our humans, Emil and John?"

Uriah called to Peter's guardian, "Ulysses! Stay outside and watch over those two till we get back!"

"Sir, yes sir!"

———————————————

As the four angels took position around their charge, the crowd parted before him.

Through the leading of his Father in the spirit arena, Jesus positioned himself for the task ahead. Through his Father's eyes he *saw individual spirit creatures and their operations*, those accessing the human arena through a natural thing or person. He watched himself *perform a procedure* in the natural, which in turn *affected both the spirit author and natural enabler...* before he actually said or did the chore.

Lifting his gaze to a place above the Temple gateway, Jesus focused on the spot where Herod's Roman eagle had been mounted. Looking like oily feathered black vultures, a cluster of leering demons clung to the Temple wall by way of those ancient splintered anchor holes.

In the spirit, Jesus saw himself take off his outer robe and hand it to John.

Removing his outer robe, Jesus handed it to John, "Hold this for me, and wait out here with Peter and Emil for ten minutes before you come inside."

In the spirit, he saw the nearest demons run for cover as he walked towards the Temple door, he saw four angels accompanying him, and his spirit self broadcasting brilliant light.

Jesus stepped towards the Temple door. Several people moved out of his way.

In the spirit, he saw himself uncoil the whip from around his waist and it became a lightning bolt in his hand.

He removed the whip from his waist, held onto the handle and let the coils fall to the ground.

In the spirit, he saw himself approach the Temple gate, one of the vulture-like demons above the door flapped up to escape. He saw himself draw back with his whip and crack it across the bulkiest part of the vulture's body.

Sparks flew in all directions as the demon was blasted from the sky; it fell to the ground in a tangled mass of feathers and flesh.

Those standing close to Jesus stepped away, as he drew back with his whip and cracked it into the empty sky above them. People from two hundred yards away turned to the sound of lightning striking its target.

In a blur of motion, Malbec's flashing sword turned the remaining cluster of vulture demons into a discomfited mess, feet, hands, legs and torsos thudded to the ground, and then sizzled up in smoke.

In the spirit, Jesus saw himself step over the chunks and feathers at his feet and enter the Temple, a path cleared before him.

Jesus walked into the Temple.

In the spirit he saw, just inside of the Temple and hulking at a table, an obese demon, sitting with an unjust set of scales. The table was covered with pinkish, pig-like flabby demons drooling on the gold and silver coins piled up before them. He watched himself throw the table against the closest wall. Demons scattered in all directions as he cut them to shreds with lightning flashing from his hand.

Just inside the Temple walls sat a moneychanger at his table. Jesus took hold of the table corner and threw it up against the wall. Tracking unseen targets, he cracked his whip in several directions.

Gold and silver coins bounced across the floor.

Falling to the floor and rising furious, the money changer, coming in from behind, lunged at Jesus with a dagger blade.

Spinning to his right with his whip hand rising, Jesus' backhand up-cut blow caught the money changer beneath his chin, with the heel of his fisted whip hand. His second and third strikes were with the last foot of his whip.

Uriah's downward stroke slashed the demon's incoming spear point from its main beam shaft, the chunk of metal tinkled to the cobbles.

As Uriah's blade came back up, his second strike cut off the demon's head, it bounced across the floor while the headless corpse collapsed. Twenty feet apart, the miscellaneous parts immediately began to bubble up in stinky smoke.

His demon momentarily gone, the scared and bleeding money changer ran from the temple. His assistant, crawling on all fours, was gathering up the scattered money when his robe pocket snagged, and inadvertently tripped a lever latch releasing a pen of lambs.

Frightened, and caught up in the surrounding frenzy, one lamb burst through the gate and all the others followed. The stampeding herd of little woolen creatures made a sweeping arc through the Temple, upsetting several vendor stands and sending people with their trinkets crashing to the cobbled floor.

Jannes and Jambres dashed after their fleeing herd of sheep, shouting as they ran. Petrified, the bleating lambs scattered in every possible direction.

Addressing the intruders in his Father's Temple, Jesus roared, "It is written, my house shall be called a house of prayer for all people! But you have turned it into a den of thieves! Get your vendor stalls and these animals out of here!"

Jannes and Jambres caught two lambs each and held them by their back legs, their front feet pawing the ground, trying to get away. The two men drug them back to their pen, their furry little lamb heads bouncing on the cobbles as they slid along.

In the spirit, Jesus saw himself persuade the men to release the sheep and leave the Temple.

Leaning over the sheep fence, the two had the lambs by their fur and were about to drop them down inside the fence, their robe material stretched tight over their hinder parts.

Two powerfully driven blows convinced the men to release the lambs and run screaming for the door.

Now...

See who will stitch that up for you...

"I said out! Take the animals out of here!"

The Temple guards, trained to respond to the higher authority, had been unresponsive up until this point. At Jesus' command they each picked up an assortment of animals and left the building.

Several Passover pilgrims remained to watch as Jesus continued moving through the Temple, cracking his whip at tables and walls and sometimes just snapping it into the air. Sometimes he hit a lingering merchant making his way for the door.

A crowd was gathering outside of the Temple gate, but they were staying a safe distance from the doors.

The watchers were faced with a tremendous contradiction of terms. What they saw first were Priests and vendors running from the Temple, many were bloodied and limping, and next came guards carrying lambs and doves.

What they heard was something totally different.

There was screeching and howling, from the fighting and dying of creatures, mixed with the sound of thunder and lightning in the sky above. The crowd of people covered their ears... protecting themselves from the horrible noise... while they looked around at clear blue sky... searching for the source of the screaming, smashing and crashing.

They didn't understand.

What their eyes saw were people fleeing a building, but what they heard was all of hell breaking loose and being cut down.

They kept their distance.

After a time, they were all wrapped in silence.

Following such tumultuous noise, the silence was deafening.

No one moved.

Finally, two men stepped out into the empty space in front of the Temple doors. They were the would-be assassins Jesus had just healed, the same ones who had been sent to kill Mary, Martha, and Lazarus.

One of the two turned to address the watchers... he said, "People of Israel! We were dying from the wounds we received as a result of our wickedness... but the God-man... Jesus... he forgave us our sins... and healed us of our wounds!"

There was movement among the crowd. It was those who were damaged or wounded, sick, or blind. They were making their way to the leading edge of the crowd and Temple gate.

The speaker again addressed the people of Israel who were moving forward. "I believe... this same Jesus who forgave and healed us... he will also heal and forgive you!"

The two men turned and entered the Temple; they were immediately followed by people with needs. The dinner bell was ringing and they refused to be late.

Jesus was standing in an almost empty House of Prayer.

Only a handful of faithful pilgrims had remained inside, they felt somehow safe, as if they had been rescued from an unseen enemy. He wrapped the whip around his waist once more as a belt, but still saw all things through his Father's eyes.

The two repentant men whom he had healed entered the Temple.

Close behind them came the hopeful... people who believed their freedom had arrived. They sensed deliverance from gnarled arthritic hands, paralyzed legs, disease and demonic torment.

They each came praising God that Jesus the healer had come to town.

Jesus saw them coming.

Yes!

This is going to be fun!

In the spirit arena Uriah shouted to his unit, "Ready yourselves comrades! Here comes the second wave! At all cost... guard the people! Cut them loose from every enemy! Make full use of each opportunity which they and Jesus give you! And if a demon steps across the line... send him straight to hell!"

Jesus moved into the approaching crowd of people, stripping each one of satanic cargo... sickness, disease, fear... plus every demon's poison plant which had afflicted.

To the people who were missing parts or pieces... physically damaged, Jesus restored them all. He passed out arms and legs like a waiter serving guests at a table.

To a hunched over old woman, he asked, "And you, mum, what will you have?"

The old woman answered, "Peaceful movement with perfect posture and pleasant sleep, my Lord."

"So be it," answered Jesus as he gently placed his right hand on her shoulder and directed the life in him to flow into her.

The same brightness of life that filled Jesus surged into her... and she received total healing with perfect posture and peaceful movement. She began to dance around the room.

Many of the healed ran out of the Temple to find their friends who were sick, broken, or damaged. This was the time of Passover when the size of the city grew by more than half a million people. Pilgrims from all over the nation of Israel and beyond were gathered in Jerusalem for this celebration of deliverance from bondage and for worship of their God. Now, with the health, healing, and restoration that Jesus was passing out to them, they had present reason to celebrate. Those people entered the Temple by the hundreds... and Jesus healed them all.

To a blind boy of twelve, Jesus said, *"Look at me with both of your eyes!"* and the boy looked up to Jesus.

To the woman who had only one leg, he said, *"Stand upright on your own two feet!"* and she stood up and went to skipping around the courtyard.

So went the entire morning and early afternoon, all those receptive to his healing touch or words of life were healed and restored to life.

In between the waves of life and godliness in motion towards the receptive, and the flow of people into the Temple, Jesus would switch to teaching them, or telling them stories. When more sick or damaged people would come forward, he healed them all. When Pharisees or Chief Priests would try to stop him... or try to stop the people from receiving... Jesus simply confronted their twisted hearts... telling a story all the people understood, firmly placing a cork into the mouth of the wicked.

This was the day of, *"Grand Finale,"* and he was finishing his race in absolute victory.

From the center of the soul, Jesus delivered from the garden of God, and there was plenty to go around.

CHAPTER 45

Simon sat in the midst of memories as he watched the first torch be lit by Benjamin. In his lifetime, he had transcribed the entire old covenant three times. Psalms and Proverbs he had copied several more times. Now pictures painted by the words he copied paraded before his eyes.

Born in Bethlehem...

Called out of Egypt...

Survived the slaughter of the innocents...

There must be hundreds of prophesies which surround and identify our messiah...

Fifty, I'm sure I could list at least fifty that have already been fulfilled...

My own skin speaks volumes of who Jesus is...

I was dying of leprosy...

Not a good way to go...

He even gave me new fingers...

How nice...

And then there's Lazarus...

Four days dead...

Think about that.

It was into the midst of Simon's memories which Jesus entered as he joined him at his veranda table.

As Jesus settled into his chair, Simon's thoughts came into clear view and proper order. Next, God's Holy Spirit covered Simon like a blanket, and inspired him to speak words from the Psalms of David to his Lord.

Simon said, *'Thy throne, O God is for ever and ever: a scepter of righteousness is the scepter of thy kingdom. You have loved righteousness, and hated iniquity; therefore God, thy God, has anointed you with the oil of gladness above thy fellows. And, you, Lord, in the beginning have laid the foundation of the earth; and the heavens are the work of your hands: They shall perish; but you remain; and they shall all wax old as does a garment; And as a coat you shall fold them up, and they shall be changed: but you are the same, and your years shall not fail.'*

"Yes, amen, I receive that, thank you, Simon."

"It was as if Spirit Helper pointed his finger at me and said, *'Say this.'*"

"That is the way he is, and then it was up to you to say what he set before you. That was your choice, to respond to his leadership, or to let it slide."

"How will I hear from him after you finish your chores? What will change?" Simon asked.

"You understand you are a spirit, you have a mind, and you live in your earth suit?"

"Yes, talking with Lazarus about his four day adventure has helped clarify the differences between spirit, mind, and body."

"When you are born of my Father... your mind and body... they will not immediately change, it will be *spirit you* which will be born of God."

"True... but the life of God in me should shine out through me."

"Very good, Simon, I like the way you think. So how do you believe Spirit Helper will communicate with you then?"

"To deal with me through my body would be the lowest form of communication; I think many things would have to be out of place in my life... for him to have to resort to the lowest level to deal with me."

"So far, so good," answered Jesus, studying the food sitting before him and picking up some grapes. "Keep going."

"To talk to me through physical words would be nice, but the enemy could easily counterfeit that with just a voice. Also, it would be of minimal strength. I believe Spirit Helper will prefer to deal with me through my *spirit self* that has been born of God, the place where he will live."

Simon's last statement caught Jesus' attention, "What do you mean the place where he will live? Where did you get that thought?"

"For thousands of years the presence of God has dwelt within a Temple made with hands, the Holy of Holies within the innermost part of the Temple. I believe that is a picture of what is to come, the Spirit of God, Spirit Helper dwelling within each one of the sons and daughters of Almighty God. In other words, the Spirit of God, dwelling in the perfect and complete *spirit me...* through the new birth."

"You do go right out to the edge of the cliff and stand there... with your face to the wind."

"What fun is it to do something I can do on my own? I would much rather do something with you... something I can't do without you. If you taught me how to build a set of wings to fly with... then I would listen to your words, and I would build the wings according to your words. With your words to hold me up, I would step off of that windblown cliff and fly."

"Hm..."

"We, Mary, Martha, Lazarus, and I, know who you are, Jesus! The Christ! The Messiah, the Son of the Living God! There are hundreds of prophecies in the written word about you! The word of God become flesh! Well over one hundred of those prophecies have already been fulfilled! Within the next few days hundreds more will be fulfilled, and many of those are too hard to look at... I can only say that we add our faith to yours... for what you must face and do."

"That, my friend, is worth much to me, thank you,"

Then he added, changing the subject, "The three siblings, they are safe, yes?"

"Yes... Esther has been having the time of her life... running between the house and cave, catering to their every whim!"

"Good, very good... but be aware, I expect that hard rock cave will be a very dark place in a few days."

"What do you mean? How will it be dark?"

"Not to worry... those three made to me a promise... to walk with me where I'm going... and even though I will be miles away, Spirit Helper will give to them some picture... to see a thing the eyes of man cannot see... and he will also present some way for them to help me."

"Okay... ah... yes... no worries... hmm... tomorrow is the preparation day of Passover, what will you do? Would you like us to prepare a dinner for you... and your disciples, here? We are well able and it would be an honor to arrange a dinner for you."

"Thank you Simon, but they are completing a part of their journey as my disciples... we will have an appropriate meal in Jerusalem tomorrow. Afterwards they will prepare for Passover."

"Yes... I suppose that would be correct. But the Passover meal when the lamb is eaten, you won't be there for that, will you? You will be lifted up by then."

"You speak the truth... but you can do that because you are a student of the word."

And then there was a silence that hung in the air.

Finally, Jesus removed it by saying, "You asked me what would change... with the way Spirit Helper communicates with you."

"Yes... and?"

"You must now associate with my Father and me according to the new covenant which I am cutting... no longer according to the old. You can learn from the old covenant, but don't eat from it anymore... your life is in the new."

"Hum..."

"First, I will show you an example of what you can do with what you have now... pour what you have in your cup into my cup."

"Okay," said Simon, and he picked up his own cup and emptied its contents into Jesus' cup. It added to it, but it did not fill it.

"What you have done is to give me what you have. When you are born of my Father, you will have the ability to receive the fullness of Spirit Helper. If you receive his fullness… and learn how to direct the life of God in *spirit you,* towards me or someone else or just towards your regular chores for that matter, you will be able to pour out of your *spirit self* an unending flow that will never run dry. Out of your *spirit self* will flow rivers of living water. Look forward to that. When you and those around you… learn how to add your rivers together, it will be an unstoppable flood of life and godliness. Do that in one accord and you will take the gospel into all your world… you will deliver the good news to every creature… you will cover the earth with life and godliness!"

Simon remembered, "It was written by Moses, that God swore an oath saying, *'As surely as I live, the whole earth will be filled with my Glory'.* Is there a connection between the fullness of the Spirit and the earth being filled with the Glory of God?"

"If the born of God people take their place and do their part… and if they make correct use of what I am getting for them, they will bear much good fruit! The sons and daughters of God bearing good fruit is what brings my Father glory! Not only is there a connection Simon, but that is how it will happen."

From the center of the soul, before the seed ever sprouted, before there was any visual evidence of something growing, its roots had penetrated the earth; they became an anchor to the plant and had established a food and water supply.

CHAPTER 46

Sunrise arrived with no dew on the grass.

Dry evening air did not transition, no moisture had arrived, and the road between Bethany and Jerusalem was just as dusty as it was the night before.

Morning light was shining on their backs as Jesus and his disciples approached Jerusalem. Twenty-six flapping feet created a small cloud as John left the road to inspect Jerusalem's fig tree which Jesus had cursed the day before.

Sunshine's horizontal beams of brightness only intensified the tree's condition. Green leaves had transformed to a crackly, crispy brown; every pretense of life exhibited by the tree had drained completely down and out.

Leaving Bethany road to follow John, eleven others approached in amazement the withered fig tree. Plucking a leaf from its branches, John held it in his hands. Studying it closely, he closed his fingers around the leaf and squeezed… listening to it crackle and crunch. Opening his hand, dozens of fragments fluttered to the ground.

"Jesus! What did you do to this fig tree?"

Jesus circled around the tree to face its deadness, with the Temple again in the background. "Have the faith of God… and you will not only do what I have done to this fig tree, but if you say unto this mountain, be removed and cast into the sea… and shall not doubt in your heart… but shall believe that whatever you say shall come to pass, you shall have whatever you say."

Whacking his hands together to knock off every last bit of brown leaf fragment, John asked, "And how can we get this, faith of God, where does it come from?"

"When you are born of my Father, the faith of God will be in you, not in your body of flesh, not in your mind, but in *spirit you* that has been born of my Father. It will then be your responsibility to let that faith flow out of you and change your mind, your body, and the world around you. You speak to the storm and demand it to stop! You speak to the mountain and cast it into the sea! You speak to the disease and command it to die! You speak to the missing leg and tell it to be!"

John cringed, looking at his hands, and then at the faces of those around him. "We are to do that? Who are we?"

"It's not who you are, it's whose you are! It's not what you are, it's what you carry! You will be sons and daughters of my Father! You will carry his nature and character in you! You take the gospel into all your world!"

"And how do we know what to change?" asked John.

"When you and the others asked that I teach you how to talk to my Father, what did I tell you?"

"You identified that we will call him our Father, and to call for his will to be done on this earth as it is in heaven."

"You must know what his will is; you must know him to know his will. Next, do your part in changing what is not his will! He wills that all be saved and come into the knowledge of the truth… all people, all knowledge, and all truth! He wills that you prosper and be in health, even as your soul prospers! Make disciples of all people… not subordinates or dependents… disciples! This new birth makes all men equal! One!"

"Who is Israel, but he who is born of my Father and does the will of my Father!" Jesus said as he turned away from the fig tree.

Overwhelmed with what he could not do, and a weight he could not carry, John remembered how Peter looked… when he stepped out of the boat… into the middle of a massive storm… when he walked on the water… for a little while. Only a moment later they all watched as

Peter began to sink... slowly... as his fisherman's knowledge worked against him...slowly sinking... in water up to his armpits, somewhere above the lake bottom twenty fathoms below.

John understood the same wide-eyed desperation which Peter expressed, yelling "Jesus, save me!" as his feet desperately tried to find foothold substance, with windblown waves crashing into his face, sinking into the raging sea.

John blurted out the words, "Jesus, we can't do on our own what you want us to do! You are leaving too soon! We can't do this without you!"

"Apart from me, you can do nothing. Don't be apart from me."

Paradox, thought John, *sure, walking on water is easy, just don't get wet.*

"Yes sir, that's exactly what I was thinking."

John pushed against his memory of Peter flailing around in white capped water, of wind-whipped waves twice the height of a tall man. It was the picture of Jesus he wanted to see, one dead calm spot of water around the man that neither rose nor fell. When the boat dropped into the gullet of a wave, walls of water had blocked their view of Jesus, but when they rode up on the crest of a wave they looked down to see Jesus take the hand of Peter.

Amazed, they watched Peter rise up and stand in that same calm spot with Jesus.

Next, with a boatload of disciples bobbing around like a cork in a hurricane, Jesus rebuked the wind and gave peace to the sea.

The wind stopped, the sea went flat, and a perfectly dry Jesus helped a soaking wet Peter over and they climbed into a sodden boat with eleven men that had the appearance of drowned rats.

It was when Jesus climbed into the boat with his disciples, and the several hundred gallons of water sloshing around in the bottom of the boat, that his feet had finally gotten wet.

From the center of the soul, in the garden growing there, all that the good gardener ever did was to manage the conditions, and give the seed a protected space to grow. The harvest is in the seed.

CHAPTER 47

Tiny toes, like little fingers, gripped the greenhouse wall, inside, and just above the door.

The little creature posted himself at the primary bottleneck for every bug that tried to find a way inside. Its silky green, tree-frog skin had somehow transformed to a mottled gray... to match the weathered wood to which it clung.

Ben's first stop was the same as every other day, the chicken coop door... and he had learned to stay clear of the fliers with their flapping wings.

There was no more picking eggs. Every hen that wanted to hatch a clutch of eggs would be allowed to set; Matilda was just first in line.

Ben tied the door back and got a full scoop of feed to spread for the bird's breakfast and then went in to look at Matilda's brooding face.

She must eat sometime...

But I have never seen her leave her nest.

Matilda tipped her yellow beak back and forth, and eyeballed the nose and eyes which intruded inside her space.

A peck on the nose would send this newcomer packing...

Might not be the best idea...

But I'd like to do it just the same!

Bug off you featherless creature!

You're breathing on me!

Working through his morning rounds, the greenhouse was next in line, and so was mixing up another batch of Mary's special plant food.

He stepped through the door, turned around, and looked up.

Yup, the chirping little bug hunter is still there.

Humph…

You got to be good…

To stay away from all those chickens!

"You be good and eat all the bugs, Zapper! Mary said I am to watch out for you… and not to let any chickens in here, so you must have earned some special right or place, or something. So… if it means anything to you, you are safe here with me."

Ben went on to mix a gallon of water with a scoop of the brown stuff, and a half of a scoop of the green stuff, and a cup of the smelly guck from the tall bottle. He stirred up the mixture and dumped a tablespoonful on each inside plant and two on each outside plant.

Next he took the donkey cart (with no donkey) by its two side-rails and pushed it over to the well and began filling water jars.

Watering plants is a never-ending chore!

And what am I?

A rain cloud!

Into the life of every plant a little rain must fall?

Humph…

But nothing lives without water.

Rainwater was precious and every drop that could be directly captured was funneled into some container. Well-water was good, but it had to be brought up one bucket at a time from thirty feet down. The dry season was over a month away where they would see no rain for maybe ninety days or more, and the water-level in the well may drop five feet.

Lazarus should be back here before the dry season arrives…

I hope…

Two days without rain meant someone had to pour one quart of water on each plant, and that took half a day.

Lord God!

Ben stopped for a moment and placed his hand over his heart.

Lord God…

Jesus stopped a storm!

And said we could do the same…

What about calling for rain?

I don't want a storm…

Is this something we could do…?

Do I just stand up straight and talk like Jesus?

Rain… gentle rain… come here… now?

Hum?

Much easier than five hours of watering the garden!

Mid-afternoon arrived before Ben had given vitamins, food, and a drink of water to every plant. Standing just inside of the greenhouse door looking at a young spikenard, a drop of sweat ran down his arm, dripped off his elbow, and landed on the plant.

Humph…

I wonder if my drop of sweat constitutes as part of its feeding… or watering?

He turned his eyes towards Zapper the tree frog's domain, looking for the little bug hunter, but he had retreated into a shady, cooler place.

Life without water is not possible…

One week without is certain death…

Jesus continually speaks of living water…

I wonder what he means?

Is that like a spring which bubbles up from among the rocks?

I know where lots of those are…

Ben put the donkey cart and the other stuff away, latched the greenhouse door, and took one last look around the yard, surveying and taking inventory of chickens and chores. Satisfied his work was done, he walked the path towards Emil's distant flock of sheep and goats.

Maybe Emil knows what Jesus is talking about…

His rivers of living water.

Ben found him sitting in the shade of the *twin sisters*, two matched and ancient olive trees near the top of a knoll. From that spot, for hundreds of years, shepherds had rested as they watched over their sheep and goats. Ben sat down in the grass next to Emil's dog and leaned back against one of three large marble-shaped rocks.

"You know as much about it as I do," answered Emil to Ben's questions. "You've heard the same words I've heard. *'It's better for you if I go away, for if I go, I can send Spirit Helper to you.'* We both have heard him say that several times, and then there is the *'Out of your belly shall flow rivers of living water.'* What it all comes down to mean is yet to be understood, but he has said one thing that definitely gets my attention."

"Oh, yeah? What's that?"

"The things that I have done, shall you do also, and even greater things than these shall you do because I am going to my Father."

"That thought is more than I can wrap my mind around, so I don't try to understand it. I just choose to believe what he said."

Emil announced, "Yesterday, I saw the two men who were waiting in ambush for Mary."

"Yesterday? That was another water-the-garden day. I was so tired by the time they got back from Jerusalem… I lit the torches for the walkway… went home and just fell into bed… woke up this morning with my sandals on."

Several young sheep were eating with their noses stuck in the grass… slowly moving over a small knoll… soon they would be out of sight.

Emil gave one short whistle blast and got Clipper's attention, the dog looked towards his master who with one hand pointed towards the wandering sheep, and with his other arm stretched high, made a circle in the air over his head.

Within two minutes Clipper had those sheep back within the circle of the fold.

"What do you expect?" responded Emil. "You're doing the work of three people, but it was Mary who asked you to do this for her wasn't it? She wouldn't trick you into doing their chores… I told you before… she has set her eyes on you, boy!"

First, the blood drained from Ben's face, then it turned beet red. He changed the subject back to the two would-be assassins.

"Were they holding onto darkness," questioned Ben, trying to recapture his dignified voice, "or were they looking for the light?"

"They were almost dead… the wounds had gotten infected… had an oozing green puss coming out of them… stunk too… the smell of certain death, but they were repentant for what they did and what they intended to do."

"Hum… I guess that's good… but you said that they were almost dead… am I to understand they are now alive and well and doing fine? What happened?"

"Jesus happened… that's what… healed them both, just tiny scars to help them remember to be nice… but they will never forget what happened next."

Ben looked over at Emil waiting for him to continue, but his thoughts had brought him back to the Temple, in his memory he was watching Jesus working with a whip.

He kept cracking that whip at something…

Focused on a spot…

Tracked it through the sky…

Then…

Whack!

Wham!

Kaboom!

I wish I could have seen what he cut down!

"Jesus had that whip with him… snapped it into the sky a few times… then took it into the Temple. From where I stood outside… it sounded like all hell was cut down… crash, smash and kaboom! Put to route on a fast track back to where they came from! Some of the merchants were all bloodied up… came limping out the doors… those are the ones still holding onto darkness!"

"What happened next?"

"The two would-be-assassins rang the dinner bell… they stood up in front of everyone… said what they had done… and how Jesus had healed them anyway. Then they said Jesus would do the same for anyone. For the next few hours… hundreds of sick or broken people went into the Temple… but only healthy and well people came out."

"Did he do the thing where he gives people new arms and legs and eyes and stuff? That's just so amazing when he does that!"

Emil's memories brought him back to the Temple, watching as freedom was birthed in people.

My second cousin's dull and cloudy eyes turned sharp green and then focused!

He gawked at me and called me by my name!

Many entered the Temple with only one leg but left with two...

Crippled up arthritic hands transformed to trim and youthful!

Emil answered, "I think that you could cook a cow, with all of the crutches left behind."

"What happens now? Next... you know... tonight... soon it will be time to go and light the torches."

"Hum... that's right... you weren't there last night... you don't know."

"No... I was so tired I could hardly stand up."

"Too bad... you missed it."

"Missed what? What's going on? What did I miss?"

"It's a good thing that you stopped by to see me... 'cause I know."

"Emil!" Ben flustered. "Come on, what do you know?"

Emil only gave Ben a *cat-that-ate-the-canary* look as he chewed on a piece of clover.

"Come on Emil! I don't have time to play twenty questions... I have to go and get the torches for the walkway ready... that takes me over an hour."

Emil continued with a note of sadness, "Jesus is staying in Jerusalem tonight... he and his disciples are having a dinner there... and after the dinner his disciples will prepare for Passover tomorrow."

"Oh... oh, pick."

"I know something else," added Emil.

"You do? What is it?"

"We have been invited to Stonehouse... there's food... and something special."

"What? Then... let's get these sheep and goats back in their pen... and get going!"

"No need."

"What? Emil... come on now! We need to get moving!"

"Moshav should be here about now," informed Emil as he scanned the horizon for his nephew. "He will look after them until I return. Besides... I'm all cleaned up and ready to go... you're the one who better hurry... you smell like a bad onion."

"Oh, man! Is Mary going to be there? I would think they could come up out of the caves. With all of the travel that goes on around Passover, it's very hard to keep track of anyone. Mary, Martha, and Lazarus don't want to be found... and I have sort of allowed some misleading information be let out... about the three of them and a cousin's family in Galilee."

"They'll be there," answered Emil, as he motivated Ben to action. "But you better do something... or stay downwind of them... Mary would rather have you tell her how busy you've been... than to smell how busy you've been."

"I'm gone," answered Ben as he got to his feet. "If I run home and you walk over, you can stop by and get me on your way there, I'll be ready."

Thirty minutes later, the two friends were walking the path where Ben had lit a row of torches the night before.

CHAPTER 48

Silence was the sound emanating from a single wooden pulley slowly turning around the oiled iron shaft that held it captive. Six strands of braided leather wrapped themselves around, up, and over the well-worn wooden disk before descending into the cavern's blackness down below.

Two small but calloused hands gripped the braided leather rope restricting its rate of decent, protecting the cargo it carried. Practiced fingers eased their burden to a flawless landing of its precious cargo, not spilling a single drop.

Resonant words from a woman's voice called out into the empty silence, "Lazarus, your rose-hip tea is ready!"

Lazarus got up, walked over and opened the dumb-waiter door to retrieve his tea, then stuck his head inside the shaft and said, "Thank you, Esther. Oh, and could you send me some of those biscuits to go with this please?"

"Sure thing, Laz," she replied… with her head inside the chute… her voice a muffled echo in her ears.

"And some of that honey butter your mom made."

"It's all gone, but I could make you some more."

"Would you, please?"

Esther looked down the black hole the dumb-waiter would soon come back up through, she took a moment to consider a thought and said, "Lazarus, where are your sisters?"

"Downstairs, they have closed the door to their rooms," he answered into the vertical passageway, "and are getting ready for this evening's meal. We get to come up and see some daylight!"

Esther wondered out loud, "What have you been doing?"

"The usual, I have some of Simon's scrolls, Psalms, Isaiah, I usually only take two or three out of the scriptorium at a time. Why? What are you doing?"

Feeding you…

And talking to you through this chimney.

"Just finishing up my chores. I fixed the greens for this evening's meal. Do you want me to send you something more?"

Send me something?

Lazarus considered her words, thinking of something too big to fit into the dumb-waiter and tried another tactic. "No… no, thank you."

He paused a moment and said, "However… I would like to show you something… but I can't send it up through this contraption… Simon's orders."

"Well… since Simon said," replied Esther through the passageway. "I will be right there."

Within five minutes Esther was walking through the wine-cellar doorway with a container of honey butter and two biscuits in her garden-chores shoulder bag. She closed the door behind her. Through years of habit she stood in absolute silence, looking, but mostly listening, just as a deer would survey an empty meadow for a time before venturing into a vulnerable place.

With her left hand she opened the closet door and stepped inside and pulled that door shut behind her. Now she was alone inside the wine cellar closet. Esther reached up and released the latch in the top right corner and pulled the back *wall* of the closet towards her and pushed it to her side. At her feet was black hole darkness. She leaned forward and looked down the stone chimney. The room below was bathed in candlelight. She reached across the blackness and grabbed an upper rung with her left hand, stepped across the hole onto the ladder and silently moved down into the caves below.

"Two biscuits, Lazarus, that's all you get. We have made a *Celebrate the Sonlight* dinner for the first day of Passover that starts tonight before the Passover Feast Day tomorrow, and I am determined to get you to that dinner hungry!"

"Esther, I am a man that works hard with his hands! It takes fuel to keep this machine running in proper operation!"

"Thinking is working? That thought don't work when I use it on Simon."

"He is only looking out for your best interest."

"And I, for yours," said Esther. "You don't want to get chubby... sitting around, waiting for time to pass."

"I'm not wasting time! I'm wisely utilizing every moment here in Simon's library! He has first generation copies of several Psalms... and parts of Isaiah! But I don't read from those, they are far too precious, I read from the scrolls he has copied... excellent work, I must add."

"I feel the same way about the old scrolls... besides; I would get a beating for touching the old ones. I have used up a bunch of candles though... reading through the words of David and Moses... and my book... the one named after me."

"I think it was the other way around Esther, you were named after the Queen who rescued the people of Israel."

"Think what you want to, Laz, but I heard Jesus talking, and very soon God is going to be my Father... and I am going to be his little girl! He's going to hang my picture on his heaven castle wall! That's what I am thinking."

"I saw her, the real Queen Esther, that is... and her uncle... we talked a lot... nice people."

"Is she pretty?" questioned Esther as she tipped her head while batting her eyes, smiling as she asked, "Does she look like me?"

"Esther, you said it backwards again... although you do look very much alike."

"Mama told me that we did, but she said that from the eyes of her heart."

"Well, I saw her… and I talked to Isaiah and David only two weeks ago… about what they wrote hundreds and hundreds of years ago… and now I am here reading what they wrote! Doesn't that bend your brain a bit? It bends mine."

"Lazarus, you should have noticed by now that my brain is very flexible. They are just as now as we are now, only they are there and we are here. Mary said Jesus is going to go and get them soon. I think about that instead of what it's going to cost him to go and get them… You told me that you wanted to show me something… What did you find? You talked to Isaiah, what did he say? Did he say more about what he wrote?"

On the table in front of them was a scroll, one Simon had copied, it was written in extremely sharp penmanship, and it was obvious that Lazarus was guarding it. Any food stuff he had was on a separate table… and a damp cloth was there to keep his fingers clean.

"You know what Isaiah wrote?" questioned Lazarus.

Esther hesitated, "Well…yes…Simon taught us to read just after he bought me and mama… but I would like you to tell me what Isaiah said and wrote."

"Hmm…" responded Lazarus with one eyebrow up, "When I talked with Isaiah, he said that when you were to see Jesus in a crowd of people, it would be just like seeing any other man."

"Well… yes… I can understand that… but I do think that he is rather ruggedly handsome… in his own way."

Lazarus continued, "Isaiah used Saul, Israel's first king, as an example, he stood head and shoulders above those around him and he looked like a King. Jesus looks like the farmer down the road or the sandal maker's cousin."

"And you found where he wrote about that, where? What did he write?"

"Right here… *he has no form or comeliness; and when we shall see him, there is no beauty that we should desire him.*"

Lazarus stopped reading but Esther continued, "*He is despised and rejected of men, a man of sorrows, and acquainted with grief.*"

Lazarus had shifted his weight in his chair and moved his hand; it was covering what Esther was *reading*. He looked back over his right shoulder to see where she was looking, it was at the ceiling.

She kept going, "*And we hid, as it were, our faces from him; he was despised and we esteemed him not. Surely he has borne our sicknesses and carried our...*"

Lazarus interrupted, "Esther... I thought you knew how to read? What are you doing?"

"I'm practicing," answered Esther turning to look at Lazarus' face. "I memorized this part." And then to the look in his eyes, she added, "but that doesn't mean I understand all of what he said... maybe you could help me?"

"Well...hum... how about we look at this together... and," he added, closely watching her eyes, "I will correct you if you need it." No flinch, only smiling, happy kindness.

Hum...

That's good...

She is kindness...

We can do this together.

"Okay," answered Esther. "That's good for me."

"The part that I read," informed Lazarus, "has happened, what you said from memory hasn't all happened yet, but we are in the middle of it happening. This entire section that Isaiah wrote about is being fulfilled right now, this week. We are at the center of all time! ... Everything... past, present, and future revolves around this one moment! And we are here... living in it... and we know it!"

Ester said, "It is Jesus who is the center axle, and what he is doing right now is the hub, and everything else is the wheel spinning around it!"

"Then it would be important to hang on to Jesus and not let go."

The sound of a clicking latch downstairs caused the two to look towards the circle stairway and bedrooms down below. The sisters came up the steps with Martha leading the way; Mary was walking behind and examining her work on Martha's hair. One curved flowing single braid formed from hair as thick as corn silk.

Esther exclaimed, "Very nice, Martha! Simon will like that, for sure!"

"Have you two set a date yet?" Lazarus asked.

"Not yet... too much going on too fast."

Lazarus responded, "I know what you are saying... I'm trying hard not to think about it... but the harder I try not to think of it... the more that I do think about it... because I remember what David said when I talked with him... and what Isaiah said... and then I go and read what they wrote... and then I think about that while I try to think of something else... and... and there is a lot going on... does that make any sense... at all?"

Esther observed, "Wow Laz! I think that we need to get you out into the sunshine... really quick!"

Martha agreed, "Yes, going upstairs should change our thoughts, at least for a little while."

Laz jumped up, offering, "I will go first, and open all of the doors, and would you come last Esther, and close them all?"

"Sure thing, Laz, lead away."

CHAPTER 49

Sundown brightness of late afternoon affectionately greeted the three siblings leaning against the veranda guardrail, soaking in sunshine's penetrating warmth. With a slight breeze caressing their skin, their eyes were gently closed while adjusting to the daylight. All three were sponges of God's goodness.

Arriving from the stables, Simon addressed his friends, "You have only been in the caves a few days, and you behave as if you're starved for the sun, wind, and sky."

"We live outside," Martha answered, "I hadn't thought much about it before, but the only time we are in the house is to eat and sleep. I know that's an exaggeration caused by thinking in extremes, and the caves are truly beautiful, but I have missed the sunshine and bright warmth of God's creation."

Simon expounded, "Hmm… yes… what he has made never ceases to amaze me. It all works together so intricately and moves forward in perpetual motion. Plant one kernel of corn and get hundreds in return, or buy a few chickens and they want to multiply and fill the yard."

Still marveling at the beautiful rock-rimmed canyon sunset before her, Martha continued, "I am looking forward to calling God my Father, it's truly an awesome thing Jesus is doing. Purchasing for us what we could never acquire on our own. Simon, soon I will be able to call you my husband, and that is breathtaking, but to call almighty God my Father! This is overwhelming beyond my imagination!"

Across the ravine and above the cliffs, a pair of eagles cut zigzag paths through the clear blue sky, playing 'catch me if you can'.

Mary interrupted their sweet talk with her observation, "You could come down and say hello Simon… the ladder works both ways you know."

"I plan to join you in the caves tomorrow, about noon."

Lazarus wondered, "But Simon, tomorrow sundown starts the feast day of Passover, the killing of sacrifice lambs begins in early afternoon… and I'm completely clueless how to deal with what I know is happening!"

"I hear you and agree Lazarus; we will prepare the house for the day, but not the lamb for the slaughter. I am quite sure Jesus will not have a Passover meal tomorrow, he will be the Passover meal."

Martha was listening closely, silently, holding Simon's right hand with her right hand… unaware her knuckles were turning white.

Lazarus continued, "That's an odd but fitting choice of words Simon, Jesus has spoken many times about his death, burial, and resurrection. It should be common knowledge, but I'm quite sure his closest disciples don't comprehend what he is going to do."

"Humph… yes… John is the closest in understanding, but he still holds some fuzzy thoughts."

Martha finally spoke up as Esther arrived, "You two have acquired a very unique understanding, because of where you have been, and what you have studied."

"Yeah, Laz," piped Esther, "I've heard people say they've been to hell and back… and it's not that you went to hell… you could just see it from where you were!"

"Esther, that's not funny, hell is a horrible place, and from what I understand, it will be even worse later!"

"I didn't say it to be funny; I was saying people joke about the place. The Sadducees say that neither heaven nor hell exists. If people knew what you know, they wouldn't do the things they do."

Relaxing her grip on Simon's hand, Martha responded, "It would be nice if that was true, but the same people who want to kill the three of us, want to kill us for that very reason. They know Lazarus was four days dead, and that Jesus raised him from the dead."

One of the eagles landed in a scraggly tree across the canyon with a fresh but lifeless rabbit, the other landed close by with a ground squirrel.

Esther answered while watching the eagles tear into their dinner, "That's too sad, and now that you say it I know you're right, but it's hard to understand someone being so stupid!"

Lazarus spoke up, "That's rather blunt."

"Yes it is, and this time I mean it just like it sounds! It's not that they aren't the sharpest knife in the drawer, but they couldn't cut butter on a hot day!"

Simon was looking into the distance and the Jordan River valley. The baptizer declared a powerful but simple message which left no room for compromise. The hearers either totally received the message, or they completely rejected his words. "You, Esther, are absolutely correct, and what some people choose to believe and do... it denies all evidence and logic."

"We are surrounded with piles of proof we have seen first-hand... with our own eyes!" Mary exclaimed.

Lazarus, remembering his stone table conversations in Adam and Eve's rock garden picked up on that thought and added, "Absolutely, and yet the most powerfully persuading reality are the vast number of prophecies declared and recorded... about Jesus our messiah... some from hundreds and thousands of years ago... all coming to pass... right here and now... as we live and breathe!"

Hannah approached the group saying, "Lord Simon, Emil and Benjamin have arrived, and the meal is ready whenever you call for it, sir."

"Now is good, you and Joseph will be able to join us as I requested, yes? That would make a total of nine. I had Joseph give everyone else a leave of absence for the next seven days."

"Yes, sir, and the table, serving dishes, bread, and wine, all have been set to match your request."

"Thank you, Hannah," to Emil and Ben he added, "Looks like you two made it just in time, let's go to the table."

Martha was seated across the table next to Simon, watching Esther slowly walk into the room to find her place and sit. She had a bewildered, twenty-mile stare stuck to her face.

"Esther? Is there something wrong?"

"Why?" asked Esther, while glancing at each one seated around the table and looking up at her. "Why don't they know?"

Martha pressed her for an understanding, "Why? Why doesn't who know what?"

"Why don't people know what Jesus is going to do? It's not like he's tried to hide it… I mean, like, almost every Prophet has written about him… and I have heard Jesus say things like *'if I be lifted up I will draw all men unto me.'* That's pretty plain he's talking about a comparison between himself and that serpent on a pole… the one Moses put up… when they got bit by all them snakes… I hate snakes!"

Simon questioned his servant, "Esther."

"Yes, Master Simon, sir?" squeaked Esther.

"How do you know all this?"

Esther tiptoed silently behind Ben and Mary's chairs, pretending to escape.

"Esther!" said Simon in his Master voice.

Esther stood up straight and flat-lined her answer, "Well… I was just using what you gave me… you taught me and mama to read… and I did something with it. You took out scrolls to copy… and I read them. Not the old ones, only the new ones that you or the others made… I didn't use all them candles just to look at rocks and caves and stuff!"

Simon tried to deliver a corrective grump-faced glare, faltered, bit his lip, and slid his right hand over his cheekbones, catching his index finger on his nose; it hung there a moment and then he said, "Wax well spent, Esther."

"Well, thank you, Master Simon, sir!" Esther joyfully replied, "I made the salad!"

"Will you sit down now?"

"Yes, sir," she replied and slid into the chair between Lazarus and her mom.

When silence returned to the room, Simon stood, raised his hands and face and said, "Almighty God, creator of heaven and earth, possessor of heaven and earth, we welcome you here in this place and in our lives. We are grateful to you for your provision for us and the table set before us. We call the food blessed... and to you we say, *'thank you'*. Against all odds, you have knitted us together as a family, and we together hold before you, our Lord Jesus, understanding parts and pieces of what is sitting on the table before him, and what he will soon take part in. With all that is in us, we add our faith to his, to yours, for all that he must face in the chores he must complete. He who always was and always will be, he allowed himself to be placed in a body like ours, to become our Passover Lamb... for the purpose of destroying the works of the enemy, and purchasing from you for us Zoe, life as you have it. Awesome God, what you have chosen to do, amazing, for you chose to make man in your image so that we could be born of you, awesome God! It is before you, always, and forever we bow our knee, so be it, Amen."

CHAPTER 50

According to Simon's request, no one needed to get up and serve during the meal, everything was either on the round timber table where they were seated, or on three small serving tables within reaching distance.

"Simon, why did you choose noon tomorrow to join us in the caves? Why noon?" Martha asked.

"The timeline prophesies... the Passover Lamb... and a comment Jesus made. According to what I believe the timeline is, whatever's happening, it will be sometime after noon tomorrow. And I think it would be okay for all of us to be there... that is if the rest of you wanted to join us."

Benjamin answered quickly, "I'll be there."

Joseph spoke up, "So will Hannah and I."

"Joseph?"

"Not to worry Hannah, more than one pregnant woman has gone up and down that ladder."

Hannah let out a slight gasp. "You know?"

"I suspected... and your daughter isn't very good at keeping secrets."

Hannah penetrated her daughter's protective *happy* bubble with a *look*.

Esther brushed off her mother's corrective frown, "I'm going to hang out in the caves with my pregnant mother! How weird is that?"

"I will be in Jerusalem." Emil said.

Lazarus was chewing on a muffin but he answered between bites, "I can't bring myself to go there, I know all too well what will be done to him... and he told me it would be of no value for me to be there."

Emil explained, "I do understand what's coming... but I was there only minutes after he took his first breath of air on this earth, and I believe that I need to be there when he takes his last breath also."

Mary thought out-loud, "You have always known who Jesus is; you are so blessed to have watched him all these years!"

"Mostly from a distance, but from the moment his angel first announced his birth on earth... yes, I have known! What he will face is absolutely horrible... but after three days he will defeat death, hell, and the grave. He will be raised from the dead! He will take captivity captive... he will get my wife and son... plus all of the others, and take them to his Father! It's so very close!"

A single hot tear escaped and slid down Emil's weathered face, "It's almost over! And it's almost begun!"

With a voice of understanding and comfort, Mary asked, "Emil, I heard you saw the two men who were at the house... the ones I hit with my coin purse, they're okay?"

"Now they are... after Jesus healed them, otherwise they'd be dead by now. The wounds had gotten infected. Watch for them, I'm sure that as much as they wanted to hurt you before, even more they want to help you now. I believe they will be among the first to get born again."

Taking a sip of wine Martha asked, "I wonder, what it will be like... to be born again?"

Mary imagined, "I feel like I am looking into a pool of water, waiting as I stand on a cliff ready to jump in, and I am thinking, *Is it cold? Is it deep? What's in there I can't see?*' I'm not sure what *born again* is... but whatever it is, it must be good!"

"The things written about the new birth are amazing, but what Jesus has said about it is mind-bendingly awesome!" Emil added.

Ben observed, "You know Emil... sometimes you don't talk like a goat herder."

"True... sometimes I wax eloquent and deliver an address as a Shepherd of Sheep. You should ask my sheep about it... I talk to them all the time, and I tell them why I take their spring lambs to the Temple... something that I will never have to do again... thank you, Jesus!"

As the evening moved by, Simon reached around and took a platter with a loaf of bread on it, set it on the table, broke the loaf in half, and put both halves back on the tray. Next he retrieved a large goblet of wine and set it next to the bread and said, "Jesus declared, *unless you eat my flesh and drink my blood, you have no part of me.*"

"Yes, that's right," agreed Benjamin. "That's when most of his disciples left him. They didn't have a clue what he was talking about."

This is so uniquely different, considered Esther looking on, *I am a guest at the table and my words are welcome, I may speak without fear of consequence,* she said, "They don't get it cause it's too simple. He is the word of God become flesh, I eat his words, and he is my Lord. Sorry, Simon, you bought me, the flesh and blood me, even though you have been more of a daddy to me than anything else, but *spirit me* belongs to Jesus, or at least that's the way it will be in a few days."

"I wouldn't have it any other way; I did what was necessary to rescue you and your mom. As for eating the word of God, every word Almighty God ever said, Jesus is. When Abraham cut covenant with God Almighty, and it was recorded that *a smoking furnace and a burning torch passed between those pieces,* I am convinced Abraham saw their footprints in that blood, God the Father and Jesus the Son with Spirit Helper watching over it all to bring it to pass! If you want to see the Father, look at Jesus. If you want to see Jesus, look at the Father. Spirit Helper is the *Muscle of God* and the *Revealer of Truth,* watching over his word to perform it."

Lazarus identified, "So, we feed on the word of God, can someone also reduce to simple terms, *drink my blood?* I think I know what he means, but to put it in ten words or less is a challenge."

Mary spoke up, "Lazarus, Jesus' first miracle, remember? Turning the dirty water into wine, the picture of the born of God new birth and *the same blood flows through us all?* Blood is a picture of Spirit Helper, so Jesus said *unless you eat my flesh,* (consume the word of God), *and drink my blood*, (somehow receive, accept, and walk in the help of Spirit Helper), *you have no part of me."*

Simon agreed with an admission, "I don't quite understand all of the *drink my blood* part yet, but I think you're on the right track Mary. Things have been unfolding in front of us at a very fast pace lately."

Hannah was also experiencing the newness of being a guest and not a slave, it was a feeling she had not experienced since before her ride north, in the belly of the slave ship. She spoke from the training of her past life.

"Look at some of what blood does, it's the primary agent that brings life to every part of the body! If a part of the body is cut off from the blood supply, it dies! When you breathe in air, your blood takes that air to every part of your body. When your blood is full of air, it's red. That's the color of it as it's moving away from your lungs and heart, but when it has delivered its cargo and it's on its way back to your lungs and heart it turns blue, it has to go back and get more air. It was much harder to see this where I came from because our skin is so dark, but it's much easier to see on those with light colored skin, like yours, Mary. If you are embarrassed for example, blood comes to the surface of your skin and it turns red. The same thing happens to me, but because of the color of my skin, it doesn't show nearly as much."

Mary asked, "So when someone gets cut, why is it always red? I have never bled blue, it's always red, and I have never seen anyone else bleed blue!"

"As soon as the blood has air touch it," explained Hannah, "the blood picks up its cargo of air and turns red again. Have you ever seen someone hold their breath until they turn blue? I have. Sometimes children having a tantrum will hold their breath until they turn blue and pass out. They used up all of the air, but when they pass out, they start breathing again and the blue goes away."

Mary was looking at Ben. He had his left hand wrapped around his right arm just above his elbow. He was squeezing hard as he opened and closed his right hand. The blood vessels of his right forearm were getting all bulgy and blue. Go figure.

"You're on to something, Hannah," Emil identified, "and I'm sure the answer is in there somewhere. I'm trying to remember where and how it's written about the blood of grapes; I think there's a connection."

"The blood of grapes?" questioned Mary. "What or how does that fit in?"

Emil answered, "When covenant is cut, people drink wine from the same cup as a representative of blood, you know, the blood of grapes, wine, blood covenant!"

"What about food, the food we eat goes to where it needs to go by what, our blood?" Ben asked.

Hannah was a young woman again, in the midst of training by the best in her homeland; the words from her teachers rose up from memories long forgotten. She now spoke those words to those who had become her friends.

"Every individual piece of our bodies is taken care of by our blood. Blood takes the elements of the food we eat to where it needs to go, the same with air. Blood also carries warrior blood that fights against things like infection or sickness. It takes things from outside and brings them inside. If someone was dying of thirst and you put him in the water, all that would happen is that he will be wet when he dies. But put water in his mouth and the blood will take that water to where it needs to go and he will live. You can also put some things on the outside of your body that will affect a cure that if you put on the inside of the body, it will kill you. Esther hates snakes, and justly so, but if you take the poison that a snake injects into something when it bites it, and drink it instead, it won't hurt you. But if you take an egg from one of Martha's chickens and inject the white part of that egg into a person, like a snake would do, it will kill that person just as sure as a snakebite. When Jesus talks about blood, he has to be talking about Spirit Helper flowing through us like blood, feeding and taking care of every part of us, individually and collectively."

"I remember," Emil said, "where it's written about the blood of grapes. It was when Jacob was close to leaving this earth and he called his twelve sons in to prophesy over them. It was with Judah, at the part where he spoke of Shiloh, a reference to our Messiah coming from the descendants of Judah. It was something about his clothes being washed in the blood of grapes, and he said something about wine in the same breath."

"Emil, try and remember. You have probably read those words a hundred times!" Simon said, trying to pry it out of him.

Emil had been looking at the ceiling.

Moving his gaze to the table, he reached over and broke off a piece of bread and dipped a corner of it into the wine. Rotating the bread, so as to not drip wine on the table, he drew back his hand and ate the bite of bread.

"I've got it," he said as he leaned back in his chair, "*The scepter shall not depart from Judah, nor a lawgiver from between his feet, until Shiloh come; and unto him shall the gathering of people be......he washed his garments in wine; and his clothes in the blood of grapes.* The question is, what does it mean?'"

Martha said, "Look first at what we do know. The primary elements are Jesus and Spirit Helper, Jesus being from the lineage of the tribe of Judah and being covered with or soaked with the blood of grapes, or wine. Maybe something like blood covenant or covered by or soaked with Spirit Helper?"

Simon broke off a piece of bread and dipped it in the wine, "And, both Joseph and Mary are of the House of Judah and the House of David. This is very important because Jesus is the adopted son of Joseph. Mary was a virgin when the word of God was planted in her womb; Isaiah wrote, *Therefore the Lord himself shall give you a sign; Behold a virgin shall conceive, and bear a son, and shall call his name Immanuel.*"

Benjamin continued by saying, "The Lord God had this plan set in motion from before the beginning, and from the moment that Adam and Eve broke covenant with him, he began recording it for us. He had Moses write, *And the Lord God said unto the serpent, because thou hast done this, thou art cursed above all cattle, and above every beast of the field; upon thy belly shalt thou go. And dust shalt thou eat all the days of thy life: And I will put enmity between thee and the woman, and between thy seed and her seed; it shall bruise thy head, and thou shalt bruise his heel.*"

With a piece of wine-dipped bread in his hand Lazarus added, "Yes, he had the plan to rescue us from before he made us, and he also gave us markers, prophesies, to help us identify who our Messiah would be. He had to be a descendant of Abraham because the Lord God had it recorded, *And I will bless them that bless thee, and curse them that curseth thee: and in thee shall all families of the earth be blessed."*

Simon said, "He is the God-Man, all God and all man… he always was and always will be… but because he will die for us, Spirit, soul, and body, he will also be the first one to be born again. David recorded it for us saying, *I will declare the decree: the Lord said unto me, Thou art my Son; this day have I begotten thee. Ask of me, and I shall give thee the heathen for thine inheritance, and the uttermost parts of the earth for thy possession."*

Emil helped himself to more bread and wine saying, "Absolutely, and he had to be born in Bethlehem, as recorded in Micah, *But thou, Bethlehem Ephratah, thou be little among the thousands of Judah, out of thee shall he come forth unto me to be ruler in Israel; whose goings forth from of old, from everlasting."*

Lazarus swallowed a bite of bread and said, "We must also remember John the baptizer, for he cut a path in front of Jesus, and Malachi spoke of him, saying, *Behold, I will send my messenger, and he shall prepare the way before me: and the Lord, whom ye seek, shall suddenly come to his temple, even the messenger of the covenant, whom ye delight in: behold, he shall come, saith the Lord of hosts.* There will never be another like John the baptizer."

"When I was a little boy," Simon remembered, "I saw Jesus just after they returned from Egypt, and it was Hosea who prophesied, saying *When Israel was a child, then I loved him, and called my son out of Egypt."*

Martha broke off a piece of bread and dipped it in the wine saying, "I was there also when he returned from Egypt. I was only one year old, but it still counts because I was there!"

"There are also the words of Jeremiah," Emil said, *"Thus saith the Lord; A voice was heard in Ramah, lamentation, and bitter weeping; Rachel weeping for her children refused to be comforted for her children, because they were not.* My son was only one of many, but he was one who sealed that prophecy forever!"

"Emil," Martha remembered, "you saw Jesus when he was only minutes old, but those who brought him gifts arrived when he was almost two. The prophecy of their arrival and the presents they brought is recorded in Psalms, *The kings of Tarshish and of the isles shall bring presents: the kings of Sheba and Seba shall offer gifts."*

She continued saying, "Everywhere Jesus went he fulfilled what Isaiah declared, *The Spirit of the Lord God is upon me; because the Lord hath anointed me to preach good tidings unto the meek; he hath sent me to bind up the brokenhearted, to proclaim liberty to the captives, and the opening of the prison to them that are bound.* He stood up and read this in Synagogues all over Israel, and he lived it everywhere he went!"

"This is the place where we are now!" identified Esther, holding a piece of bread as a ribbon of wine dripped down her wrist. "Isaiah said it, *He is despised and rejected of men; a man of sorrows, and acquainted with grief: and we hid as it were our faces from him; he was despised, and we esteemed him not.*"

Joseph said, "And we will have to look at what is coming, he will be betrayed by a friend. David said it, *Yea, mine own familiar friend, in whom I trusted, which did eat of my bread, hath lifted up his heel against me.* This will happen within hours."

"This happened only hours ago," Hannah added, "God through Zechariah declared it would happen, *And I said to them, If you think it good, give me my price; and if not forbear. So they weighed for my price thirty pieces of silver.* I'm confident the traitor will choke on it!"

Mary said, "Many will lie about Jesus, it's how they do what they do. David said it, *False witnesses did rise up; they laid to my charge things that I knew not. They rewarded me evil for good to the spoiling of my soul.*"

Esther was observing a part of her mom that she had never seen, it made her feel all warm inside to hear freedom in her mother's voice, "The traitor will pay a terrible price, but the money will go somewhere else, because Zechariah also said, *And the Lord said onto me, Cast it to the potter: a goodly price that I was prized at of them. And I took the thirty pieces of silver and cast them to the potter in the house of the Lord.*"

Ben remembered, "This was only a few days ago, Zechariah also said this about Jesus, *Rejoice greatly, O daughter of Zion; shout, O daughter of Jerusalem: behold, thy King cometh unto thee: he is just, and having salvation; lowly, and riding upon an ass, and upon a colt the foal of an ass.*"

"I hate snakes," Esther announced, "but I know what Moses did with the serpent on a pole, and what will be done to Jesus. It's recorded in Numbers, *And Moses made a serpent of brass, and put it on a pole, and it came to pass, that if a serpent had bitten any man, when he beheld the serpent made of brass, he lived.*"

Simon had noticed the transformation of Hannah and her daughter, and he heard Spirit Helper speak to him… spirit to spirit, *do not be afraid of this, it is a good thing.*

Simon then expounded upon the thought presented by Esther, "Isaiah added to that, telling part of what Jesus is getting for us, *Surely he hath borne our grief, and carried our sorrows: yet we did esteem him stricken, smitten of God, and afflicted. But he was wounded for our transgressions; he was bruised for our iniquities: the chastisement of our peace was upon him; and with his stripes we are healed.* Jesus is going to get the most terrible beating, but he is doing it for us!"

"This is one many people want to have happen now," Emil said, "to kick Rome out and to make Jesus a flesh and blood king, but it will not happen for a long time. From a Psalm of David, *The Lord said unto my Lord, Sit thou on my right hand, until I make thine enemies thy footstool.* It sounds like Lord God is calling for Jesus to wait where he is until his Father finishes something, that something being causing Jesus's enemies to be His footstool."

The loaf of bread was gone and the wine goblet empty.

Simon said, "Esther, would you see to it that they get safely back to their rooms in the cave? Then close and latch the doors on your way out."

"Yes, Simon," answered Esther.

An eyebrow went up as Simon looked at Esther asking, "Esther, are you okay?"

"I am fine, sir, I think my compliance is a side-effect of the wine. I will get them tucked in and be back to my room in a few minutes."

"Good, morning comes early, and we will see everyone by noon, except for you, Emil? When are you heading to Jerusalem?"

"Now."

"Then go with God and be safe, my friend."

CHAPTER 51

Crimson colored against a backdrop of once-bronze skin, ribbons of red trickled their winding way to mottled cobblestones, smeared with blood upon the ground. From hate-inflicted stripes, those scarlet streams joined in rivers as they oozed their winding way through gaping wounds torn by a fragment-loaded whip.

The attack had been unyieldingly savage, and even though both Isaiah and David described this portion of unfolding horror, Emil's stomach had turned upside down. He braced himself against a supporting column while wiping off his mouth.

Morning sunrise had brought the preparation day of Passover into full and deliberate motion. Jesus the Christ had been fully examined and the sacrifice of lambs had begun.

Working his way through the wolfish crowd, Emil maneuvered towards a position where he could look up into the face of Jesus.

Chained to a post with his arms up-stretched he was collapsed against its splintered surface.

From behind the guards and ten steps away, Emil dropped to the ground and caught the silent pain-filled gaze of Jesus.

CHAPTER 52

Approaching the sixth hour of the day, and from his home's front stone steps, Simon watched for Benjamin. Joseph, Hannah, and Esther had already descended into the candlelit caves within the rocky cliff on which his house was built.

Come on Ben...

Where are you?

Simon was watching south, towards the home of his friend, encroaching shadows appearing over his right shoulder caused him to take a gander north.

Pillaring purple clouds were piling up, bulgy things, rippling green and ugly, with the eerie, stagnant sound of pre-chaotic silence. A storm front was sweeping down Jordan River valley, bursting over their mountaintop divide, both Bethany and Jerusalem would soon be swallowed up.

What the...

Where in the world...

You weren't there five minutes ago...

He saw a running form to his left.

Benjamin?

In the time it took Ben to cross the valley floor, midday sunshine brightness was consumed by swirling green, boiler-head clouds.

Then wind hit them like a hammer!

"Simon! What's going on? It's almost noon but it just turned as dark as night!"

Surrounding air temperature immediately crashed and both men ran through the house, swinging storm shutters closed and locking them with crossbars.

The soldier's calloused fingers clamped onto the first rusted spike, he wrapped his paw around the blood-stained iron. Pressing its point into soft tissues just above his victim's wrist, he drew a two pound hammer back and slammed the spike through retreating flesh. The rusty iron passed between bones and severed tendons before sinking deep into a wooden post. He swung the hammer for a second blow and struck the spike again; the massive nail's iron head was now tight against his captive's wrist.

Glancing back towards Jerusalem, Simon shouted above the roaring storm, "It's the serpent on a pole! Jesus has become sin for us and they have nailed him to a tree!"

Lighting candles to just move through his house, Simon peeked through the shutters and out into the blackness.

God has put out his hand to block the light…

To hide the punishment he's pouring out upon his son!

With the house locked down, both men made their way to the wine cellar and then into the caves below. Climbing down the ladder while holding candles, Ben sort of limped along, grabbing with his right hand from rung to rung.

Watching his burning candle as he entered the cave, Simon saw the flame get squished, as if it were coming under pressure. As he descended, the flame of fire got more compacted, and even though there seemed to be the same amount of light, it didn't move as far.

"Benjamin, what's happening?" Mary asked, "It feels weird. We keep setting out more candles and lighting them, but it still feels dark, and why did you come down the ladder with a candle?"

The same bloodied hands picked up a third and final nail from the dirt at the soldier's feet... only this spike was larger... longer. With practiced blows this spike was driven first through the ankle bones of one foot, then stacked upon the other, driven through the bones of the second foot... and anchored deep into the post.

Ben answered Mary's question, "Its black as night outside! I was running towards Stonehouse, and in the time it took to cross the valley floor, the sky went from high noon to the dark of night... and the air, it became cold, thick... and heavy!"

Esther exclaimed, "David said this would happen! *They pierced my hands and my feet.* They have nailed him to that pole!"

"Augh... augh!!!!"

The sound of burning anguish moved across the cave's rough stone floor. Esther and the others turned towards the grief-filled noise.

It was Lazarus.

He looked like a blob of melted candle wax, his body drooping over his knees.

"He knows what's being done!" said Martha.

Simon countered, "Worse than that, he knows what's coming next! He not only read what David wrote, he and David talked about it! He knows all about the soldiers who beat Jesus and then nailed him to the tree! Lazarus has seen the demons behind the men! *Many bulls have compassed me: strong bulls of Bashan have beset me round. They gaped upon me with their mouths, as a ravening and a roaring lion. I am poured out like water, and all of my bones are out of joint: my heart is like wax; it is melted in the midst of my bowels. My strength is dried up like a potsherd; and my tongue cleaveth to my jaws; and thou hast brought me into the dust of death.*"

Esther shouted at them all, "We must keep our promise! Collapsing like a broken box won't help Jesus at all!"

Four Roman soldiers… straining… picked up the tree, with Jesus nailed to it, two more directed its base into a hole, dug among the stone. With practiced ease they positioned the tree vertical, before they dropped it down. The three foot free-fall sent the post to a thudded stop at the bottom of the hole, but all the weight of Jesus sent tearing pain throughout his body… as flesh tore and bones ground into the rusty iron spikes that held him captive to his cross.

"What do you mean Esther?" Joseph asked.

"We can add our faith to his! We all know pieces of the living word of God! Truths that have come alive in us! Like a seed planted in the ground comes alive in the dirt it was buried in!"

"She's right you know," Mary said, "it's true he will suffer horrible things to pay for our sin and purchase our salvation, that's true! God said it, it will happen! We cannot, and should not try to change that! So, what can we do? Cry? Feel sorry for him? Feel sorry for ourselves? The bucket full of tears I cried over the death of Lazarus… it did not grow one bit of help to get him back! Now Jesus is going to die a terrible death! He will go to hell for three days and nights! But he will defeat death… and rise from the dead! All of that will happen… whether we add our faith to his or not! But the next time I look into his face… he is going to know I did not cave in to fear, or some selfish feelings! When I look into his eyes, he will know he has a sister who stands with him! And believes in him!"

Pushing down against the ankle spike to raise his body slightly, Jesus pressed to pull in a deeper breath… pain traveled with piercing sharpness throughout his arms and legs. Then drawing in to fill his lungs, the skin of his back tore loose from the bloody bond that glued him to the tree.

Mary went over to Lazarus and knelt beside him, she put her left arm around his waist. "Come my brother... get up and stand with us... we will do this together."

Lazarus bunched up the sleeves of his robe and used them to rub the tears and slobber from his face. After a time he looked into Mary's face, he bit his lip as he nodded his head and together they stood up, saying, "Yes... together we will do this... together."

Mary continued, "Lazarus, remember, when Jesus and John were at our house... and Jesus lined Martha, you and me up in a row. He said that we would look like him? I thought it was great... except I wanted to keep *my* nose?"

"Yes... I remember... you had quite the duck-faced look on your face! And I think Jesus got a mouth cramp... from trying so hard not to laugh!"

Mary kept going, "Right now, even though Jesus is going through a transition of looking like us... he told us about the other side! He will win! He is becoming sin. Not just a little sin, but all sin! For us... and everyone like us! Isaiah said it, *All we like sheep have gone astray; we have turned everyone to his own way; and the Lord has laid on him the iniquity of us all.* Every bad thing that anyone has ever done is being dumped on him! The same as if he did it. We just need to look at what comes next!"

The nail-driving soldier leaned a ladder up against the cross, and once at the top he drove another smaller spike through a board. Each thudding blow sent showers of dirt into Jesus' wounds and streaking pain spasms throughout his body. Standing at the base of the cross the soldier surveyed his work, the sign said, King of the Jews.

Simon agreed, "That has to be what's happening… and he also has to be receiving the penalty and consequences for every twisted thing that ever will be done. So it's past, present, and future… one payment for always and forever… made by one perfect God-Man! Isaiah said it, Yet it pleased the Lord to bruise him; he hath put him to grief: when thou hast made his soul an offering for sin. The man who never sinned… never broke covenant with his Father… not even one time! The one who has the blood of God, not man, flowing in his veins! He is paying for all my sin!"

Hanging between heaven and earth, he was not alone; there was a thief on a cross to his left, and a thief on a cross to his right, from that place Jesus cried out, My God! My God! Why have you forsaken me?

"The bloodline comes from the Father, not the mother!" Hannah exclaimed, "That must be part of the reason his body had to be created in the womb of a virgin. The seed planted in the womb of Mary was the word of God!"

"And we will be born of that same seed!" said Joseph.

Hannah agreed with her husband, "Yes… yes we will! Jesus will be the first begotten from the dead, but we will only be moments behind him! Isaiah also spoke of this. He said, *By his knowledge shall my righteous servant justify many; for he shall bear their iniquities.* The King giving his life for the slave."

Esther added, "And many of the prophecies are about the wonderful things he has already done!"

"Like the way he always told stories," Lazarus shared, "God didn't just use David to tell of the horror that would happen to Jesus, he also said, *Give ear, O my people, to my law: incline your ears to the words of my mouth. I will open my mouth in a parable: I will utter dark sayings of old…*

I mean, isn't that the way Jesus always talked when there was a crowd around? He always had those old codgers scratching their chins and nodding their heads."

Adding to the words of her brother, Martha said, "David also talked about how Jesus would treat people. *The Lord lifteth up the meek: he casteth the wicked to the ground.* Emil told me about how he cleaned out the Temple with a whip… again. There was a few wicked who hit the ground that day!"

Once the soldiers were sure they had inflicted enough pain… they were required to speed things up. The feast day of Passover Sabbath would start at sundown, and they had to have the dead bodies down before then. They broke the leg bones of the thief on the right to speed up his death… it would come in minutes now.

Simon identified, "And he arrived right on time. Daniel prophesied that it would be four-hundred and eighty-three years after the decree to rebuild the city of Jerusalem that Jesus would arrive, and when you go back and add it all up, Jesus arrived right on time! Four-hundred and eighty-three years after the decree was given, the angel of the Lord was standing in front of Emil and the other shepherds, announcing the birth of Jesus! And I think if you looked closely, you would find it was on exactly the same day. That's just the way he is!"

The soldiers circled around to the thief on the left… and using an iron bar as a club, they broke the legs of the second thief… it took several blows.

"Amen, brother!" shouted Esther, with a tentative glance at Simon. "Hi, Simon, …ah…it's only a few days away…I thought that I… I would try it out… you know, to see how it sounds…you know… yes… Simon?"

Remembering the guarded joy expressed by Esther and her mother at their dinner the night before, Simon replied, "Who am I to think what Almighty God is doing is not perfect and correct …my sister!"

"Yahoo!" shouted Esther, while looking at Martha standing close to Simon. She said, "Master brother! We are so near to the finish line! We should celebrate! You ought to kiss her again!"

Lazarus said, "Yes, I agree! Rejoice! Our mourning must turn into joy, for praise of the Most High God stills the avenger! Jesus is finishing this war beyond all wars as the absolute winner! Every moment he walked on this earth he has spoken of these things as though they have already happened!"

Simon recalled, "It was my friend Nicodemus who snuck off to talk to Jesus in the middle of the night. Jesus told him *And as Moses lifted up the serpent in the wilderness, so must the son of man be lifted up: That whosoever believeth in him should not perish, but have eternal life. For God so loved the world, that he gave his only begotten Son, that whosoever believeth in him should not perish, but have everlasting life. For God sent not his Son into the world to condemn the world; but that the world through him might be saved.* It was more than two years ago that he spoke those words!"

The soldiers moved in to examine Jesus… he looked already dead… but they had to be sure. An old front line soldier took his spear, razor sharp with a blade as big as his hand, he moved to Jesus' right side. Starting below the ribcage he shoved the spear up through his liver… through his diaphragm… all of the way up and through his left lung… blood and water drained out.

Mary remembered, "For the joy set before him… he talked about that. He is so much looking forward to bringing us life! Life everlasting and full of glory! It's amazing the depth of love he has for us! And for people he has never even met! People that haven't even been born! Jesus said it was for the joy of what's coming that he is able to endure this cross! Since the joy of fulfilled love is the picture and strength he is pulling on to get through this... how much more should we pull on the same power ourselves?"

Simon was feeling the pressure of immanent death, he pushed against it with the fullness of life, "In the past God spoke to us through the prophets, but now he has spoken to us by his Son! The one who is the brightness of his glory and the express image of the Father! Jesus is the one sent to purge our sins! He is the one that will sit on the right hand of the majesty on high!"

Distant thunder rumbled. Lazarus put out his hand and touched the cave wall and felt a slight vibration. Heads turned towards the source of the sound, and then, more thunder from the direction of Jerusalem.

"Joseph?" said Hannah, looking around the room.

"Yes, my love?"

"What's happening?" asked Hannah. "It's getting darker, even though we have more than twenty candles burning in this room!"

Within the growing darkness, Ben looked into Mary's face, watching silent tears streaming down. He reached out and pulled her close as she buried her face into his shoulder.

Joseph answered, "It's almost over."

The cave shuddered like a shivering man pummeled by icy winds! The cave floor dropped... and stopped!

"Simon!" shouted Martha caught off balance, grabbing at his arm.

Light flowed out of the room... leaving with heavy air... down and over the wall... falling from sight... and then came total blackness.

Every candle in every room was snuffed out, unseen smoke rose in swirling curls.

Simon said, "Don't move, we will be okay! Just stand still a moment, Jesus said something would happen here and not to worry... He wanted us with him... without standing there and staring at his body. Even though we are miles away, this place is somehow tracking with him!"

"He is dead then," Esther said.

From somewhere in the cave's darkness, Lazarus answered, "Yes, spirit, soul, and body, but we will not leave him now! In three days he will rise again! We will look into the eyes of our Lord, God, and Brother!"

Simon asked, "Esther, you are closest to the ladder. Can you slowly move that way?"

"Yes, Simon," answered Esther, sliding her feet across the floor. "There, I have my left hand on it now. Follow my voice and just shuffle your feet so no one trips."

"Are we all here? Mary, are you okay?" Lazarus asked, sliding his feet and reaching out into the darkness.

"Yes." Mary sniffed. "I'm fine. I've got a hold of Ben's elbow."

"Hannah?" questioned Simon.

"Not to worry," answered Hannah who had focused in on Esther's voice and was slowly moving towards the sound. "I needed to be here too, Simon."

Simon said, "I will go first and find some light. It will only take a moment." He maneuvered to the ladder in total darkness.

Looking up as he climbed through the stone chimney, there was only blackness.

Esther blinked her eyes trying to adjust. "It's black as the inside of a cow," she said to no one in particular, and then, "Simon, you still with us?"

"Yes," he answered, feeling for the latch. "There we are… okay… hey, look at that!"

"Look at what, Simon?" called Martha. "What do you see?"

"The lamp up here," answered Simon. "It's still burning… and it seems like there is light coming in from outside, late afternoon light!"

"Okay," replied Martha. "We are coming up. Hannah? You ready?

"Yes, Martha," replied Hannah, feeling for the ladder rungs. "Thank you."

Joseph followed with each one slowly making their way out of the blackness. Esther was last in line to close and latch the closet door.

The War Is Over | 333

CHAPTER 53

Only moments after the hands and feet of his Messiah were nailed to a cross, the noontime sky went to nighttime darkness.

His friend was so badly beaten that as he looked at him now, Jesus no longer looked like a man.

Emil positioned himself so as Jesus pushed against the nails to draw in a deeper breath, he would enter his line of sight. John and Jesus' mother stood in another key location, Joanna and Mary Magdalene in a third.

Jesus...

We are here...

You are not alone...

Emil stood in silent thought and consideration...

All my life I have been a shepherd and raised countless sheep...

I've examined hundreds of newborn lambs...

For eventual delivery as spotless sacrifice...

Although a shadow of you,

Their blood could not remove but only cover...

Somehow you take away our sin...

A thing no lamb or common man could ever do.

While keeping his eyes on Jesus, but entering into a memory... Emil walked back in time... to a nighttime sky... where he was a young shepherd to a field of sheep.

And Emil remembered what he saw and heard.

The first element to invade my space was light...

Fast, bursting from the midnight sky...

Falling stars burning towards me!

But then they slowed...

And took on shape...

Transforming...

Giant men like burning candles...

Flying...

Without wings...

But they were flying, floating...

Never setting foot on ground...

And then I heard the voice...

A booming rain-barrel voice...

The leader spoke...

"Fear not! For, behold, I bring you good tidings of great joy, which shall be to all people. For unto you is born this day in the city of David, a Savior, which is Christ the Lord! And this shall be a sign unto you; Ye shall find the babe wrapped in swaddling clothes, lying in a manger!"

Emil's memory replayed the dark blue sky, a sky which filled with hundreds and thousands of angels, light tracers entering in from every direction, each one covered with multi-candle brightness!

They praised the goodness of God Almighty, flying like giant burning birds, streaking through the black and purple sky!

As they sang and praised the son of God, becoming explosions of light, coming together in tight clusters, and then soaring up into the sky and blasting out in starburst patterns, singing, shouting, *Glory to God in the Highest, and on earth peace, good will toward men!*

Frozen to the ground I stood and watched them...

Thunder in my ears...

Awesome exploding wonder before my eyes...

Starburst patterns of absolute precision...

Magnificent colors of red, white, green and blue...

Transfixed, Emil stood and watched the light-show scene replayed for nearby shepherds, and then breaking loose his feet he ran through grassy fields to a Bethlehem stable to see the savior they announced.

At a cave stable, Emil was one of six shepherds ushered in to see the newborn baby, one or maybe two hours old, bundle wrapped in a manger bed of hay.

And then, suddenly, the war between God and man was over.

CHAPTER 54

In the place of protection a new resident arrived, a thief, one of two who were crucified with Jesus. The man was standing, looking down at legs which only minutes before had been broken in several places. He bent them at the knee and began to bop around, he held up both hands and studied them, checked his feet also.

The nail holes…

Where did they go?

For nine close friends Simon's home had become a meeting place. For the siblings it was their hideout, to Hannah, Joseph and Esther it was their home, Simon informed both Benjamin and Emil they were always welcome… they could come and go as desired among their chores.

Presently, only two were out and about, and the kitchen was totally quiet.

Lazarus and Mary were relaxing on Simon's veranda, soaking up some sunshine. Benjamin was still doing their greenhouse chores, but with most of Jerusalem celebrating Passover, the three felt little need to hide in the caves… they had even slept the night in Simon's guest house.

"Lazarus."

"Yes, Mary."

"What time is it? How long has it been?"

"It's the ninth hour of the day, mid-afternoon of the Passover Sabbath, the second day of Passover. They started in on Jesus yesterday morning about sunrise, and they had him in the tomb by the time Passover Feast-Day Sabbath began at sundown. Tomorrow is the weekly Sabbath, and according to the law, we can't even walk to Jerusalem to check on anything until the day after tomorrow, not that I would want to… why?"

In the place of protection two visitors arrived, although they looked like men, they were not descendants of Adam. They were larger, thicker, carrying ability far beyond that of mortal man; they were angels, and they proceeded directly to the narrows.

"What's happening to him now?" Mary asked.

Lazarus replied, "Mary… I don't want to think about it!"

"My brother… dressing wounds or setting broken bones or killing chickens are all things I don't like to do, but I do them anyhow! This is not a time to hide; I need to know what's happening to Jesus now!"

"You already know Mary… he's in hell… being tormented by the demons I saw across the divide! I stood there with David, in fact, I would expect David and the rest are there right now… along the edge of the divide. Strange… I hadn't thought of that before."

The name of the lead angel was Michael, Chief warrior of God's armies, the second was Uriah.

"What? What didn't you think of before, Laz?"

"People, at the narrows, they're probably lined up there and watching... not that they could see Jesus... but they could yell across the pit... remember? I told you about the beggar and the rich man."

"Hmm... yes... the one named Lazarus... makes me wonder."

"Wonder what?"

"I wonder what's happening to the people in the place where you were... the protected place."

"Why? Why would anything be different for them now? Jesus is on the other side of the pit, I doubt if they could even get a glimpse of him."

"Lazarus... Satan's kingdom...? They think they've won."

The second thief crucified with Jesus finally arrived at the door of his new home. At the moment his legs weren't broken... and there were no holes in his hands, but he was experiencing the strangest sensation of falling, wind whistling past his ears, an end over end free-fall tumbling towards a matrix of small, black, elongated islands surrounded by glowing red rivers.

The ground came screaming up to meet him and his body slammed into jagged black lava rock, his left foot bounced back up on impact and then landed in one of the red rivers. Numb with pain he heard a bubbling, sizzling eruption emanating from the proximity of his left foot. Yanking back his leg the thief screamed with horror, the skin of his left foot slid off and he gawked at his own sparkling white foot and toe bones.

In the place of protection, David, Jonathan and Mordecai stood in silence, their hands wrapped around vertical iron bars of their protecting fence, their eyes burning into red-rimmed blackness on hell's side of the pit.

Thunk...

Bang...

Smack-bang-rattle...

Bang-bang-bang...

Thunk-smack-bang.

Michael addressed the residents, "When did they start?"

Jonathan answered, "About twenty-four hours ago, pounding on their chains with rocks and stuff... trying to get loose. At first it was just one or two of them... now they've all set to it with a vengeance."

"What happens if they break loose?" Mordecai asked, "Can they get across the pit?"

Bang-bang-bang...

Grawrrr!...

Schrawrrr!...

Aghhhh!

Uriah exhibited some skepticism, "Don't know... we've never been at this place in time before."

David asked, "Why don't we see any of the topside demons here... the only ones we see are locked in chains."

"They cannot come in here," Uriah responded, "or more accurately, they won't."

"Those in chains gave us reason to rid the earth of them forever. Demons can't actually make a human do anything, they're not allowed, people must always have a choice," Michael explained, "as for every other demon out there... this place is surrounded with a living grid-work containing membrane valves, what you could call gates, or one-way doors... once they're in here... there's no way out. This two-part place was created as an interim place of protection for you... and incarceration for them."

Mordecai wondered, "A one-way demon filter? Could they break a hole through it? A hole from the other side... coming in? So they could come and go as they please, could they do that?"

"Many years ago Lucifer's transgressions were multiplied when he entered covenant with a serpent," Michael explained, "and then with man. Their appearance and abilities transition the instant they enter in this place... they become what they are... and they are on their own... they lose their ability to levitate, they fall like a rock, and chains materialize upon them as they fall, the chains pull them to a vacant place where they are anchored... held captive."

Jonathan agreed, "Yes... I have watched this many times! Sometimes the chains pull them through the air for some distance before they lock into the lava rock!"

"What if the demons topside think they've beat us?" David asked, "What if they believe Jesus is dead forever?"

"Then they don't know my Jesus," answered Michael.

Michael turned and spoke again, "Uriah."

"Sir?"

"As this plays out... it is imperative we follow our instructions to the letter... obeying the thought and intent of our Master... even if his instructions to us seem... odd... at the moment."

"Sir... yes sir... I am returning to my post... now."

Outside Michael's field of vision... a short distance away, two fallen angels hover, observing, poking at the waters.

In the backwater counterpart of Abraham's Avenue, near the place where residents and demons were dropped through the filter and into hell... an arrow shot away... they are watching... inspecting... wondering.

He is dead...

Or...

Is he just pretending?

He is locked inside this place...

I can read his spirit heartbeat...

His broadcast signal...

It emanates from hades...

And the eternal light inside him has gone away.

Hum...

So he died a dead man...

Full of sin...

And I have won.

"Loki, call in some… volunteers… maybe twenty at a time… or only ten… no need to spook the troops without some plan or purpose. Keep them separate… tell them they get to run a special mission for their master."

Only minutes later a group of ten appeared.

A demon with jet black hair and a white stripe down the center asked, "Sir?"

Presenting an image of ultimate care for his soldiers, Lucifer answered, "Jesus is defeated… and we are here to rescue your brothers… our brothers chained inside."

The contingent's leader spoke again, "Oh wise and all powerful Lucifer… how can we obey your commands… if we get but only close… we will be sucked inside?"

"Walk along the water's edge… on fallen trees above still water… cautious, yes of course… we must not lose even one brother of us all."

"Sir… Master Lucifer…"

"You appear almost human… what do they call you?"

"They call me Skunk."

"Hum… yes… of course… Skunk… if through the course of your mission you fall inside… we will surely come to rescue you… and your men. Jesus has been defeated… and there are words I desire to present to him… in person… since he is now my slave."

Skunk swallowed hard with wide eyes and then responded, "Sir… yes sir!"

Skunk and his nine were standing on a berm; below them were the waters… the living grid-work… seeming like a giant honeycomb, with each cell being fifteen feet across. The grid-work frame appeared quite solid… flat on top… about two inches wide… tan in color with a three-segment, flesh-like, leathery-floor which was about four feet below the honeycomb frame.

Sliding on his butt, Skunk shuffled his way down the embankment… his right foot coming into contact with the honeycomb grid as a drop of sweat rolled down his forehead and dispersed among the hairs of his left eyebrow. He pushed himself to a standing position and inched along… haltingly… both arms outstretched to maintain his balance.

The six-sided cells presented a consistent eight foot long straight section and then a sixty degree corner… straight section… corner… straight section and so on. Skunk wound his way along until he was two cells away *(about thirty feet)* and then followed two consecutive left turns where he was then facing his master. He stopped at a corner… where he could have better balance, his feet placed on adjoining walls.

Perspiring profusely, his tunic boasted blotchy stains.

"No worries… brothers… come on down!"

Dutifully complying, the nine gained access to the grid at four distinct locations… and spread their way across the narrow frame.

Hesitantly Skunk asked, "Lucifer… ha… we're still here…what's next?"

Martha, Hannah and Esther stepped out on Simon's porch hearing only the last portion of Lazarus' and Mary's conversation.

"Who thinks they won?" Martha asked.

"Satan and his demons," Mary answered, "we understand some of what Jesus is doing… because we know he will rise from the dead… but Satan doesn't have a clue of what's coming next!"

Hannah exclaimed, "David and the others are so close to going home! I can only imagine what it will be like for them; it's almost worth dying for… just to be part of it happening! Almighty God will say *'It is enough!'* And Jesus will come alive with an explosion of life right in the middle of hell! He will tear that place apart! A magnificent blast of absolute light in the midst of the darkest dark!"

Esther enthusiastically agreed, "Right on, mama! The other Esther who looks like me is going to get to see Jesus rock that place!"

"They are all there," Lazarus added, "Moses, David, Samson, Adam and Eve! They are watching for Jesus… cheering him on… he is alone, but he is not alone!

A spark of light caused Michael's head to turn and tip up, the focus of his comrades followed.

A heavy leather demon filter door was kicked open, and a demon had fallen through.

The eyes of all four were locked upon the thing before the screams of the falling creature reached their ears; squalling, bawling, and then screeching… roaring, a quarter mile away.

Refracting light from a band of white came in and out of view, as tumbling through space the demon plummeted… growing larger… transitioning to a gross and vile ugliness as it fell. By the time it reached the ground it appeared much like a dragon… but with short, stubby, bone and leather wings… lethal front leg raking claws… muscly massive rear legs… totally covered with shiny black scales, and one bright stripe of white horns which spanned the distance from its toothy head to its long and pointed tail.

Locking chains did not materialize upon its legs as it fell, neither did it hit the ground and bounce, but Skunk rather slowed before impact, to a gentle and peaceful landing.

CHAPTER 55

Topside, Lucifer and Loki both tried to catch a view… but the doors had closed too quickly.

Lucifer barked demands, "Tell me what you saw!"

A balancing demon closest to him answered, "I couldn't see a thing! You wasted Skunk's life for nothing!"

"You impudent little coward! Loki… kick him in!"

Responding to his Lord's command, Loki bumped the accusing demon with a long and skinny pole.

"Ah…! Aahh…! Aaaahhh…! Aaaaaaaaaahhhhhhhhhhhhhhhh!"

Thump…

Whoosh…

Pelf…

Lucifer shouted orders at his volunteers, precariously balancing on the beehive demon filter grid, "Now watch him as he falls! Or you are going next!"

Eight petrified and sweating demons scrambled to observe what happened as he entered… but the doors again too quickly closed.

"Lord Lucifer a plan! I have a plan!" exclaimed a fear-filled brother in hopes of saving his own neck, "When the door opens… we must throw something bigger in! Some trees, boulders… or a house! To block the doors… so we can see inside!"

"Make it so! Do it now, go and get…"

Stopping mid-thought… and momentarily returning to his mild-mannered mask, Lucifer checked himself and said, "No… you eight stay right where you are… Loki… acquire another set of volunteers, scavengers… give them a list… and see to it everything called for be quite dry… and grossly flammable! Trees, beams, houses, I don't care! Tear a town apart! We are going to have a celebration fire! *Jesus is dead and I am God!* We are going to burn our way through the gates of hell!"

Skunk landed softly in his magnificent and beastly form, and wondered at the smokin' hot body of the human lying next to him. A large patch of skin was burned off the human's left shin, ankle and foot, but as he watched… it was slowly mending.

Amazing…

Rejuvenation here in hell…

And it's so fast.

He took survey of those around him, those who looked similar to he, beating on their chains with rocks, chewing on them also, trying to get free.

There are no chains on me?

I am in hell…

But I am free.

Skunk, in his present agile form, bounded from island to island, easily avoiding those tiny red molten lava streams.

Humph…

They are only here to keep me warm…

How nice…

I never cared for being cold.

Finding a vantage point of observation, where he could see two fences and a pit, an assortment of humans on both sides, plus the ceiling chute which he had fallen through, Skunk settled in to observe… and think through a thought.

Evening passed and so did the morning, as time found all nine gathered around the plank table in the House of Simon discussing the merits... and oddities, of salvation.

Ben asked, "What happens when we become forgiven children of God? What will hold us from going wild... if not the fear of punishment, or the fear of being an outcast or thrown into hell?"

"I will try to answer Benjamin's question," Hannah spoke out, "with your indulgence, Simon."

"My indulgence? Surprise me."

"Alright... if I wanted to, I believe you would let me leave this place... true?"

Simon answered with lonely eyes, "That would be a sad day... but I would let you go... and leave a free person... and give you proper supporting documents or necessary tattoo."

Hannah then expounded, "Ten years ago when you bought Esther and I, we were stripped naked and standing on the meat-market auction block. Because of those who were bidding against you, I know that if you had not rescued us by buying us, I would have been raped to death for their profit, and so would they have done to Esther. It might have taken five years or maybe ten, but that death was our future. But instead you bought us and loved us... not with the world's kind of love... not like my old master... he would tell me he loved me, when he took me to have sex with him... I knew he was only lying, he was only taking from me. You Simon, you have truly loved Esther and me, and yet you have never even presented the thought of sex with either one of us. At first we worked for you because you bought us... and rescued us from hell... you gave us life... but eventually that changed. Now we work for you because we have learned to love you... we have seen you, your kindness... and we are grateful for, and enjoy, the life you have given to us... I believe somewhere in that thought is the beginning... or part of the answer to your question, Benjamin."

Hannah placed the room into silence, but eventually Esther spoke up, "Hum... wow, mama."

Emil pushed their thoughts another way, "I believe the other end of our question is this: is the payment Jesus is making for sin enough or not? Either it's true Jesus is making one payment for all sin for all time, or, his dying nailed to a cross and going to hell for three days is not enough, and we must also be punished by God for what sin we have done. In all of the lambs and goats that I have brought to the Temple for sacrifice, it was the goat or lamb that was examined to see if it was a perfect sacrifice, not the one it was offered for."

Loki and his crew had been busy, plus, they had broken every law of God along the way... but felt no reprisal. Most actions taken were done without human authorization or interaction; they even directly killed or damaged several humans through their actions.

Houses had been broken up, doors and their frames removed, ceiling beams pulled out... trees ripped out of the ground... even a few boats were thrown into the pile; as a mountain of dry wood collected on top of, and around, God's honeycomb one-way demon filter.

Emboldened, Lucifer was pleased, his eyes glowed red... "Light it up!"

Within Skunk's view of observation was one more loose and roaming demon, his friend called Pug, bumped into hell the same instant as Skunk touched his razor-claw feet once more on solid ground.

Pug was a slightly chubby demon, who through his falling transformation still maintained his wide, flat head and beady eyes.

Pug?

What are you doing?

You were never very fast...

But the humans you are chasing are slower still!

Behaving like a cat with a nest of baby mice, Pug seemed to be enjoying his playful antics.

From Skunk's seat of observation, he counted the time lapse before the torn dismembered humans Pug was playing with… were once more restored to functional and active movement.

———————————————————

Lazarus was in a fit of dismay, he threw his arms back over his head and grabbed his hair at the nap of his neck as he shouted, "And what is being done to him now is even more real! His flesh has been peeled away… and it's Jesus' Spirit Self that's being torn now! It's a spirit, soul, and body payment for a spirit, soul, and body redemption!"

Esther's vivid imagination reached out and touched those thoughts, her mind's eye pictured what was happening to her friend… and wondered at his feelings; she jumped up, slapped both hands over her mouth, ran to the corner of the room, and emptied her stomach out in a waste-basket.

Hannah stood up… walked over to her daughter and knelt beside her on the floor. Taking the apron from around her waist and she gave it to Esther to wipe her face… and wrapped an arm around her.

Martha was sending her brother a '*do not talk like that*' look, but she continued. "It's beyond imagination… to think for one moment the price Jesus is paying to his Father is not enough! He is absorbing the full measure of God's wrath towards man's sin! Because of that… there must also be something stronger than the fear of punishment to be used as strength against doing what I know is wrong!"

Emil considered, "Jesus made it through this battlefield called earth without breaking covenant with His Father even one time. He, Jesus, is paying the price as the sinless, spotless Lamb of God, or as John the baptizer said it, '*The Lamb of God that takes away the sin of the world!*' But how did Jesus do it? How did he keep from sinning?"

Hannah looked back over her shoulder and said, "He has the blood of God, not man flowing through his veins!"

Emil said, "Yes… but he also drew breath into the body of a man! He faced every temptation that is common to man! Every temptation that is possible for a man to face… he endured it all, without caving into sin… not even one time!"

Simon pointed out, "Every rope has an opposite end. What's on the opposite end of fear?"

Lazarus considered, "A rope has three strands my friend. We have been kept in check by the law with fear of punishment from an angry God. I wonder if our answer is being delivered to us on the opposite end of the three strands of that rope?"

Martha was perplexed, "You think we can go to the opposite end of those three things? Fear of something we don't want to happen to us by an angry God? And we will find our answer? I only wish it were that easy!"

"What?" Mary questioned, "Believing something good will come to us through a loving Father, is that so hard to look at as an answer? That's where you stood with the words Jesus gave us… before he called Lazarus out of the grave!"

"Those three things, fear of punishment by an angry God," Lazarus remembered, "They are often used by people like a club, or pry bar, to manipulate those around them."

Martha said, "Yes… but…"

Emil interrupted, "When I was a young boy… working with my grandfather, I sometimes would get to stumbling around, trying to figure out how to do something, making the chore much harder than it needed to be, and he would say to me… ***Boy, get your butt behind you!*** Maybe our answer is that easy. Jesus turned the water into wine, you know. I believe the faith, hope, and love we saw Jesus walk in so consistently… is the wine our spirit self will be transformed into… and we will carry our Heaven Father's nature, character and ability inside us!"

In the place of protection, Anna was leading several residents down an embankment and towards the narrows.

A half a mile away and slightly left, a growing yellow brightness was emerging through the distant ceiling, and it cast a light into the depths of hell which they had never seen.

Screaming, howling demons, appearing like giant winged lizards, all teeth and claws, they were ripping at their anchor chains... pounding, smashing, jerking while they slapped at hell's human residents with their spiky tails.

Oh dear God in Heaven...

This is the most horrific ugliness my eyes have ever seen!

Almost to the narrows now, she watched what seemed to be burning trees fall through the ceiling. Spinning, tumbling, twirling, and leaving streamers of sparks behind them as they fell.

On the floor of hell a burning fire was building up... and then as Anna reached the narrows, an entire boat and burning ocean fell through the ceiling.

———————————

Skunk, with one eye on the flaming ceiling, anticipating the hoard which was sure to soon come pouring through, Skunk's other eye was on his chained and roaring brothers.

Us two free and all the others chained?

I don't think so...

Safety is in numbers...

It's time to initiate my plan.

"Pug! You're alive! Over here... come! Together we can set the others free!"

It only took a minute for Pug to comprehend his part in Skunk's grand plan, and one more minute to put it into motion.

Skunk bated a chained demon to lunge towards him... and as the chain snapped tight Pug bit the creature's leg off, just above the shackle!

Screaming at those who crippled him, the demon roared in pain but rolled away quite free.

The first instinct of the three legged creature was to turn on his attackers, but they were quite already gone. His second response was to lick the bloody stump… which to his surprise was already growing back.

By the time Skunk and Pug had '*set one hundred free*', the first freed demon's leg was restored… to full form and function.

David turned to Michael saying, "I don't like the look of that."

Mordecai observed, "Michael… Jonathan… they are gathering at the fence!"

Anna watched their actions across the pit, searching their intentions… and seeing what wasn't there, "David… the fence… it's not barking blue fire anymore when they touch it! Those monster creatures… they're trying to find a way across… to come over here!"

CHAPTER 56

Once the honeycomb structure caught fire it burned fiercely, overloading the senses with sight and sound... roaring up in flames taller than most trees.

Lucifer shouted orders above the din, "More wood! Trees, beams, houses! I don't care what it is or where you get it... if it burns, throw it in!"

Then two hours later it finally happened.

First a piece fell here and there a little... a post, a tree, a log... some creaking and a little groaning... and then the earth collapsed... an entire circle section of the honeycomb grid gave way with one colossal, "Snap! Crack! Crinkle! Whoosh! Boom! Poof!"

The falling cloud inferno cast sparks a hundred yards in all directions!

The bigger chunks fell one hundred feet and there collected, whereupon, spurred on by the lava streams in which they landed, the fire flamed hotter, higher, consuming everything and every creature nearby and underneath.

Massive warbling heat waves came back up through the burned out section, shimmering, rolling... distorting every sight seen across and through them.

Lucifer screamed, "Yes! I've broken through the gates of hell and into prison!"

Loki watched his master through the fire, his face and form perverted, stretching… shrinking… his voice muddy through the heat waves with the madness of his obsession.

"I will set my warriors free! I will drive a stake through the heart of Jesus! I will anchor him to the stones of hell forever! I will slaughter the ones who think… *that he is so special!* Then I will go find his father… and finish what I started so many years ago!"

He maneuvered, turning, glaring down the hole, straining to see through the heat waves and flames of fire.

Among flickering candles and silent shadows friends were chatting… and waiting for what they knew would happen next.

Simon said, "It was at the feast of tabernacles, Jesus spoke from the prophets Isaiah and Jeremiah, he stood up and shouted it out, he said, *"if any man thirsts, let him come unto me, and drink! He that believeth on me, as the scripture says, out of his belly shall flow rivers of living water!"* He was quoting from Jeremiah where Lord God said, *"For my people have committed two evils; they have forsaken me the fountain of living waters, and hewed them out cisterns, broken cisterns, that can hold no water!"* And from the voice of God that came through Isaiah, *"Ho, every one that thirsteth, come ye to the waters, and he that hath no money; come ye, buy, and eat; yea, come, buy wine and milk without money and without price!"* Almighty God identified himself as living water and the source of spirit food to eat… and Jesus said that the ones who believe on him… we will have his rivers of living water flow out of our spirit selves!"

Martha said, "I am trying to remember what Jesus said about this, when he was at our house, just after he raised Lazarus from the dead."

"Martha? He spoke to you personally about this?"

"Well, yes…something about after I am *born of God,* choosing to let the life of God in me to flow out of my *spirit self*… or your *spirit self.* But it's as you have said before, we are talking about a room we haven't walked into yet."

Mary longingly remembered, "When Jesus talked about these things… he made everything so clear and easy to see. I hope this *Spirit Helper* he spoke of will help us see things clearly again. I like cloud-free thoughts, not fuzzy thoughts. I like my thoughts to be crisp… and precise!"

Esther was muddling around in a thought, "When morning comes, it will be halfway through the first day of the week… the third day Jesus spoke of… how will we know when Jesus comes alive again? And from when do you start counting three days and nights? Is it three full days and nights, and like how tomorrow started a few hours ago at sundown? He said *that as Jonas was three days and three nights in the belly of the whale, so would the Son of man be three days and three nights in the heart of the earth.* They beat on him for over six hours! Doesn't that count for something… when you are counting time?"

Those watching at the fence had been intent in one direction… and never realized they were surrounded until they were.

Every resident in the place of protection had been moving… down the hill and towards the pit… to stand against the hoard.

Queen Esther silently arrived beside her uncle.

John the baptizer was not so quiet when he placed both hands upon the fence; he shouted words of victory right past the monster dragons to his Messiah somewhere within hell's expanse.

David, Jonathan, Mordecai, Anna and Michael, each turned to survey those who gathered. All of God's people who had left their earth suit were come together, thousands deep for miles in both directions along the gorge.

Hell's collective observance of Skunk's stretch-bite-snip maneuver was first met with anger… then acceptance… compliance… and finally with desire. The still chained demons were calling out… pleading… to be rescued next and bitten free.

Following Skunk and Pug's example, several of the *'free and foot restored resident dragon demons'* went off in pairs to set their brothers free.

Watching Skunk from high above and dropping to his hands and knees, Lucifer crawled up to the opening's edge, his head tucked within a cooling, circling, updraft, created by the rising heat-wave's movement.

Skunk?

Is that you down there?

Beneath a row of white horn crowns?

Pug?

You too?

Ugly Pug in a handsome dragon body?

You both... look... so... majestic!

So fantastic!

But what about your wings?

They're rather puny...

As Lucifer observed, Skunk, like a young eagle in its nest, reared back, rose up and flapped his bone and leather wings.

Although they could not lift him off the ground, the air-wash from them raised up a cloud of sparks from the fire's base one hundred feet away. The swirling sparks rose up and passed as racing streamers only inches in front of Lucifer's sniffing nose.

Oh yes!

Wow...

Beautiful!

So very nice!

Although your wings are not yet fit for flying...

They are growing grandly!

This is bigger...

Bad'er...

Then when I flew through Adam's garden...

The day I took these puny humans as my prize!

Desire climbed into Lucifer's eyes as lust spread throughout his body with each breath... remembering Skunk's transforming passage into hell.

Loki bumped Skunk in…

And he was not damaged…

But instead transformed…

Hum…

What would happen now?

One of his remaining *volunteers* was crouching right beside him.

Lucifer glanced at those around him, wondering, calculating.

Hum…

No one's watching.

With the slightest movement, Lucifer gave a push and then cried out, "Oh no! Help! Someone… catch him quick!"

But it was far too late, and none could be the demon's rescue.

With all eyes watching, the screaming demon tumbled, and transforming to a majestic dragon he landed gently, but he landed in the raging fire's center.

Lucifer watched in horror… as the beautiful new dragon suit began to smoke, squirreling around violently until at last the scaly skin began to bubble and burn away.

Augh!

This is true sadness…

What a waste!

We must find a better way!

He shouted down the open hole, "Break the fire up! Kick it all apart! You must put the fire out so we can come inside!"

Hearing their master's voice, many of hell's prisoners were instantly set to motion, quickly, although cautiously, tearing out burning trees and timbers from the fire.

To his topside demon leader Lucifer instructed, "Loki! A chain… we must have a chain! An anchored climbing entrance in… and… yes! I know! There must have been an anchor chain from the boat you threw inside! Send for someone to get it! Bring it in…"

Lucifer scanned the space around them, and pointing at some boulders he instructed, "Hook the boat anchor between those two side by side boulder rocks! And drop the chain inside!"

His demons, (each anxious to receive their own dragon suit) instantly retrieved the chain and hooked it in the rocks.

"Yes! Now throw it in! Throw it in!"

Clank, clunk, flooooo..., swish, dit, dit, dit, dit, toonk!

The chain dropped into hell with the final end whipping back and forth... whacking several unsuspecting demons about their scaly dragon heads.

Still crouching topside, Lucifer surveyed his chain's hanging place; it swung inside the fire's edge.

"Pug! Quick... Pug... before it gets too hot! Catch onto the chain's last link and pull it over! Away from the bed of coals! Pull it over!"

With his teeth, Pug latched onto the swinging chain and backed up, pulling it towards the iron fence, the bottomless pit, and watchers in the distance. Maneuvering, selecting an open landing spot before him, Pug then planted his dragon feet and stood waiting.

One quarter mile away, over an iron fence, across an almost bottomless pit and then over another iron fence Mordecai asked a question, "Ah... Michael... you are the only angel I see in here... aren't you going to bring some reinforcements in here with us? There must be a bunch of you guys around... somewhere... you know... ah... just in case?"

"Nope."

David eyed the league of demon dragons across the pit and looking nasty, "Ok... hm... how long... um... before Jesus... you know... comes alive again? And what... what will happen when he does?"

Michael answered, "Patience David, he almost has his head inside the noose."

CHAPTER 57

Lucifer knelt at the edge of hell's honeycomb demon filter grid; a new world stretched before him and he smelled pleasure in the distance.

With a taunt anchor chain beside him and the burnt-out hole before him, Lucifer shifted his position and lay prostrate on the ground. With his left hand he grasped the chain to keep from falling, and his head he eased down through hell's prison fortress ceiling.

Somewhat upside-down and looking backwards, he first examined the scene close to him…

Hmm…

Most freed demons have their bitten feet grown back…

The rest are in a restoration process…

And what's that?

The '*that*' he spotted was God's treasure in the background.

A fence, a pit, and another fence?

And then what, god's protected humans?

Humph…

Not for long…

We will take them for our sport!

Nothing but a hungry dragon's play toys!

That's what I am thinking!

Feeling rather frisky, Lucifer entertained a playful imagination, which planted a pleasant picture in his mind.

Hum…

I'll bet transforming to a dragon, would cause a person to get awfully hungry!

Cautiously, slowly, Lucifer shuffled himself around while holding tightly to his chain… he sniffed the air…

Hum…

He sniffed again… his nose twitching.

Humph…

Nothing…

All is well…

Just a gentle warming airflow rising up now…

Yes, all is well.

Feet first, Lucifer eased his body over the edge and into hell.

Suspended just below the ceiling… captured by imaginations of a glorious future which hung before him like a prized golden apple… Lucifer didn't notice what he had just slid by; the first phase mending restoration of the demon filter grid was taking place, one foot above his head.

Drawing in a deep breath he exhaled slowly, continuing his journey, arm over arm, link by link descending down the chain; wrought iron sliding against his leather leggings, feeling cool against his thighs, legs wrapped around the chain.

On the lava rock below him his minions were still scrambling, breaking up the fire, creating an ember-laced smoky-column rising upward.

Descending further, Lucifer entered the chain's curving portion, and the weight of his growing body swung him slightly, turning, to be facing Pug, the pit, and God's treasure in the distance.

The chain's last link was created exceptionally large, and Pug had simply hooked the iron ring over a lower canine; it slid down almost to its base. He then closed his massive row of upper teeth over the iron and locked it in, leaving regular chain links protruding from his mouth.

Now Pug's eyes were closed tight and he was straining. Lucifer's changing transformation was causing him to grow quite heavy, and Pug focused his attention on holding Lucifer back from landing in the fire's burning coals.

As Lucifer's change continued, a tail grew down and wing buds sprouted, skin changed to scales, and the man's face distorted to a snout. Fingers transformed to giant claws and massive, rippling muscles burst out all over, but what this transformation caused to Pug was a chain pulling harder… more intensely every second.

Pug swallowed hard and reopened his eyes slowly. Looking down his nose he focused on individual links and then followed them upward, as the lopsided pulling caused his head to turn slightly sidewise… and his feet were sliding… slowly towards the fire.

Lucifer's tail felt the approaching heat and he beat his wing buds franticly, forcing into present tense reality his final transformation. The bone and leather wings grew quickly, pushing out tree size bones and massive sheets of leathery membrane, like the sails of a giant warship.

The mind of Lucifer was not keeping up with his rapid makeover into a winged and flying dragon. He cried out in fear at the thought of being burned alive in the fiery coals behind him.

"Aahhhiiii!!!"

With Lucifer still clinging tightly to the chain which Pug was fastened to, his wild flapping caused him to rise sharply upward, which jerked Pug violently forward, and then threw Pug into a face first dive that landed the subordinate demon beneath his master's airborne feet.

Behind the pair, Lucifer's wing-wash first caused the remaining coals to be fanned to a fervent-red brightness. Next, as the massive demon dragon began to slowly settle down closer to the ground, the wind-storm air-flow caused the remaining fire to be blown away. Giant billowing cinder clouds of sparkly fire rose up behind him, and the majestic dragon landed gently on ground blown clean by his massive flapping wings.

On the northwest corner of Jerusalem, outside the city walls but inside a little cave, one faithful angel maintains his silent vigil.

Uriah examined the chiseled stone walls, ceiling and floor that surrounded him, and the silent form that he now guarded. Although even now the cave was little more than a spider hole, it had been cut and expanded to be the grave of a wealthy man.

Just before sundown three days ago, the tomb had been given by that rich man to be a resting place for the body of his Lord. The body Uriah now guarded belonged to his own Commander and Chief, the same one who commissioned him to this assignment 34 years before.

Among the instructions Uriah received for his mission was one which required him to continually protect and serve until the appointed moment. At that time, and the declaring of the words '*I Am*' by his Commander and Chief, he had been ordered to withdraw and maintain a one mile perimeter, leaving Jesus alone at the center for a period of 18 hours.

Doing nothing for 18 hours was the most difficult thing I have ever done...

I could have cut the heart out of every wicked one among them...

In only minutes of their time!

Instead he obeyed his Commander's instructions for the higher purpose of his maker.

Uriah allowed himself to illuminate the little cave with a brightness level of 4 to 5 candlepower. The dim light seemed appropriate to silent waiting and remembrance, his master being in a place where he could be no help to him at all.

Looking through the stones and earth surrounding him, Uriah observed the entire watch of human guards who were assigned to secure the tomb, were still standing in their places.

Pitiful puny humans!

You have absolutely no understanding of the power you are charged with holding back!

You could not stop the rain from falling...

And yet you think you can hold back the one who made the earth the stars and sky!

Ignorant idiots!

Uriah silently mocked their foolishness while at the same time he understood the soldiers also served the purpose of witnesses to an undisturbed and sealed tomb.

Looking through the ceiling and adjusting his focus to the sky above, Uriah studied a primary constellation and its relationship to the rotation of the earth.

It was 87 minutes to sunrise.

CHAPTER 58

Beautiful, shiny black interlocking scales, overall body armor, fantastic teeth and claws, rippling, handsome, and provocative muscles, plus giant, powerful, 'take you anywhere you want to go, fold'em-up, tuck away' wings.

Lucifer was a complete, offensive-defensive masterpiece.

I am bigger…

Bad'er than when I flew in Adam's garden!

Looking down his long dragon snout he caressed his body with his eyes.

Yes!

I am an awesome sight!

Strength beyond measure…

A lean…

Mean…

Almighty God…

Kingly machine!

Groogrrrroo…gr…ggrrrr…

With an empty stomach!

While all who watched him paid him homage *(for he was their master)* and he pretended not to care, he did pay close attention to those across the pit.

Lucifer examined the wings of those who bowed before him.

Humph…

Kind of runty wings…

Maybe I should command them to fly across the pit…

Just to see what happens…

Some might fly a little…

Before they fall into the pit.

He cranked his head around to examine his own bone and leather wings, and then compared them with his soldiers.

Magnificently beautiful!

My wings are by far the best…

As they truly should be.

Them and theirs?

Humph!

Pitiful excuse for dragon wings!

They need more hot and zesty sauce…

And time cooking in the oven…

Ha!

I think I made a funny…

Soaking up the praise of those who bowed before him, Lucifer evaluated his immediate choices.

Pillage god's treasure and tear his people into tiny shreds…

Or…

Drive a stake through the heart of Jesus and anchor him to the stones of hell forever!

Hmm…

Work before pleasure…

Or pleasure before work?

Lucifer strutted himself, grand and regal.

I am the winner…

The Majestic…

Imperial…

And Magnificent dragon!

I am God forever!

He addressed his demon-dragon horde.

"I am your God! And you are the soldiers in my army! I came to set you free!"

A cheering chorus surrounded his words, heaping praise upon him.

"I will lock your jailer in hell forever!"

Much more cheering burst forth.

Lucifer reached down and retrieved one of the chain and collar sets which had held a demon captive. Then, holding tightly to the chain, he unfurled his mighty wings and shot straight up into the air!

Snap!

Zing!

Bam!

He ripped out the chain's giant stake-out spike and held it up with the locking collar.

All his minions cheered, "Yes! Take the stake and drive it through the heart of Jesus! Lock him to the stones of hell forever!"

Lucifer absorbed their praise while flying… hovering… fifty feet above them. Then, from that place, he focused in on Jesus' spirit self broadcast signal, to search out and destroy the world's creator.

Half a moment later he turned his dragon head as he locked onto the Jesus signal. It was miles north, into the depths of hell.

Seeing fire in their leader's eyes, his people shouted, "Yes! Seal Jesus as twice forever dead! Do it now, and you will be the eternal King!"

Then… with half a wonder floating in his mind…Lucifer flapped his wings and flew off… towards Jesus' broadcast beacon signal.

From high above the ribbon-red lava streams of hell, Lucifer acquired a better understanding of his massive impact upon the residents of hell… or the total lack thereof.

A circle spot, something like a red bulls-eye target, was the place where he first landed… covering an acre or two of space.

Skunk and Pug had set about a hundred demons free, and those had set free another thousand, but that is where his impact ended. The freed dragon demons had turned to fighting with each other, or else they were gathered at the fence, trying to get across the pit, straining to molest the apple of God's eye.

This is not good...

I must seal the death of god forever...

And I must do it quickly...

I must establish absolutely my total and complete control!

Lucifer was able to recognize Skunk and Pug after their dragon transformation through their distinctive features, and now as he flew north he was also able to identify the transformed demon-dragons still in chains below him.

They were demons he had sent on missions, demons he had pushed across the line... demons he caused to leave their first estate... to violate the will of man... crossing to a place where God's angels could justly lock them up in hell forever.

Lucifer shook off his troubled thoughts and pushed on harder... towards the Jesus beacon somewhere in the distance... but he could not escape the memories which plagued him from down below. He was flying through some sort of progressive timeline going backwards... all in order but going backwards... observing those who were removed from the earth... as punishment for overriding the will of man.

The bulls-eye spot where Lucifer first landed contained the most current demons to be anchored to the lava swamps of hell. The ones he saw below him now were imprisoned about two thousand years before... and he flew on, deeper into hell.

There were demons which had brought forth centaurs, birthing perverted imaginations of all types. Half man and half horse or goat, half dog and half woman... or a wolf transforming to a man... creatures looking human which drank the blood of man. Some demons orchestrated building the pyramids of Egypt, others, the works of Nimrod, or that of Ishtar and her whoring husband... producing countless products of Satan's mind... Baal/Satan worship... perverted pleasure sex... with anything that moved... the blood and fire sacrifice of babies... sacrificing babies up to Satan... inside and outside of the womb.

My greatest victories...

Plus my creation of the Gods of Greece and Rome...

A living breathing legacy of my crowned achievements…

I see my recorded history written up in my incarcerated demons…

And forever sealed in the carcasses of God's rebellious humans piled up below…

Successful works of my hands and of my mind…

So…

Why am I not celebrating?

CHAPTER 59

Naked, beaten, and lying in a tangled pile, Jesus floated in and out of consciousness. Halfway between destruction and recovery, his eyes fluttered open.

Oh God my father help me!

Save me from the dragon's mouth!

From his claws and the horns upon his head!

Around him, nothing stayed where it used to be, everything was moving.

Each lava rock island contained a chain-anchored dragon, but the islands were shifting, moving on a liquid bed of lava. Through their movement, what was once a safe spot could suddenly turn and be within the reach of a different demon's claws.

Dragging himself with his one functional arm, he pulled his body back from a shifting lava stream... and from a hungry set of eyes.

Floating on his bone and leather wings, Lucifer was circling, searching out his prey.

I'm close, very close...

I can almost smell you Jesus...

And taste your blood upon my tongue!

Where are you?

Banking left he set his wings, dropped his elevation fifty feet and cut a swooping path above a row of slowly shifting islands.

Yes!

There you are...

Got'ya!

Ha! Haaa! Yes!

Seeing Jesus, Lucifer's right hand automatically gripped tighter to the massive iron stake he carried. His left hand clenched the chain and collar fastened to the stake.

Pulling up his wings, billowing like the sails of two ships, Lucifer landed softly at Jesus' feet.

Humph...

This is the one I was afraid of?

The one who caused me so much fear?

Humph...

He is a thing of nothingness...

Of no count...

Lucifer tossed the chain and collar to the side but held tightly to the stake.

Absolute victory...

I can smell it...

I can taste it!

Unseen by Lucifer, a set of black claws reached out and took solid hold of the discarded collar.

With both hands, Lucifer clenched the giant iron spike, and raised it high above his head.

Drawing in a deep breath, and relishing the moment, Lucifer prepared to drive the pointy end through the chest of Jesus, and anchor him to the lava rock below.

Standing silently...

With his arms upraised...

And with no warning...

The chain draping back from the iron stake snugged tight...

And then… with a steady pull on the chain… by the collar-holding demon… the black-clawed demon pulled his *master* over backwards.

Caught completely off balance, Lucifer flapped his wings up to catch himself from falling.

But given his most desired attack conditions, the lurking demon struck!

Crunch!

Scrunch!

Snap!

Lucifer's right wing was completely bitten off…

And he screamed in pain, "Yahaaah!"

Swish!

Slice!

Four massive claws, sharper, stronger than the best of steel, raked down the chest, shredding Lucifer cleanly to his ribcage!

"You left us there to die!" shouted his attacker.

Dazed and groggy, with blood all over, Lucifer gazed at his attacker, "Wha… who… who are you?"

Whoosh!

Swoosh!

Whack!

Whack!

Whack!

Lucifer's majestic dragon suit was turned almost completely inside out.

"In the garden… Adam and Eve… do you remember them? Do you remember me? I was there! We followed you! And you deserted us! You led us to rebel against God! God? The most good and kind of all! I was such a fool to follow you!"

The creature chained in place screamed a scream which rattled the very foundation stones of hell, "Aughhhhhhhhhhhhhhhhhhh!!!!!!!!!!!!!!!!!!!!!!"

Lucifer was thrown back, just slightly out of reach from the razor claws. "What's wrong with you! Don't you know? I have won! I have beaten god! Jesus is dead and I have won!"

The War Is Over | 371

The guttural voice responded with deeply mocking words, "Lucifer, you too are such a fool! Tell me of the mighty battle fought for you to enter in this place… how many thousands of my brothers did it cost!"

Eyeing his dismembered right wing from twenty feet away, and a useless pair of legs, the once mighty Lucifer weakly responded, "On the earth… on a cross… I killed god… Jesus' spirit self died dead!"

"The sinless, spotless lamb of God? And you think that he is dead? Can't you read and comprehend what God has said? Hundreds of prophecies spoken about the trap he laid… which you have broken into! You have broken into hell you fool!"

Hiding, time was working on his side, Lucifer began to mend, parts and pieces were growing back together… pulling in… and he could move one toe a little.

Straining at the end of his chain, the monstrous creature towered over the eviscerated frame of Lucifer and spoke louder still, "*It pleased the Lord to bruise him*… does that ring a bell? *His soul shall make an offering for sin*… Lucifer… what the hell do you think Jesus was doing here, you fool! *He shall see the travail of his soul and shall be satisfied!* You have played his game and lost Lucifer! *By his knowledge shall my righteous servant justify many; for he shall bear their iniquities! Therefore will I divide him with the great, and he shall divide the spoil with the strong; because he hath poured out his soul unto death!*"

"Lucifer… Jesus has won… he has beaten us all!"

Parts were pulling back in… Lucifer slid his hulking body across the ground and lay beside his wing… trying to get it to glue back on… rubbing up against it.

Faster wing… a little faster… faster if you please!

He pulled his leg up an inch or two, bending at the knee.

CHAPTER 60

Those watching at the fence had been intent in one direction... and never realized they were being surrounded until they were.

Every resident in the place of protection had been moving... down the hill and towards the pit... to stand against the hoard.

Queen Esther silently arrived beside her uncle.

John the baptizer was not so quiet when he placed both hands upon the fence; he shouted words of victory right past the monster dragons to his Messiah somewhere within hell's expanse.

David, Jonathan, Mordecai, Anna and Michael, each turned to survey those who gathered. All of God's people who had left their earth suit were come together, thousands deep for miles in both directions along the gorge.

For several minutes they watched in silence what played out across the pit, until one massive dragon rose up on bone and leather wings. It circled around a bit until it seemed to acquire a target, and then made a bee-line, flapping its wings and flying off, into the depths of hell.

David spoke to anyone who chose to listen, "I found it quite a challenge... to put into words the understanding and pictures Lord God showed me."

Anna was one who listened, "You are speaking of the Psalms you wrote?"

"Yes… some…pictures of this I saw… a glimpse here and there… of Jesus… as he approached the cross… and while he was on it… and what happens next."

Anna expounded on his thought, "Yes… I suppose… and if you declared a '*thus sayeth the Lord*'… and it did not come to be… you would have been stoned for your… ah… misrepresentation."

David smiled slightly, "Yes… being stoned for presenting a lie as a '*God said*'… that was always a consideration. Just ask Isaiah, or Jeremiah… all will say the same… no one wants to die by being stoned."

Across the pit, the demons, although they could not yet fly, were quite determined to get to Anna's side of the pit. They resorted to piling up debris, smoldering timbers and trees from the fire which they had torn apart… they worked together to build a bridge over the narrows.

Anna turned away from watching their struggling efforts to look into the eyes of her friend David, "Yes… and?"

"Ah… your Simon… things will change for him… soon… and for many others."

"*My* Simon?"

"Yes… *your* Simon! Anna… it is no secret! You had no children on your own… but you raised him in those caves as if he was your own… and you look in on him every chance you get!"

A daring demon… carrying a large long pole, long enough to finish their bridge across the pit, he was cautiously maneuvering out upon the existing bridge structure they were building. He carried the tree like a giant balance beam in his mouth.

Anna folded her arms and said, "Okay David… I'll bite… what happens next?"

"*Thou hast ascended on high, thou hast led captivity captive;*"

"Yes David… we already know that part… Jesus is coming to get us and take us to his Father… that's why as we are watching these goofy demons… we're watching and thinking… it is so foolish what they are trying to do!"

Just then the daring demon lost his footing, the log dropped down, impacting the timber structure with his jawbone caught in-between. There were some crunching sounds as his jawbones shattered… then he scrambled for a scampering moment before both the smoldering tree and demon tumbled end over end into the bottomless pit.

"Anna… you know there's more… *Thou hast received gifts in the man; yea the rebellious also that the Lord God might dwell!* Anna! Isn't that amazing… Lord God's very DNA nature and character! He is going to impart an equal, blended portion of himself into each one of his kids! He is going to birth an equal part of himself into the spirit self of everyone who through Jesus' death burial and resurrection becomes one of his sons or daughters!"

Above the gorge the '*sky-ceiling*' cracked, manifest with splintering sounds of shattering rock announcing Almighty God's arrival. Fragments and discomfited chunks whistled through heavy air into the pit. Distant stone-to-rock crashing impacts marked their decent into the abyss.

Much to the dismay of the wing biting demon, Lucifer recovered quickly. His wing reattached, the wounds healed, and in only minutes he came back bigger and more awesome than before.

Out of reach from every chain-anchored demon, Lucifer strutted about, ruffling his wings, flicking his claws, stretching out his muscles.

Clawing the ground in front of Lucifer, the wing biter did not cower; instead he pulled towards him, straining against his chain, his head and snapping jaws weaving side to side just inches above the lava rock.

Lucifer scowled down at him.

Humph…

You belong in chains you traitor!

You disgust me!

Standing high above the snapping wing biter, Lucifer felt the fullness of his strength restored , and he also fondled the stakeout spike which he still held in his right hand.

Lucifer spat the words, "You are a pitiful excuse for a brother, demon!" and he allowed the stakeout spike to slide down, leaving six feet of chain from his hand to the long narrow chunk of iron.

With the chain clamped tightly in his dragon-claw hand, he lifted up the spike, allowing it to swing freely; it weighed as much as a chubby human.

Lucifer shouted, "Die like the dog you are!" and he swung the chain roundhouse, bringing the iron crashing down on his tormentor's head, which slapped the stone below his jaw.

The spike struck squarely and quite centered, splitting the demon-dragon's head in half lengthways, from his nose, to back between his fuzzy ears.

Lucifer swung the iron a second time, and then a third, completely severing half the dragon's head from his brain-splattered body. Picking up the bloody half-head by a canine tooth, he threw it into a liquid stream of lava.

The half-head smoked, sizzled, and smelled like a burnt breakfast of toast and eggs.

"Now Jesus... where are you?"

Lucifer held the bloody chunk of iron like some trophy, a trinket treasure won at the games in Rome. He swung it around his head, listening to its low throated whistle.

Playing dead only feet away, Jesus focused on the sound to track its movement.

Finding his target, and staring at the head-down limpish body, Lucifer roared his hatred out, "This ends right here and now forever Jesus! Everything you ever wanted is only mine! All the people of the earth are in my kingdom! I can tear them... shred them... I can eat them for breakfast... and I don't even care! Take that with you as you die!"

Lucifer had brought his nemesis to this final moment, and he redirected the swinging iron to bring it down on Jesus' puny human form.

As the low-pitch whistle of the flying iron changed slightly, Jesus quickly rolled towards the half-head portion of the dead wing-biter dragon.

The iron missed its target and struck stone instead.

Shards of rock blew out in multiple directions, while Jesus hid behind the dragon's bloody half-head.

Lucifer shouted, "Quit your squirming you furless rodent!"

Pulling up the chain, Lucifer swung the iron again at his elusive target... but the scrambling Jesus rolled left this time... and grabbed tightly to wing biter's jawbone... just above the canine, the half-jaw remaining portion of the dragon's head.

Lucifer's swinging iron struck again... and missed... sort of.

The iron's heavy impact was a twisting blow, but it finished the primary separation of the dragon's jawbone from wing biter's head.

With his right hand locked around the jawbone, Jesus lifted as he twisted... ripping muscles... snapping tendons, then with one more twist, a tug, plus a little cutting with a rock shard, Jesus ripped his jawbone weapon free.

It was a twenty pound club... three feet long... with a handhold space between the last canine and first molar... strips of flesh still hung to it in places, a chunk of scaly skin remained on one side.

Armed now, Jesus maneuvered and boldly faced his attacker.

Lucifer laughed as shouted, "Ha! What's that you have? You're going to fight me with a toothpick!" and he swung the iron to clip Jesus in half at the waist.

Jesus dove in towards Lucifer's feet... swinging his jawbone as he went.

The first impact from his jawbone struck a left toe... shattering the connection between the last joint and its claw... the second impact was a smash hit on the biggest right toe.

Lucifer screamed in pain and clenched up both his feet.

"Aaaiihhhh!!!!!"

Rolling, Jesus spun around behind him and found Lucifer's dragon tail pressed tight down on the lava rock... helping to support and balance the massive body.

At three places Jesus struck in quick succession... not smashing the tail off entirely, but rather breaking the bones inside it... leaving all the nerves intact... and still sending signals... communicating to the dragon-brain the tail's absolutely painful condition.

Protectively whipping his tail around, Lucifer lost his balance, and tipped over... falling to his right side... and exposing his left ear slightly... which Jesus struck quite squarely, exploding its base structure... and ripping loose a big chunk of scalp and ear.

Instinctively, Lucifer dropped the chain and brought his hands up, protectively covering his handsome dragon ears.

Sort of lying on his back now, the creature roared again in agony... tipping his head back... to where it rested solidly against the stone... his snout pointing straight up.

Intense pain flooded Lucifer's senses and he clenched his mouth shut... as Jesus brought his club down through the center of it, shattering most of the dragon's teeth... chunks and bloody stumps flew out in all directions.

Screaming violently, Lucifer threw his head from side to side.

Watching closely, Jesus timed it nicely... raising his club, he completely smashed off the dragon's other ear.

Writhing in total agony, Lucifer accidently let himself roll downhill and into a lava stream... and although only his body's lower half fell in, the heavy lava locked his wings down, pressing them tightly to his body.

Paddling with his rear feet he tried to push against something solid, but there was nothing... so he reached out with his front legs... where Jesus was there waiting.

Once Lucifer's front feet had a sure hold... and were pulled tightly... Jesus... repeatedly brought the jawbone down precisely, smashing Lucifer's finger-claws into shattered little pieces.

Recoiling and sort of hunched up, Lucifer pushed his head down, to where his jaw was solidly set on the rocky island.

Seizing his opportunity, Jesus crashed his club down, striking top dead center on Lucifer's scaly head.

Then pulling the club back and turning it around in his hands, he drove the jawbone's nine inch canine tooth through Lucifer's left eye... and then used it like a pry bar... to break through into his skull and stir his brain around.

Lucifer, with half of his body sizzling, bubbling, and anchored in a red lava deep fryer, he drifted in and out of consciousness.

The topmost portion of lava, cooled slightly by the dragon's bulk, solidified and locked the wings and body into place.

Jesus retrieved the chain and collar set and drug it over to Lucifer's massive, but decimated frame, he was lying on his belly, the three foot long snout pointed to his left side.

Jesus spoke his thoughts as he finished off his chores, "Lucifer... it was for one primary purpose I came to this earth in a man suit."

Then, taking hold of the chain's big, round, last link, he pulled the first part of the chain back through the link to form a loop.

"To destroy what you have done."

He slid the loop over Lucifer's snout and then circled a dozen wraps of the chain around the dragon's mouth.

"To destroy the covenant you cut with Adam to use his authority."

Next, lifting up the iron stake attached to the chain's far end, Jesus stuffed the pointy end into Lucifer's mouth, down through the middle of the chain loops, and crammed it into the back of Lucifer's throat.

"And to abolish the deal you made with the serpent to use his body."

Then using the stake like a giant pry-bar, he began twisting Lucifer's head over and around... till his head was facing backwards...

"Lucifer... Satan... your user days are over!"

And then he pushed harder... until finally... some certain sounds... and some movements... were felt and heard quite clear.

The creature in a dragon suit looked out at Jesus through one good eye... with his head twisted around... doubled back backwards... but he was speechless.

Tic...

Tic...

Cheeeeeee...

Spiccc...

Click...

Spic...

Stretch...

Streeeettttttcccchhhhh...!!!

Snap!

"Loser!"

Back at the narrows all eyes turned upwards, ready for the announcement of forever change.

Starting from beyond the distance of their hearing came the crashing, tearing, reverberation, of massive lightning bolts passing through solid stone, superheating and shattering everything in their path, they ran a parallel track between the two iron fences in the sky-ceiling above the pit.

For the space of one breath, God waited, and then he delivered the words each member of his kingdom so intensely desired to hear, words released from within the stone-shattering lightning he clothed himself with.

"It is enough! It is done! Jesus! Messiah! God Almighty! Life Be! Live Life Forevermore! Always and Forever Life!"

380 | Mike & Dianne Heintzeman

CHAPTER 61

Listening closely to a rumbling emanating from far beneath his feet, Uriah determined it to be miraculous and not natural; Lord God was making his presence known as he traveled through the earth.

Moving to the tallest part of the little cave, Uriah turned his face towards the form of his Lord and stood at full attention, his hair brushed the stone ceiling.

Until this moment he had refused to examine the condition of the body. Although not one bone had been broken, most were out of joint. His King was torn, damaged and diseased to the point that he no longer looked like a man. In all of time he had never allowed a human on his watch to be so damaged by the enemy, and yet he was obeying orders when he allowed this to happen. Uriah considered what he could do in just five minutes of their time... to the people and demons responsible for what lay before him.

In the distance was a burst of light, one puff of brightness from deep within hell's domain. Millions of eyes strained to watch, and then they saw another more pronounced burst of brilliance. A massive jolt of Zoe Life dumped into the dead spirit... bringing life rejuvenating, heart pumping, word of God spoken, Holy Spirit fire flowing through his veins.

Mordecai, Esther, David, Anna, plus every other face and name focused on and witnessed the explosion. The detonated radiance became a towering pillar of bright glory-fire, shattering and dispersing all darkness. Above the pillar of fire was a mushroom cloud of brightness, it towered up against the earth.

Blasting forth from the fire's base came a moving wall of light.

Beginning at its central starting point, the shock wave of glory violently blew out in all directions, throwing every demon's face into the rock-strewn dirt. Creatures bumped and skidded; they tumbled into rocks and bounced off boulders, blown back by the brightness of the glory emanating from the first begotten from the dead. Reborn in the depths of hell, it was the resurrected Jesus Christ.

The wall of light explosion started at the central core of Jesus' transformation, and moved out equally in all directions.

Watching the progression of the initial shock wave of brilliance, and seeing its effect upon the inhabitance of hell, Queen Esther, Mordecai, and all the other watchers braced themselves for its impact on them. It was only one second, or at the most, two away.

As the shock wave struck the iron fence on hell's side of the pit, it scooped piles of bloodlust hungry demons like they were grains of sand gathered in a bucket, and then dumped them over the fence and into the pit.

Anna studied their whirling, tumbling decent, till they fell out of sight.

Wondering of their immediate future, Queen Esther found herself remembering her life upon the earth, a time when one man's blessing had been another man's curse, when the punishment of the guilty became the protection of the innocent.

The giant wave of judgment rolled across the gorge.

Mordecai reached over and held the hand of the niece who had been placed in his care so many years ago.

And then closing their eyes it struck them.

Full-force waves of glory covered and enveloped all those who had been forever watching, and waiting for their Messiah. Like waves of liquid love, an announcement of what was to come. Their deliverer had arrived.

Moments passed in silent splendor for every watcher above the abyss, as they breathed in the glory of their God.

Mordecai slowly opened his eyes to observe the scene before him. Near him were joy-filled faces eagerly awaiting the arrival of their King Jesus. Across the pit every creature's face had been laid low and thrown into the rocky dirt. In the distance, more than a mile away, stood one lone figure, a light in the midst of darkness. Jesus, clothed with a long white robe, a wide band of gold draped across his chest, Jesus coming to his people.

Step by step through the crumbled chaos came King Jesus, King of Kings, Messiah. Fallen soldiers, wicked warriors, residents of the kingdom of the damned all kissed the dirt and hid their faces from the glory of the Lord.

One murmured word whispered through the darkness, uttered by the fallen. One word spoken by every fallen spirit as Jesus drew near and then passed by.

Prickly sparkles danced down the back of Mordecai's neck when the sound of latent worship reached his ears. One word sounded by a thousand voices every second, every step brought broken voices with one word spoken as he passed by.

"*Lord.*"

Queen Esther heard their worship, "Uncle, every spirit in that serpent's kingdom! They only say one word as *our* King Jesus walks by! They say, "*Lord!*" Well I say '*Lord*', because he is, and always has been my *Lord! King Jesus, You Are My Lord! King Jesus, You Are My Lord! Thank You Jesus!*"

It only took one small hole through the wall of glass to let all of the bottled up emotion come pouring through.

Millions of believers, a countless number of voices erupted in praise to their God.

"King Jesus! King Jesus you are my Lord! You are my God!"

Overwhelming gratitude rolled like thunder throughout the cavernous expanse.

Jesus came walking victorious through the dwelling place of the damned; fallen spirits released their one word of submission.

Praise-filled joy, overflowed from waiting believers.

Sounds of rolling thunder washed over thankful hearts as the joy-filled saints timed their praise to the speed of sound. The wall of believers was four miles long, and they praised God like the white-capped waves of the sea, like waves coming together in crashing sound, *"King of Kings!...Lord of Lords!"*

Then they worked it through together, starting from two miles out in both directions, starting from both ends at the same time, four miles apart, *"King of Kings!"*

It was one shouted phrase started from both ends in tandem, four miles apart and coming together in the middle eight seconds later, in a massive, crashing wave of praise to their King, *"King of Kings!"*

From across the divide, Jesus raised his right hand. There was something in it. Queen Esther could not make out what it was. He put his hand down.

Another shouted phrase was starting, again from both ends, here it comes, *"Lord of Lords!"*

Rocks fell out of the weakened ceiling above the divide. The entire place shook as the crescendo waves struck each other at the center, as millions upon millions of voices simultaneously smashed into each other, bursting forth with Praise to their God.

At less than a quarter of a mile away now, Jesus raised his left hand, there was something larger in that hand, and something dragging along behind. Queen Esther tried to make out what it was, she couldn't tell; it looked weird. Something like a big ball with bed blankets dragging along behind, she looked at Mordecai.

"Uncle, what has he got in his hand? And what is that... dragging along behind... that... thing?"

Mordecai reasoned, "It looks like a ball-thing... that has a face, it's hard to tell."

"Hang on," he said, "Here comes another wave!"

"King of Kings!"

The sound crashed together, causing the rocks that they were standing on to tremble.

Jesus raised his right hand.

Queen Esther announced, "Those look like keys, but I still can't make out that other thing, but whatever it is, it looks very crude."

"Lord of Lords!"

Mordecai declared, "It does have a face! I have seen a painting of that face before!"

Queen Esther gasped, "Uncle! It's the serpent! Jesus has Satan by the neck! That big round thing is his head!"

David shouted, "Yes! You rock, Jesus! ... Jesus! Jesus! Jesus! Lord of all!"

Queen Esther said, "Oh, that's so gross!" and then she shouted, "Rip his lips off! And feed his liver to the fish!"

"King of Kings!"

Across the scorched earth landscape of hell's domain Jesus continued on, his left hand clamped tightly around the neck of Satan. Lucifer's authority structure was shattered, his magnificent dragon-suit was gone, and the powerless body of the deflated Satan dragged along behind.

"Lord of Lords!"

In Jesus' right hand were the keys of death, hell and the grave, everything Adam had lost, plus all of what Jesus had won. In front of Jesus cowering demons, their faces tight to the dirt, they crawled through rocks and trash to get out of his way.

"Oh look Uncle! Satan's smashed body! It's oozing stuff out of it! It looks like just the empty skin, with no shape, like a worm!"

Satan's mouth still functioned, but his neck bones were smashed, his head kicked off at a grotesque angle as his powerless body flopped along behind.

"King of Kings!"

As King triumphant Jesus passed by hell's inhabitants, those who had been kings on earth, or lords of war, the once powerful Pharaohs, were now things of nothing. They were cowering, hiding, surrounded by the people whom they cursed.

"Lord of Lords!"

Now, within just feet of the fence Jesus stopped, facing the millions of people who waited for him. He held up both hands displaying victory's spoils, keys in his right hand and a deflated Satan by the neck in his left hand. Raucous cheering burst forth from the celebrating watchers.

Next, Jesus turned back to face the multiplied millions of hell's inhabitants, still holding Satan by the throat in his left hand, and the keys in his right hand.

"Uncle?" questioned Queen Esther. "That person at Jesus' feet, is that Judas, the one who betrayed him for thirty pieces of silver?"

"It is, what's left of him anyhow, he as all those with him, caged in a never-ending cycle of torment and repair."

Jesus held out the wormlike body with a head… and dropped it in front of Judas, as it crumpled and rolled, the head sloughed around and stopped, eyeball to eyeball with Judas.

Judas shrieked and tried to bolt, but a watchful demon, *(a demon looking very human, with an odd white stripe through the middle of a head of black hair)* slapped him down, and held him face to face with his chosen king.

Turning to look upon his waiting sea of people, Jesus raised his hands for silence.

Then, turning back to the inhabitants of hell, Jesus said, "Know this!" His voice rang out for all to hear. "The price for sin has been paid in full! But you are here! And you will remain with the king that you have chosen… forever! At your conception upon the earth, the knowledge of God Almighty, the understanding of who he is, and what is like him… that knowledge was placed within your spirit self! But by your choice… within the garden of your heart… you rebelled at God Almighty! You rebelled at his leadership! You chose another king! You are here for the sin of rejecting me… and by rejecting me… you have rejected the one who sent me!"

Satan's decimated form was lying powerless on the ground by Jesus' feet.

"Behold the King! And behold the king whom you have chosen!"

There was sound of a ruckus close to Jesus, a resident fighting with a skunk haired demon… and begging to escape the place.

Jesus answered Judas saying, "No… it was while you walked the earth that the choices were made which last forever. There are only two kingdoms, there are no others. The kingdom you belonged to when you left that place… it is the one you will spend forever with. Each and every person will share their king's reward."

CHAPTER 62

Out of a guardian's habit, Uriah initiated a full spirit, soul, body diagnostic scan. Spirit and soul of course were gone; the physical portion of the mind had been functioning at 18.7%. Viewing this, Uriah wondered why his Commander ever allowed himself to be placed within one of these fragile... and so terribly limited bodies.

He switched to DNA sequencing to identify body characteristics and heritage. *Father...*

Almighty God...

I can't go any farther back than that.

Next, he identified the mother.

Mary...

Of course...

I already knew that.

He then pigeonholed markers and tracked the mother's contributing DNA back through King David.

The following step was to consider cause of death, he started at the blood supply, and it was depleted to 4% of its original volume. From where he stood, and without touching the body, he began a visual layer by layer observation.

The tearing caused by a spiked whip had been excessively brutal; lacerations covered the form from head to foot.

A spear thrust had been a center hit on the liver, slicing up through the diaphragm, creasing the bottom lobe of one lung and almost severing the left lung in half. The pericardium surrounding the heart was still engorged with fluid and would have exerted extreme pressure on its functional pumping before death.

Any one of a dozen conditions could be listed as cause of death.

Turning his back to the inhabitants of hell, Jesus continued walking towards the redeemed.

From the perspective of the watchers, Jesus walked up a ramp they couldn't see that went over the iron fence. He kept on walking over the fence and above the pit on a bridge that wasn't there. Once Jesus was standing about midway across the pit and slightly higher than the iron fences, he stopped and addressed his people.

"In a moment we are leaving this place. Once we're gone, I must first stop by the tomb to collect my earth suit, which will then be transformed into my heaven suit. I have a few chores to complete there, and then I will take you to my Father. With my Father I must complete my duties as High Priest of the new covenant for it to be set in motion. Then you too will be born of my Father."

Jesus gave his words a moment to be planted in the gardens of those who listened, and then he continued on.

"Considering this is a one-time event, I am also giving you a one-time opportunity. Some of you may desire to look in on those who are close to your heart and still walk upon the earth. You have a short time to do so. For those of you who choose to take the scenic route to my Father, do not be concerned about getting lost along the way, you will be tied to me and I will pull you to my Father."

"Come," Jesus said and he stretched out his hand.

Instantly, a line of light connected from Jesus to each and every person he had purchased. Not one was missed or forgotten, every spirit in the place of protection was immediately connected to Jesus by a line of light.

The very next moment the millions of watchers found themselves above the city of Jerusalem, very early in the morning.

————————

Uriah went back to DNA sequencing to confirm that the son of David who carried a curse was not in the ancestry.

Nope...

Not there...

But I already knew that too.

Looking again at the brain's functional capacity at just 18.7%, Uriah was lost in thought when the ground beneath his feet shook and the digital input that he had been observing spiked off the charts past 100% brain capacity. A blast of white light threw him back against the cave wall.

"Wow!" Uriah shouted, "Jesus, Master, Lord! You're back!"

Jesus sat up pulling a towel-like cover off his face, "Catch you napping did I, Uriah?"

He tossed the towel to Uriah and continued, "Almost 34 years and I only see you one time... in the garden four days ago... where have you been?"

Uriah folded the towel neatly and set it down, "I was never more than ten steps from you my Lord, up to the '*I AM*' mark you gave me. You just never needed much help... that's all."

"Do you have the earth clothes I told you to bring?"

"Yes sir," Uriah answered, handing the bundle to his Commander and Chief, "but I don't understand why you want these."

"Earth rules, I still have a couple of chores to complete here before we go to my Father."

Jesus continued, "Would you like to make an announcement... to the guards outside... that we have won?"

"Yes sir!" Uriah responded with a little too much excitement, "I mean... ah... yes sir... it would be an honor... to do so."

"OK, these are the rules of engagement, you can startle them to the point where they pass out, but don't touch them, clear?"

"Can do captain," said Uriah with a grin on his face, "ready?"

"Ready," answered Jesus, "go for it!"

Uriah focused his energy and drove his heals into the stone floor so hard that he split the earth and shot up through the cave roof without even disturbing one grain of sand.

He blasted up through the sky to the place where almost all oxygen is gone and adjusted his brightness level to full illumination. Next he focused on the soldiers guarding the tomb and fired straight back to earth looking like a flaming missile.

To the soldiers guarding the tomb, they were first shocked to an adrenalin rush by the trembling of an earthquake. Next, a sonic boom that rattled each rib cage caused them to step back and look up... to see what? A flaming meteor heading straight for them with maybe two seconds to impact. Their elite warrior bravado melted like wax as they froze in fear.

The two seconds till death turned to three as the white hot meteor slowed down, and was transformed before their eyes into a flaming warrior.

Being back dropped by a dark blue pre-dawn sky only accentuated Uriah's reentry to the earth's atmosphere. His heavy impact arrival jarred the bones of the now panicked soldiers who watched this heavenly warrior snarl at them, and with one hand he rolled away the giant stone covering the cave door.

Next, Uriah drew his sword and swung it at the face of each shaking soldier, who, as the blade passed by, just fell down. Observing his workmanship over his shoulder Uriah stepped back down into the cave.

Jesus had been watching the spectacle from inside the cave and took note of the look of satisfaction covering the face of his faithful friend.

"Feeling a little better now... are we?"

"Sir, yes sir! Better! Yes sir... just needed to burn off a little steam... I didn't touch a one of them... but they all fell down!"

Jesus said, "Choose one from your team and stay here at the tomb for one hour. To those who come looking for me, tell them that I have risen and that I will meet with them in Galilee."

"And what of the cloud of millions who are watching us… and waiting for you in the sky above? I recognized several, David, Mordecai, Queen Esther and many others."

"Oh… you saw them."

"Hum… kind of hard to miss."

"I am taking them to my Father. They are all the Faithful ones whose bodies died before today."

CHAPTER 63

Three from the cloud of millions had been watching one of their own walking towards a large stone house, several others from their group walked through the streets of Jerusalem. Now they turned their attention to the tomb where a flaming angel had, only moments before, landed, scared an entire watch of soldiers to oblivion, and stepped into the tomb through the door.

"The soldiers are waking up," observed Queen Esther, "Those boys are up to their armpits in alligators... they're in trouble and they know it!"

Mordecai said, "They have only been unconscious for two, or at the most three minutes."

"But they have no comprehension of how long they have been out," David explained, "their minds can't tell them if it was three minutes or thirty."

Queen Esther wondered, "What will happen to them? In my kingdom they would be executed for falling asleep while on watch... plus they sort of failed at their mission... Jesus is more than... just... *alive.*"

David responded, "I expect the same thing will happen here... permanently decommissioned."

"You mean they're going to kill them?"

"Yes... unless their commander can negotiate some sort of deal."

Slowly, unconscious soldiers began to come around; they observed each other and their surroundings. No one damaged... no one missing... except... they looked to the tomb entrance, the stone was rolled away. Two soldiers closest to the tomb went inside, and then a third, they came out slowly, shaking their heads, and went directly to their unit commander. After a few moments of discussion the entire watch of soldiers headed towards Jerusalem.

"Mordecai, did you notice how many of our troop took the scenic route Jesus spoke of, and are walking around down there?" David asked.

"The number, I do not know, but when you look closely you can spot each one. They are tethered to Jesus by a skinny beam of light... and there is a glow about them... they even show up through buildings and stone. I can see thirteen... no, fourteen, walking the streets of Jerusalem... see?"

In the early morning light, three women approached the tomb, leading the group was Mary Magdalene. Nothing they saw was what they expected, the soldiers that had been charged to guard the tomb were nowhere to be seen, and the massive stone covering the door was rolled back. Mary bent over to look inside. The tomb was completely empty, and the cluster of women began to panic. They ran to find Peter and the others.

"I see them!" exclaimed Queen Esther. "Just follow the beams of light; they lead straight to each one!"

David was amazed, "Wow! Just look at the faces of the people who recognize them, they are some kind of surprised!"

"I see one, a woman, way over there, about two or three miles east, can you tell who it is?" Queen Esther asked.

"Phaneul's daughter," answered David, "That's Anna... our Anna!"

Queen Esther quickly glanced around, "What? I didn't notice she was gone... she's running up the path to that big stone house... Oh

David! That's the house of Simon! ... Where the other Esther is... the one who looks like me... David, Uncle Mordecai... she is going to see her Simon!"

——————————————————

Fiery eyes clouded Mary Magdalene's vision as she ran through pre-dawn darkness; anger pushed her past her cramping side.

Do this!

Don't do that!

It's the LAW!

Now three days of delayed reaction had only left her with a hollow heart and empty grave. Frustrated emotions surfaced, emotions planted about religious minions who continually preened among some new decree.

Haven't they done enough already?

First they murder him!

And now they go and rape the grave?

A stolen body and an empty tomb?

Mary fought with thoughts from those who told her what she should believe, scratchiness gnawed upon her heart.

They must have paid off the soldiers...

Paid them off to steal his body!

Filthy creatures!

Probably dumped it in some garbage pit...

Or buried it in some desert ravine...

Damn them all to...

Auagh!

It's not like we need another martyr...

To build some shrine...

To mark the grave...

Auagh!

Waves of tumbled memories churned within her mind, of what was and is and is to come. From the author of her second chance, she remembered words that bubbled up, words that he had spoken; they struggled to the surface of her mind for just one breath of air.

Mary Magdalene reached a stone barn, where Jesus' select group of grown men… were hiding like frightened children… she ran up to the small door.

"Peter!" hollered Mary as she beat upon the door, "Peter!" she yelled pounding again with both hands, "Peter!" she shouted and stepped back… preparing to confront whoever answered.

Anna ran towards Stonehouse, hunting Simon, Mary Magdalene pounded on a heavy timber door, hollering for Peter…

The three watchers in the sky were torn with which one to follow after… until they realized that somehow, they could watch and hear both women while hovering where they were.

Queen Esther was focused on the youthful looking Anna arriving at Stonehouse; she was walking up the steps. "I hope Simon will recognize her… he was only a small boy… four or five years old when Anna's body died."

Mordecai agreed, "Yes, and her earth suit was about worn out, well over one hundred years old. That old body looked a lot different than the real Anna does."

Queen Esther observed, "When her body was about thirty or thirty five years old, it would have looked close to Anna's spirit self."

David contemplated, "Anna is quite aware that Lazarus is a good friend to Simon. She only asked Lazarus a few questions, but she watched him closely, she was seldom more than twenty feet from the man the entire time he was with us."

Seeing Anna pass through the home's outside wall and enter Simon's room, Mordecai added, "Anna was studying Lazarus to gather understanding about Jesus and Simon, of that I'm sure. She's quite confident of who she will find… she will not be disappointed."

"I'm coming!" declared a voice, "hold on I'm coming… don't tear the door down!"

Mike & Dianne Heintzeman

Mary Magdalene heard a crossbar being removed and the door slowly opened, a disheveled Peter stood inside.

"He's gone!" she said gasping between breaths, "the stone was rolled away! And his body wasn't there!"

Other male voices mumbled from inside and John stumbled out the door looking of sleeping in yesterday's clothes.

"The soldiers?" John asked, "Where are the soldiers?"

"I don't know," answered Mary still gasping breaths, "I didn't see any, I didn't see anyone! It was only me and two others who went there! And…" standing near the step, Mary glanced around her, confusion settled on her forehead, "I don't even know where they are now… I thought they were right behind me?"

Peter was doubtful, "And the body of Jesus wasn't there? Are you sure you went to the right tomb? Maybe you got turned around in the dark. There were more than two dozen of those Special Forces soldiers guarding the tomb; they wouldn't just run away you know… they could be nearby! Did you let some follow you?"

Mary Magdalene was furious; she shifted the direction of her flowing emotion, "Peter! Do I have to get my mother to go back there with me? When are you going to quit hiding?"

John finished tying on his second sandal and started trotting off in the direction Mary had come from, he looked back over his shoulder and said "Well? Fish or cut bait Peter."

"Oh bother, I'm coming… slow down!" Peter responded, trying to catch up.

"No…" John replied over his shoulder, "You get your body moving!"

Mary followed a few steps behind Peter… just to make sure that she didn't lose either of the men.

As they ran, Peter continually scanned his surroundings, looking for soldiers or guards of any kind.

Six minutes to cover a one mile return trip was a bit longer than Mary's run, but they still made it back shortly before sunrise.

John got to the tomb first… but just stood there looking at the massive stone and the open doorway.

Peter arrived and scooted down, right into the tomb, "You're right Mary," his voice a muffled response from inside, "there's no one here."

John stepped in there with him... scratching his head... trying to remember something.

Why aren't the soldiers here?

Where did the body go?

Hugh?

I know he was dead...

Dead a dozen different ways.

Peter and John maneuvered through the doorway and out again...

They started walking for the barn.

"What?" called Mary, "You're leaving? Just like that... you're going back?"

Peter replied, "Mary... there is no one here... we'll be at the barn."

"No, no, no!" said Mary standing at the doorway, "This is all wrong! It wasn't supposed to happen like this!"

Watching the men leave, Mary slumped back against the door's cover stone... she slid to the ground in a lump... weeping... her body quivering as she cried.

CHAPTER 64

She stood watching the sleeping form that held the one spirit closest to her heart. Glancing over to the bedroom window, she observed the faintest hint of morning sunrise. Aware of her fleeting moments, Anna spoke the first words that she had uttered upon the earth for almost thirty years.

"Simon... it's a new day... time to get up, sweetheart."

"Nana?" The sleeping spirit answered as his mind began to wake, "Anna! Is that you? How is it that you are here?"

"Yes, Simon... this is the day we have watched for!"

"Jesus, he is risen? But I don't feel any different... we have been waiting... and watching... we were in the cave... all the candles went out. He died... but now you are here... he must be alive!"

"Jesus is alive! Alive forevermore!" Anna answered, wondering for a moment... how to say of what she knew. "He defeated Satan... Jesus drug Satan's sorry... carcass... across the lava swamps of hell... he bruised the serpent's head and deflated him of his power!"

"Yes! Yes! Yes! Thank you Jesus!"

"Jesus made a spectacle of him... and his crummy kingdom... he broke the serpent's neck... took the keys of death, hell, and the grave... the only thing left working is his mouth!"

Simon sat up in his bed, rubbing his eyes and peering through the darkness… towards the voice of his childhood friend and guardian.

Simon spouted, "Tell me more! What happened?"

"He bought for us salvation from his Father!"

"Did you see it happen? Nana, tell me what you saw!"

"I saw him rise from the dead… right in the middle of hell!… A shining light that smashed out all darkness… he sent darkness to its knees!"

"Where is he now?"

"In just a few minutes he will fulfill his duties as the High Priest of the New Covenant before his Father."

"And then? We can get born of God?"

"Immediately after the new covenant is ratified… we both will be born of God!"

"And Jesus will be our Savior Brother."

"Absolutely! And Almighty God will be our Father!"

Simon grabbed his robe, threw it on, and tied it off. Next, he pulled his window curtain back, to let in the first early morning light… and to see his friend who had been so long gone.

Turning back at the voice, Simon faltered. "What?… Who are you?… I…"

"Simon, close your eyes… and listen to my voice."

Like the little boy that always obeyed, Simon closed his eyes and listened.

"Hear my words," said Anna "We knew this would surprise you."

"Where is my Nana?" demanded Simon, "You sound the same, but you look no older than me!"

"Your spirit self knows who I am. It was my body that got old, not me."

Simon swept from his mind the religious clutter and traditions that obstructed his vision… and opened his eyes. He studied the face of the young woman standing before him… remembering her voice, her mannerism.

Closing his eyes again, and from his spirit self he whispered, "Lord God, help me see!"

Simon opened his eyes and reached out his hand, to the one who held his hand... so many years before.

Anna reached out to receive his grasp... knowing there would again be surprise in his eyes.

"Nana!" declared Simon, as his hand passed right through hers. "You knew that would happen!"

"I wanted to come and see you... but I knew this would surprise you."

"How come you don't have a... flesh and bone body?"

"A heaven suit? Jesus is the first, he just got his, and I, from what we understand, I will not get mine until you get yours... many years from now."

Simon wondered, "Isn't that a little odd?"

"Just different... I can touch another spirit... but I will not eat food until we all eat together... at our Father's table."

"We, all nine of us, we were there in the stone cave when Jesus died. We must have had more than twenty candles burning, but they all got squished out at the same time!"

Anna replied, "I was there... with several million of us... when Jesus came alive! His Father declared it done! The war between God and man is over! The sin-price has been paid in full, and Almighty God blew the breath of life back into his son!"

"Where is He now?" questioned Simon.

"He just entered back into his earth suit, and transformed to his heaven suit. Only a moment before that, he was speaking to us while hovering above the pit... between us and hell. He told us that during this one-time-in-forever occurrence, he was giving us a one-time-in-forever opportunity. For a few minutes, as he completed some chores on earth, we could look in on someone here."

"Then you only have a little time."

"Yes... and just know this, my love. As you were one of the cloud of witnesses, cheering Jesus on, I am one of the cloud of witnesses, cheering you on!"

"Nana?" wondered Simon. "You are starting to sparkle!"

"Simon!" called Anna as she turned translucent sparkly and reached out for him. "Goodbye, my love! There is treasure hidden for you in Jesus!"

"Nana!" called Simon, shielding his eyes from the brightness of her disappearance.

———————

Moments passed and her crying subsided to sniffling tears, Mary Magdalene gathered herself up, and stepped down into the tomb.

Peacefully sitting where the body of Jesus had been were two angels, Uriah, and one other.

Uriah asked, "Why are you crying?"

"They have taken away my Lord, and I don't know where he is."

"Why do you look for the living among the dead? It is as he said it would be… he is raised from the dead."

Her mind was on overload… she couldn't process… Mary tipped her head to the side, as if it would help to comprehend the man's words, but it didn't. In a daze she left the tomb to look for Jesus outside.

The gardener arrived and she asked him, "Sir, if you have taken away the body of my Lord, please tell me, so that I can go to him."

"Mary," he said.

"Teacher? Lord God? It is you! You are alive!"

Taking a step back Jesus said, "Slow down Mary… don't touch me yet, I have to go to my Father first."

"What? You haven't seen him? Why not? Why are you here and not there?"

"I had to come back through this doorway first."

"And me Lord? Is there something I can do for you… here… now?"

"Yes, Mary, there is. I want you to tell my disciples that I am going to my Father and your Father, to my God and your God. Tell them to go to Galilee and I will meet with them there, at that place."

"Is God my Father now? And are you my brother?"

"By the time you see Peter and the others, it will be done."

Mary slowly exhaled, took hold of the long sleeves of her robe and wiped the slobber from her face, "Okay… I can do that."

CHAPTER 65

From the Heavenly Holy place, the real, from where the earthy tabernacle was copied, Lord God said, "Thou art my Son, this day have I begotten thee. Let all the angels worship you."

Lord God continued, *"Thy throne, O God is forever and forever: a scepter of righteousness is the scepter of thy kingdom. Thou hast loved righteousness, and hated iniquity; therefore God, thy God, hath anointed thee with the oil of gladness above thy fellows. And thou, Lord, in the beginning hast laid the foundation of the earth; and the heavens are the works of thy hands: They shall perish; but thou remainest; and they all shall wax old as doth a garment; And as a vesture shalt thou fold them up, and they shall be changed: but thou art the same, and thy years shall not fail."*

"Father, it is done, and I present to you my blood of the new covenant."

"With excellence, you have completed everything required and have purchased the fullness of salvation for each and every person ever conceived on earth," answered Lord God, "I accept the covenant that you have cut."

"And my request?"

"You have asked of me," Lord God replied, "and I give to you the heathen for your inheritance, and the uttermost parts of the earth for your possession."

Lord God continued, "Each person that shall declare you are Lord, and will believe in their heart that I raised you from the dead, shall receive power to be born of me. They shall be my sons and daughters; through you they shall be new creatures and their sins will I remember no more."

All of heaven observed as elements of the covenant were declared, all were blessings of the covenant, for Jesus had become a curse for us, and had been raised to newness of life, he had conquered sin and death.

Jesus said, "As you have sworn, the entire earth will be filled with your Glory."

Lord God replied, "And so shall it be, sit at my right hand until I make your enemies your footstool."

"As you sent me, even so shall I send them, as your sons and daughters, called, equipped, empowered and anointed," Jesus said.

Lord God declared, "You have taken captivity captive, you have received in each individual man, ability and attributes, DNA of Me, so that I might shine through them as each one is born of me. I will walk in them and they shall be my sons and daughters."

Jesus answered, "You have taken away the first covenant, so that you might establish the second."

Lord God declared, "My laws will I write in their newborn spirit selves, and in their heart will I write them."

Jesus answered, "You shall be Father God unto them and they shall be my people."

Lord God said, "You are the vine, they are the branches, in you they shall bear much fruit."

Jesus declared, "And they shall fill the earth with Your Glory."

Lord God said, "You My Lord, you have saved the best wine for the last."

Jesus said, "You shall be with them, always and forever."

Lord God answered, "The same Blood flows through them all."

Jesus answered, "As they receive and walk in the fullness of Spirit Helper, they will be empowered to fulfill the callings that I have for them."

"So be it," they said, and light, glory, life everlasting full of glory blasted out in every direction. The new birth became instantaneously available to every person on earth and a present tense reality to every human spirit in the heavens.

The new birth seed of the Word permeated every watcher in heaven, every person Jesus had brought from the place of protection to his Father. Abraham, Isaac, Jacob, John the Baptizer, David, Jonathan, Mordecai, Queen Esther, Anna, plus each and every one of the millions instantaneously became born of Almighty God, now sons and daughters of Almighty God. The brightness emanating from God's Heaven blasted out through the galaxies and penetrated distant stars. The most magnificent occurrence of all time was now an accomplished fact, the new birth, born of above, born of God.

EPILOGUE

With more of an interest in listening than walking, Mary Magdalene carried a message of words for disciples, but she listened intently for the voice of her Lord.

Halfway between tombs of the dead and the timber door she had pounded on hours before, she heard Jesus call her name.

She dropped to her knees and raised both hands to the heavens.

"Thank you Lord Jesus that you are the Christ! Almighty God, thank you for putting life back into my Lord... and raising him up from the dead!"

The dead Mary spirit was instantly transformed, becoming a *daughter-of-God-spirit* with fullness of life. The seed had taken root, and the word of God had filled, covered, and given her Life.

Jesus and Uriah met at Stonehouse an hour after sunrise.

Standing in a room adjacent to the kitchen they stayed in the spirit arena, hidden from the eyes of men. They were observing the condition of seven friends.

"We are going to approach this in a step by step manner," Jesus said, "this is a training exercise and you are going to start with only surface observations."

"Understood, what level do you want me to dial down to... and please don't say human... there is any number of limitations you can place on me without being restricted to that lack of ability."

"My friend... I was there for 34 years... it will do you good to *pretend* for a few minutes."

"Sir, yes sir... hm... I am sure it will do me good."

Slight smile wrinkles appeared in the corner of Jesus' right eye, "Patience Uriah... you might learn something new... start with this, tell me what you see."

Although Uriah was bothered to even momentarily function within the limits of an earthbound human, he of course put a smile on it and obeyed.

He observed no more than what Martha would have seen. Three siblings in their mid-to-late twenties, a dark brown skinned, Ethiopian woman with her mixed race daughter, there was also two men who appeared to be in their early thirties, with physical characteristics of Jewish heritage.

All were displaying different levels of emotional disturbance.

Uriah observed and presented Jesus with the information.

At the sight of the old shepherd his sheep moved forward, listening for his voice. Emil reached up and slid the first of three gate-poles back as he spoke to individual sheep by name. "Snowflake, Sundance, are you ready for some breakfast? Today is a special day, maybe I will get for you some leaves from a tree."

Emil moved towards the gently rolling hills of the Twin Sisters; two old olive trees with three large, backrest-rocks near their base, it had been a week since their last visit to the trees. Sensing his course of direction, Emil's sheepdog motivated his sheep along.

Emil waited for the day to unfold. He had seen the birth, life, death and burial of his Lord, now he would see the resurrection fullness too.

Approaching his destination, the sheep spread out across the hillside munching their breakfast as Emil knelt down beside the rocks.

It was sunrise of the third day.

In his mind, Emil imagined the steps of a High Priest as recorded by Moses. The High Priest carrying the blood of sacrifice into the Holy of Holies within the veil, Cherubims guarding the mercy seat, the very presence of God in the place.

But Jesus did not walk into a copy here on earth, he entered the real, with his own blood, the perfect sacrifice, once and for all. Examined and offered up, a spotless lamb and a serpent on a pole. Jesus had become sin for us; the sinless, spotless, Lamb of God, had paid the price for us all.

As a small boy would lean against the shoulder of his father, Emil leaned against the rock at his side and said, "I accept and receive the covenant you have cut for me my Lord, it is the great exchange. I give to you my beat up old life, and I receive from you the life you give to me."

"Those are good and acceptable observations," complemented Jesus.

"Thank you sir, what's next?"

"Bring your ability level up a few clicks, but only look into their physical bodies for observations."

Again Uriah dutifully complied and presented a detailed report. It was confirmed that the siblings did have the same mother and father, plus all three were virgins and in excellent health.

His report also presented information on the other four.

Esther's father of the flesh was an Egyptian, and her mother was pregnant, sixty-eight days into gestation, a healthy boy, Hannah's husband Joseph was the father. Simon's great, great, great aunt was indeed Anna and both Simon and Esther were also in perfect health.

Crawling on the office floor Ben rolled up his bed as he looked through doors and greenhouse flowers to the sky beyond. Observing the coming weather conditions, he set in upon his chores in the cool of the morning.

Lowering twenty five feet of rope into the well, the clay jar touched water, tipped to the side, sunk, and Ben started pulling it back up. In a mindset of remembrance, he looked to the east; the sun had risen up above the hills.

Jesus is alive!

He jerked his hat off and waved it back and forth, shouting at the morning sky, "Jesus, you did it! You did it Jesus! You paid for us all! You beat the devil and rose from the dead! You did it Jesus, you did it all!"

Jesus said, "You have again presented acceptable observations."

"But... I can't say that I have learned anything *new* yet."

"Don't be concerned, you haven't missed anything... yet. Bring the scan level up to the mental or soul arena."

Uriah stood for a moment or two in silence, turning his attention to each individual member of the study group before responding.

"Each one of the seven is of varying intellectual capacity, but all are a ways above average, a unit I would be pleased to be assigned to."

Jesus commented, "Beginning to wonder what your next assignment will be?"

"The thought had crossed my mind; you made me to be a field angel."

"You stand among the best."

"Thank you sir," replied Uriah as he returned to his observations.

Continuing on, Uriah understood that Hannah had been an assistant to both a midwife and a doctor... blood and its function fascinate her, and she was a quiet person who continually looks for understanding on how things work. He noted that her baby carried a similar DNA makeup of slightly higher capacity, but then he found what he believed he was sent to look for, an anomaly present in all seven.

"Sir, I see an anomaly."

"And what is that?"

"The natural progression of each individual has been enhanced, as if... as if a filter had been washed... or a light was broadcast into a dark room. This change occurred at almost the same instant for each, less than an hour ago, the tools that each one is using are the same, but you could say the knife is being sharpened."

Jesus acknowledged Uriah's observation, "Interesting analogy... now bring the scan all the way up... and look at them... the spirit person... each spirit self... but Uriah, don't let them know we are here."

Uriah stepped back to look at Jesus...

Wondering...

Sir?

It takes a direct order to sidestep a primary directive...

He then turned back to face the seven.

Uriah naturally let his gaze fall on the human he stood closest to, Martha. She was standing, leaning, with her hands and head against a wall.

With his God-given ability, and from five feet away, he examined her spirit self.

A moment later, Uriah jumped back, reacting as if he had accidentally touched a lightning bolt. With troubled eyes he looked at Jesus, somewhat bewildered.

"Sir, I... I don't understand! She... her spirit self... she... she looks like you!"

"Uriah my friend... maybe you should look again... or check someone else in the room."

To help him focus, Uriah closed his eyes tightly... and put his hands over them for a moment. Next... he slowly shaped his hands together in a circle... so that he would be looking through a tunnel... with one eye only... at one individual person... one human at a time.

Concentrating on each of the seven, Uriah methodically clicked through his examinations.

Moments later, perplexed, he put his hands down... slowly... while staring at them... willing his mighty angel hands to stop shaking.

Uriah spoke in a whisper, "Sir... they all look like you! Similar to how I examined the siblings and concluded they resemble each other... with the same mother and father, an assembled blending of generic traits, but here Lord... I look at each spirit self! Lord... they all look like you! I see an equal-volume-fullness of your Father in each of them!"

Jesus asked, "Have you learned something new yet?"

"I will say I am learning something new… it may take some time… to comprehend the scope of my observation… sir."

"Understandable; we will help you with that."

"Thank you sir… all assistance in that arena will be greatly appreciated."

Jesus changed the subject, "Are you ready to know of your next assignment?"

"Sir?" responded Uriah in a somewhat unsteady voice, "I believe so sir… is it the son of Joseph and Hannah?"

"No… Simon and Martha's firstborn."

"But… they are not… they have not… ah," Uriah faltered.

"True, but I believe they will marry soon. They are my friends, and giving them you… to watch over their firstborn… this is my wedding gift to them."